A
WORLD
OR
TWO
OVER

A WORLD

OR TWO

OVER

GOLMAH
ZARINKHOU

Visit her website at golmahz.com.

Edited by Shawna Hampton and Fija Callaghan.
Cover art and design by Story Wrappers.
Interior map art and typesetting by Travis Hasenour.

ISBN: 979-8-9924254-1-3 (Paperback)
ISBN: 979-8-9924254-0-6 (eBook)

First Edition February 2025.

For my parents,
who fed me my first stories.
For my imagination's first ever partner,
my little sister.

And for anyone who's ever
had to escape into or out of their
own mind using a book.
Here we go again, together.

CONTENTS

INGRESS

THE LAND OF PORTALCRAFT

THE SIMMERING SEA

VOIDSRANGE

Mount Onstel

Onstel Valley

THE SKY REALM OF MADDOOINNE

Northern Portal Mines

Border River

King's Pass

KING'S PASS TRADING VILLAGE

WEST SKIA VILLAGE

FARROW'S FORGE

Thornhaze Forest

EAST SKIA VILLAGE

TWISTED FORGE

SOUTH SKIA VILLAGE

Orelio's Arbor

SHADOWLANDS

N
W · E
S

EMBERLANDS

VOID VALLEY

Southern Portal Mines

FALLEN FIELDS

LINEAGE TREE

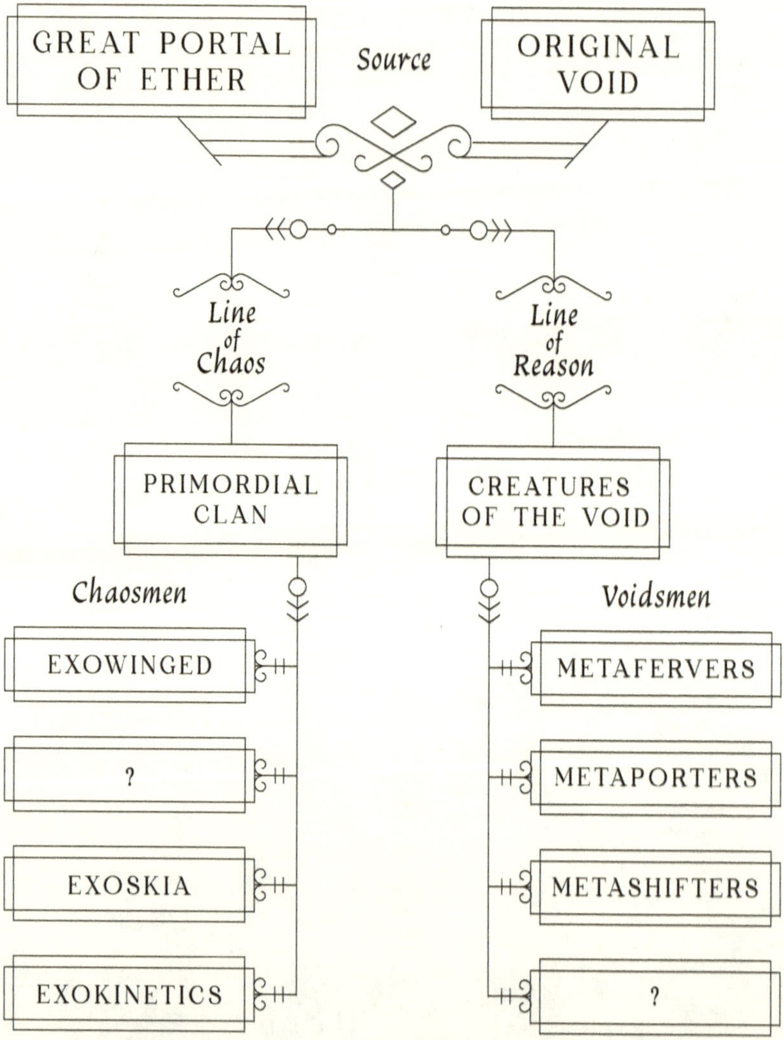

GREAT PORTAL OF ETHER

Source

ORIGINAL VOID

Line of Chaos

Line of Reason

PRIMORDIAL CLAN

CREATURES OF THE VOID

Chaosmen

Voidsmen

EXOWINGED	METAFERVERS
?	METAPORTERS
EXOSKIA	METASHIFTERS
EXOKINETICS	?

GLOSSARY
OF TERMS

Void:
> a poorly understood, intangible substance

> a spark of life that some Ingressians consider to be the soul

> note that *external* void pools have also been documented and used by voidsmiths* for message carrying

Ether:
> a coppery, chaotic substance tangible and visible to chaosmen

> part of the natural composition of everything and everyone

> the concentrated, main component of a portal

Source:
> the origin of an Ingressian's powers

> two confirmed sources exist: the internal void known as the Metaself and external ether known as the Exoself

> descendants of the Line of Reason draw on the Metaself while the Line of Chaos taps into the Exoself

> Ingressians are referred to as either Metas or Exos depending on their source, the layman's terms for the more classic epithets of voidsmen and chaosmen

Designation:
› a label denoting a group's specific use of their source, as in how their source control manifests into an ability

› following long periods of geographical isolation, likely due to portal travel, the original two lines gave rise to different designations, e.g., Kinetics and Fervers.

Portal:
› a gateway full of heavily concentrated ether

› may be visible (patent) or invisible (veiled) to the naked eye

› may be naturally occurring or crafted

› based on how they enter, bodies are flipped along the axis of the portal at the exit, which usually drops them to the ground from a few feet in the sky

* A voidsmith is a trade and therefore not to be confused with voidsmen, as these smiths are usually a designation of chaosmen called Exoskia.

PORTALS

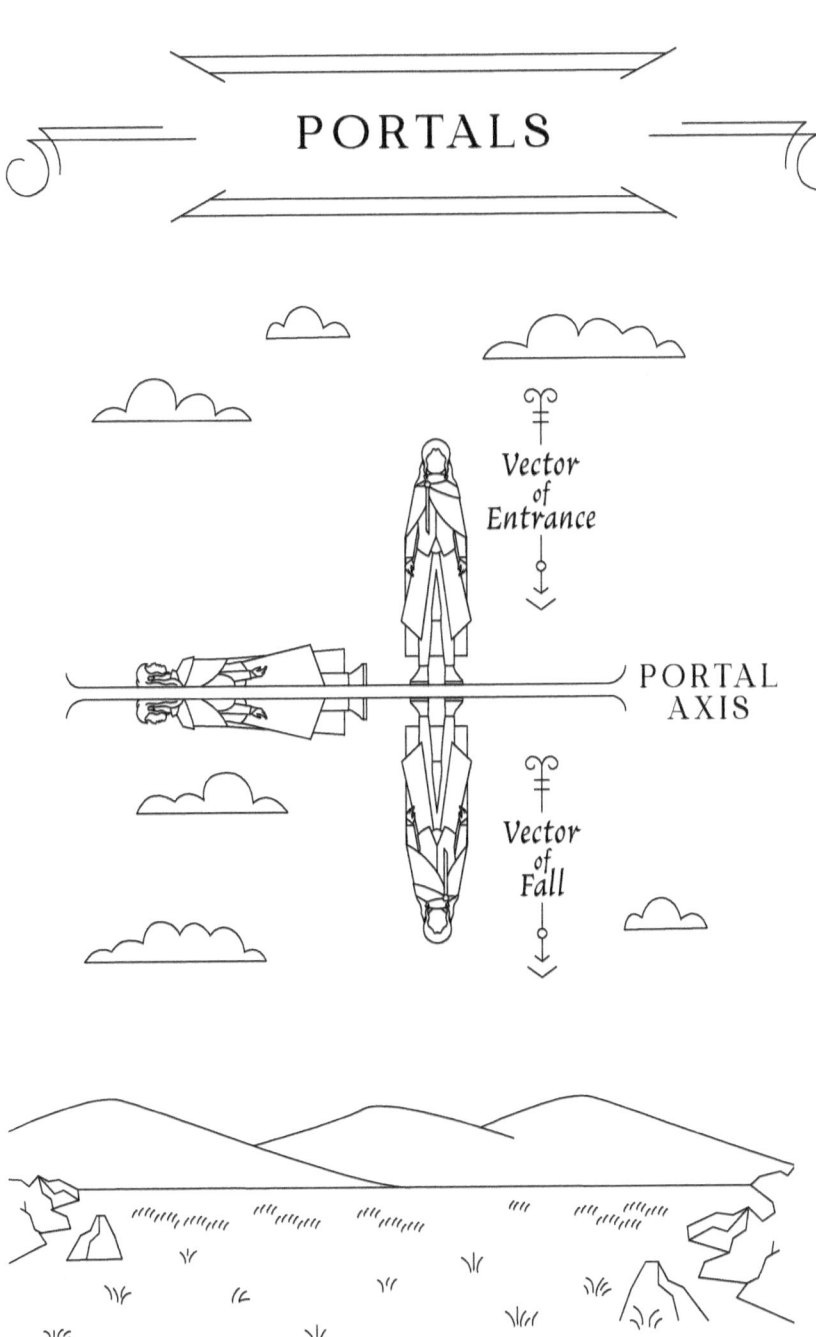

Vector
of
Entrance

PORTAL
AXIS

Vector
of
Fall

PROLOGUE

Sweat from white brows dripped into the blaze below.

The First Elder drew in a ragged breath and hovered high to escape the heat. Feathers rustled throughout the largest cavern in a series of tunnels, where the Winged High Council completed preparations. He glanced down as fifty of his senior clansmen knelt, their furled wings cramping from the long-held position.

Outside, a blood moon glowed with embers of the primordial ether, a warning of spellcraft long forgotten but underway, just as gems in the obsidian walls around them glinted with reflections of a titanic fire.

The First Elder staved off the ache of all he felt forced to do. All the death he caused to save his own kind. And all the suffering it would cost his little great-grandson this time around.

He murmured as he pointed with the primaries of his wings at the mounting inferno, and barely managed to dodge in time when the hottest section of its flames, whiplike ropes of blue, shot into the air around him with great threatening cracks.

Fifty wings snapped open in tandem, wingtip to wingtip encircling the unruly center and forcing it to heel.

His son looked up, torso pouring with sweat, and nodded at the First Elder, who understood that as permission to destroy their family with his next actions.

"As we spell it be," intoned the First Elder, his old heart heavy as he pulled on the planes of ether only he could see, patterned so well they had enslaved his dearest brethren for years, and grabbed a new fold to draw into his existing design.

It stood out like a copper spiderweb in the air, gleaming at the corners beside other such planes of manipulated ether that twisted and turned, their edges connected to each other with filaments thinner than silk. Overall, this gorgeous, dimensional arrangement often left him just as entranced as he was desperate to alter its geometric meanings.

How something so awful could look so lovely still disturbed him. He was about to make it lovelier still.

"So mote it be," he finished, placing the new fold with great care between the others.

"So mote it be," replied the Winged.

The fire swayed, air draining from the room.

An entire race far south of the Border River clutched their crying children.

Blue ropes hissed with fear and suffocation.

Distant victims gasped in growling anger.

The blaze shrank into a single tapered finger of blame, then shook and sputtered.

Bodies convulsed, their selves severed.

The fire blew out. The room blinked to pitch. Void Valley went silent.

And the First Elder wept to hear the echoing screams, not of phantom, faraway beings cursed, but of his toddling great-grandson just woken from the agony of losing his Guide.

That same sound would echo in his mind for months, until he jumped to his death with closed wings, the only way he could think of silencing the screams.

But the tortured forget.

Abandoned pain does not end. It transfers.

PART
I

SPINOR
FALLS

CHAPTER
1

RISING TO ADULTHOOD

Night falls here like a demon on dragonback,
Never quite ready to consider a different tack,
Ignoring the gloaming
To race toward morning
With the ephemeral haste of some infernal insomniac.

O nce upon a winter solstice, a couple youths courted trouble instead of each other.

One was turning eighteen, and the other had just gotten them arrested.

"I expected *him*, but what are you doing here?"

Willow glanced up in silence at the familiar, raspy voice. She hoped that Detective Jessica Reid secretly shared the island's general fondness for her as the only fatherless girl in Spinor Falls, despite being detained like this on the eve of her birthday. When she *should* have been out celebrating her upcoming age of freedom, Willow sat behind an interrogation table in the most sterile room of the town's watchtower, rubbing at red wrists bound with scratchy rope.

"Lovely décor, Detective," said the fellow suspect seated to Willow's right.

"Only the best for frequent guests," snarled Reid as she leaned forward from her own seat to remove their binds.

"Well, the emptiness of it all makes me feel oh so powerless. Even the candlelight is at the other side of the room. By that very striking two-way mirror."

Words oozed from Zephyr's mouth as though from some sluggish fountain of archaic disdain. Limbs outspread on an iron chair balanced on its pointy rear legs, he stared through long, dark pieces of hair spilling over amber eyes that were never quite capable of masking his scrutiny of the world.

"Speak up for the scribe," said the detective. "Verbal responses only." Zeph nodded.

Reid turned to the pinch-faced woman in the corner clutching her quill like a fluffed-up spear and announced, "Date: winter solstice of the waning crescent. Time: two hours and twelve minutes past dusk. Location: Enforcement Room Three. Detective Inspector Jessica Reid interviewing Zephyr Norwood and Willow Erifson. Sheila Sherrington present as scribe."

She paused. "Zephyr's guardian has encountered some serious financial trouble," she continued as the boy's lips pursed, "and it's perfectly reasonable he would conspire to fix it."

Zeph lifted a brow. "You're attractive when you're textbook."

Willow snuck an angry glance at him from below her lashes and pushed the hair out from behind her ears, covering her face in one fell swoop of auburn so deep it shone brown.

Zeph chuckled when his chair slammed forward.

The detective's voice rose. "You stole a small fortune's worth of silver cutlery. We have three eyewitnesses."

"Oh?" asked Zephyr. "How nice for you."

Reid leaned back, her neck veins straining with frustration. "They saw you both with the stolen merchandise."

"With it or next to it?" he shot back.

"Excuse me, boy?"

"You heard the question, Detective."

Reid slapped her palm against the table. "They saw you standing by the silverware one second, and empty shelves the next."

"Oh, then we must have done it. Naturally. Even though we were apprehended in seconds with nothing but a shopping basket. Your evidence is foolproof. That's why we're in this room, yes? Because your job was done the second you heard such damning accounts?"

Silence fell hard around them but for the scratch of a quill on parchment attempting to keep up.

Reid crossed her arms and legs. "Pure silver does not just disappear. Tell me what happened, Zephyr Norwood. In detail. Now."

His eyes slid to the right. And stayed there.

Reid shifted. "Willow, you're six years his junior. You'll be considered an adult in just a matter of minutes. Are you going to follow his lead forever? Willow, look at me."

Standing, she grabbed Willow by the chin, exposing the starburst scar beneath her pale jaw to the flickering candlelight.

But Willow continued her worship of the floor.

After a beat, Reid let her go. "Fine. Boy?"

"We've established I'm twenty-four," said Zephyr, his gaze unmoving.

"Where is the silver? How is what happened in Moran's store possible? How did you do it? Look here."

"I could tell you what happened. But why must I look at you?"

"Explain. Now." Hands on her hips, Reid took a heavy step back from the table.

Willow's head rose at the especially nasty tone of voice. No islander could find much use for Zephyr Norwood, often looking at him the same way Reid now did across a polished metal table that shone with their hazy reflections. And while Willow hated seeing the evidence of her friend's alienation, she was determined to use it to their advantage.

With a huff, Zeph closed his eyes and interlocked both hands below his chin in thought. "Oh, alright…it was a ghost."

"A ghost?"

He deigned to give her one more nod.

"Out loud."

"Yes, a ghost."

"A ghost who enjoys fancy cutlery for the afterlife cuisine?"

"If only. He owes a debt of silver," said Zeph, picking at the frayed ends of his sleeve, "to the man who murdered him."

Reid frowned as Willow helped Zephyr tear off a loose thread. "I need to speak with Willow alone," she said, but at that very moment, the room went black—the candelabras clunked over in unison, wicks extinguished and smoking.

The detective turned her back to them to bellow at the mirror, "Who's back there?"

With their interrogation cell gone dark, more light reflected in from the room past the mirror than from theirs, suddenly rendering the observation area visible from where they sat.

It was empty.

Sheila dropped her beloved quill to cover her gaunt face with parchment.

Reid noted the lack of onlookers with livid wonder. "That's enough fun and games." She grabbed a chair and pulled it over to look Zephyr straight in the eye. "Sheila and I are the only enforcers on duty during the solstice. I know this. You know this. That leaves you two as the only possible culprits. Yet again."

"I hardly think I'm two people," said Zephyr, staring straight back, "although it's flattering you consider me such a sizable presence."

Reid grabbed the youth by the lapel of his well-worn coat.

"Is this sort of aggression really necessary? You're angering the spirits that be." He pressed a hand against his temple in mock woe, just as the table between them lifted.

Everyone stood up in alarm.

The metal flipped and flew with such force it soared over Reid and crashed against the mirrored wall, suspended there as if stuck.

Willow pressed herself against Zephyr, her eyes glued to the sight.

"The ghost," he whispered, dragging the words out, his own eyes wide.

Sheila dropped her arms to reveal a nose streaked with ink. The detective herself stood and tugged at the table legs without success.

Voice low, Zeph wondered, "The murderer must be in this room. Is it *you*, Detective?"

Shiela ran out the door.

But Reid looked determined. She placed a foot against the wall for support and gave another big pull with both hands. This time, the table came with her, hovering just enough not to crush her as she fell. Retreating in a crawling backward scramble, she screamed while it followed close against her body. The table crowded her all the way out the door, where it remained, blocking the exit.

Zephyr and Willow glanced at each other. A moment later, once they could hear Reid's heavy boots running away, Willow sighed in relief.

The table fell, slamming abruptly to the ground, just like Zeph's iron chair had earlier. He gave a sharp nod and the pair jumped over it, taking a detour into the observation area.

Willow hopped and shrieked with glee. "All the records should be in here, including my birth papers."

Zephyr patted her head as he nudged her aside.

"We have to be quick," he said, rushing over to the corner where a mountain of scrolls sat, divided into sections.

But Willow hovered at his shoulder, heart racing and foot tapping. "Look for Mother's family name."

"I know, boss," he said with a mock salute. "Seems like they've ordered them by year first, then alphabetically."

"Move so I can help."

Kneeling beside him, she rifled through parchment after parchment, unfurling them in a rush and wincing at the paper cuts she endured along the way, until finally, she held one up like pilfered silver, the blood from her fingertips trickling into its yellowish cracks.

"Let's see it," said Zeph, taking hold of one side as she did the other. They looked down.

Zeph pressed his shoulder against hers. "I'm sorry, Willow."

"His name is missing. Even here. Legally, it *must* be here. But they didn't even bother to write in the section for my father's name. Why?"

"I don't know. But I suspected as much."

She blinked back tears. "You did?"

"Doesn't really seem like anyone knows who he is. Does it?"

Willow sucked in a breath, the disappointment so overwhelming she had to hold in the swelling scream.

Zeph pulled her up with one hand and cupped her face with the other. "That's why I have a better birthday present for you. Follow me."

"What?" Willow watched him walk off with confusion.

"Feel for a smoother brick than the others and give it a push," instructed Zephyr, running his hands across the room's single brick wall. "It should be one of the red ones."

Willow searched until she encountered a loose brick. One fierce push triggered the hidden door to slide aside.

She looked up at Zeph with delighted wonder as he sauntered past her wearing a grin.

They entered a stone stairwell and climbed in tight spirals under heavy darkness, with only their hands against musty walls for guidance.

Halfway up, the texture against their palms turned smooth again as they passed thick iron doors rumored to lead into the island's treasury.

"So did you have to flirt with her?" Willow's voice cut through the gloom.

Zephyr chuckled. "You said to make her lose her temper. You didn't qualify how. And it worked. We got in, didn't we?"

Once the final door came into view, Zeph wrapped an arm around the girl's waist to pull her into a blustery night—

Where the entire island lay before them.

"Oh," breathed Willow, owlish eyes brimming with tears.

Like the spokes of a wheel, eight massive hills radiated in each cardinal direction from this point, the highest tower of the town square. Glinting bodies of water carved the land to pieces, and lantern-lit pathways curled around each occupied hilltop. Homes sat amid the landscape, no element carved or chopped down for space. Cliff walls burst into the living areas designed around them just as entire foundations fit atop old stones never cut away. Nothing on the island intruded, only joined.

One hundred feet above ground, on a landing with no railing, Zephyr clutched a drainpipe and watched Willow step, untethered, below clouds of black and blue to take a deep breath of wintry air.

She lifted an arm, coppery eyes glowing golden with the moon, and felt her body rise to hover a few inches into the sky. Despite the thrashing winds billowing through her cloak, she had never viewed Spinor Falls so clearly.

Willow could only move what she could see. And now she could see it all from the top of the town's highest watchtower, embedded with a great clock that began to chime midnight.

"Happy birthday, nestling," said her accomplice. "Let's see how far your powers truly reach."

CHAPTER
2

OUR
HALLOWED
HILL

Let me tell you of some other place.
With some other rules.

$$v = 1.5w \qquad x = z + v \qquad 0 \le v \le 27$$
$$y = z + w \qquad 0 \le w \le 18$$
$$[z] = years$$

T en years ago, in Spinor Falls, the island welcomed its first
visitor in living memory.

Although it was less of a welcome and more of a concession.

Because on the day that old Robert Larsen first spotted
Zephyr Norwood stumbling along in his strange clothing, the
boy was not a Norwood. Fourteen years old, and yet he claimed
to remember nothing but his name and age. Not a hill tribe. Not a
house. Not a hallway. Nothing.

The council met in town directly to decide the boy's future in
Spinor Falls.

The eight members tossed their names into a cast iron pot,

and Councilor Norwood of the Southwestern Tribe accepted Zephyr for his son. He grasped one dusty shoulder with long, manicured fingers to present the newcomer to his recently wedded wife and their household.

But each evening, the youngster crept out of his large new home, rushed past the river cottages, and headed west. He had his eye on the tallest hill of the isle.

Eight-year-old Willow stewed over her stew and wondered how it might seem steaming merrily atop the bald head of the snake currently wooing her mother. Or perhaps a suit of armor could escort him into the washroom and lift the horrible man up over the chamber pot.

"Sterling," Mother was saying to the reptilian invader of their ancestral home, "when do you think your new seafood establishment in town will open? Your uncle continues to change his estimate." Brow raised, she tapped the broadsheet in her hands.

Mother only ever talked sense, only ever read about sense, and only ever paid attention to sense. And apparently, her senses considered newspaper headlines a romantic topic for dinner conversation. Willow tried to focus instead on the snow flurries dancing beyond the floor-length windows surrounding one-half of their circular dining room.

"In a couple months, Rora. Maybe three," said Sterling with a nod at Willow. "You will both be very welcome on opening night." He paused and looked away. "I thought it might be better to wait until then, but now I see that, well, three months is a bit far off, isn't it?"

Hope bloomed bright upon Mother's face. "Oh, yes, very far off."

Sterling stood from the table and knelt before her.

The snake withdrew a diamond ring from his pocket, and through the clarity of her terror, Willow realized her world had shattered.

As had the windows.

Willow stormed down the Western Hill with her arms swinging and feet dislodging every pesky pebble in her way. Her cherished hill, like a chubby baby giant curled up on its side, looked as lumpy as it stood high. More rocks jutted from the rippling green grass than from any other promontory, but at a certain angle, where a mouthlike indentation punctured the hill's leeward base to form a hollow, the sleepy giant yawned.

Willow hoped it might swallow her up as she sat, sheltered from nature and her mother's fury by the protrusion of a flat, black rock. Instead, she discovered a human form already in residence.

"What are you doing here? This is my hill," said Willow, drawing herself up like Mother in a council meeting.

"Hills don't belong to people, especially children," drawled a voice from within the shadows.

"I'm not a child."

"You whine like one."

A growling sort of huff erupted from her throat as she fell to her knees and charged at the lanky figure.

He fell back in place, visibly amused by her passionate launch. Once her brief rage melted, the boy wrapped an arm around her waist to quell the sobs echoing off the walls around them.

Willow rubbed her nose against his too-thin shirt, sniffed, and pulled away, large eyes peering into his almond-shaped ones with keen interest. "Oh, are you that Zephyr boy? Your dad was complaining about you."

"Was he?"

"He says you're weird. Everyone says you're weird."

"How polite of everyone." Zephyr leaned farther back against the rock wall.

"Most people like to be right, not polite."

"Odd, isn't it?"

"No."

He cocked his head to the side, rustling hair black as a raven's wing, and squinted. "Well, you *are* one of them."

"Aren't you?"

"I have my doubts."

"That would explain why you're so hated."

"Thank you. Seems you're learning to be a proper adult. But you've gotten glass in your hair and snot all over my jacket. So, sensible or wild? What'll it be?"

She smiled up at him. "Don't know."

"Well, either way, welcome to my yawn with an awning."

"Oh," she cried. "You see it too? I told Mother our hill likes to yawn, but she told me I was being 'fanciful.'"

Zephyr shook his head. "Sounds like you annoy people as much as I do."

"Uh, almost."

"Yeah, almost."

Her new friend disappeared for the next few days, though she often waited for hours in their meeting place. They had agreed to call it their *hallow* and, at Willow's insistence, forever ban anyone else from entering. Restless, she decided to walk by again on the sixth day, but arrived to the sight of four schoolchildren tossing slurs and snowballs at the space with glee.

"Devlin Norwood, stop that right now," she shouted at their de facto little leader. "What's wrong with you?"

Ten-year-old Devlin, with his large mop of blond hair peeking out of a shiny red snowcap, paused to stick out his tongue. "None of your business."

"My hill, my business."

"It's your mama's hill," he said, but dropped a massive ball of snow. The other boys followed suit.

"Well, I'm Mother's heir." Willow walked closer, the best way she knew to show off her half-inch physical advantage.

"Exactly," Devlin said and turned to the wall of ice and snow barricading the hallow. "You hear that? Blood heirs get everything, and you're a nobody."

Willow gasped and scrambled back. "What've you band of babies done?"

Devlin stomped his foot. "Nothing."

She fell to her knees and began to dig through the barrier with both her little hands. "Get over here and help me." But when she looked over her shoulder, the troublemakers had run off into the evergreens of the nearest valley.

"No, no, no, no," the girl chanted. "Can you hear me in there?"

She stood and considered breaking the rules on purpose for once. She plunged her arm up to the shoulder in snow but could not reach a void in the worrisome wall of white. So once the children had scuttled out of view, she lifted her numb hands and focused. Nothing happened until she grew frustrated enough with that fact.

She took the ball of frustration and shoved it outward. Snow erupted from the space with such force that ice chips cut her cheeks, and though she paid it no mind, an exploding piece would forever leave a scar the shape of a starburst beneath the right angle of her jaw. Willow trembled, dragging out the familiar body of a loathed young teenager twice her size.

"Zeph? Hey, Zephyr. Open your eyes."

Chin dripping blood, she choked back a sob at his blue-tinged skin and labored breathing. In the eternal winter of Spinor Falls, even children could identify the basic stages of hypothermia. Pulse present but irregular, Zephyr needed immediate medical attention.

Mother forbade her from using her powers outside the home, where others might discover her child was an unexplainable oddity, but Willow decided to break the rules some more.

Placing her coat underneath the boy and holding on to its hood, she managed to hover him just above ground as she dashed up the mountainous hill, all the while hoping it looked from afar as if she were simply dragging him.

Willow held on tight to Zephyr and the power zinging through her veins. "We'll see those boys in court. Enforcers will drink their blood for supper. See if they don't," she muttered.

Zephyr's eyelids fluttered as if triggered by her chatter. She stopped talking to navigate past black ice and boulders. Fatigue curled about her limbs like a bothersome, fat feline until at the first sight of home, Willow collapsed into the snow.

She woke in Aurora's arms.

"Mother," Willow whispered, lungs afire. "Sorry."

The striking woman, slender with flaming ringlets of waist-length auburn hair, poured numbing and antipyretic potions down her daughter's throat. After patting Willow's bloody skin clean, she said, "Keep your eyes open for me, dear. Come on now. Tell me what happened?"

Willow fell back asleep trying to explain. She reopened her eyes at the familiar popping of a wild cherrywood fire casting its bone-deep warmth into her skin. With one arm looped around her daughter, Mother dozed behind her in the large corner chaise of the Western Estate's master bedroom.

Zephyr, the girl noted, had found the strength to sit up against the large iron bed frame across from them.

"How did they trap you in there?" she whispered.

"I fell asleep inside. I often do." Limbs awkward as a baby bird, he stepped out of bed to face an ice-encrusted window too opaque to see beyond. When the boy tilted his head, firelight accentuated a jawline no longer quite round with youth. "Then I woke up, choking for air, everything dark and with no way out. I lost it, only to wake up in shock all over again."

"Because you didn't know where you were?"

He turned around. "No, because I was in the air, flying up the Western Hill."

With Mother's comforting body asleep against her back, Willow found the nerve to say, "I did drag you pretty fast. Must have felt like flying."

"Only flying feels like flying."

"You're being silly."

"You moved a person with your mind. I will never tell anyone you can do that, and neither should you." His eyes locked on hers.

Willow would never forget the intensity of that stare. Years later, the meaning behind it would bewilder and propel her into the unknown.

Mother always said not to tell. Just let them say strange things happen in Spinor Falls.

Let Sterling Dermott tell people a blast of wind once struck the Western Estate so hard it rained glass shards and convinced him he could never live there.

Let the graying Western healer pretend *she* harvested all sixty bunches of willow bark left on her doorstep during the great fever outbreak.

Let storeowners prattle on that Willow was so adept an infant climber, she had often scrambled up their rafters behind the great Councilor Aurora's back.

For it was not until she found her own child screaming in a closet about ghosts at the age of six that Aurora herself accepted the truth. Flying fabric and singing curtains swayed to the floor once her child fell asleep in a pool of mental exhaustion, but not a single second prior. And though they worked on tamping down her abilities during months of endless self-quarantine, Willow could not sit still when her mother stopped eating.

The eight town councilors, settled on the highest hilltops of the island, each bore responsibility for the microeconomy of their tribe's terrain. The Southwestern councilor lived closest to the large lakes and supplied the island with the bulk of its fish. The Northern councilor's earth proved most fertile for farming, and the game ran plentiful in the rainforests of the Eastern's valleys. But other tribesmen struggled to feed their people, some more so than others.

Aurora made do for years by trading timber, until the fever outbreak meant she could no longer deny that, as the smallest territory by far per capita, hers lacked the labor and supplies to match its abundant resources. But with hunger at its peak and their once vibrant young men in sickbed, tiny Willow tossed a small ax out her first-floor window and leaped after it into a snowbank.

She trudged into her heavily thicketed backyard for the first time in months and put the control she practiced so hard in her room to use. A couple dozen trees felled, chopped, and stacked later, she ran back home to request a tarp for seasoning more firewood than the town market had seen in weeks.

The westerners were too cold and hungry to ask questions then.

Zephyr had a million now.

The day after she rescued him, he helped her design firewood stacks with better air circulation and coverage from the snow.

And when he tossed a block of wood at her, she naturally sailed it back at him with her powers.

"You have to control that instinct better," warned Zeph, catching it one-handed.

"I know." Little Willow pouted. "But why can't everyone else just be like me?"

"Maybe someone is."

"Silly."

"Somewhere off this island, there could be people like you."

Willow looked him in the eye, cocked her head, and laughed. "There *is* nowhere else."

"Life began right here, then?" He looked around with a hand in his pocket. "This is the center and entirety of the universe?"

"Yes." With a definitive nod, she took the wood from him to place it neatly with the rest.

Zeph followed her, step for step. "What do you see when you move things? Are you doing anything specific?"

"Do you want to learn? I'm sorry. I wish I could teach you! But I just focus on something and believe it can move. Because why not? It does."

He huffed a laugh and crossed his arms. "Even when you were bringing me up the hill? That's all you did?"

"Yes, but that was *really* hard. I can't get you or Mother to lift up high, just maybe hover a little."

"So people are tougher to move than things?"

She thought about it. "Much tougher. So much. Even moving my own body makes me tired. Can I practice on you now, though? Mother hates it when I try on her."

He stepped back. "Sure."

Aurora interrupted them with a shout from the door. "Don't forget Zeph has to check in with his family. Take him home!"

"Ugh," groaned Willow.

Skipping off, she escorted Zeph to the Southwestern Estate to explain the situation of his absence to Councilor Norwood. She expected a semi-frantic household that mirrored her mother's reaction to their late arrival home yesterday, yet the Norwood family all sat in peace before a steaming lunch of cured elk meat slices and pounds of multicolored fingerling potatoes in the formal dining room.

"I see now, thank you, Willow," the councilor said as he ruffled her hair outside his estate doors, their jeweled panels bearing the Norwood crest of scarlet waves on a backdrop of blue. "Please relay the depth of my family's gratitude to your mother as well."

Frowning, the girl asked in a rush, "Sir, how will Devlin be punished?"

Behind his guardian, Zeph rolled his eyes.

"We will determine a fitting consequence," said the councilor, stepping back into his looming entryway with a nod.

Dismissed in that wordless way adults lay aside their minutiae, Willow bowed her head and ambled for a while down the long, salted path leading to the western side of the sun-dappled hill upon which the eldest councilor resided. Sighing, she stopped in her tracks and glanced back to see Zephyr facing a bay window upstairs, with his legs drawn against his chest and Lady Norwood gesticulating before him with the self-importance of an etiquette mistress delivering her daily sermon.

The girl turned to face the house with an elfish grin. The adjoining stable roof appeared to reach just below the third-story window in question, and if the Norwoods did not consider that an invitation for trouble, she thought, they should really reconsider their architectural choices.

She ducked inside the stables, evaded the sleeping young stable hand with ease, and climbed out the rounded window of a hayloft onto the roof. Using a bit of power to keep from slipping on the wet tiles, she ascended with slow steps to just underneath her destination and huffed when her head barely reached the sill. She vaulted upward, relying on her abilities to reach higher and land softer.

"Hi," she mouthed at her jumping peak, waving outstretched arms at Zephyr behind Lady Norwood's back.

His eyes widened as she dropped down.

"It's me," she said soundlessly in the air again.

Zephyr looked like he was choking.

Up she flew, wild and laughing, and down she went, making faces at the skinny boy. On her fourth airy zenith, Lady Norwood was gone and Zeph lay doubled over on the floor. Willow latched on to the sill to yank up the glass.

"You alright?" she piped, hanging on with blanched fingers and feet dangling in the air.

The boy looked up as he coughed out, "You're insane, nestling."

Willow took it as a sincere compliment, especially since she had never before seen him smile, so she grinned back, much too young and sheltered to fully comprehend those fresh red marks on his face.

CHAPTER
3

SECRETS
BEST
SHARED

I imagine your face in this dancing flame
Lighting up caves of hoarded gems,
Where paupers breed and die.
I wonder if you're safe so far away,
Broken in ways I may never disclaim.
So I lift the Veil and vanish through time
Past a film of ether, yours and mine.

Willow crossed the threshold of adulthood into a nightmare, one of recurring dreams that came like visions. Vivid and frightening and full of more questions than information. Always ending with that same hypnic jerk, a sick sensation of falling in her sleep that felt like a nasty mind trick.

Each time in this dream, she waits above the falls at the northern edge of the island, by the highest and steepest drop into the surrounding waters, where scattered whirlpools rage at the base. The world seems to end there. No islander can safely cross the churning salt water around them, nor had they ever considered the idea until Zephyr brought it up in a public council meeting.

But she always stands in the same spot within her dreams. Sometimes alone, sometimes clutching a large hand that seems to hold another world of answers. Never does she wonder why, only when. And not until a gust of wind floats her forward to dangle in midair—only to let go with an abrupt disregard for her will—does she fall awake.

The first of those dreams pierced the bubble of her eighteenth birthday. That morning, Willow's eyes snapped open and she shot upright, surprised to see the stirrings of dawn beyond the cottage she built to mark this year, the age of legal maturity on the island. Today had been her first in this bed, and as she lifted a hand to the windowpane, she wondered how strange dreams could find her on such an auspicious day, even as the details and drowsiness ran off together.

"Oh, good, she awakens." A deep drawl sauntered up to her ears from below-stairs.

Willow looked past the railing by her bed at the ground floor. "Zeph, what are you doing here?"

He brandished a long black cape with a sweep. "The festival begins in an hour. Remember?"

With a shriek, Willow jumped out of bed and stomped downstairs. "Hold on. I can be ready to leave in just a few minutes."

"I knew you'd oversleep after last night," he said. "It was taxing to practice your powers from such a height. But you did well."

"I've never been so scared and pleased at the same time." She slammed open her closet doors and practically jumped inside. "We should break into that tower more often."

"No. Now that you're an adult, the legal consequences would be more severe."

She fell over trying to pull on her shoe, a leg in the air. "But you've been an adult for six years."

"And yet you've always led me straight into sin with your master plans," he said, leaning over and tweaking her nose.

"Well, you *are* the perfect cover."

"You just like playing the part of an angel on the devil's shoulder," he sighed, "and speaking of which, it's time for more feigned villainy."

"And now, with a cackle, I die," Zephyr proclaimed, one hand pressed against the center of his broad chest.

Heat poured off the stage in unbearable, visible waves when he fell to mass cheers. Dressed entirely in black velvet robes that trailed in multiple distinct curls behind him, Zephyr dropped so well to his death beside a bundle of burning branches that a long, sustained howl pierced the thunderous clapping.

A large white hound named Nimmi yowled at the dais while Councilor Norwood and his wife, Zeph's adoptive parents, struggled to keep him from jumping to Zephyr's aid.

"I must admit, he makes a great Orelio," said the girl standing to Willow's right, just up against the platform edge, so close that few people could withstand the heat. Areida Sampson, first daughter of the Northern councilor and the haughtiest female Willow ever did see, stood tall, with an aquiline nose and cat-shaped blue eyes, all wrapped in tight, gauzy finery like a solstice present. The young woman tossed a red rose at Zephyr's feet as the performers took their final bows.

Willow's eyes narrowed. Areida rarely complimented anyone, least of all Zephyr Norwood. But she bit her tongue and walked off to help Lady Norwood, now alone, calm down her distressed old dog.

Pushing her way through the throng, she spotted Mother escorting a stumbling Niles Sampson into a seat before the ceremonial pyre, one stacked higher than the largest pine in her forests and set right in the middle of the stage, the very center of the island and perilously near Zephyr's staged collapse.

No one envied his role, and so he was allowed to have it.

The longer the wood stayed aflame, the more auspicious the coming year. The pyre lighting during the intermission of the play commenced the festivities by symbolizing the funeral of everlasting darkness, honored each year with this ninety-minute performance of the fierce struggle for warmth when the prodigal sun refused to make so much as a momentary appearance under Orelio's influence.

Willow watched Zephyr head straight for Nimmi, but Lady Norwood held the hound back with a tight grip.

"I can take him for a walk," offered Zeph.

"You're not fit to take anything," said Lady Norwood, thin as a rod and back just as straight.

He smirked. "I take your insults just fine."

The older woman flashed a sudden, bright smile as Willow called out, "You may hand him to me, lady."

"Ah, hello, Willow. Or should I call you Miss Erifson now? Happy birthday."

"Thank you, ma'am. And happy solstice to you."

"Same to you, dear. Keep this one out of trouble for a night, won't you? The others are waiting for me."

Lady Norwood thrust Nimmi's leash into Willow's hands, gathered her skirts, and joined a group of women presumably avoiding their husbands for the night.

Willow at last stood before her friend in his scorched performance robes, no doubt retained for nefarious effect, to smile up into that solemn, large-featured face and find herself surprised at his height, even after a decade of running wild alongside him.

Lifting onto two legs, Nimmi swiped a tongue up Zeph's face.

"This would be cute if it weren't so irrational," said Zeph to the overeager dog he was quieting with a tight, two-armed embrace. "Someone must really love you."

A voice behind Willow intervened before she could check his back for burns or offer the traditional congratulations.

"Greetings, oh Orelio, Shadow Man and Purveyor of the Eternal Eve."

"Evening, Miss Sampson." Zeph's eyes roamed over Areida.

"You looked pretty dashing up there."

"As I committed mass murder? Why, thank you."

Areida stepped forward to place a hand on his chest, her height nearly a perfect match for his. "Sometimes the dark can be quite seductive."

"Even if it's literally evil personified?" he asked, leaning closer.

She laughed, a tinkling sound as hollow in its beauty as the dead redwood Willow felled yesterday for the pyre, then bent forward to spill a silly secret. "I've always been drawn to that—well, let's say that depth of character you portray at the festival. Orelio for five years running? According to my father, *the* Northern councilor, that's an impressive record. And we all know he lacks for nothing in life, not even historical recall."

"Yes, yes, we get it. You're rich," Willow huffed. "So am I. Now go away."

"Excuse me, child?" Areida whirled upon her. "Where is your parental supervision?"

"Babysitting your father. He drank too much ale."

"How dare you? I could—"

Nimmi let loose a world-ending bark.

"He's hungry. We should go. You know, before he dies and I'm blamed for it. Excuse us," Zephyr cut in. He grabbed Willow's hand to pull her toward the long double row of food stalls along an alley of the main bazaar declared free of charge tonight for festival performers. "Since when do you get into status contests, nestling?"

She looked away. "I don't. She's just always been Miss Hoity-Toity of the Northern Farmlands, and it finally got to me."

"Okay," said Zephyr, drawing out the word while reaching for a skewer of spiced chicken from Robert Larsen's ancient kabob stall. The old northerner threw him a suspicious look from beneath bushy white brows but could say nothing to break their traditions in public. Zeph took three more helpings.

"Can you eat all that?" she asked as they moved on.

"I can if it makes the veins in Larsen's temple pop."

"Fair enough. Hand me a beef one. And about Areida—I did nothing wrong."

"I didn't say you did." He handed her a skewer and tossed Nimmi an uncut steak the size of the hound's head that he'd taken from behind the stall. Larsen looked ready to reach for a weapon before some customers pulled him away.

"Yes, but what was that all about? What was she even doing?"

"What do you mean?" he asked.

"Why would she talk to you? And like that? What did she want?"

"You're an adult. As of today, in fact. You can figure it out."

"She was…Well, she was flirting with you. But why?"

"People can flirt with me, Willow. I exist on this plane, same as you."

"No, it's just that she's never up to any good," said Willow, throwing up her hands. "You know I think she's the one who poured water over an entire stack of our fully seasoned oak last year."

He shrugged. "Blaise was flirting with you yesterday during lecture."

"Huh? No," she said, bemused at the turn of conversation. "How would you even know? You were busy teaching us about something or other." An assistant professor of mathematics at the Academy, Zephyr lectured often, with a zeal he hid from others when he was in public, unless he was eating. "I found your view of integrals quite derivative by the way."

"Hilarious. You need to pay better attention to everything, or I'll be failing you."

"You would never, and besides, Blaise has no interest in me. Although I am pretty bad at recognizing romantic advances. I admit that." She strolled faster past the stalls, fingertips brushing along the smooth carts.

"You're usually pretty brilliant."

"I'm terrible." Frowning, she looked back at him. "I called Daniel Kindling a fool when he asked for a convenient date to call at the house because I thought he forgot what day of the month it was."

"Your face distracts men."

"And I never recognize flirting when it comes to myself."

"Like a sun shining too bright."

"I do often seem to burn the people around me. But only by accident." She plopped onto a tree stump and sighed, head in her hand.

"You *are* terrible at flirting."

"Huh?"

He laughed. "Nothing. Let's get some more food."

Zephyr, mountainously tall and eternally famished, dug into food with a relish Willow never quite mastered. And each year, he insisted on sampling from every stall, cart, and fire pit within a two-mile diameter of the central town square.

Tonight, the air hung heavy and rich with the scent of everything from roasting meat dripping beside spears of sizzling fish to mounds of popped corn covered in toffee to pots of bubbling malt cider. The main pathways looked and sounded more congested than ever; nearly the entire population of Spinor Falls was in attendance as merchants peddled their wares with gusto, expecting to make more tonight than on any week of non-festival business. Willow heard the most enterprising of the lot offer to hand deliver items so tribesmen could make extravagant purchases without ending their celebrations.

Perched atop a hay cart to stare at a very heated interplay over dry-aged beef, Willow wondered at her love for such a raucous time of year. She settled on the quaint smokiness pervading Spinor Falls—the puffs of gray twining about people's legs, the cages of embers radiating their luminous warmth, and the swollen fireflies dancing without fear through it all.

"Willow, what's this I hear about last night?" And just like that, her cozy feelings faded. Aurora stood, vibrating with rage, before her. "And where's Zephyr?"

Zeph shot her a panicked look from across a mountain of candied fruit. Willow shook her head very slightly in caution. He shoved an entire glazed orange into Nimmi's panting mouth and ducked.

"Mother, may the fires be blessed," greeted Willow, pasting on a smile.

"I will bank your fires right now if you don't explain how a child of mine was arrested on the most auspicious night of her life."

"You say arrested. I say questioned and released."

"On your first evening free of my house. And you put Zephyr up to your foolishness as well. Doesn't that boy suffer enough?"

Zeph materialized. "Thank you for understanding the situation. As usual, Councilor Erifson, you are ever wise and—"

"You! How could you?"

"But you know she put me up to it." He pointed at Willow, who glared daggers back.

"I asked you to look after her," accused Aurora.

"And how can I do that if I don't follow her?"

"Excuse me if I don't bow before the King of Loophole."

Willow laughed until Mother shot her *the look*. "Sorry."

"How many of our rules did you break?"

Willow understood. "I didn't use my powers on anyone else. Promise."

"But you did use them outside our estate?" Mother looked ready to kill. "The both of you are in more trouble than you realize. I've just now been informed there's a public council meeting scheduled in two weeks' time, and your names are listed on the agenda. *First* on the agenda."

Mother took in a deep breath and crooked her finger at Zephyr until he bent to her level. She patted his flyaway hair into order before handing over a large package wrapped in butcher paper. "Take this platter home for your lunch this week. The McKays were hiding them from the performers."

She kissed his forehead, and Zephyr looked ashamed for once.

Answers. The greatest promise of all.

For weeks after the solstice, Willow sought them in her dreams.

Her questions grew hazy in the light of Spinor Falls. But during sleep, she could sink into an unknown where the key to her greatest desires finally seemed within reach. Where her powers and her self made sense. Where the whirlpools below an overhanging cliff always spun in hypnotizing circles.

And where something beyond them glimmered.

She would reach for that glimmer each time, her heart aching, and topple over into an abyss.

As Zephyr washed off his chalk-drenched hands with icy river water, Willow stood beside him, squinting into the murky foliage of dusk.

Whoops and hollers sounded from above, where the Western valleymen dwelled in fragile-appearing cabins constructed of reinforced wood and rope all throughout the lowland forests of the western section of the island. Living off the earth and their councilor's kindness, valleymen were the poorest of the poor, but Willow knew their children laughed the loudest, especially at her.

None of their families could pay Academy tuition or otherwise afford daylight hours away from work. Instead, Willow tutored them on literacy and Zephyr covered mathematics, the funding for their education secured by Zephyr after his insistence six years ago on a curriculum tailored for this subset of the population. Willow had watched him annoy the council into agreement, overloading them with paperwork and filibustering enough meetings until he got his way.

Aurora gathered her tribe's valleymen in community safe houses on her grounds or in her estate during the worst of the weather. And now, with the sun warm upon the top layers of snow, they had returned to their place amid the leaves and wildlife with a sloughing restlessness.

Willow loved to see it, tired though she was herself.

"You look a bit green," Zephyr noted, standing up and shaking off his wet hands.

Willow groaned and leaned her head on his shoulder. "Such a long lesson you gave today," admitted the girl. "And I don't feel well."

One hand came up to cradle her head. "You flashbacked to the fall."

"All these years, and I still can't shake it."

Her fall of years past had cut through her childish fearlessness, her body, and her mind. She recalled the utter peace at the top of the bleekmere tree she had scaled in this forest, the peeling black bark over a bright red base, the lack of thought and worry, the bleeding tension from her muscles, even the brilliance of the view, and then nothing but air cutting past her face as she plummeted to frozen soil.

She no longer remembered the pain, only Zephyr's panic and his body draped over hers as he threatened each valleyman who tried to roll her over with such ferocity that many of the adults here still looked away at his approach.

"Zeph?"

"Yes?"

"Why do you think it was so hard to tap into my powers after the fall?"

"You were scared." He sighed. "As a child, you always insisted your powers worked just because you believed they could. Falling so hard taught you to doubt. I think growing up does that to everyone, really."

Aurora had tried for weeks to get her out of bed, or even to use her abilities to move healing limbs about the house, but those early attempts had failed.

Nothing was harder for Willow to move than a body, and she supposed there was some earthly justice to that truth about her powers. She still could only hover a few inches, unlike how, as a toddler, she practically flew into the rafters.

"I'm not like everybody at all, though! Why am I so very different?"

Zeph smiled, of all things. "I haven't heard you ask that since you were a child."

"Mother just shuts down when I do. Her eyes glaze over before she walks away. But I want to know. I *have* to know."

"And I like to think you will someday. You're my best student. You'll figure it out."

An insect chirped loudly in the night. Willow took a moment to listen, her head a mess, as she built up the courage to tell him about her troubling dreams.

"Does anything frighten you, Zeph?" she asked softly, just as—

A teenage boy dropped from a branch onto Zeph's back, howling like a wolf, draping them all in a blanket of snow. Willow bent over laughing as Zeph cursed.

"Damn it, Davie. Are you wounded or something?" Zeph said, trying to shut him up.

"Hey, I'm your best student, not Willow," Davie growled into Zeph's ear, strangling his teacher in vengeance.

Face red, Zeph promised, "I'll believe it when you show up to class on time."

Davie howled again and ran away.

"Do valleymen ever grow up?" asked Zeph, stomping off.

"Nope. He's my age, believe it or not." Willow smiled, brushing away tears as she fell in step with her friend. "And we better be careful. They really do have the sharpest ears."

"I'll remember that."

She took his arm. "I'm sorry for the emotional detour. I think the lack of sleep has been getting to me."

"Oh?"

She steeled herself. "Yes, this odd dream has been coming to me over and over again recently. Probably just remnants of trauma, but why so many years later? And though I can't remember what I see, once I fall back in, I know I've been there before."

"Funny you should say that."

"Funny?" She turned to him with her eyebrows raised.

He lifted a hand. "No, listen, I keep meaning to tell you the same thing, except I know what I've been dreaming. Could be because of you, but I'm standing by the waters up north, on that steep cliff a few miles up the road from Oar's cottage."

Her heart skipped a beat, stray memories now slotting together, as she asked, "And then you fly forward?"

"Yes, as if some force like the wind is pushing me over."

"And yet you hang over the water for a moment."

His eyes burned into hers. "The shortest moment, just before I—"

"Fall," they finished together.

Neither spoke again until they reached the Western Estate.

A few feet from the door, however, Zeph turned to her. "I think we should do it."

Willow froze in place beside him, spine straight and gaze forward. "No, you don't."

"You didn't ask me what I mean."

She hurried through the doors and all the way to her mother, refusing to look back.

"Mother."

Panting, Willow stepped into a massive bedroom, where Aurora stood before a mirror, draped in jewels. A floor-length emerald evening gown complemented her red hair and sea green eyes so well, Willow had to touch the heavy brocade fabric for herself.

"Are you going somewhere important?" she asked.

Aurora finished fastening a large pearl earring as she replied, "Dinner with the Norwoods."

Willow made a face in the mirror. "Why? They're so stuffy. And Lady Norwood looks like a scarecrow."

Mother's voice grew sharp. "They are my peers, Willow. Yours too someday, once you take my seat."

"Don't say that!"

"Why not? It's the reasonable order of things. I will die"—Willow put her hands over her ears—"and you will take over."

Willow slammed her hands down. "I don't want it. I'd rather have you."

"While it's nice to know you lack the blood thirst for power, dear, the world will take me from you one day. Organize your mind to accept that when it happens."

"No. Look at you. You're young and healthy and beautiful. That's not happening."

"Not now. But one day," she said, stroking a soft hand along her daughter's hair.

Unwilling to discuss it further, Willow leaned against her mother, staring at their reflections. "Why is my hair so much darker than yours? And my eyes so gold instead of green?"

"You don't only get your genes from me, dear."

"Then who—"

Aurora was walking away, moving already into the connected study.

Willow sighed and followed. "So why the dinner?"

"It's time to discuss Zephyr's situation with the Norwoods. They've ignored our traditions long enough. Zeph is well past adult age, yet they haven't given him any land to take as his own. They shame him this way."

"I remember. Councilor Norwood agreed, but his wife vetoed the decision. She doesn't even like Zeph, but she prevents him from leaving their house."

"Well, our conversation tonight must go one way. They will claim that as an adult, Zephyr is no longer their son under the council guidelines on bereft minor support. I will then kindly agree and offer him space on my land."

Willow gasped in delight. "You're backing them into a corner. Publicly."

"Exactly. Into a corner of shame. Using their own tactics against them."

"Brilliant."

"Thank you." Aurora curtsied, a playful gesture she learned from Willow. "But it's not an empty threat. I am quite willing to give him the land."

"Bless you, Mother." Willow wrapped her arms around Aurora so she could look away as she said, "I have something to tell you as well. But it's a little embarrassing."

Aurora pulled back to look her timid daughter in the eye, one regal brow raised and ready. "Tell me," she ordered.

"I have this dream," said Willow, heart in her throat. "Or I've been having this dream. Where I stand on a cliff."

"Ridiculous. Go on."

"And then I'm pushed forward, or I leap. There are answers in the water, so I chase them." Her voice grew smaller at the storm in Aurora's gaze. "Could there be any truth to this?"

"I did not raise you to be an idiot."

"Yes, but—"

"I taught you to think."

"Yes, but, Mother, sometimes we have desires that defy reason. Look at what I can do. There is so much I need to know. And maybe I've been imagining those answers past our borders."

"There is nothing past our borders."

"I know it's just a dream, but I'm scared because it calls to me. I find myself standing on that cliff and wondering—"

Aurora whirled to face her. "You say you're afraid of heights, and now you want to jump off a cliff? What are you trying to tell me, Willow?"

"Nothing, really, just that this urge has grown a little frightening. And the dreams so constant. I'm *scared*."

Aurora looked so stricken that Willow apologized, saying, "At the end of the day, it's only a dream. A metaphor, basically. It's nothing. I'll forget all about it soon."

"Do not put me through this again, Willow. When you fell off that bleekmere tree—"

"I won't."

The dreams did not stop. They worsened. Blooming like wildflowers, over and into each other. Sometimes haunting Willow after waking with a dark taste in her mouth. A mixture of hope and terror and desire.

Until one day, she took a stroll, lost in her thoughts. Found herself admiring the sun-dappled water. Looked down at the sheer drop below her and felt no fear. Raised both arms with the wind. Lifted a foot.

A voice called out to her from Oar's cottage. She gasped and fell back. Sense returned, and she ran home, horrified.

CHAPTER
4

COURT OF
PUBLIC
OPINION

In this sleeping kingdom of yours
the world should stand still
and yet it burns

Willow often wondered how the stones of the Academy were laid to create such a behemoth on an island of modest dwellings but always forgot to ask. Today, it loomed ever larger as she walked in its shadow, hyperaware she would return midday to venture into its bowels and answer the summons of the town council.

"Willow, did you hear the news?"

She glanced up to see Moira Halifax, with her trademark haphazard curls and pregnant belly, hanging out of the upper window of the town smithy, waving her red scarf in the dimness of early morning. Willow dropped her shopping basket to wave back.

"Did you burn your drapes again?" she guessed, crossing the lane toward the smithy.

"Hush, you menace. You're fortunate I like you."

Willow curtsied in mock gratitude.

"Now listen to this," continued Moira. "My mother was up at the Northern Estate and heard it from Mrs. Sampson, who heard it directly from the couple when they asked her blessing. Joseph Morningstar and Loretta Pearson are engaged to be wed. Of all the blunders this season. A valleyman promised to a councilor's niece? I said to my own husband this morning at the breakfast table, I said, where will they live? A hill or a hole?"

"Maybe they'll take to the sea, and teach us all a thing or two," said Willow.

"Please. Chances are higher I'll give birth to piglets," chuckled the young woman, laughing a touch too hard and clutching the windowsill.

"Be careful, Moira. When are you due again?"

She nearly fell out of the window this time, trying to recall. "Oh, I can't be exactly sure. Must be soon."

When a drizzle of rain landed on her cheek, Willow urged Moira to shut her windows and return to the warmth of her hearth. She picked up her basket and continued the walk home, feeling uneasy. Before she could untangle the threads of her own feelings, a second voice called out her name.

"Devlin Norwood," she greeted without looking, "how are you and your high horse this morning?"

He brought the large steed he rode to a stop beside her, its golden mane glinting in the weak morning glow just like its rider's gold-spun hair. "What a coincidence, Miss Erifson, I was just headed to the Western Estate to call on your mother. No need to carry all that on foot." He offered her a gloved hand and a gamine smile.

"Why so formal?" she asked, glancing up into his cornflower-blue eyes, which always seemed so pleased with the width of their narrow view. Devlin had changed a great deal through the years, yet in few ways that mattered. The same features—catlike eyes, heavyset brows, long face—housed on a lankier frame, carrying a haughtier personality, with meager practical skills. These days, he doted more on his mother and idealized less his father, yet he never seemed much attached to anyone.

His grin somehow widened. "It's the duty of a well-raised man, but it seems having spent so much time with the island's sole orphan, you've forgotten."

"Don't you two have the same parents?"

"Do we?" he asked and withdrew his hand.

"If you think I enjoy being teased by people with no connection to me, you're not just mistaken, you're an idiot."

"No connection? Isn't my brother your dearest friend?" he drawled.

She resumed walking. "Oh, so now he's your brother?"

"Legally."

She stopped. "Monsters really don't change their stripes."

"I think you'll find that is not the saying."

"Dev, whoa there, where are you headed?" interrupted Willow's Academy mate, Amos McKay, bringing to a halt his own glossy white horse primped with bright flowers braided into the curls of its thick forelock. Amos tossed Devlin a suspicious look. "You're up early, you know. For you. Have you ever even seen dawn break?"

"I have business. A gentleman is always up early when there's business."

"What romantic drivel have you been reading? Don't answer that. I don't care. Tell me, is this actually about business or pleasure?"

"A pleasant business, you could say. And you? You're up early too."

They seemed to size each other up a moment, Willow noted. And without so much as a greeting from Amos or a farewell from Devlin, they called out, "Race?" and sped off to the west.

"Such gentlemen," she muttered.

But on reaching the brow of the Western Hill, her family estate now visible, she noticed their stable boy busy brushing down many more horses than her mother owned.

"Colin," she asked, "what's going on here? Is that the Tyson carriage?"

"Yes, we have quite a few visitors this morning, my lady."

"But it's barely light out."

She stomped through the main doors, halting at the sight of an entire garden of flowers and foliage bursting to life in the vestibule. Jade plants in ornate pots, a full trellis of flowering vines against a wall, bouquet upon bouquet of thorny winter roses, and even out-of-season aquamarine lilies covered all available space but for a small preserved pathway leading into the house.

"Mother," she called. "What is all this?"

When no answer seemed forthcoming, she headed for their main receiving parlor, where the servants attended to seven well-dressed young men, including Devlin and Amos. They stood upon noticing her slack-jawed presence.

Aurora floated over wearing her perfected public-persona smile—warm, demure, but assertive—and said, "You've finished running your errands, then? Come in. Come in. You see we have visitors."

"*We* do? I thought people were here to see you," she said, wary in a new way and conscious of how sweaty she must appear after a trip into town. "Hello. And please excuse me."

Objections rang through the room.

"Darling, come sit a moment. You remember Paul Canter?"

Her mother led the introductions and steered the conversation, though not so well that it veered away from the boring and uncomfortable, for a full half hour before facilitating her escape. "Go on and freshen up a bit while you check on that sandwich tray for me, Willow, would you? The service bell isn't working." She leaned forward to take Willow's teacup and whispered, "Check the library first."

Bemused, but grateful, the girl all but ran out the parlor door.

After a quick wash and change of clothes, she did head for the library, hoping her mother meant she could steal away some time in there. But once more that morning, she stood dumbstruck in a doorway.

Zephyr's large form was sprawled across a wingback chair by the fire, a pile of books and plates scattered about. Except he who wore the same sensible outfit day after day now sat in a fitted tan waistcoat over ebony dress pants the exact shade of his thick hair, which was brushed back but somehow still tousled over his forehead.

"Hello, nestling, why are you scurrying about your own home?" he asked, not looking up from a large leather-bound volume on the side table.

She walked over to sit between his feet by the fire, folding her arms on his knees so she could prop her chin atop them. "This damn day has barely begun, and it already feels like a whole week."

"You're just experiencing the natural side effect of idiots—they stretch hours out like laundry, until you want to toss them into fire to dry or burn. Preferably burn."

She felt her own ears begin to burn but admitted, "Speaking of clothes, you look very handsome today."

He looked down at her blushing, squashed face. "My thanks to your mother. She bought this for my first council meeting a few years ago and had it tailored again for today. I've come to pick it up."

"I'm a bit nervous, Zeph."

"Don't be. They'll be gone soon." He stroked a calming hand through her hair.

"No, fool, about the meeting. I know it's just a slap on the wrist, but it's going to be so embarrassing." She paused. "Although, why *are* all these people here today? At the same time, and so formally? They're not coming with us to the council meeting, are they? It seemed rude to ask anything of actual importance in there."

"You mean you don't know?"

"Know what?"

Zeph knocked his head back against the chair in exasperation. "Let's see. Since today will be the first winter council meeting, it's also the first official day of the courting season. You turned of age on the solstice, so your guardian may now endorse a darling suitor to escort you to the spring festival, that lovely day of love and frolic in the sun— or icy rain, more like."

"But that's not for months."

"Seems you're just that popular."

"Or just that rich." She pressed her face into her arms.

"Ever notice this book?" he said, never one to indulge in the upper-class privilege of self-pity. He thumbed to the first page, on which exactly three lines were printed, and then flipped through the rest with alacrity.

"Why are most of the pages blank? It's such a big book for nothing," said Willow, frowning at the waste of paper.

"These as well," he said, picking up more examples. "I'll write a story in one of them for you instead. How about—There once was a girl named Wilhelmina, who could never quite locate her pashmina. Then one day, she just ran away, and we were all left wondering, 'Have you seen her?'"

"That was atrocious."

"Yet I've been working on it for ages. I'll never claim to be any good. Only eager to help you stop thinking about those leeches in the other room."

She leaned her head against her fist. "Write me another poem."

"Absolutely not. Did you talk to your mother about the dreams?"

"She said I'm crazy."

"Of course she did."

Willow laughed. "Well, did you talk to the Norwoods?"

"They said to jump."

"Really?"

"Of course not. I'd never talk to them about anything important."

Light footsteps preceded a manservant with a tea tray, who trembled a bit from the herculean weight of its contents. "My lady? Your mother requests your presence in the gray parlor."

Zephyr barked a laugh and stood. "Guess there's no helping you now. I must be going. Willow, either I'll return for you in an hour, or I'll see you in court. Meridian, I can help you with that and grab my coat on the way out."

Meridian held the tray tighter to his chest, well aware Zeph would consume half the desserts before they ever reached the parlor.

"Why do I have to suffer through their company alone, on today of all days?" asked Willow through gritted teeth.

"They're hardly here for me," pointed out Zephyr, plucking a biscuit off the tray.

A thought struck her. "Well, don't you have to say goodbye to Mother, *today of all days*?"

He groaned at that and tossed her a glare, but he did walk her back into the lion's den. Heads swiveled in their direction, lips tightened, and eyes fell with a collective swoop upon Willow's hand tucked in the crook of Zeph's well-dressed elbow.

Zephyr strolled right in anyway. "Dear, dear, why didn't anyone tell me I'm so beloved? No, hush, Devlin, no need for words of brotherly devotion. I've only come to thank our host and take my leave."

Devlin smiled with the warmth of a dead fish. "So beloved."

Willow jumped in. "Have some tea first. Mother, he can't leave without a cup, can he?"

Aurora took in her daughter's pleading expression beside their friend's weary resignation and sighed. "One cup, Zephyr, dear?"

"Of course, my lady."

"Come sit beside me as Willow entertains her guests," said Aurora, motioning Paul away from the window seat adjacent to hers with the compliment, "I thank you for your thoughtfulness, Paul, in helping me send my congratulations to the Pearson family."

Willow growled under her breath at the treachery of confiscating her sole ally to the corner, but she took her failure and her seat in stride. "I heard the news from Moira just this morning. She seemed quite worked up about it, although I don't think she has ever met either one of the affianced couple."

Amos cocked his head. "What newlyweds they'll make. Like a pair of confused Northern chickens."

Alex Rochester, a valley dweller of rare fortune hailing from the same area as the groom, leaned in to their circle to confide in low tones, "The Morningstars haven't announced the news yet in the Northern hamlets. Very unusual. Likely unhappy with losing their only son to an uneducated climber."

Willow kept her head down to replenish the tea and announced, "I hope their devotion to each other proves you all wrong."

Devlin dared reach over to lift her chin with a fingertip. "You have a generous spirit."

The room silenced in surprise at the gesture.

"He sits so straight for such a crooked person," said Zeph loudly into Aurora's ear, sending her hand flying to hide a smile.

The familiarity of that display did not go unnoticed.

And when the party parted ways so that Aurora could leave early for her council duties and Willow might prepare for her summons, no guest missed the peck Aurora bestowed on only one boy's cheek in farewell.

A piece of blue hair ribbon floated over to Willow as she took another look in the mirror and cocked her head. Pleased with her new council attire, she summoned a couple of pins to secure the ribbon she'd bought that morning and hummed while placing the finishing touches on her appearance. Locking the rear entrance to her cottage, she flounced down the garden path toward the stables to check on her horse, not wishing to arrive too early but knowing that if she left any later she would be late.

She stopped first to check on her personal, favored stack of split cherry wood and lifted a piece to her nose, noting instinctively even before taking a sniff the decreased weight, peeling bark, and shift in color—light and woodsy, she confirmed.

The seasoning was coming along well, so perhaps another couple months of decent weather and it would be dry enough to burn by the end of winter. She imagined herself for a moment sitting in her favorite chair beside a sweet-smelling blaze as she gazed out at the colorful plants bursting through snow in expectation of spring.

Something stirred in the air, quick to raise the hair on the back of her neck. She turned, unsure and uneasy. A splash cut through the soft gurgles of the brook, and she felt pulled forward along the water into the tree line. She suspected more timber-related sabotage afoot, and she tread lightly in hopes of finally capturing Areida in the act. But there, by the widest and deepest portion of the brook, far from the Erifson firewood, a group of her morning visitors loitered. Devlin was notably absent, but the rest of them remained.

Amos shifted to the right, and what she could then see sent her running.

Three of the brutes had forced Zephyr's head beneath the water, while Amos held his legs in the air. Zeph twisted, his dress pants smeared in mud, and managed to kick Amos in the chin. But the tall man's grip held firm.

"No!" Willow screamed, hurtling toward them.

Amos let go, prompting everyone else to drop Zephyr's body into the water like hastily hidden evidence.

Willow waded in to grab her friend's torso and drag him out, but she slipped on the wet rocks of the bank. Muck in her mouth and dress drenched, she crawled forward to pull Zeph into her arms. His face frightened her with its pallor, and she patted his cheeks in terror-laced déjà vu until, after a moment of stillness, he coughed up a stream of water.

"Zeph! You're okay," she cried.

"Just suffocation, my old friend," he laughed and spat out some gravel.

Willow charged to her feet and looked around. Most of the men had left. "Amos McKay, we will be filing high charges at the council meeting. Make no mistake. Your own father will be forced to order your arrest."

"Oh, please," he scoffed, knowing full well no one would believe the duo in legal trouble over a councilman's son.

She wanted to topple them all. "Why? Why do any of this?"

"He's never really understood his place, has he?" said Jeffrey Rudets, a sliver of a young man who would never have dared take on Zeph alone. None of them would. "Dressed up like a pauper prince."

"His clothes? You nearly killed him because of his clothes?" More slowly, she enunciated to herself, "You nearly killed him because of his clothes." Shock vibrated through her so severely it seemed she could barely stand still or feel the cold. She glanced at Zeph, catching his breath with harsh heaving sounds, and for the first time, she realized why the morning news had upset her so much. Few people here would ever consider him valuable, suitable, or simply just enough.

Fine, then. Amos seemed the broadest of the group to her. She stepped away and took a leaping jump onto his back, clamping one arm tightly around his neck. They struggled for a moment, with

Willow's face pressed against crunchy, gelled hair as she fought to stay on the beast.

Zeph was chuckling just as hard as he was shivering.

She finally clawed off Amos's vest while sliding from him and waved her suede prize in the air.

"Zeph is going to need this," she said. "Seeing as how you've ruined his waistcoat. Now off with the pants."

"Why, you little minx," said Amos, smiling. "Like mother, like daughter, it seems."

"You complete ass, take off your pants," she shouted. The group broke into laughter, so Willow reached for her powers to show them that yes, she could force them off, just as Zeph's ice-cold hand closed around her ankle.

Still panting on the ground, he said, "You're no expert on men's fashion, nestling, so I have to tell you—I'm about three sizes larger than he is."

But she was incensed and illogical, and she darted at Amos so abruptly he fell over into the water. Growling on top of him, she promised, "I'm going to make sure your whole family knows what kind of degenerate swine they raised."

He flipped them over and submerged half her head, a slimy hand around her throat. "What would you know about family? You've only got a spinster whore for a mother."

Zeph's foot slammed into the man's jaw at that moment with a jarring crack. "And that's enough fun and games. Get fucking lost."

By the time Willow was back on her feet, the men had scattered.

"Our clothes," she moaned, taking in the mess. "And Zeph, we're going to be so late."

"But there's a bright side," he said, picking something small off the ground. His lips curled as a black look crossed his face under all that dripping hair. "I knocked out a tooth. I do hope it was a front one."

The largest man on the island, a veritable toad in shape and a dragon in size, stood guard whenever council was in session. No one could quite remember hearing him speak. And few knew where he resided out of work hours. But any soul could identify him from afar; he struck a secret, unaccountable fear in them just by browsing in the bazaar.

Willow really did not want to ask him for late entry into court. So Zeph did it.

"Hey there, Yonsoon, we have a standing appointment, so if you could just, you know, open that there entrance, we would like that."

Silence.

"No? How about for a kiss? Willow, do the honors?"

She shoved him.

Yonsoon sneered at this pair of huffing, drowned young rats with matching towels wrapped about their heads and, in the boy's case, wearing sopping clothes under a woman's cloak that dripped dirt onto the floors of his antechamber, the otherwise most elegant public room in the building. The sentinel spread his feet wider before a set of ceiling-high double doors and made no move to unlock them.

"Please?" Willow piped up. "We're so sorry for our tardiness *and* for how we look."

"I look the same as usual." Zeph motioned to his blackening eye.

The girl pursed her lips. "You can clearly see we were accosted on our way here."

The large wrinkles of Yonsoon's pudgy face scrunched up in thought, but he must have allowed her logic for he grunted his assent and removed the padlock with a scale-covered key. He knocked a classified, oft-rotating pattern.

A minute passed as the three of them stared at each other.

Until from within, ushers swept the doors open in creaky harmony.

Zeph gathered their towels and tried handing them to Yonsoon. Both plopped to the floor. "Thanks again, friend."

A multitude of startled eyes stared back at the duo like beleaguered bats in a cave. In the utter silence, Willow noted only a handful of empty gallery seats among the rows upon rows of oversized benches behind the stand; no person's legs ever seemed long enough to touch the ground when perched atop them.

Willow looked up, straight ahead, searching for her mother amid the controlled chaos of this cold place, where she felt ashamed and uncertain over her unpressed old clothes and wet hair.

Constructed of a soot-black mineral, the excess running over in odd places, the chamber looked forged entirely by some giant, untalented ironsmith, and it all led up to the Bowl, a rounded platform in the front, above which each councilor presided in loge seating, the boxes organized in tiers to form the circle of a compass. These eight hooded men and women looked indistinguishable from the rear of the gallery, seated as they were up front in their black, scarlet-trimmed gowns. But Willow knew Aurora must be peering down from the Western box; her own eyes, half-filled with adult shame and half with childish need, locked on its scooped-out, molten shape.

Sure enough, Mother's voice rang out, "Zephyr Norwood of the Southwestern Tribe and Willow Erifson of the Western Tribe are now called to the Bowl."

Willow placed her shaking hand on Zeph's elbow as they marched up, noting Areida Sampson seated in the front row, draped in yards of artfully arranged taffeta. She winked at them. Willow bared her teeth.

They reached the stand. The depressed, rounded nature of the platform made it difficult to enter or leave on one's own, and the last person who had been called upon, Melvin Shaw, waited to exit with their help. Zephyr held out his arm, but Melvin placed his fingers into some of the melted imprints on the Bowl wall and reached for Willow with his other hand. She steadied herself against Zeph to yank the man up and out.

After Melvin was clear of it, Zeph slipped down into the Bowl and reached for his friend's waist so they too could waddle over to the flat center.

"So annoying," whispered Zeph.

Councilor Ignatius Ren of the Northwestern territory, a long-faced man of middle age with dark blond hair, raised a hand, with his arm bent at the elbow to signify which councilor spoke. He commenced proceedings in his throaty, cracked voice. "Thank you for hailing our summons, albeit at your own pace."

Scattered snickers slapped Willow in the face, but she squeezed Zeph's arm to prevent him from characteristically speaking out of turn.

Ren lifted a sheet of parchment with his other hand as he continued, "You can be at no loss to understand why we have called you before the council. Two weeks ago, you were questioned on suspicion of theft and abruptly released. The town sheriff has requested the council consider the case after certain 'unprecedented developments,' as per the official report. The charges against you are as follows: grand larceny, destruction of police property, violent assault, and conspiracy to deceive law enforcement. How do you plead?"

"Not guilty," Zeph and Willow said together, stunned at the charges.

Councilor Erifson dropped her hood, a frown on her face, and glanced up at Ren's box. She motioned with her hand. "As the silverware Zephyr and Willow were accused of stealing was recovered the very same evening, locked in the store safe," she clarified, "we will be throwing out the charge of larceny. However, we were told there are some strong concerns regarding the night in question."

Ren intoned, "Detective Jessica Reid and Enforcement Scribe Sheila Sherrington, both of the Eastern Tribe, are now called to the Bowl."

The two women slipped down from the other side. Reid looked away from them, but Sheila tossed a very imperious glance at the charged pair.

"Are they going to do what I think they're going to do?" Willow whispered.

"It appears so," Zeph said mildly. "We really misjudged the fallout on this one."

"Your comments are ever so helpful."

Reid squared her shoulders and greeted the court. "Bright be the judgment."

The chamber boomed back, "Bright be the judgment."

"Councilors, my gratitude for your assistance in this matter and for your swift response to my request. What I must relate today may seem shocking and highly improbable, but I ask that you take into consideration the fact that my testimony can be fully corroborated by Ms. Sherrington."

Zephyr whispered, "You have to try and choke her from a distance."

"I haven't done that since you broke my wooden horsey," said Willow.

He glanced heavenward. "Suffocation really is my old friend."

Reid plodded through the events of the interrogation, some people laughing or gasping as she spoke apparent absurdities in her sure, commanding voice. Finally, she admitted, "The boy tried to convince us it was all the workings of some indebted ghost."

"Now, Willow. Choke her," Zeph said, his voice pitched low.

"I can't."

"Do it. Just make her faint. Quick. Before she talks about what you can do."

She looked up at the urgency in his eyes, felt the sense of panic beating its pulse in her stomach, and directed her ability at a still-speaking Reid. But just as she imagined her power wrapping about the detective's throat to press against her carotid arteries, Willow called it back.

Reid finished up, saying, "At that point, I retreated from the room and the suspects were effectively dismissed."

Willow could feel on her skin Zeph's accusing eyes, her mother's shock, and the councilors' silence.

As Aurora's gaze of liquid fire rained down upon them, Zeph declared, "Do you have any evidence of the insanity you just spewed?"

Reid turned to him. "Do you deny it?"

"Deny what? What is the accusation? Demonic revelry was not one of the initial charges, so I'm sure we're all confused here."

"You tried to kill us with that table!" she accused.

"So now you're adding attempted murder?"

"There's always been something wrong with you, boy."

"Once again, I must remind you that I am currently twenty-four years of age. Why, then, am I a boy when you speak to me but an adult when I'm tried?"

Councilor Norwood cut in. "Silence, the both of you. Rebuttals come after the councilors' cross-examination of the accused."

Councilor Vesta of the Southern Tribe, a rail-thin woman with steely eyes the color of a thundercloud, motioned to speak. "I will second his question, however. Are you proposing the boy tossed that metal table at you, Detective?"

"Not physically, Councilor, because I admit he did not raise a hand."

"What evidence do you have, then, that he caused it? Or of it happening at all?"

Reid's expression hardened. "I am law enforcement, Councilor. My testimony itself is evidence."

"Let me rephrase. What is it you believe actually occurred the night in question, and why?"

"I do not wish to speculate, Councilor."

Vesta pointed at Sheila. "Then, Ms. Sherrington, we must turn to you. Does Detective Reid's account differ from yours in any way?"

"Only slightly, my lady, as I have more concrete evidence to present." The slight woman shivered a moment before unrolling and lifting a large canvas. Of Zeph with glowing red eyes. "I submit my official portrait of the interrogation."

Reid tried to grab it.

Sheila dodged and shrieked, "The boy is possessed. There is no other explanation. This is exactly what I saw. His eyes grew redder and redder as the night went on."

"Orelio have mercy," said Vesta, laughing. Soon, the entire chamber tittered along with her.

"Nestling," said Zeph slowly, "I think the mad woman has saved us."

Aurora saw their chance too and took it. "I submit a motion to dismiss the charges against Zephyr and Willow in light of insufficient, and frankly, outrageous, evidence."

The councilors paused for a moment, but one by one, they began to second her motion. As the fifth councilor raised a hand for the majority, Willow hugged Zeph, joyous, just as a familiar voice rang out with a lisp, "I second the charge of violent assault against Zephyr Norwood."

Amos McKay strode unbidden up to the Bowl, with Jeffrey and Alex at his side. "Permission requested to enter the stand."

"No, thanks, it's a bit crowded in here," Willow called up.

"Permission granted," said Councilor McKay. "Make your testimony."

The three young men jumped in, and Willow got a good look at Amos, his puffy lips and chin crusted over with blood, as though stung by a gang of honeybees. He had done nothing so far to mop himself up.

"Bright be the judgment," he said and, without waiting for the customary response, continued. "Councilors, I testify that Zephyr Norwood accosted me outside of the Western Estate just a couple hours ago. He held me down and kicked me in the face until he knocked out a tooth." His sibilants strange and speech whistling, he pointed to a missing upper central incisor.

"You should have looked for it and popped it back in immediately," advised Zeph.

"You see? He is not denying it. And what a disgusting suggestion, you moron."

"I can't deny your tooth is missing, no. Never said I caused it."

Amos sputtered. "Do you have any idea the emotional and physical and functional"—Willow struggled not to laugh at the sight and sound of him—"and aesthetic value of such a tooth? Well, do you?"

Councilor McKay, the square-jawed and stocky leader of the Eastern Tribe, found the situation of his heir's battered face much less amusing than Willow did. He pointed a finger at Amos's friends and asked, "Are these men here to corroborate?"

"Yes, sir," parroted Alex and Jeffrey.

"Councilors, may I speak?" Willow asked.

"No," said McKay as Aurora answered, "Yes."

Vesta broke into a cold smile and raised a hand. "What an unprecedented situation. I recommend Councilors McKay, Erifson, and perhaps even Norwood, recuse themselves from this matter."

The three councilors agreed, but not without some muttering.

"Is that good or bad for us?" Willow wondered out loud.

Zeph just shook his head. "Makes no difference. Not if it's about me. Watch." Louder, he said, "Councilors, my rebuttal?"

But at that moment, Councilor Sampson of the Northern territory, the oldest and often least-engaged member, seemed to awaken from his slouch to stretch his old bones and lift a hand. All sounds in the chamber died off as his voice rumbled through it with the timbre of a tomb come alive. "A more clear-cut case I have never seen."

Zeph tensed.

Sampson rearranged the long beard in his lap and glanced down at the accused. "The boy's record is clearly that of a delinquent, whereas McKay has been a stellar example for our young men."

"Sir, Zephyr's record at the Academy is faultless," objected Willow.

"But his overall record is not. And this is a council meeting, not a lake. Did he go swimming to prepare?"

"If you would only let us explain this entire—"

"Silence! Willow Erifson, I caution you. There has always been a darkness in your friend that you fail to see." Sampson stood. "Now, my suggested ruling is as follows. The boy should be hereby terminated from his post at the Academy."

Willow glanced at Zephyr in panic.

"Father?" a soft voice spoke. Behind them, Areida Sampson was on her feet too. "He also runs a free program in the valleys, remember?"

Councilor Sampson's deep voice somehow deepened. "Ah yes. Thank you, dear. So which position would you prefer to lose, boy?"

Zeph spoke without hesitation. "The Academy."

"No," said Willow. "That's a paid position. Sir, leave him his livelihood at least."

"Willow, kindly shut the hell up," said Zephyr.

"I can't believe you."

"I can't believe *you*," he spat.

Sampson's eyes narrowed. "Both, I should think. Violent behavior coupled with these public outbursts must not be tolerated in the educators of our children. The valleymen should not suffer just for being poor."

Zephyr snapped.

And for the first time in public, he roared, not to be interrupted by anyone, "Rulings and charges such as these are meant for private hearings. Why, then, did the council summon us for a public one? And has anyone allowed me to defend myself? No. Has anyone cared to notice the black eye that half this room, including two councilors, can verify was not present this morning? No. Has anyone on this council besides Aurora Erifson called me by my name?"

He glared at Sheila and Reid, now cowering by the Bowl wall. "No. Well, then, I say a final fucking goodbye to all of you and your decade of baseless character assassination. I'll see you when I see you."

Zephyr, tall enough to reach the Bowl edge, climbed out, arms rippling with the effort of pulling himself over in one smooth movement. He landed in a crouch before Areida with undisguised venom pouring from his eyes, and without waiting for a council vote, stormed out of the chamber.

CHAPTER
5

WATER UNDER
THE BRIDGE

Feel this moment, so redolent
Of fresh regret, a bit of pine,
Or some cement, and strangled weeds
From which does form
This petrichor'd post-decennial storm

Night had fallen, and so had she on the way home.

"Thought I'd find you here," said Zeph, nothing but his legs visible to her from her spot in their hallow. "What was that in there, Willow? Do you even give a shit about our program?"

Willow looked up, eyes red. At the sound of his voice, she crawled out to sit against the slope of the Western Hill.

"They've always been uneasy with you at the Academy," she admitted. "We should have seen this coming. I mean, staff members say you stole Willoughby's books after his death, just so you, and only you, could take his job."

"Oh, they do, do they?"

She wiped her eyes on a muddy sleeve to avoid meeting his. "Some even say you may have killed him."

"Wow, if they say so much, they must be right."

Willow dropped her arm in exasperation. "Of course they're not right, but must you antagonize everyone? It helps them feel validated. And some of those people literally get to make the law of the land."

He started pacing. "Well, *you* could have nipped all this nonsense in the bud. You could have stopped anyone in that room from talking, yet you protected no one but yourself today."

"It didn't feel right," she protested, her powers whipping hair against her face with the turmoil of agitation and shame. "What if I caused permanent damage? How could I hurt other people just to protect us, Zeph?"

He laughed in her face, his expression twisting. "I thought I did my best to show you how right and wrong are never mutually exclusive, but I fucking failed, didn't I?"

"What are you going on about?"

"Exactly. You understand so little."

"How dare you?" she cried.

"And it's not always my fault, you know. This sure as shit is not. You got me arrested. You scapegoat me constantly here."

"I do not," she said, springing up. "We took advantage of your *pre-existing* reputation, and that doesn't make it all my fault. You're older than me. You've had a decade to be seen as you are."

They devolved into shouting.

"And how's that?" he asked, arms spread wide.

"As someone who makes utterly no sense at all. For one thing, where do you even come from?"

"You too, huh? Well, you and that bunch of xenophobic freaks in their molten black lair"—his voice rose as he turned around to yell in the direction of town—"can just shove it where the sun don't shine. Oh, wait, you don't need to, because nothing warm ever shines long enough in this icy hellhole."

"Go cry a river elsewhere, like to your jerk of a father."

His nostrils flared, and his rumble of a voice lowered and shook when he said, "That man is not my father."

"Then who is?" She sucked in a breath as soon as she said it.

When he finally turned to face her, fire and brimstone flashed in his darkening gaze.

She took a full step back.

"In this forgotten place, where no one comes or goes, who's *your* father, Willow? Where's the father of the wealthiest heiress on the island?"

It stung. So much so that her lungs fought for breath. "He...I don't...know...he prob—" Large gulps of air. Knees hitting the ground. A panic attack she could not reason away, even as part of her finally realized she'd never asked him that question so that he would never ask her the same.

He took a step in her direction, but she let loose a scream so feral he stumbled back in surprise. Clouds of dirt and stone hurtled down the slope over their hallow. Zeph ducked below the rock awning, but it too started to tremble, worrying Willow enough that she pushed herself to her feet, shook the tears from her face, and ran off, growling.

She awoke from the dream, its shape clear and solid for once despite her instant sobriety. But this time, phantom waves continued an urgent crash against her ears as shadows swayed in threat along her bedroom walls. In disturbing sync, her heartbeat pounded while her head spun faster and faster, until she swung open a window and vomited over the sill.

Early morning frost lessened her nausea enough to seduce her outside. She snatched her heaviest cloak off a hook and stumbled down the stairs to the ground floor, where she moved to the right and felt worse, moved to the left and felt better. So out through the north-facing door she went, heaving in air and swaying like a drunkard in whichever direction best eased her pain.

She had climbed and descended the Northwestern Hill, traipsed straight through the Rens' beloved cauliflower patch, and initiated her ascent of the Northern Hill by the time her mind realized where her body was taking her: in a straight line to the north despite the level route available through the lowlands. She refused to wonder why, not when the discomfort ebbed only as long as she carried on.

About halfway up that final rise of the Northern Hill, she could see embers in the night.

With her abilities, she lifted her aching body to float faster toward the source, coming to a sudden stop when she found it. Had she not recognized the massive cottage not far from the hill's zenith, the screeching pitch of Areida's sobbing would have been enough.

The five-year-old home built entirely from Erifson firewood lay in ashes under the stars. A few flickering licks of flame were still alive in the snow but under attack by the small crowd of northerners holding buckets of water.

Willow hid behind a roll of the hillside, in curious shock, as the last standing beam of the foundation fell like an afterthought.

Lady Sampson held her daughter back as she shrieked. There was murder in Areida's eyes when she seemed to stare right through Willow's hiding place. The youngest Sampson toddled over to clutch the girl's skirts and wail.

"What a tragedy," a young man not far from Willow whispered to his father.

The man snorted. "No, you weren't in court today. This was deliberate."

Overcome with growing nausea and unable to watch more, Willow fled.

The sun soon joined her journey to higher elevation; true north meant the height of this hill, the only one where the terrain ended at the bluffs over the tallest natural point on the island.

Once she crested the final peak, a swath of tangerine-orange sky streaked with blinding yellows and pinks outlined a grim figure at the cliff's edge. He faced the water with no cloak or protection from the stinging cold.

Her own body calmed at the sight of him.

"Zeph?" she whispered, too low to hear, yet he turned.

"Morning, nestling."

"So, I'm 'nestling' again, am I?" she asked.

He smiled in what almost seemed an apology. "This is sooner than I hoped. But I guess I had far longer than planned."

He wasn't making any sense, and when he looked down at his feet, the dread she should have felt earlier burst into the air between them.

"Come over here, Zeph." She tried for firmness.

"No."

She stepped forward, but his hand shot up in a clear warning to halt. Everything around them had fallen so silent, the entire encounter like a fatal secret from within which she could hear neither the whirlpools beyond the bluffs nor the wind stroking through Zeph's hair.

"Why do you think we've been dreaming the same dream for weeks now, nestling? Hasn't it bothered you?" he asked after a long pause.

Her lips trembled. "Please step away from there. Oh, Zeph. Just forgive me, won't you?"

"I wish we hadn't fought yesterday. Really paints what I'm about to do in a different light."

"How can you sound so sane?" she cried. "You're standing on the edge of a cliff."

"Yes, and I'm about to ask that you literally follow me off it." He glanced behind him and chuckled.

"But why? You're scaring me."

"That's fair. But think hard, nestling. I know you also dreamed something different last night—plucked feathers drifting around you as you fell. Isn't that right?"

She shook her head violently. "Stop this. Stop it right now."

"That means it's time. Time to go."

She reached out to him with her powers, knowing she had never been good at holding on to people, especially when she felt so afraid. Oh, but she tried. She tried to hold tight.

"You matter to me in ways you will never understand if you stay here. You matter in ways no one will understand if you do. I saw you in that damn courtroom yesterday, hesitating to stop the detective. Tell me this: Deep in your heart, didn't you want them all to know and accept you for the extraordinary person you are?"

"Why are you asking me all these questions?" she said, her knees shaking. "I'm the one so confused I'm about to vomit again. What have you been keeping from me?" She waited, but he refused to answer. "Zeph, did you set fire to Areida's cottage?"

He cocked his head. "Yes."

Tears pricked at her eyes.

"Don't cry for that viper. She understands nothing of struggle or loss. And her ladyship has an entire estate waiting for her to claim."

"Look, it doesn't matter"—she held out a hand—"because I'll help you sort it out. I swear. You don't need to jump."

His voice grew soft, more soothing. "I won't die, little one. Not from this. And neither will you. Maybe I should have prepared you better. But your actions must be your choice, and I can't stay any longer. The warning bell is ringing."

"Do you mean the dreams?" At his silence, she shouted, "I want answers, Zeph. You have them, don't you? About everything, even my powers, that you just won't give."

"Come with me and get them."

"Please. Please don't."

"Remember something for me, won't you?"

She started sobbing.

He smiled. "No one can do exactly what you do. Don't tell anyone what you can do to people, anywhere."

"I don't understand you anymore." Hysteria set in as she reached for him, extending her arm almost out of its socket. "Did I ever?"

"You could. I swear, you could if you follow me. This is the most important loophole I've got. Please."

Zeph held out a hand as well.

He did not jump.

He fell.

Backward he went, in such slow motion, and yet too fast for her to register the action in time. She pulled at him, too distraught to do a proper job, so there he went, right over the cliff. And there she ran, right after him.

PART

II

TO INGRESS

CHAPTER
6
RETURN
ARRIVAL

Come take a flight of fancy
Through swirls of foam and fields of green
Come where the people fight
Over magic's wild delight
And the children only fear
A step too far from what is near

W illow bolted upright and screamed from the pain. Her body felt decrepit to the bone, as if it could not move yet had anyway, her muscles unable to bear the defiance. She plopped back down, terrified to drown or choke or hit her head against a rock by the whirlpools.

But softness, of all things, met her from behind, and a scream caught in her throat, turning at once into a panicked sob.

Blinking in confusion, Willow realized she could not turn her head. And a translucent coppery sheen seemed to ripple around her, the colors of the world muted behind it.

Her strange vision settled on a roof composed of what

appeared to be straw. Odd thoughts trickled through her brain: *How does it protect against the cold? Or the spread of fire?*

She spent a long while trying to slow her racing heart.

Until a pair of wide eyes framed by fluffy white brows appeared above her.

"My stars, she's awake!" said the woman to whom they belonged. She shrieked again, calling out, "Jerald. Did you hear me, old man? I said she's awake!"

"I'm coming. I'm coming," came a different muffled voice.

Is he underwater too? No. It's dry. Too dry.

"Oh, ducky, you're alright. Don't panic." The woman tilted Willow's head toward her with a gentle touch as she settled into a chair at her side.

Willow could now see an ax in the corner, a dining table, a few squishy chairs, and a funny-looking rug. *How did I come to be indoors?*

A man shuffled into the room from a doorway that led outside, spilling sunlight across the floor as he entered. He stood tall, built solid yet thin, and nothing like an old man but for the cloud-like patches of hair on his balding head.

"What were you shouting?" he asked just before he took sight of Willow and dropped the bundle of crops in his arms with a gasp.

The woman chuckled. "Like the dead come alive, no?"

"Didn't think I'd see the day, not after fifteen years," he whispered.

At that, the world spun and took Willow away with it.

When she regained consciousness, Willow's body felt shot through with warmth, and it lay arranged in a plump chair by a small hearth in which no wood burned. Her chest ached. Her vision remained altered. Again, she could not move.

The older woman sat across from her, knitting in apparent peace beside a tea tray. "Welcome, dear." Another wary smile. "Can you speak?"

The words rose like glass shards against her throat, but Willow managed, "Who're you?"

"A caretaker, of sorts. But mostly a Skia farmer near a trading village. I was told you wouldn't remember any of what that means. My husband and I will have to start from the beginning."

"Over here, dearie," said the man called Jerald, who was sitting on the floor with his back against the woman's legs. Struggling to see him, Willow cast her eyes as far downward as possible, restricted by the distance they could travel in their sockets.

He leaned over and placed a cup against her lips, tilting her head back to drink.

Willow kept her lips pursed, resisting the only way she could against this stranger.

"It will help your throat muscles and ease the ache of speaking. Your muscles have fallen out of use. But we'll get your limbs moving and your feet dancing again, so don't you worry about that. Won't we, my Evie? Now, what all d'you remember, miss?"

Willow took a sip of something foul and immediately rasped, "Where's he? Where's Zeph?"

"Who?" asked Evie.

Jerald frowned and shook his head. "Don't know anyone by that name. What's his designation?"

Tears filled her eyes, and Willow inhaled as deeply as she could. "What'd you mean? Fifteen years?"

The couple glanced at each other.

"That's the beginning I mentioned," said Evie.

Willow's breathing grew harsher, ragged.

"We don't know a Zeph, but a boy did drop you off to us fifteen years ago. Skin the color of bone, that one. Amazing he could even fly with you. Said you might never wake, but paid us very handsomely for your care. A king's ransom, really."

"How young was he?"

"Barely a teenager, I'd say. Thin. Winged."

"Winged? As in…he had wings?"

"Yes, and you can read about his kind in here." Jerald held up the book in his lap, moth-eaten and as old as Robert Larsen in appearance. "He left it for you. *The Primordial Clan of the Great Portal: Volume I.* A very precious edition, stamped with the reviewal seals of many famed scholars, all quite dead. I'm told that adds to their clout."

Evie's face grew pinched. "We thought the Exowinged a myth until your captor scared us to the Hub and back casting his shadow through our door. We assume he did this to you, and we have no clue why. We'd never be stupid enough to ask a royal mage his reason for enchanting an innocent at the behest of his precious king."

"But he said you would wake one day and need a medic, so here I am." Jerald smiled at her and bowed his head. "Farmer by day. Physician by night. At your service."

Evie puffed out her chest. "My husband held the role of chief medic for our clan until the diaspora sent us packing. Sent most of us packing…" She trailed off, catching the confused, panicked look on Willow's face.

"I'm not in Spinor Falls?" Willow finally whispered in fear.

"No, dear."

It took a few minutes to calm her back down, Evie patting her face dry and Jerald covering her in a blanket so heavy it felt like liquid metal.

"We're not doing this right. How's about a light walk outside?" Jerald offered. Willow made no sound to accept his ridiculous offer, instead feeling frozen in time as it coldly passed her by. "I'll grab the hay cart."

Soon, she was half-reclined against a stack of straw beside Evie and soaking up the warmest sun she had ever felt on a ride through strange, multicolored fields. Before them, Jerald lugged the cart with tan arms under a white short-sleeved shirt that was so thin, Willow could not imagine anyone ever bothering to sew such a useless thing back home.

"Maybe we should have a horse do this," cackled Evie.

"I pull smoother than any horse, my lady," Jerald shot back. "The outdoors are a better place for serious conversation anyhow. I've always said so."

"When have you *ever* said so?"

"Didn't I just?"

"Your version of 'always' disturbs me. Then what did you mean when you promised to always love, honor, and cherish me?"

Jerald laughed and continued his stubborn march ahead.

Their banter sent another pang through Willow's chest. She jolted out of her shock into another panic. "Please. Please tell me what's going on. I jumped off a cliff, and suddenly I'm here. Where is here? What is here?"

"Why in the Shadow's name would you jump off a cliff, dearie?" the woman asked. "Are you sure that happened?"

Jerald stopped moving. "Hush now, Evie. Don't question her reality. It might not be good for her."

"Actual reality is good for her, that's what. Prescribe some, you old turd."

He pushed himself into a sudden sprint, Evie laughing in delight as they fell back against the hay, the wind a harsh force that soon slapped their faces red. Minutes later, they reached the edge of the fields and barreled through the last plot of head-high vegetation.

"Look there, little lady. That's the main trading village for a hundred miles, or so it's said." Jerald came to a halt and pointed off into the distance, where gray fumes and tallish buildings slunk into the sky.

"It's ugly," decided Willow. "I want to go home. Take me home."

"Now, ducky," began Evie.

"My name's Willow!" she shouted to the sky. "Willow!"

The cart shot into the air. Evie screamed, and Jerald swiped at the cart with his arms in a desperate effort to grab the handles.

"Honey, hold on," he cried.

Willow and Evie shook, spasmed, and spun with the cart as bursts of hay showered the field and a stricken Jerald followed them below, hollering, "Breathe, Willow! Tie yourself down to the earth. Come back."

Willow flung herself through her thoughts instead. She liked it up here. The clear blue and soft light. She avoided looking down because the relative flatness of the land below was not very nice at all. No lumpy roads. Not a true hill in sight.

"Curses, girl!"

Could I just float this useless body all the way home?

"She's afraid of heights. Please. Please, girl. Lower the cart."

In the eye of her mind's storm, Willow managed to see through the whirling torment of pain inside her just long enough to notice the old woman's terror. Centering herself like Zephyr often preached in their meditation sessions, she lowered the cart onto a plot of cabbage. Jerald fell upon them and snatched Evie away, though the lady's viselike grip on the edges of the wood held firm.

"Kinetic. She's a freaking Exo pusher," sobbed Evie into her husband's neck.

That caught Willow's wayward attention. "I'm a what?"

Jerald glanced at her in frustrated pity, but his positive nature seemed to win out. "Guess this means I don't have to pull us back home, eh?"

They leaned Willow against the cart and spread out in a bedraggled patch of monstrous-sized daisies. Jerald had plucked a couple of rainbow-colored heads of cabbage to feed Evie, but Willow refused to open her mouth.

"We call this place Ingress, or more formally the Land of Portalcraft," Jerald began once they had settled in the tall, warm grass, his eyes softening with the hazy touch of rote memory. "Little is known of how we came to be here, but most historians believe it started with the Great Portal of Ether opening beside the Original Void, merging and exploding together at the Hub to litter the land with portals and populate it with two main branches of people and powers."

Willow's heart banged against her chest. "Powers? You mean there are others like me here?"

"Oh yes, although you gave quite a display for someone so young."

"Quite," muttered Evie. "And to think, that devious boy hinted at you being one of us. Of course he would, now that I think about it."

Willow wanted to scream while she stared down at her paralyzed arms, but instead asked for forgiveness in her quest for answers. "I'm sorry for the loss of control, ma'am."

That seemed to soften Evie a bit. "Considering you've been with us so long, I can't really hold you accountable for the atrocities of your people, can I?"

"But I don't understand. Just who do you think my people are?" asked Willow, but with an impatient edge she just couldn't dull.

Evie rose for a stretch and to dust off her skirt with angry patting motions. "The Exokinetics, of course. Simply put, they're the sort of Exos who can move objects in the world around them."

"So there are truly others like me here?" wondered Willow.

The couple nodded. They allowed her a long moment to take in a shaky breath and follow a loose thread of thought until she discovered what nagged at her. "You mentioned portals. This place is full of them?"

The couple nodded.

"They take people from one place to another?"

"Usually without their consent," laughed Evie.

"So that must be how I got here, then?"

"Maybe," said Jerald, but he did not look convinced.

"What?" prodded Willow.

"Nothing."

"Go on, then. I won't pass out again so soon…I don't think."

Jerald offered her a leaf, and this time she accepted the fresh, sweet-tasting vegetable out of absentminded impatience.

Jerald smiled and said, "Well, we don't know of any place called Spinor Falls, but I admit it's not possible to know of much past your own neighborhood in these parts. People who travel run the great risk of never coming back. And it's often only the stupidly rich who try it, with their very expensive, very unofficial maps."

"But your account of my time with you makes so little sense," she said with her mouth full.

"How's that?"

"Why would someone impair me like this only to pay buckets for the lifelong care of a medic and his wife?" she demanded.

Evie snorted. "The Winged have their reasons, some more sinister than others. The way their mages manipulate ether remains poorly understood." She lay back against flowers and earth only to hiss, "It's commonly considered sorcery. And they use it for the benefit of a genocidal race."

"We don't know that for sure, Evie, dear," said Jerald. "We don't even know how many of them are left."

"You thought all the rumors of the Flock were nonsense until you met that child with the hideous black roots sprouting from his back."

"He was no assassin. He left her in our care, Evie."

"He kindly left her cursed, with a body that aged but completely stopped functioning. Not even a heartbeat this whole time. I almost buried her once."

"Evie!"

"So," Willow jumped in, too excited to feel disturbed, "why agree to the request of a Winged boy?"

Evie turned her head to look at Willow, smooth yellow blooms pressed against her wrinkled face. "You were so young. We didn't have the heart to turn you away."

"And we needed the money."

"Jerald!"

"Evie!" he teased.

Willow smiled for the first time since entering this recurrent nightmare of paralysis. "And what sort of people are you?"

"Exoskia," said Evie, sitting up straighter. "We can manipulate and meld with shadow ether."

"Huh. Well, you really lost me that time."

Jerald held up a hand. "Time to be the medic I claim to be. It's getting late, and we've overwhelmed you enough. Let's head back, get some dinner going, and rest up. You'll find many more answers in that book of yours, I promise you. And we'll be here to fill in the gaps."

He plopped a frustrated, embarrassed Willow back into the cart before sweeping his wife up into his arms and stepping in as well. He turned to Willow. "Go on, then."

Willow didn't know whether to laugh or cry, but she transported them all back to the little double-storied house, all strange angles and leaning to one side, with Evie's eyes closed and Jerald whooping his exhilaration the entire way.

Some sort of veggie stew bubbled over the lit fire for dinner as Willow inhaled her book, floating before her tired but determined eyes. It had gilded edges, which Jerald said implied near-ancient age due to the scarcity of gold.

With the help of its glossary, Willow struggled through the first chapter of clearly high-level scholarly work that assumed a basic understanding of terms she had never heard. Willow was about to slam the book against the wall when Jerald burst in.

"Willow, come along," he huffed. "Quickly."

She glanced at him in fury. "How?"

"Oh, right." He tucked her into his arms and rushed outside. "A neighbor just reminded me about tonight's show by the trading village. I think it would be perfect for you."

Willow decided she did not like being carried like a sack of potatoes through the fields. Offended, she endured the bumpy trip in the dark with her eyes closed. The sounds of strange birds and insects grew softer the farther they went, and very soon, Jerald was placing her down onto dry soil against a bale of hay and arranging her head for the best view.

When her eyes fluttered open, she could see a grand booth with curtains set up ahead and clusters of children gathered with lanterns in the grass before it.

Sitting cross-legged just ahead of her, Jerald explained softly, "We're at the very border of the East Skia Trading Village, where they stage marionette shows for the children each night. I heard this evening they're doing *The Fox and the Phoenix*. That's why I want you to watch very closely. It's starting."

Even the children had grown quiet with anticipation when a deep, gruff voice from behind the booth spoke. "Once upon a time, the world was full of portals. That time never ended, for time rarely does. And when younglings looked outside and dreamed of more, their parents tugged them closer, knowing too well that in a land of unchartered and unseen thresholds, only the foolish go wandering. And only the lost appear from the ether."

The curtains opened with a flourish.

A large phoenix puppet stretched its wings, marionette strings dancing to produce the effect, while the narrator continued. "Mother Phoenix burst out of the Original Void at the beginning of time and brought order to the universe"—the stage lit up—"but this angered an older and more chaotic force."

A cloaked, shadowy reptile hopped onto the stage. It contorted until the hood of the cloak fell off to reveal a hideous, bloodied eye.

The children in the crowd gasped as the character howled like a wolf.

"Father Orelio lived within the darkness of the Great Portal, a primitive form of life long ago, and he had no interest in bending to the will of a phoenix."

Willow stared, recognizing the name from her childhood fables, and burst into silent, homesick tears.

The reptile asked the phoenix, "What are you?"

"What are you?" the phoenix replied with suspicion.

They circled each other, pouncing back and forth on their strings until they collided. The fight worsened, pieces of the puppets breaking off until they finally fell away from each other.

The narrator continued, "She was born from order, and he was chaos. The calm void and the roiling ether. Opposing sources. So they took pieces of each other in that first battle and fled."

The puppets moaned, injured, on opposite sides of the stage.

"Unable to find common ground, Father Orelio and Mother Phoenix governed different regions of the universe, where the two separate lines of our land's ancestors formed: the Primordial Clan came from him and the Creatures of the Void from her. The Clan and the Creatures would clash over the years, evolving into their modern forms as Exos and Metas."

Jerald cut in, saying to her, "Never call the Metas 'creatures,' Willow. It's highly offensive."

"Shut up, Jerald," grumbled a parent nearby.

Willow's lips quirked a bit as the storyteller continued. "Ether is in all the things we can touch: our skin, our homes, our soil. It is the coppery plane we can see around us, a source of power outside ourselves that, as Exos, we have the ability to control. Our source name comes from the very external nature of our powers.

"But the void contains a spark of life, an ancient power coursing throughout our bodies and our land. It is not right to manipulate the void, whether it's internal or external. As a form of life, it should be left alone, but Metas don't respect that. They can play with this power, using their internal void to ruin the world."

The curtains closed and reopened to a new set. The narrator stayed silent as a little fox pranced through a dense forest, even its whiskers twitching from the tug of thin wires.

It rushed into a tunnel, where a family of foxes stared back at him.

The narrator began:

"Long ago, a young kit found its mother crying in their den. All his siblings and parents were sick, so sick they could barely move. Mother Fox knew the younglings would die without help. So she called out to her one healthy kit, 'You must bring us a bunch of the bright yellow flower with blue dots in its middle. The one that grows in threes within the woods. I will boil it to save your brothers and sisters.'

"The kit nodded and returned to the forest, frantically searching through clusters of flowers. It sniffed black ones and purple ones and white ones and pink ones, but never found the yellow ones.

"He grew scared as night began to fall and a strange noise reached his ears. He had not noticed the bird watching him from high above the trees until it began to sing. Red as a phoenix, with the same sort of tail feathers, she cried such a terrible song that the fox grew even more anxious."

The kit growled at the bird onstage to stop.

"Why are you crying, little fox?" asked the bird.

"I need the yellow flower with the blue dots in the middle that grows in threes. Or my family will die."

The bird cocked its head and asked, "What will happen if they die?"

"Well, I will be alone."

Willow's tears fell again, hot and fast, as she tried not to make a sound. But inside her, something very loud screamed in pain.

"What will happen if you are alone?" asked the bird.

"I don't know. I'm just a child."

"What will happen if I help you?"

"We'd all be saved! So can you help? Please?"

"Well, as a Meta, I'm a reasonable sort. You have given me reason enough to help you find these flowers."

The kit danced and jumped over to stand beneath the tree where the bird perched. "As an Exo, I thank you."

"This way."

The bird flew, marionette strings flapping its wings slowly at first, then faster. The kit had to rush to keep up.

The narrator spoke again, "The kit ran faster than Mother ever let him, bounding off in such haste that he could not see the bird and keep an eye on the ground at the same time. Something gave way beneath him, and he slipped through a portal."

The children in the audience cried out.

"Like all portals, it dumped the kit into the sky so that he fell to the earth. The bird was able to fly gently down instead. They landed beside a grove full of the yellow flowers with blue dots. The kit laughed in joy and rolled in the beautiful blooms, gathering a large bunch and coming to a stop before the bird."

"I'm ready to go back," said the kit.

"You will have to find your own way. I know only how to fly in that direction," replied the bird.

It cawed, a cackle in the sound, as the audience booed.

"You tricked me," said the kit.

"I did what I promised. You only asked for the flowers."

The kit's anger visibly swelled and swelled.

He lunged at the bird while it blithely cleaned its feathers. In anger at the bite, the bird spewed fire—actual fire alighting onstage—that burned down half the field and nearly scorched the fox. But the kit was fast. It tore off the bird's head, throwing it out into the crowd as someone began to douse the blaze in the background.

Some of the children started crying. Willow glanced over at Jerald in question, and he shrugged. "Damned bird deserved it," he grumbled.

The narrator quieted them all with his next words. "The kit sat there beside the bleeding bird and thought of his dying family. He fell into such despair and desperation that he tugged at his fur with his sharp teeth. He tugged at the carcass. He even tugged at the flower roots beside him. Until, in the depths of his pain, he tugged at a shadow so hard it lifted off the earth and over onto him.

"Covered in shadow, he managed to meld with its ether. Using this new power, the kit disappeared into the earth and searched the land safely without fear of portals. One day, he appeared from out of the shadow right near his family den. How did he do it? What sort of powers did he display, children?"

Little shouts came from the front row, too low for Willow to understand.

"Yes, he was an Exoskia, just like you. Our kind can travel unnoticed by using shadow ether as cover. But the dangers of the world around us remain very real.

"The story of the fox and the phoenix is a classic we therefore pass down to you. Remember always to watch where you step, beware the tricksters, and trust your own powers above all else. Good night, little ones."

Jerald scooted over to Willow during the smattering of clapping little hands. "Well?"

"There should be an age limit to this," she whispered, confused and forlorn.

The hot night air felt different against her wet cheeks than the constant chill of her childhood home. Even this simple disparity made her want to yank the silly marionettes by their strings and tear into them with her teeth.

Jerald squeezed her shoulder and explained, "It's more important that our younglings understand the harsh reality of Ingressian life. Too many mothers and fathers lose family to childish wandering each year. It's enough to drive an Exo mad with fear to reproduce."

"And the Metas? They're the villains in your story?"

He sighed. "Metas are close to extinction, Willow. Be wary of them. They distort the truth for their own purposes. Don't you think it's better to be stupid than use your mind the way they do to justify their own ends?"

"But the fox attacked without trying to find a solution. It could have reasoned with the bird to help him again. What was right about that?"

"You're an Exo yourself, Willow. Don't talk like them. A Meta will just play mind games with you."

She could only watch as people put out the remaining licks of flame onstage, and felt a strange, hot bubbling in her own veins.

Willow was quiet on the way back as Jerald explained, much more kindly than she took it, how he and Evie had left her in a corner all these years, like a stowed-away broom meant to take up as little space as possible. They covered her in blankets and checked on her twice a day. Her body needed nothing else while in some sort of coma, a spell that defied even their logic, as they protected her useless shell of a person for fifteen years.

Humming, Jerald entered the little double-storied house with Willow in his arms to see Evie fuming. Gone silent, he placed Willow by the fire and casually walked upstairs.

Evie pointed to a bowl on the side table and said, "You seem to have fine ethereal control, so spoon it up yourself."

The woman dashed off, following Jerald.

Willow could hear them arguing for a long while afterward, Evie's voice carrying down to her. "How could you take her there? We have no idea who she really is. We can't trust her with our people's secrets, you fool!"

Jerald spoke lower, and it was harder to hear him, though at one point he mentioned something about "just the basics," and Willow trusting them enough to stay "or we lose that income."

So, when he returned to put her to bed, Willow resisted. "I can do it when I'm ready"—he laughed at that—"or I'll sleep here."

She wanted to read her book anyway.

It was a good thing she did because she understood it much better this time around. The fire was dying down by the third chapter. By the fourth, Willow had lost all the breath in her body.

"On Sentience," the chapter was titled, and it began, "The Exoself is a source restricted to the external world by definition, and as such, can exert no power over a sentient being. That is an ability restricted only to those with control of the Metaself."

But Willow's kinetic powers had always allowed her to move people around as well as things. Even to move herself.

The book fell to the ground.

No one can do exactly what you do. Don't tell anyone what you can do to people, anywhere.

Zephyr's past words cut through the nighttime silence.

Where is he? Where's Mother? And what must they think happened to me?

She summoned a mirror off the mantelpiece and stared at a face she recognized only as an old acquaintance. Tracing her features with a teary gaze, she noted how she had visibly aged: young yet, but no longer a teenager.

She sobbed for hours, unbidden sleep offering the only escape from her suffering.

CHAPTER
7

BATH TIME

Close your eyes but keep open your ears.
Heighten your senses and soften your fears.
Beware the monster beneath your bed,
And don't you forget to check overhead.

—*Ingressian nursery rhyme popularized*
in the Shadowlands

Throughout all of recent memory, Ingressian offspring had been forbidden to nurse wounded birds. No toddlers ran after pretty butterflies with jars. No adults bred avian creatures for message carrying in a land where flight presented the utmost advantage. "Because when the Flock come for you," parents taught wide-eyed children in their beds, "their wings make the softest sound against the floor, which you must never mistake for anything else."

Younglings across the land, who would never meet thanks to separation by those dastardly multi-furcated portals, all fell asleep to phantom whispers of brushing feathers, hyperaware of leaves thrashing in the wind or the rustle of a cat slipping across their covers.

Stories of bloodthirsty bogeymen may have risen from kernels of truth, but common sense should have suggested that long-lived, clandestine monsters would never let their wings drag.

And so when the tallest of the Flock stalked through a cemetery much too surefooted for an amateur assassin gone unseen for so long, his traditional garb was stretched across massive inky wings that not once met the ground.

His brethren wondered how he knew where to go or how he felt safe on soil yet so foreign to him, but trust in their own kind was all they had left. Two of them hurried to catch up.

"Dark tidings, Zeph," whispered the brother on reaching his side. "Retrieval is now the secondary objective."

Zeph halted. "And the primary?"

"Final retribution," said the sister. "I've been ordered to bear witness."

Zephyr's eyes narrowed. "Let's be off, then."

The other two glanced at each other in brief concern before she said, "I brought a satchel for the long flight."

"No."

"No?"

"Short journey. Bidirectional and non-furcated to the Twisted Forge." He furled his wings into a tight cocoon behind him and ran with great speed at an unmarked grave, where he jumped in headfirst, disappearing into the portal's ether as if sucked into the Original Void.

Brother and sister shared a questioning look before she followed.

At the exit, the pair burst vertically into the air and opened their wings, taking flight over swamps full of unmapped portals. Just a mile south, in the deepest portion of a thick cluster of trees, stood a small cottage beside a sleeping forge. They landed after an aerial sweep under cover of darkness proved unremarkable.

Wings tense, they peered through the cottage's single large window at what appeared to be a small dining room.

She glanced over at her kin's still profile. "He always says he must bathe our hands in blood as early as possible."

Zephyr motioned her away, his eyes on their goal, left abandoned beside a sleeping dog in the corner of the silent room. She fell back just as he touched the windowpane with his middle finger, the glass dissolving from the point of contact outward until he could step over the sill.

A few paces past the magicked threshold, he paused to inspect a leftover meal on a wooden table. Steam puffed over a full teacup.

Without sound, a man slammed into his chest from out of the shadow before him, rolling them onto the floor.

He swung his head away to avoid a dagger in the face and flipped the man over, trapping him below, only to stare into the eyes of an Ingressian legend of a voidsmith.

After a beat, he grabbed hold of the fist clutching a dagger against his stomach, breaking the smith's wrist with a crunch and shoving it up and into his chest, burying the blade to the hilt.

Life bled out of the legend.

Wafting back onto his feet with a single thrust of his wings, the assassin faced his target to complete the retrieval. "Come along, child."

CHAPTER
8

SHADOW OF
MY SHADOW

The Primordial Clan of the Great Portal branched into modern-day **chaosmen** or in layman's terms, **Exos.**

> Further subdivided by the quality of their powers into designations, e.g., Exoskia and Exokinetics.

The Creatures of the Void branched into modern-day **voidsmen**, or in layman's terms, **Metas**.

> Further subdivided by the quality of their powers into designations, e.g., Metaporters and Metafervers.

*Note that abbreviated source precedes designation.
Source: Meta or Exo.
Designation: Skia, Kinetic, etc.

—The Primordial Clan of the Great Portal:
Volume I, *Chapter 1: Classification*

Learning to walk proved no easier the second time around. And without the use of Willow's powers to aid her disused limbs, the entire process bordered on damn near excruciating. She would not risk breaking her promise to Zephyr, now that she more fully understood its meaning. Ingressians so far did not strike her as the most open-minded sort, and if an Exo who could use her power on living beings was not something they had ever seen, she would not be the first to show them.

The first few days, Jerald guided her through strength exercises, massaged her muscles, prepared nutrient-rich elixirs, and mixed an array of pungent salves that he said included a decade-old, exotic ingredient saved just for her. She improved, but the pain of a fishhook pull at her chest remained a constant ache.

After her first solo steps, she dredged up the courage to ask, "Why continue to go to all this trouble for a Kinetic?"

"Deals struck in the Land of Portalcraft are not broken without consequence, Willow," Evie said, nose in the air as she helped Willow into a seat placed outside for her benefit.

"And we get the money in payments," called out Jerald, knee-deep in mud and grinning from ear to ear. Evie chucked a spoon at him.

A couple weeks after that, he took her on a stumbling but brisk trip farther than she had yet been able to walk herself.

"Today, we secure you a decent map. No Ingressian child leaves home for the first time by herself without one. Ever," said Jerald.

"Don't you consider this area home?"

"No. It's just a trading village."

The sun had sunk low, glancing over the horizon in goodbye to paint rows of crops in the pink-and-green colors of an Ingressian gloaming. Willow lay her head in the thick grass and listened to another of Jerald's lectures begin. She enjoyed his fatherly tone, though she would have rather licked horse dung than admit it.

"Two warnings," he was saying. "The most important thing to remember is that there are no portals within these fields, but as soon as you reach my property border, it's best to follow the dirt path down to the village to avoid all the ones leading to the Shadowlands."

She felt a tap on her head.

"You listening?"

"Yes, sir," she mumbled, turning face down and pulling one foot over and onto her head in a satisfying stretch. "And how many portals are there?"

"Four in the immediate area, but only one is bidirectional, so it's not a simple jump-back-in-and-return sort of situation, alright?"

She nodded into the dirt. "And the second warning?"

"Using your powers in the village is acceptable, but do nothing to draw attention."

"Meaning?"

"No moving anything bigger than a barrel unless you want trouble. The Exokinetics highly covet power, so they'll wonder how you slipped their notice. You'll get to see more Exoskia, traveling Kinetic traders, and the odd Kinetic patrol. But keep away from anyone else because they might just get you arrested."

"Why do the Kinetics get to police a Skia trading center anyway?"

"It's not like they ever asked our permission, kid."

Cryptic enough, she decided, that she made a mental note to internalize her powers better, effective immediately.

Jerald tugged her up with a jaunty flourish before setting off on the winding dirt path overrun with bothersome little pebbles ahead of them. It seemed to go on for miles.

"Take a look over here," said Jerald after a minute or two. "Portals can be either patent or veiled, as I'm sure you've read by now, meaning they're basically visible or invisible to the naked eye. Patent ones will obviously present less danger if you know what you're looking for. Let me show you."

He stepped off the path and knelt by a sizable puddle of dirty water. "Now, youngling, run your hand just over it, but don't touch. Then tell me what you see."

Willow obeyed. When Jerald just looked at her, she did it again until she noted, "There's no reflection."

"That's right. And they don't lead very far, ranging from a few paces away to a couple miles or so."

"Wow," she said, sitting down to see better. The surface had a liquid-copper sheen, too molten and perfect to resemble actual water from up close. "So why don't people just leave a marker by all the known portals for public safety?"

He looked at her like he sometimes did when thinking her childish. "That would take trust, not just in the people who left the markers but also in the travelers who may come across them. Ingressians have little reason to help strangers navigate our territories. And we expect native residents to know their way around."

They resumed their journey to town, and after a couple miles, she was ducking under the shade of a massive tree that draped itself over a considerable stretch of the road. When the cramping in her legs advanced to pain, she fell behind and glanced up for walking-stick material. Lifting onto her toes, she reached for a promising branch.

Her already failing legs gave out, sending her tumbling off the path with a muttered curse.

Landing against a massive, spotted tree trunk, she called out, "Jerald!"

He turned back to her, eyes wide with alarm when she made to stand, placing a palm on the ground for support.

The earth collapsed, her hand sinking into it just before all of her did.

Willow felt a rush throughout her body, as if she were being both pulled apart and smashed for an eternal fraction of a second, only able to breathe once she emerged on the other side—body sprawled out and free-falling as she looked up into a dark sky.

Dropping a few feet to land on her back, Willow rolled over in pain with the branch still clutched in her hand.

Jerald landed beside her—nothing there one moment, a man shimmering into existence just above her the next.

Too worried to feel dumbstruck, Willow pled, "Tell me that was the two-way portal."

"No such luck, foreigner," he replied, turning from his side onto his back.

"My chest hurts so damn much," she gasped out.

"People react differently to portal travel. But entering like you did was not the best idea."

"Why?"

He ran a hand over his face. "Think of a portal like a tunnel running through the ground that spits you out at the end going the same speed as when you fell in. So it's best to enter slowly and backward. That way, when you exit out, into the sky, you're horizontal and facing the earth, which gives you more time and visibility to shift your body to its safest landing position. Which is?"

"Well, you landed on your side."

"Exactly."

"But can't I just step into a portal?" asked Willow.

"Not unless you want to land on your head."

Willow lifted herself onto her elbows and thought about it. "So if I step in, my head actually exits first?"

"Yes, because your exit position in the sky will always be the flipped version of how you entered—flipped along the axis of the portal, that is."

At Willow's confused look, he laughed.

"Just do exactly as I say: enter backward, wait until you erupt from the exit portal—which will be right as you start to feel the drop—and immediately check the ground. Quickly. So you might avoid falling on something dangerous. Or, in case it's not a typical short drop, you can try to land on something soft. But usually it is, so Skia like to turn our bodies to the side. Others prefer landing on their feet or back. Our way will spread out the force of the fall and allow you to roll out of the impact when you hit the earth, unless you suspect more portals are close by."

"Okay," she groaned, overwhelmed and imagining herself landing flat on her face like a stupid foreigner, "well, what now?"

"We're a hundred miles or so west of our trading village, but at least there's a portal nearby that'll take us back to the outskirts of it, which does mean it's off to the Shadowlands we must go." He sighed. "Evie will worry when we miss dinner. And kill me when she realizes where I'm about to take you."

Willow rose with the help of her costly stick, and she stuck so close to Jerald's side this time that he laughed and flung an arm over her shoulder.

They were headed to the homeland of the Exoskia, where Jerald's kin had lived until about thirty years ago, he explained, when reports spread of how the Kinetics ordered the mass destruction of every Metaferver alive.

"That led to the diaspora of my people," he was saying, leading them through a thick forest unlike anything in Spinor Falls—darker yet lush, with brightly colored, thorny blooms the size of her head. "Clansmen left their tribes for the first time in living memory and dispersed throughout the land, as Evie and I did. We did our best to stay close to the portals leading home, as you have so graciously proven, but far enough to make a run for it if they came after us too."

"You expect fellow Exos to harm you?"

"We don't believe the murders in Void Valley were purely out of bigotry. Exokinetics may despise Metas for their insularity, but they mistrust *any* foreign powers."

"Insularity?"

A burnt orange bloom with long whips hanging from its center swayed toward Willow. She lifted a finger in curiosity.

"Careful there, that manducaré bloom can smell your blood," Jerald said, taking her cane and whacking the floral threat back with a whoosh. "My great-uncle Frederick once lost a finger to a yellow one. But then again, he did lose his limbs like he lost his maps."

"You were saying about the Fervers?" she asked, trying not to think about being eaten by something with petals.

"Ah yes, well, no one knows the exact location of Void Valley. We only know where it's not, and that makes its phoenix-born people a unique threat."

"Phoenix-born?"

"We sometimes refer to the Metafervers as phoenix-born. You've read about them, no? How their bodies turn to fire, and how some of them can even throw that flame? As the very first Metas, the Ferver designation is thought to have arisen from Great Mother Phoenix herself."

"And the Kinetics figured out where her descendants live?"

"Yes, but they haven't seen fit to share the information, or any information, really. They live cloistered in the clouds. The hypocrites. No offense."

"None taken, I guess."

"And here we are."

Through the last of the trees across a flat clearing, she could see man-made structures that turned out to be strangely leaning watchtowers. The city perimeter had no walls, only multiple towers spaced apart and strangled by skeleton-like gray vines, curling and overflowing with more of the carnivorous manducaré flowers, these a deathly shade of lavender.

"There are two veiled portals in our immediate area." Jerald slipped his arm back over her shoulder. "So stay close."

They set off across the barren field lightly coated in ice that faced the city, as Jerald pointed out the general positions of those hidden portals.

Halfway, a dim light flared brighter in the nearest tower just before Willow scrunched up her eyes and moaned in pain.

Opening her eyes, she choked on a scream.

Five cloaked men had surrounded them, with their blades drawn.

"Short-range portal," explained Jerald.

"Present yourself," said a man with more mustache than hair.

"Hello, sir," she said. "I'm—"

He shoved the gleaming edge of his weapon against her neck.

"Uh…I'm Willow."

"Oh, then I'm just Bill, ain't I?" grunted another man wrapped in white fur.

"Nice to meet you, Bill?"

Their tallest interrogator, pinned everywhere with medals and evidently the leader, gestured for the others to tighten their circle. "Your *source*, girl?"

Jerald stepped forward. "Not to worry, men. She's an Exo. We'll just be on our way."

"Her designation first, medic."

Jerald hesitated, but Willow flicked her hand and swung the sharp metal away from her throat in an arc so wide it sank into a manducaré high on a watchtower. "Kinetic," she said, then turned to her companion. "Please note that was no bigger than a barrel."

Jerald looked his age for once as he hung his head.

The leader motioned his men to stand at ease, though his face was suddenly harsher than his words. "Welcome, Exokinetic. Your visit surprised us during the evening watch, but I remain," he said, touching his chest, "James Alden of Skia Clan Rooh, Head Warden and Keeper of the Shadowland Towers, at your service."

Jerald bowed his head. "Warden, we were just heading for the portal back to our trading village. No plans to overstay our welcome."

"Then you must have the honor of an escort."

"Escort? Boy, I used to treat your baby colic."

Willow laughed as the man glared and pointed behind him in a clear order to start walking.

The other watchmen returned to their posts while the new trio strolled through deserted streets, where deformed buildings cast coiling shadows by bending forward in what seemed a precarious attempt to stroke the ground.

It smelled to Willow of wet stone and a foreign winter, the sort of petrichor that stings.

But strangest of all was a tree so large it had no end. Willow could see it once they passed through a thick barrier of its hanging leaves, the kind that swept the soil in the wind. Half-hidden in darkness, a gnarled mammoth of wood and foliage rose to the sky at the center of this obscure community, covering entire establishments and homes, yet also appearing to house some within; man-made windows and doors shone along its vast trunk, dotting it with light from afar.

"Its roots extend throughout the entire town," said Jerald as he knelt to pat a patch of it bursting through the ground. "Our eldest and most vulnerable live directly within Orelio's Arbor."

Alden's sharp voice cut through, "Sell us to the devil, why don't you?"

Jerald's fist tightened at his side, but he said no more.

Satisfied, the warden resumed walking. A slick shock of gray-ing blond hair, severe face, and wide-set shoulders lent him a rough, animalistic air unsuited to his unhurried persona. James Alden took the confident strides of a jaded commander, and he kept his eyes on Willow as if she were a loose predator.

A young couple caught Willow's attention with their tinkling laughter as they leaned against the sidewall of a pyramidal house, their bodies pressed close.

The boy looked over at Willow and rolled his eyes.

"Audience," he muttered to his lover. Bending over, he snatched at the shadow of a lamppost and pulled it from the ground like a cloak over them both. The shadow stretched from the earth to gather around the couple before snapping back into itself. Shrouded, the two disappeared from sight.

Willow froze, shell-shocked once more, until Jerald patted her shoulder.

"Nothing prepared me for seeing your powers," she confided.

"Stop staring. In here," he whispered.

The Steelie Sprig Inn and Bar, announced by a small lacquered sign, stood before her, doors built into the very base of Orelio's Arbor, its full girth much wider than could be determined up close. Jerald placed her hand into the crook of his elbow and essentially led Willow up carved wooden stairs into a tree trunk, right to where James held open the bar entrance with the hilt of his sword…and stared her down.

Willow used her powers to make sure her legs did not fail her as she walked past his cold face.

"Maurice, our visitors here request use of the trading portal," Alden called to a large man inside behind an elaborate bar littered with odd little pots of bubbling and boiling brews.

Jerald burst out, "I'm hardly a visitor."

Maurice looked them over after sliding a foul-smelling concoction down the bar table. "Kinetic, then?" he grunted.

Alden nodded as Willow huffed, the mystifying turns of her life morphing from distressing to irritating in this brightly lit space full of lanterns filled with trapped fireflies.

A loud shriek startled her. A couple at the bar openly flirted as they arm wrestled before a small crowd. A group of youngsters huddled on a rug by one of the metal-gated fires—one for each wall of the cramped square room—and about them, claw-footed tables hosted people bent over frothy drinks and steaming meals. Lanky as stretched taffy, the townspeople nearly all possessed pale and narrow faces with catlike eyes tipped upward beneath light hair, as did Jerald and Evie, Willow now realized.

She was glad, at least, to see that the peculiar, acute angles of the outside world were replaced here with the obtuse smiles of tipsy villagers.

The female of the wrestling pair tossed back her golden locks and leaned forward, saying to her competitor, "Give up the map already. Your arm's shaking like an itty-bitty porcy leaf."

Willow's curious gaze whipped back around when Maurice barked at her, "So you come through Thornhaze Forest, girl, instead of an official visitor's portal and expect free access to our people's resources?"

Jerald burst into explanation about their misstep as she stood silent. Zephyr had never begged for a crumb as an orphan, and neither would she now.

Alden leaned against the counter, with his back still military straight. "Be reasonable, Maurice. Don't you want her gone?"

Willow's body aches had worsened the more they walked, her chest now cramping with a relentless, roiling mass of pain not so different in quality to her monthly courses. Noting nearly all the barstools as taken, she used a concealed dash of power as the others were talking to hoist herself onto the remaining seat, right beside the victorious arm wrestler clutching her map, its corners glinting a silvery gray in the firelight.

"Lovely, isn't it?" asked the girl.

Willow figured she could be no older than twenty. "Oh, yes. Is it, um, a good map?"

"Well, that depends, doesn't it? It's so beautifully untested."

"Right. Yes."

"Well, let's find out." She lit a nub of candle wax from her pocket and placed a corner of the map's thick parchment into the center of flame. The edges recoiled into blackness.

"Oy!" called a server. "No open flames in the Arbor."

The girl stanched the fire before it could spread and laid her head on the table. "Well, that's unfortunate."

Confused, Willow patted her shoulder in support.

"I was really hoping for an unofficial map, maybe even a valuable fake. But look, it's only got the Shadowland outskirts and a bunch of common trading villages. And the portals are all correct." After barely a moment, the girl brightened and rattled off, "I'm Astoria Sutcliffe of Skia Clan Murr. But you're new. How have we not met? Are you visiting family? What's your name?"

Willow held out her hand. "I'm Willow. Nice to meet you."

"What's your clan, then?"

"Astoria, my dear, how are you taking to your new in-laws?" cut in Jerald, popping up behind them and not waiting for a reply. "Please do remind your husband to take his turmeric tonic and eat less meat. Now let's be off, Willow."

Astoria touched his arm. "What's got you spooked, old man?"

"No, it's just—" began Jerald as he turned just so and caught sight of the map. "Say, how much would you take for that?"

"Well, it's quite a rare find, and I only just acquired it."

"Rare my arse, youngling. Those are some nice scorch marks."

"Ten starters."

"Five."

"Done."

Barter complete, Jerald yanked up the stone divider leading into the bartender's quintessential inner sanctum and pulled Willow away as she waved goodbye.

"She was always a shit negotiator," he muttered.

"See you in the Hub," called Astoria, waving back at Willow.

She smiled at her in vague agreement but asked Jerald, "Where's the Hub?"

"Where I said all of existence started, remember? So it's nowhere now. Just a saying, like 'see you later.'"

Past an archway into darkness, Willow only made out shelves full of blades, crossbows, quivers, and the like before a hand clapped over her mouth and rough cloth slipped over her eyes.

She reached for her powers, unable to use them blind.

"Hush, pretty princess, you're safe," she heard Alden say. "Leave it on or you're not leaving."

"Just a precaution to protect the portal location," came Jerald's voice at her side. He took her hand and steered her along for what seemed an age.

"Sorry," he whispered in her ear, out of breath, "we have to take the unidirectional one so they know we can't come right back through. Heart of the tree. Not long now." She heard a jangle, perhaps of keys. "Mind your leg. That's a step. Now through here. Higher. That's it. Well, goodbye to you both. See you at the next trade fair. Remind everyone that I've replenished my supplies. Now, dear, don't forget to fall *gently* backward through the portal."

A light push, and her entire body went cold, pinpricks stabbing her being into a fever pitch of pain that heightened until she could take no more—just as it ceased.

Grass and ground slammed into her face. She tore off the eye covering and sobbed with a relief greater than the trauma of her landing. Because the pain in her chest had decreased along with the pricks.

"You didn't try to turn, Willow."

"How could I? I had a blindfold on. How dare you treat me like that?" she burst out, noting Jerald already beside her.

"It was just—"

"What? Your stupid prejudice?"

"Now see here, it's not prejudice after scores of people have been murdered."

"Seems to me those are just rumors like everything else around here. And why am I to blame for the decisions of some far-off monarchy anyway?"

Jerald went red as a tomato, but he said nothing more as he directed them home along the pebbled path from which they had earlier strayed. Strange creatures squawked at them in the dark, but the Exoskia embraced shadow, and Willow was too angry to be afraid. Or perhaps too lost.

CHAPTER
9

GREAT FLARE
OF EXECUTION

I should fix my relationship with time
It has been brought to my attention
The way we see each other may be toxic
Look how he takes no interest in my desires
But with a tritely tragic tick
I watch his every passing.
Nothing I do for him *seems lasting*
Everything he does for me *feels lagging*
I should fix my relationship with time
But he moves so fast—I'll only almost catch him.

S kia children popped in and out of shadow throughout the trading village, bursting forth from out-of-place silhouettes that moved beneath people's feet like frantic fish in a sunny lake.

Willow suspected a game of hide-and-seek at play when one youngling, barely five, bloomed headfirst out of the ground to plaster herself against her legs.

"Please," said the girl, ducking under Willow's cloak. "Hide me. I wanna win."

Willow patted her little head and promised. Over the past eight months, she had developed a soft spot for the strange Skia younglings despite her total lack of experience with children in Spinor Falls.

"Patrol!" shouted someone at the far end of the alley, people parroting the message from vendor to vendor along the line of carts.

The child shrieked and seemingly turned herself back into nothing.

Willow tossed her hands up. "There you all go again, pulling total emptiness over yourselves like it makes any sense," she muttered.

Everyone else had gone still, yet an old crone sifting through a barrel of overripe apples beside her cackled. "A patch of shadow is anything but empty, child. It's full of the ground's ether. Shadow is the absence of light, true, but not everything else." Her face scrunched up. "It's easier to meld with the essence of the land when it's not all muddled with the sun's rays." She tired of her stooped search and stepped back to flick her finger, the fruit sailing up to sit suspended in the air. She looked back at Willow. "Well, don't you look sad, with those red eyes of yours?"

Horns cut through the air as Willow shivered from the strange expression leveled her way.

A small group of muscled men, crossbows and broadswords hovering at their sides, marched through the crowd in bright blue coats studded with the sparkling stones of the Sky Realm.

One patrolman kinetically swung a ball-and-chain flail, slamming its spiky head into a small melon and yanking it off a seller's cart. Shaggy-haired and deeply tanned, he glanced around with a crooked smile only to say, "Back to business now."

People rushed to obey in an awkward dance of forced conversation and half-hearted bartering.

Willow turned her head to note the woman had never ended her perusal. The crone finally moved away, but not before barking, "Put that back."

A little boy froze with his hand in her skirt pocket. He ran off with a limp, the coins in his fist floating back into the woman's grasp.

"And aren't you late for work?" the crone asked Willow with a tilt of her head.

Willow's eyes widened just before she dashed off too, speeding through narrow walkways between loaded carts and stalls, not much different from the bazaars back home.

She halted in the doorway of a grungy stone building, its bowels dug deep into the ground for holding higher-level criminals, and walked in feeling like a prisoner herself. Every day for the last few weeks, she awoke in a panic, some painful amalgamation of confused, scared, heartsick, and homesick. Aimless in this place, with little purpose but to play scullery maid amid dank cells filled to the brim with innocents.

Someone bumped into her side. "Ow."

"Hey," grumbled the man. "Move it or we're both tardy."

Guarding highly feared prisoners had a unique way of setting everyone on edge.

And there in the corner, a rare pair of such people sat in adjacent cells, coated in the dirt that had migrated over them since their uproarious arrival. Rumors flew early last week of Metafervers captured in the village, just minutes before Willow watched them dragged in by the patrolmen, who had arrested each one within a mile of the other, kinetically pulling their manacled wrists forward above their heads faster than they could walk. Not yet fourteen years old, the two Fervers stumbled into incarceration without a word.

Severin, the withered head warden with the craggy face of a jaundiced toad, called out to Willow today, "Come on in, dearie."

"Morning, Warden," replied Willow.

The old man bowed his head from behind a desk and directed Willow to the mops with his usual confusing blend of respect for Kinetics and disdain for menial laborers.

Willow had wondered how he retained status as keeper of the peace in a jailhouse, until the day two prisoners touched hands through their bars. Severin fell upon them and gnawed off a finger in a blink of an eye. He spat the severed appendage into the fire, alighting a warning smell of burning flesh throughout his dungeons that announced exactly why the man deserved his name and title.

Reminded of that inhuman-yet-too-human stench, Willow sniffed some lye before dropping it into a bucket of water and pushing past her sluggish pain. Once finished burning circles and circles through the stone floor, she tended the hearth beside Severin's desk, where the stoic warden sat overlooking his underlings. Soon the chimney let loose a belch of black ash that turned Willow into a stick of soot, and worse, showed the warden that Willow could withstand being smothered in smoke without coughing. He immediately set her to cleaning out grates that had never seen a brush.

Lunch break consisted of the luxury of sitting down on the floor with a dry sandwich and instructions to keep a furtive eye on the prisoners. Willow usually leaned against a damp pillar in a dark corner, her body well-hidden as she cooled off sore muscles. Setting aside the inedible crust of today's meal, she pressed her head against her drawn-up knees to fight a headache.

The mere concept of prison confused her. Petty theft from hunger had been the worst infraction committed in Spinor Falls as far back as she could remember, so their holding cells often remained empty, graced mostly by raucous drunks. But here, bars as thick as her arms rose from the floor to the ceiling.

Across from her, Willow could glimpse the Metas this world found so fascinating, an endangered subspecies, remnants of a time beyond Willow's comprehension. The villagers felt certain this couple knew each other from before, as any fugitive Metas must be in collusion, but Willow believed otherwise.

For one thing, they had made their introductions nine days ago.

The boy, tall and stocky for his age, had been ranting on and off. The girl said not a word, but paid close attention, never bored, as if accustomed to a life of listening.

"So, you ever gonna tell me your name? Come on. You know by now I'm Gideon Eldur. You would have heard of my grandfather, the famed southern-valley swordsmith?" the boy had asked as Willow peaked out from behind her pillar.

The girl, slight and short, with steely eyes the color of moss, shook her head.

"Come on. He designed the Black Forge Scythe itself." No answer. "Well, what's your name then?" pushed Gideon.

The girl cocked her head and tossed a quick look around—assured Severin was still away on lunch break—before crawling forward a bit. She lifted her stained hands, palms facing outward, and flames spurted from her fingertips, so tapered that her hands from palm to tip were longer than her face. She wrote out her name, Vatra, with green fire that lingered in the air before diffusing into smoke.

Willow went still, riveted.

"A Flamethrower," Gideon breathed, one hand lifting toward the girl. "I've never heard of one that can do *that*, but I know there are none in my family line. Or…there weren't." His hand dropped.

Vatra pressed fingers alight with power against her throat and drew a fiery X.

"You're mute," he said.

She nodded.

"Well, you can speak better than anyone I know."

She blushed through the grime on her cheeks.

"I'm going to call you a Flamespeaker."

But as time went on, Gideon seemed to fall into a trance.

For days, he lay draped across the prison floor, awaiting his sentence, unresponsive to anyone, ignoring the worm-infested chunks of stale bread growing into a pile by his head. Vatra often tapped on the bars between them, though he wouldn't look her way.

Today, he responded at lunch break, prompting both females to lift their heads in surprise.

"Too thirsty. Can't talk," he grunted.

Vatra yanked off one of two similar adornments around her neck, a pebble on thin string, and she tossed it through the bars. Gideon looked her way at the clink and watched her lift the other one to her mouth, sucking on its stone. He mirrored the motion, realizing it would make his mouth water, as he remained splayed on the floor.

She tapped again.

"Hmm?" He looked back, raising a brow, the stone between his lips.

Vatra spun her fingers around each other, accelerating speed, a ball of fire whirling into hazy shapes between her hands. She cupped her palms side by side, and a blazing horse with orange body and blue mane rose to life atop them, prancing forward as Vatra rocked her joined hands.

Gideon shot up. "What the—?"

Vatra smiled.

Willow watched an entire show alight along those long arms. The horse morphed into a battle-ready steed and multiplied into a battalion. Vatra flicked a tapered finger. Warriors appeared atop each finger on opposite sides of the field of her forearms, before a charge commenced, the fiery bodies intertwining, clashing, and ultimately merging once more into a swirling fireball.

"How?" asked Gideon.

Vatra shrugged, watching the last vestiges of that stunning performance creep through her clasped hands in wisps of smoke.

Gideon crawled forward to clutch the bars between them. "Needs must, huh?"

She looked over, into his eyes behind the many clumped strands of her bangs, and they both grinned, the sight striking a pang through Willow's heart. She returned to her duties with a sigh full of missing belonging, missing sense, and missing just her sense of self.

By the end of shift, daylight had faded away into a mere suggestion, and in her now constant state of doubt, Willow pulled out her Skia map for reassurance of the safest route back to her caretakers: through the shortest alley first, a left at the clocktower covered in sleeping owls, an odd turnaround at the tiny inn, and finally straight through the path that led into Jerald's fields.

Nearing the clocktower, the tallest and narrowest structure in the village, Willow noticed the same little boy who had pickpocketed the crone curled asleep beside it. A tumble of blond waves fell beneath his woolen cap onto a porcelain face as smooth as a babe's.

"Hello there, little thief," she murmured, kneeling.

He opened one eye and turned away from her onto his side.

She placed a hand on his pale shoulder, taking note of his bone-thin form. "What's your name?"

"Benny," he mumbled, shrugging off the touch. "Now go away."

"Where's your home, Benny? Need directions?" asked Willow.

"I'm homeless, stupid."

"Home less? What's that mean? Do you have less of a normal home?"

He sat up. "Are you okay?"

"Am *I* okay?"

"Yeah, unless you're crazy *and* stupid, could you find a way to leave me alone already?"

Willow felt like she had been pushed, but she persisted. "I know someone who can help with your limp."

He snorted.

"Well, I do. Come find me if you ever get tired of your obvious pain," said Willow, facing him as she backed away.

Benny stuck his tongue out at her, watching her leave with suspicion.

Her own body was also filled with a strange, irrational panic that followed her through the tall grass, their stalks swaying against her in consoling sweeps.

Charging into the house, she blurted out, "Jerald, what's being homeless mean?"

"Hmm?" The man looked up from his position on the floor, where he was carving a floral design into a table leg for Evie. The woman sat before the fire, stirring dinner. Willow blew her way inside along with the cold night air and an emphatic slam of the door.

"It's just that there's this little boy, hardly ten maybe, sleeping outside."

Jerald looked back at his work without alarm.

"In the village streets. Alone." Her voice rose as she paced back and forth. "He said he was *homeless*."

Jerald bent his head closer to his carving. "Never seen him. But best stay away, Willow. He's more likely to rob you than to thank you."

"Why doesn't he have a home? Doesn't your community care for lost children?"

"And who would do the caring?"

"There are policies…procedures! Back in Spinor Falls—"

Evie called out, "That place was just a dream, Willow. Let it die."

Willow glared at the back of her gray head, as Jerald softened the blow by saying gently, "There are no such policies here anyway. Now go on and help Evie with supper."

Willow doffed her cloak, reaching for her week's pay in its large pockets, but it wasn't there. She laughed, though it was a watery sound, and hung her head.

Later that night, she awoke to cinders floating about like tired fireflies of ash and realized she had fallen asleep by the dwindling hearth.

Moving forward to bank the last of the flames, she reached out her arms just as the fire blinked back to life.

Something strange flashed across her flesh.

"I'm seeing things," she whispered.

But she tossed in a piece of wood and built up the fire. Leaning closer, she could see thin, scar-like lines crawling to life along her shaking left forearm, all twisting and coming together to form…a map?

A map of so very much. Not just of this village or the Shadowlands, but also more.

She stood up, and it disappeared; she returned to the blaze, and it reformed. Touching the tiny Skia trading village with a pinky, her skin seemed to focus on it by enlarging the location depicted on the soft, pale flesh above her veins. She let go, and it grew smaller.

"It's alright. It's alright. I'm just dreaming." She tucked her arms against her chest and fell back asleep on the rug.

The next time the boy tried to steal from her, she swung around and offered him a sandwich. He shot backward with his arms over his face.

Holding up her hands, she offered, "Come to lunch."

"What?"

"I brought this sandwich for you today, but tomorrow I'm not working. Have lunch with me at the house. Meet the medic I told you about."

He slipped forward toward her offering, so visibly dripping with meat.

She held it back a fraction. "And come earn some wages by cleaning up at the jail. They'll take anyone."

Cocking his head, eyes never leaving her edible bribe, he said, "Tell them I limp and see what happens."

"I will."

He smirked, nabbed the sandwich, and ran off with his tongue sticking out at her again.

"I always thought I'd get to see my parent's hometown, you know, the place of my people. Eat food made with ingredients they always say taste purer down south."

Vatra nodded her head, expression soft as Gideon whispered to her. He had started sitting up again in the corner of their shared bars.

Face pressed against her two hands as they gripped the iron, she uncurled a single finger to release a tiny flame. It split up into sparks.

Vatra does that all the time, thought Willow as she watched them from the corner of her eye, *as if doodling to pass the time.*

"Mom would always say the rice there has a smell, like she could scent the starchy fluffiness steaming in those huge pots outside. Can you imagine, Vat?" he asked. "I know it's stupid, but I was trying to go back. See what's left of it."

Startled, Vatra lifted a hand and tapped her chest.

"You too? Huh. Guess we should have left dead enough alone."

Vatra ducked her head, a dark frown draping her lips.

Time felt like a joke dancing in her face, except it was as nonsensical as the ones that jesters in the island pantomimes spent hours spinning for children during solstice and equinox gatherings. Willow figured time only behaved properly for people with anything useful to do. Unlike her, who only ever had never-ending questions in this strange realm.

"I keep hearing people say the best maps don't burn. Why's that?" she asked Jerald while helping him grind powdered ginger.

He handed her a larger mortar with a mix of dried herbs. "Rumors. The rumors that say the master mapmaker learned a spell from the Winged to prevent his finished works from burning. And since the few but fortunate people with his maps have lived to spread those rumors, it's hard not to believe them."

"Master mapmaker?"

"Yes, a modern-day journeyman who managed to map most of Ingress. Likely dead by now. He hasn't released anything new in the past thirty years or so. He was probably a displaced Skia of the diaspora."

"Wait. Hold on. So people other than the Winged can use spells?" Willow slammed the pestle against the table.

Jerald tossed her a look, a reminder that the pestle was made of precious bone. "Only a rare few, talented and lucky enough to meet someone with the knowledge. So far, we only know for sure of the Winged mages, and I suspect also the monarch of Maddooinne—he's the king of the Kinetics—since they're his guard."

"And you."

"Excuse me?"

"I notice you mumbling over my muscles as you massage them. Everything goes cold for a moment, and then I feel…better. You spoke to that Winged boy before he left, didn't you?"

He raised a finger. "Now don't you go telling Evie."

Time for her had lost its wings, lying broken and keening like a faceless, fallen child at the edge of the cliffs. Because as Willow dreamed of that dawn on the edge of her island, a dawn that now seemed like a nightmare she convinced herself only in waking never to remember, she screamed.

And awoke with the same echo of pain in her chest that had led her to Zeph in the far north that final morning. It prompted a question that sent her running to Evie.

"What's chest pain mean here?" demanded Willow, clutching her book to her heart.

"Here?" asked Evie, barely looking away from hanging the wash, now immune to Willow's oddities.

"In the Land of Portalcraft."

Evie finally glanced at her. "Well, it could be a cardiac issue, spoiled or poisoned food, physical injury, or most likely, my dear, you're just anxious."

"And what if it's none of those things? If the pain is a little higher, just under my breastbone. Can a splitting pain right here…mean to lead me somewhere?"

Evie put down her basket. "Oh, the Tug, yes. Sure. But that's so rare, the last one recorded among my people was over a decade ago."

"The Tug? That's not in my book." She started riffling through it, past the chapter on ether as a substance versus energy versus time, past the chapter on Metaporters and Metamorphs, past the chapter on native Exos that should have included Faeries but didn't—

"Here," said Evie, thumbing to the very last page. "It's a footnote in the glossary. Because literally no one but you needs such basic physical facts spelled out."

Guide Flare:
Combustion of pure ether at the first touch shared
between a Guide pair.
Initiates the Tug, a painful sensation that draws
the pair together across time and space.
A shared trait between the Primordial Clan and
Creatures of the Void.

"But what's a Guide pair, Evie?"

"Two people who can locate each other through that tugging feeling. When they first meet, there's a flare of power that marks the Tug forming. We don't know if everyone has a Guide waiting to be found. Guide pairs may never even cross paths in this world to realize the other person exists."

Willow broke into tears. "And you said my whole life's been a dream! Horse shit. I'm going after him."

Time finally looked up, ready to crawl forward.

Willow studied her skin map alone by the fire each night and began to hope.

She often strolled along the rooftops—the jailhouse ladder gave her access without suspicion—to stare down at the village or up at the horizon. Memorizing the skyline view from here had been the simplest way to learn the layout of her new environment at first, as the written map Jerald bought was not detailed or dimensional enough.

She adjusted her new satchel into her lap and reclined against a chimney, like she had many times before. She had packed her book, dried foods, and basic traveling supplies, like kindling and tinder, before shoving a small knife into the bag with the rest of her coins. She had sought matches and tried to trade for them, only to discover they were hideously expensive.

Now she was just left to work up the courage to say farewell to Jerald and Evie. They would likely take it poorly, losing the flow of income her presence assured them. But she refused to be tied here any longer.

Pondering whether she should just leave without giving them the chance to stop her, Willow dozed off against the warm thatch of the jailhouse roof.

She shot upright at the blaring of horns.

A parade streamed in, with bearers of flags depicting silver clouds shaped into winged beasts on a backdrop of azure sky.

"What's the Sky Realm up to now?" she murmured. Ice dripped down her spine when Gideon stumbled out of the prison in manacles before a Kinetic guard.

A crowd formed to watch Vatra pushed out after him and ushered to the head of the march. Willow followed, leaping from one roof to the next, her cloak adding considerable drag she had to counter with her powers.

They all stopped at the executioner's dais.

Time slowed, crippled. Willow sank to her feet on a sloping roof behind the scene, holding on to a narrow chimney. A simple stage towered on stilts above the crowd. And on multiple rooftops within sight stood strange hooded figures, one of whom she had jumped past herself, unable to tolerate its chilly presence. They held weapons taller even than their considerable heights and waited with the still patience of angels of death.

Below her, she could see the back of an executioner, just like the one illustrated in her book, covered from head to toe in black-trimmed white robes. He was climbing the few steps onto the stage with a loud thudding of his scarlet boots. Before him, Vatra glanced over at Gideon as a tear slipped down her blustery cheek.

"Whoa, what's that guy doing?" said a voice beside Willow.

She groaned as she met a pair of wide eyes. "Benny, how'd you get up here?"

Gasps rose from below. Willow looked back, heart dropping, to see a noose about Vatra's neck going up in flames, as well as the executioner's robes. Soon, Vatra was face down on the ground with a guard's boot crushing her spine and unable to voice her pain. Flaming robes shot up into the air, revealing the man beneath as the same patrolman often stealing fruit from the bazaar.

"You get to be second, then, Flamethrower. Hear him die first for your folly," the patrolman grunted at Vatra. He lifted a hand for the executioner's sword, and it swung toward him from a great distance out of the grasp of a hooded figure across the square, stopping to float at his side.

He shoved Vatra over the chopping block with a bare hand. Gideon called out her name as he was shoved down too, a pair of guards manually holding daggers to his neck.

Gideon turned to Vatra with a sob.

Benny started tugging at Willow's sleeve. "Is that man really going to hurt them?" He huddled against her side.

Willow could not spare the boy a glance as she said, "Don't you dare use this moment to steal from me."

Shaky little arms curled about her middle.

The executioner lifted a gloved hand, sword rising higher kinetically, blade angled for a flashy, wide fell swoop. The other guards stepped back. The once raucous crowd held its breath. And the exposed executioner began to speak slowly, enamored with his own voice:

"By order of the Kinetic Kingdom, on charges of high treason against the Primordial Clan, and on behalf of His Imperial Highness, King Soren Everly of Maddooinne, Metafervers Gideon Eldur and Vatra Sharone are hereby sentenced to death by beheading."

The man ran a finger down Vatra's neck.

"If any Exoskia harbors Meta traitors, let this be a warning of the consequences for all involved."

His right arm rose; the sword sang through the air—edge gleaming—coming to a stop mere inches from Gideon's neck.

The metal strained, rippling from the force of two opposing powers.

Willow refused to look away even as Benny breathed, "Lady, are you seeing this?" and then, "Oh, hell in the Hub, are you *doing* this?"

Unblinking, Willow pushed with a touch more effort and sent the blade arcing through the air, miles off into the distance.

The executioner stilled, then spun around. Willow had pulled Benny behind the chimney, her heartbeat quivering against her throat.

The boy shook and babbled, "It's not working."

Willow clapped a hand over his mouth.

"Guards, at attention. Search," called the executioner. The robed figures began to stalk the square, and without the mercy of a single sound, one had Willow in its clutches.

"We were just watching," she said. But it raised a warning hand and with the other, tossed Willow and Benny over the gutters to crash atop the stage.

The executioner's boot landed on her stomach. "Now would you look at this," he hissed. "A Source traitor."

Willow looked up into eyes muddied with rage. "This won't end well for you," she said, a lost part of her so angry and wild it wanted to raze the entire village.

"For *me*?"

She lifted her chin, baring her scarred jaw. "What's your name?"

He laughed, and as his large, bearded face shook in manic amusement, he leaned close to smash her face to the side with his hand. Gasping for breath, Willow could see Gideon scooting over, as he so often did in his cell, inch by inch to get closer to Vatra. His hand reached out to her in solidarity, so sweetly Willow thought she could see time pausing just to watch. Vatra looked like a living fireball, skin puce, when her fingers stretched over and claimed his—

The platform and everyone around it blew away.

Willow flew from the slamming power of some invisible force onto a cart half a mile from the epicenter. One moment passed, or maybe a million did, before she realized that chunks of rubble had buried her face-first. Unable to stand or breathe, seeing only through the slits of light around her, she tapped into her powers to free her torso and sit up. She shoved aside the detritus on her legs and with a deep breath, limped out of the cart.

Spotting Benny beside her in a pile of straw and the old crone crumpled on the ground to her left, she could hear nothing save for the ringing in her ears.

She scooped up the boy, noted his pulse and chest rising, slung him over her shoulders, and considered the ever-changing situation. Everything in pieces. Bodies unconscious or flung far enough away to be of no immediate threat. Except for the Guide pair that started it all.

She headed to the most vacant area.

"Let's go," she shouted at Gideon and Vatra, who were still crouched in the same spot, staring at each other in a daze. "There's a hidden portal out of here."

They seemed not to hear.

She tossed gravelly debris at their faces.

Vatra raised her hands, both arms abruptly engulfed in flame.

Gideon held her back. "It's you," he said in surprise.

"Yes. Me. Now simmer down and *come on.*"

CHAPTER
10

UNDERTAKER OF THE SAND AND THE DAMNED

The banished may find me
Where the damned roam free
Jailed by bars of chaos
And my company

This is just a clocktower, chaosman." Gideon looked at her with fulminant, fuming suspicion.

Willow pulled out an ax from her satchel. "What, I saved your necks but now I'm leading you to your doom?"

She took a breath, balanced the ax in her hands, and took a poor swing at the base of the structure. "Damn it. My body hurts."

Gideon stepped forward. "You're a bit weak. Let me."

Instead, the ax sailed up, and with the kinetically detailed, yet forceful, stream of power she had once used to fell trees, slammed precisely into the wood meeting the ground and did not return.

"This must be it. Stand back." Willow focused on the boards

forming the base, enlarging the ax-sized hole more easily now with her powers. "Alright, now get in."

Gideon pulled Vatra tighter against his side. "Where does it lead?"

"Half a mile within the Shadowlands. Seems the Skia like to conceal important portals. Hiding out may as well be a personality trait for them."

"And how in the Hub would you know?"

She threw up her hands. "Let's just say I got an inkling when I visited last."

"But how do you know of this portal?"

"Does it really matter? Look, the whole village will be out for our blood. This mess will just seem like damage from the flare, and no one will follow if they can't be sure of coming back." She motioned with her chin over Vatra's shoulder, where they could see some stirring in the rubble. "I'm taking Benny to safety. You two do as you want."

She lifted the unconscious boy off the ground into the circle of her arms and fell into an onslaught of portal pain, enough to wake him on the other side.

He rubbed his eyes and started crying. "Ow. Crazy lady, you stabbed me."

"I did *not*, Benny."

They had landed in what appeared to be a mesh-enclosed chicken pen without any chickens. Vatra and Gideon dropped in quick succession onto the ground beside them as she reached for her ax, glad to have it back, and noticed a woman watching them from the doorway of the attached house.

"Hello there, and sorry to drop in like this," Willow called to the woman. "May we speak with the authorities?"

The woman laughed and slipped inside.

"Odd."

"Not so much," said Gideon as Vatra pointed to a strange circle of darkness around the otherwise sunny pen. One by one, familiar and unfamiliar guards burst forth, shedding shadow, with their blades at the ready.

Willow stood straight, steeling herself. "Hello there. Head Warden James Alden. Ah, is he free? By any chance?"

"Over here." Alden stood behind them, hands in his pockets, and angry. Very angry. He practically vibrated with it as he rocked on the soles of his feet. "How did you come by this portal information?"

Willow lifted her hands. "I'm here to ask for help, not cause harm."

"Calls for help tend to involve harm."

She gestured to Benny. "I have an innocent Skia child with Kinetics after him—after all of us."

On the ground, Benny cried harder, so she picked him up as he continued to whimper, "It's not working."

"Did you take that child from his parents?" growled Alden.

Willow worked on checking her temper. "I'm not a monster just because you want me to be. His name is Benny, and he's a homeless child I met in the East Skia Trading Village."

Alden stepped forward. "Child, swallow your tears"—the growl startled Benny into silence—"and tell me if she speaks the truth."

Willow's heart skipped a beat as she rocked Benny.

Lifting his head, the boy rubbed his eyes with two shaking fists. "She fed me and tried to find me a job and then she saved those two and everything exploded and I have to go back but I can't. It's not working." He devolved into sobs, and no amount of encouragement could get him to speak again.

The warden motioned to the duo standing at Willow's side. "And whom else have you kindly brought with you?"

Gideon bowed, a bit of a formal gesture for a young man in a pen. "Source?"

Gideon sighed. Long and deep. "Meta. Same as my Guide."

A visible shock ran through the men and women around them, except for Alden. He went still, growing stonier the longer Willow spent in his presence, with no attempts at civility this visit.

"Phoenix-born? I assume, then, you're the reason for the purported flare and the Kinetic manhunt?"

Gideon stood straighter, an aristocrat shining through the smithy's grandson. "Yes, sir, Willow really did use her powers to save us from a Kinetic beheading. The boy got in the middle of it. And now we're just looking for safe passage. You understand my people's condition."

The warden nodded, his expression no less heated. "But none of this answers the most pressing question. How did an Exokinetic come by such private clan details? We've never so much as mapped this portal for ourselves."

Willow swallowed, unwilling to tell them she had more where that came from.

"The medic Jerald seemed too chummy with her, Alden," said one of the Skia. Willow recognized the gruff speaker as Bill, keeper of one of the watchtowers.

"He's eccentric, not stupid," retorted Alden.

"She mighta seduced it outta him, who knows?"

Willow made a furious gagging noise and shouted, "He told me nothing!"

That seemed to trouble the warden. "So you did try to get it out of him."

"No."

"Yes. And whom else have you told?"

"No one."

"Hmm. First things first. Bill, send guards to patch up and secure the clocktower before we have a bigger mess on our hands. I'll find the boy's kin."

"You're not calling the Kinetics on us?" Gideon asked.

Alden stepped up to the mesh, bending forward, fury finally overtaking his voice. "A portal into our homeland is a domestic vulnerability. Surely you see that? None of you will be leaving us. Ever."

"Fuck," whispered Willow, head falling back.

Another round of interrogation yielded nothing new.

Vatra just fell asleep against the table.

The inquisitor rapped the wood with his knuckles.

Gideon rapped it back. "She burned a lot of energy trying not to get killed today. Leave her alone."

And so the Skia tried tossing them into isolation cells.

Willow looked up hours later from her position in the windowless room, her supine body absentmindedly floating an inch or so above the floor in this disturbing, fully lit space, when she heard the rattling of the padlock. She dropped to cold stone.

"More of the same questions?" she groaned.

The door swung open to reveal the only Skia she would not have expected to see there.

"How could you do this to us?" cried Evie, banging the door shut behind her.

Willow got up on shaking knees. "Evie?"

"They came for us. Your damned kind came looking for you at the house, and now we've lost everything!" the woman wailed, hands fisted at her sides.

"Oh no, Evie. I'm so sorry."

The woman slammed her forehead against a dank wall and whispered, "They took Jerald."

"The Kinetics have him?"

"No, you idiot girl, he's being held by my own kind, and it's all your fault."

Willow tried to push back as the world closed in on her, tears tracking down her face. "I didn't plan this. I swear. I just couldn't watch innocent children die, not like that. Could you?"

She raised a hand, more incensed than Willow had ever seen her. "I swear to the void, I could. I'd keep my head down to protect my husband's neck, but you shoved him right into the gallows. Oh, I will see you rot for it."

"They'll see he did nothing wrong. Evie, please—"

She was gone with the snap of a shadow.

Nothing wholesome ever began with a march.

Blindfolded, cuffed, and swaying on her feet from hunger, Willow moved as directed, with too much time to think and catastrophize.

For a moment, she wondered what Mother would think to see her like this, and quickly shoved that thought down deep, knowing that every whisper of home threatened to break her to pieces. For now, she had to forget what she wanted most, or risk losing the resolve she needed to attain it.

So Willow marched on, chin up.

Evie had earlier convinced the guards to starve Willow, who heard the woman swearing loudly outside her cell that food was the girl's greatest weakness. But she could not know the state of Willow's childhood, had never cared enough to learn that Willow could withstand much harsher pangs than they had yet doled out.

She'd walked for hours now on an empty stomach below an aching chest, soldiering on for what must have been half a day, resorting to using her powers to prevent the shame of falling flat on her face.

Once they came to a stop, she could hear the nasty grumbling of a crowd mixed with the purity of birdsong.

She demanded her sight back.

Alden's voice answered, "We were told your powers are so much stronger than average—"

Evie.

"—that you once lifted a full hay cart ten meters into the sky. The blindfold stays on."

Willow could not open her eyes to see the cloth, but she knew it was there, felt it with her skin and reached for it with her powers. It barely wriggled.

"No one else has come through the portal, corroborating your claim of secrecy. But you won't tell us more, won't even trust us with the origin of the information."

She wanted so badly to sit down, minutes away from collapse. "How I know is of no danger to your people, but it is of danger to me."

Alden continued without pause. "Your guardian has no kind words for you. And as we can neither hold you here without risk of Kinetic retribution nor let you free to return to your kind, the road of your fate has forked: execution or exile."

"And what about Jerald?"

"Our kind's none of your business," tossed out a voice from the crowd.

"Gideon and Vatra, then?" she pushed.

Alden called for order but answered, "Voted innocent of conspiring against us after the many Skia reports of what happened at the stocks. They may not leave, but they will stay safe in the Shadowlands. Being Meta children, it remains in the best interest of everyone involved that the Kinetics never know they're alive. They will be trusted to start new lives with us, in hiding. Perhaps that will give you some peace."

"While you murder me?" snarled Willow.

Someone pushed her forward into a body's length of mud. The blindfold loosened, and Willow could see just over it that no one stood before her.

"You will restrain yourself, Evelyn Murr, or join the Kinetic." Alden sounded surprised.

Willow spoke with a mouth smeared in muck. "You're a coward, Evie, hiding behind my back like that." She could not get up, arms bound, legs gelatin, and torso shivering in air chilly from recent rain. "Warden, I assume by this long stroll you've chosen exile."

His voice sounded closer. "In the Southern Portal Mines."

"Do I get a final request?"

"Depends." A whisper in the wind.

"Matchsticks to help me survive. Allow me that, and I won't struggle."

A scoff. "Some portals allow nothing but a creature through, naked on exit."

"Well, does this one?"

"No travelers return to tell."

"Then how do you know what lies beyond? Southern Portal Mines, was it?" She spit out some muck. "Seems better to be prepared."

"And what would shadows want with matches? I don't have any on me."

She tried to say a forest should have something in the way of tinder, but in the end, they gave her no warning, not a single goodbye or see you later should you live, nor enough time for her to get the blindfold off. Just the sound of a roiling mass as she was lifted and shoved once again from behind, just like she had been for months now.

The Tug's pain this time was the worst by far. It ripped through her so badly on the other side that she curled into the fetal position, blindfold fluttering off somewhere, unable to so much as look around.

She only registered the graininess of sand against her cheek, until she felt something slam onto her.

She moved aside to see a little gremlin.

"What is wrong with you, lady? Why didn't you roll over?"

Benny lay in the same spot she was just in, glaring at her, his small face scrunched up.

"Benny? What are you doing here? How could they do this to you too?"

"You have got to be the strangest lady ever. Who doesn't roll over?"

"I forgot," she moaned.

He blinked. "Where'd you even grow up?"

"Spinor Falls. You ever heard of it?" she asked with some hope.

"No, is it some random village?"

"I don't think so?"

He shook his head, sitting up and tossing his arms around his knees. "Definitely the strangest lady ever. Here." He dug in his pockets and pulled out a large matchbox. "You said you wouldn't survive without it."

"Wait. You *chose* to come after me?"

She held back tears as he nodded and untied her hands.

"It doesn't really matter where I am anyway," he said, "if I can't be at that trading village. And you saved me first, I guess."

"But you're much better off with your own people."

"Yeah, but even that bunch of thick clansmen'll figure out soon I'm not one of them."

Willow rubbed her raw wrists and sat back to look at him. "Oh. Well. I guess I shouldn't have jumped to thinking you're Exoskia just because of where you lived."

"You shouldn't assume anything at all, lady. Not in this place."

"Speaking of which, where are we?"

Flatlands of sand surrounded them in a gentle darkness disturbed by no movement, not so much as a breeze, yet the sky was a silent storm pierced with red lightning. It flashed across the ground at intervals, glowing in eerie patches across a dry wasteland extending as far as Willow could see.

Whirling masses of patent portals dotted the landscape, never more than a few meters from each other, but often clustered so close together it worried Willow to think of the implications.

Benny tucked himself tighter against her side and said, "Portal mines. They're full of wild portals, but super close together. We're probably gonna fall through a veiled, furcated one and end up in hell, or worse, the northwest."

"Don't be scared, Benny. I'll carry you so that if we fall, I promise we fall together."

He swirled a finger in the sand between his legs and asked with uncharacteristic shyness, "Do you think promises are better broken sometimes?"

"I can tell you Zeph's opinion first and then mine...Wait. Shit. What is that thing?"

Something was emerging from one of the portals in the distance behind the boy, starting at first with a black mist that scoured the ground, obscuring the patent portals. A bony leg the size of a tree trunk came through, followed by more legs and a body in the shape of a massive, spidery skeleton with so many joints it contorted inside out. Its skin was a smooth, leathery brown, and its face a round eyeless thing that opened into a mouth with rows and rows of little teeth.

Willow stood up and said, "Benny, I think I have to break one of my promises just now." She picked him up and shot up over the sand, only able to manage a couple feet, enough to prevent them from falling into anything as they fled.

Benny screamed as he hung on to her neck, "What *are* you?"

136

Willow covered his mouth, backing away slowly, and whispered, "Hush or that thing might hear you."

Eyes wide, he nodded.

"In answer to your very loud question, I think I'm a Kinetic, but I'm not entirely sure."

"You're breaking a very basic, very big rule right now, lady," he whispered back, sweeping one arm out and staring at her like a god. "No such thing as a Metakinetic."

"Well, you're welcome."

They got far enough away that Willow could no longer see the monstrous thing, only more sand dunes full of portals rising up around them.

With the boy now seated on her back, she needed a plan. "Okay, Benny, since you know more about this place, I'm going to need your input."

He nodded really fast. "Duh."

"What was that thing?"

"No clue."

"You ever heard of skin maps?"

"Nuh uh."

"How about maps that show up in firelight?"

"Is this a puzzle? I usually like puzzles."

"No, Benny," she said, pulling him back over into her arms. "Just light a match for me and you'll see."

Willow lifted her forearm to the flame and watched the curling lines appear across her flesh. "See the map now?"

Benny looked closer, touched her arm, and flipped it over. "I wanna call you crazy again, but you're flying without wings, so what's crazy even mean anymore?"

"So you don't see anything?"

"Freckles."

"Funny. Well, I can see everything. From the village where we started, to the Shadowlands, to way up north, some place full of mountains labeled Voidsrange. There's just a large swath of emptiness down south past the Border River, though, that extends along the Simmering Sea."

"Oh, people call that whole area the Emberlands. Somewhere in there was Void Valley, where the phoenix-born used to live."

"The Fervers, right? I remember seeing these mines to the south of that. Uh, here." She pressed on that patch until it enlarged. "Alright, wow, looks like the portal pockets here are well-mapped, but barely any destinations are noted. Just three actually."

"How are there even two? How many times could someone come and go from here to figure all that out?"

"Maybe it's the work of multiple mapmakers."

Benny shook his head. "Only the master was ever that brave."

"Either way, two of the recorded portals are headed even farther south, and I need to go north."

"Why?"

"I have a Guide of my own."

Benny's eyes grew round with hope. "You do?"

"Yes, and he will definitely make me sick before this is all over."

"Is he rich? Can he give us lots of food?"

A hiss sounded from behind them. The closest sand dune shook.

Willow stopped breathing as a snake so large, larger than any she ever saw in her gardens emerged from its base, its body textured like thick gray rocks and eyes reflecting red from the color of the sky. It rose up, tail still in the sand as its head swayed in the air.

"Higher, lady, go higher!"

She rose as much as she could, but it was not far enough, bringing her just to the height of the massive thing, its swaying almost hypnotic, rife with the clear intention of striking.

"I can't go farther, Benny. I already feel like I'm about to fall."

He whimpered. She tried backing away and barely managed it, fighting exhaustion and starvation, her powers milked from moving too many people when affecting sentience was always harder, a principle she had only recently grasped as highly significant.

The snake opened its mouth, fangs dripping blue liquid into the portals below. "It can't move too far, or it'll fall into a portal," said Willow. "We just need to get out of its range."

But it was like flying through honey, and she knew any second now that thing would pounce.

"Stop moving," came a voice from below. "It agitates her."

A bearded man holding a bow and arrow stood on a high dune. Willow could barely take her eyes off the thing to look.

But in the next moment, it cried out with piercing shrillness, its head toppling over toward her in the air, those fangs nearing with such speed she just had time to turn her body sideways. Benny squeezed her as the monster fell past them, shot through the eye, down into a portal and away.

"Too bad. Sand wyrms have a lot of meat," laughed the man. He began to walk toward them, unafraid of where he walked despite the vigilant look in his eyes. "Hello there. I'm Victor. This patch of darker sand here is safe."

Panting from exhaustion, Willow descended.

"Wait," breathed Benny into her ear. "He sounds hungry. What if he eats us?"

Willow gripped him tighter in alarm. "People do that here?"

"I've never been *here* to know."

"I really miss home." She reached the sand but kept her hand out, palm flat, the way she had seen Kinetics use it to threaten others, and said louder, "One wrong move and I'll push you into a portal without even touching you."

"Yes, I can see you're capable of that. Calm yourself. I'm the under-taker here." He said it so proudly she wondered if he were insane.

Benny flailed. "You hear that? He lives off dead bodies. Flee. Flee."

The man laughed, a whole-body shudder. "No, no, little one. I offer help to the exiled or bury any I find dead. You'd be surprised how many corpses get sent to the mines. Anyhow, I've a fully stocked home, and I can take you there safely to rest. No one ever shows up here happy or well-fed. Did you?"

They were too desperate to refuse, but Willow worried that was the man's key occupational premise. He even carried a world of metal on his person: fishhooks attached to string, a spearhead carved of brown bone, green-tipped arrows in a narrow quiver, and a dagger or two tucked into his supple boots. Silver-haired everywhere and short in stature, he sported the body of what could have been a dancing wrestler: overly bulky above the waist with lean legs below.

"Gotta be agile in the mines," he said, leading them through the dunes. "Oh, and it helps to name the larger piles of sand. That one there is Emeline, quite a tall broad. Here's Frank, both tiny and ugly. And yes, that's my Lucy, a true beauty, with perfectly symmetrical curves."

"This guy's been alone too long," whispered Benny.

Willow snorted as she followed close behind but kept a couple inches off the ground, just in case.

"So, Victor, how did you come to be here?" she asked, aiming for conversational instead of suspicious.

He held out an arm, stopping them, before rapidly firing off an arrow into something crawling a hundred paces away. "Well, I'm probably the only one to do it deliberately." He skipped over a por-tal pocket, nabbed the lizard into a bag, and returned. "What I didn't know is it would save me from a mass killing."

Benny's head shot up. "You're a Ferver!"

"That's right, little man. And are you a mutant Kinetic like her?"

"Hey!" said Willow.

Benny laughed. "She is *so* weird."

Willow dropped him. He screamed until he realized he was floating beside her.

"Whoa," said Benny, drawing out the word.

Victor jumped into a portal without warning. Out he came a few paces away and strode into another. "Come along! Patent portals only take you so far. Just *do not* roll over on landing."

Tired enough to try, Willow and Benny looked at each other and decided to follow. After a while, it felt almost to Willow like skipping rocks. Except she was the rock.

Just behind the highest dune they had seen so far, they came to a small cabin. Victor put his hands on his hips with a proud smile. "Like every other Ingressian home, I built mine in the largest area I could find clear of portals. A full one-mile radius all to ourselves. Come in and have a bite to eat."

"Will it be snake soup or something?" asked Benny.

"Or something."

The interior was full of rugs and simple furniture, a wide-open one-level abode with no rooms. In a corner chair slept a man who looked so old, death may as well have been peeking over his shoulder.

"That there is another exile—found him just about to fall into a portal by Emeline. Arrived three years ago, and he's barely moved since," said Victor as he shucked off his gear to tuck into a wardrobe by the door.

Willow sank down onto a soft seat of fur blankets and almost cried from the relief. Her mind had a slightly harder time dropping its guard. "So why choose to live here? And how could you possibly know the area so well?"

"Maybe you tell me how in the Mother's name you can fly?"

"Nah, you first." She waved a hand.

"You."

"Nope, you."

"How about you?"

Benny's head volleyed between them, until he punched the man in the arm. "Stop it. We're tired. And she doesn't know. She just can."

"That does about sum it up," groaned Willow, realizing that without the adrenaline, she could no longer move her limbs or keep open her eyes. "Benny, c'mere," she said through a yawn. "Wake me if he proves a threat."

Victor just shook his head in amusement as Willow's eyelids slammed closed with the helpless compliance of shutters in the wind.

"So a Skia, a Kinetic, and a Thrower walk into a pub. The barkeep looks up and asks, 'Am I dreaming, or is this a joke?'"

The laughter pelted her sleepy bubble hard enough to pierce, waking Willow to the sight of Benny playing cards with Victor and the old man at a round table carved of stained bones, draped in odd animal skins, the red eyes of a sand wyrm staring straight at her.

"Am I dreaming, or is this a joke?" she asked aloud.

"Lady!" Benny hopped over to her with two steaming bowls of something that smelled divine. "It's real beef stew, see?"

She took the offering and asked between bites, "There are cows here? In the sand?"

Victor tossed down a card and answered, "Just one that cropped up ages ago through a portal. Lucky for us, I caught it before it lumbered over into another one."

The old man scratched his white beard and coughed. "I saw it from the window. Credit where credit's due, boy."

"I'm hardly a boy, Marsden."

The old man just chuckled once and lay back in his rocking chair.

"Girl, you look emaciated," Victor noted. "Which begs the question: Why such a harsh sentence for someone so young? And a Kinetic no less, the most protected of all designations?"

"Benny didn't tell you?"

"Lips shut tight on that one."

Willow tossed Benny a proud look before her face fell. She slurped up the last spoonful with a noise that would make her mother blush before answering. "We saved a couple Fervers from death in a trading village before escaping to the Shadowlands, where, and I can say this quite confidently, I am not welcome."

Benny poured some of his food into her bowl even as she tried to stop him. "I was treated well there. You weren't."

"You ate more while I was sleeping, didn't you?"

He grinned. "A lot more."

She turned back to the hulk of a man staring at them. "Is there a safe way out of here, Victor? Preferably headed north?"

"So soon? I was hoping a pretty lady like you would show up one day and care for a roll in the hay."

Benny pursed his lips as if he had eaten a tart lemon. "Ew."

Willow laughed. "Do you even know what that means?"

"Hey, I've taken care of pigs."

"You're referring to the animals, right?"

"Duh."

"Wouldn't put it past you to mean the men."

"Oh." He nodded. "Both, then."

Willow looked over at Victor and straightened her back. "All this to say, no, thank you."

"Suit yourself." And when he waggled his gray eyebrows, she laughed so hard her sides hurt.

Smiling, he placed his elbows on the table and leaned toward his new guests. "Alright, let's talk strategy, then. I know of only three portals out of here, and one does head north, but with a dangerous exit. I wouldn't risk it. Best to take the one into the Fallen Fields south of here, quite close to a portal that will then take you on north. You follow?"

"Yes, but how do you know where these three portals lead?"

"Quite the suspicious one, aren't you?"

"Can you blame me?"

He tossed her a rakish grin. "Not at all. But as you're a Kinetic, I don't want you blabbing anything about me if you ever get back to the Sky Realm, which coincidentally, is north."

"I'd only blab that you saved me."

"No." He raised a finger, a frightening look overtaking his eyes. "I'm a Meta, remember, and your king wants me dead. Letting you go is dangerous enough as it is. My sole protection is that no one who dares step foot here can get around safely without me."

He outlined exactly why Willow had kept her map to herself, knowing that such a valuable resource on her body could get her killed, and this man knew too much about her already. "Understood. If it helps, you carry a secret of mine now too."

"Well, then we can shake on mutual discretion, a deal on our honor."

They clasped hands in one firm, deep dip.

Willow did not let go. "So how do you know how to get out?"

He fixed her with a hard stare. "The master mapmaker brought me here in the first place."

"You've met him?" said Benny, young voice a touch too loud.

"Yes. And you two will need supplies if you're going that far." He leaned back and crossed his thick arms. "Weapons too. Heed my advice and drop by Farrow's Forge. The weaponsmith will trade you fairly for a travel pack and a blade."

"Ooh, I want a blade. I want a blade," cried Benny.

Willow raised a brow when Victor nodded his approval and said gruffly, "In the Land of Portalcraft, everyone could use a blade."

"You really don't need to take turns."

"It's not personal."

"Feels personal."

Willow waved her hand. "Well, you weren't nearly killed by two different designations in one day, then starved at the will of your own guardian and tossed out for dead. Maybe trusting adult Ingressians isn't exactly working for me." She stroked Benny's hair against the couch cushions and continued to refuse sleep until he woke.

"I hope you don't leave my home like that." Victor pointed at her with a tumbler of liquor from his position across from them, his arms and legs slung over the back of a chair.

"Like what? Realistic?"

"No, this world is a bombed battlefield where one wrong step will kill you." Willow smiled as he tossed her a tipsy grin. "But it's also full of more. I'll put it this way. I once asked the master mapmaker about a journeyman's decision to leave home and map this damn land. What purpose would it serve, really? It's just safer to stay put. But that upset my young friend, who told me it's never safe to live in ignorance or exile. And look at what's happened to my people, the ones who thought they were so safe in their homes."

"I could point out you've chosen exile right here."

"I need exile." He rubbed his stubbled jaw and stared into the murky tumbler. "My wife and three children fell ill about thirty years ago. Passed, one after the other. After the other. Then after the other again. Needed a place to forget."

"So the mapmaker stepped in to help?"

"She did," he said, closely followed by, "Shit."

"She, huh?"

He waved a floppy hand. "Forget I said that."

Willow shrugged, wondering if he would even remember this conversation in the morning, but interested to know most people were wrong about the mapmaker being a man.

Victor turned his back to her, fiddling with the abandoned deck of cards on the table, shuffling them faster and faster into a blur of red and black. "She found me this place, safest place to be alone outside of Void Valley, or so we thought. Even stayed a while to map the region better, though I suspect it was more to make sure I was no harm to myself." He said the last part more softly, laying aside the cards to toss back his drink. Then he flicked a hand at the fireplace as well, flames shooting from his open palm.

Willow leaned forward and touched his warm hand as he drew it into a fist. "She sounds like a good person."

"The best."

"May I ask her name?"

"Not my place to tell," he grunted.

"Alright. Well, I for one am very grateful that you stuck around to save the damned."

He was silent a moment, until he put down his glass with a *thunk*, and left her to her thoughts, mainly the realization that perhaps heroism could be entirely selfish without losing its honor.

CHAPTER
11

A CHILD'S BURDEN

Great tribes of void and clans of ether
Would rather fall than stand together.
Mind your fears and fear not your reason
Or all of you will fall to pieces
In a ruined world that craves cohesion.

—*The Seer of Tribe Starlight at the coronation*
of the first child king of the Kinetics

The patent portals in this area proved noisy. They crashed like corporeal sound waves, merging into each other to create an angry pool of portals so cramped it could almost be mistaken for one large trapdoor into the unknown.

Victor saw them off with a travel pack filled with animal skins, a tarp, water, and dry food. "The skins should get you what you need," he roared. "Especially the sand wyrm hide, great for under armor and found nowhere else. Demand two fresh blades for that, designed custom for you. Accept no less."

Willow had insisted on spending the past week learning about the landscape and helping with repairs for the house, where she used her powers to nail, board, and sharpen tools until she completed Victor's chores for the entire month; she allowed herself to take the skins as exorbitant thanks rather than charity.

She hugged Victor with one arm as Benny patted their escort's leg with an awkward smile.

"Take care, Victor. This world looks like it could use more people like you," shouted Willow through the din of portals.

"I echo the sentiment. To a Kinetic, no less." He threw up his hands. "But maybe that should teach me something. And Willow, make no mistake, your level of source control is breathtaking. Put aside moving sentience—such delicacy rarely comes along with the power of brute force."

"I wish I had a means of comparison."

"You'll find it in your travels. Just look around."

She laughed and slapped him on the arm with a blush. "Well, thank you for saving our skins, Victor. And for the literal skins too." She had a sobering thought and knelt with care onto the burning sand. "Now, about you."

"Me?" Benny pointed to himself.

"Take anything you shouldn't have?"

"Nuh uh."

Willow continued to stare him down.

Benny sighed and pulled a trinket from his pocket.

"My wedding ring," Victor said, taking it.

Willow apologized with a deep bow. "Be well, and, er, see you in the Hub," she said.

One harsh, unbidden bark of laughter escaped Victor. "Certainly, my dear. Take good care of the sticky-fingered one."

Willow held a pouting Benny as the boy waved goodbye, both falling backward once more.

The Tug pulled at her chest with the force of a running river, pushing bile from her throat within seconds of her arrival in the Fallen Fields, the farthest south she had traveled thus far.

"At least we know south is definitely the wrong direction," said Benny, patting her on the back and handing her their waterskin.

Willow guzzled down the cool liquid before leaning against the nearest tree. "Yeah, and that the master mapmaker probably has something to do with my skin map, since it matches perfectly with Victor's portal knowledge." She lit a match and checked her arm once she felt better. "Looks pretty safe here. No veiled portals for about three miles in each direction, and if we go that way, we should find the one headed north to Farrow's Forge—very north—and just one more portal away from the Sky Realm."

"Brilliant."

"But Benny, are you sure traveling with me is what you want? I'm not even sure where I'm headed, only to whom."

The boy just nodded. "I want to go with you. I can help find your Guide."

She slung an arm around his shoulders. "You have a place with me as long you want it, but you have to be honest in return. Who are your parents? Don't think I haven't noticed you've yet to tell me your designation. I didn't want to press you in front of Victor, but you're a Metaferver, right?"

He stared at his feet. "My full name is Benjamin Waylon. And I promised not to say any more than that."

"There's a lot of that going around lately. But who'd you promise not to tell?"

"Strangers."

"Am I still a stranger? If you're a Flamethrower, that could be really helpful. We wouldn't even need the matches. Why'd you have them on you?"

"Um…to throw people offtrack."

"You're lying to me. Benny?" she growled.

"Oh, look, a bird!"

"Alright, alright," she said, giving in for now. "Teach me something as we walk. Why do they call it the Land of Portalcraft? Didn't everything start spontaneously at the Hub?"

He swung his arms wide, clearly happy to switch topics. "We think so. But ancient designations used to know how to make portals, almost dig them into the earth with their powers. It took whole villages sometimes. But we don't do that anymore. Too many people died from the energy loss, and wars started over who gets to control the craft."

She hummed. "So that's why wild portals are much more common than man-made ones."

"Yup. The ones we made are all mapped out pretty well, but they're locked. Sometimes by ability. Flame-locked, void-locked, blood-locked, riddle-locked—that kind of thing. Portal classification can be way complicated, lady." He picked up a stick longer than himself and inspected it with the great care of a child, though he didn't always speak like one.

"If I didn't have to constantly run for my life, I might just die from its jarring lack of reality."

Benny shrugged his shoulders, waving the stick with dramatic flair. "No one ever defined reality for me."

"Well, how could they?"

"Exactly."

"You're a strange little boy."

"Lady, do you see yourself?" With an abrupt flick, he stuck the twiggy end up her nose.

Matthias Farrow, an Exoskia of humble birth, lived in a cottage with his eldest son at the border of the largest Kinetic trading village yet founded outside the Sky Realm of Maddooinne. The benefit of heavy foot traffic through King's Pass, the only reliably mapped route from Skia trading villages to a Kinetic one, offset the threat of working with Kinetics only by a slim margin. But Matthias's exemplary skills earned him a certain distinction, such that unlike most Ingressians, he could afford to turn away commissioners who displeased him. Unbeknownst to them, most Kinetics, however rich, always failed to purchase a Farrow blade if they made one of three mistakes.

First, they entered his home or his forge without express permission.

Second, they dismissed his family as unimportant bystanders of his work.

Third, the least common but most unforgivable offense, they feigned superior knowledge of his craft.

His son's wife, Anya, vetted potential buyers for the first transgression before inviting them in to tea. Next, his son would strum up a conversation, ultimately to ask for personal help with something that had a simple Kinetic solution just to see if the visitor would bother lending a moment's assistance.

As for today, the sky had split open a storm that had just calmed into a light evening drizzle, through which Matthias could see his next project arriving beyond the forge window. There, a little boy ambled up the safest path from town alongside a young woman of perhaps Anya's age. The boy poked his companion with a stick before thrashing it about in the rain like a sword. A strange couple as far as weapons patrons went, Matthias thought, but they certainly sought his services.

He checked the stores of iron powder, wondering if the weather would drive the pair into his home when Anya pretended not to hear their knocking.

He glanced back through the porthole-shaped glass to see the boy reach for the cottage doorknob. Matthias put down the powder. But the woman pulled the boy away with a clear rebuke, and just as they began to walk off, the door swung open.

Matthias lit the forge.

A full hour later, Evan dropped by as his father sketched with one hand, the other dangling within the void pool as it so often did.

His son, a redhead like his belated mother but with his father's unique ethereal control and broad shoulders, touched the elder Farrow's arm. "We have visitors."

Matthias's head snapped up. "I thought they'd been turned away. They arrived a while ago."

"No. In fact, you'd better come meet them now."

As Matthias stepped over the cottage threshold, he could hear the young boy loudly spinning tales, saying, "And then it tried to eat us, but I was too quick. I shoved this pointy stick down its throat until it spat us out and ran away."

"Welcome," Matthias called. "Glad you survived such a harrowing trip."

The boy's fair companion stood with a small bow and said, "Thank you for seeing us, sir. My name is Willow, and this is my son, Benny."

The youngling waved from his place, belly down on the hearth rug.

Willow smiled politely at the middle-aged smith, so tall he had to crouch on entering his own home. Matthias Farrow knew he was more tanned muscle than man, odd for one of the Exoskia, who all otherwise seemed so long and thin and pale.

After a moment of silence, the girl straightened from her bow.

Matthias hid his surprise at her respectful formality and grappled for an explanation. "What's your designation, youngling? Skia?"

"Oh no, sir—Kinetics, the both of us."

He had a harder time hiding his surprise then. And that's when he noticed it. The large iron cauldron stored upstairs now sat in the fire, the one he had promised to bring down but was always too tired by end of day to try.

Evan took a seat on the couch by his wife. Anya hardly looked up, knitting away with a rounded belly and a soft smile. It was unlike any of them to be so at ease with Kinetics on the property, and Matthias did not approve. His first grandchild was not yet born to defend itself against the opaque motives of strangers.

"What brings you to our home?" he finally asked, moving to the oversized armchair by the fire.

Willow retook her seat. "We were separated from my husband in our travels. So I'm heading back north alone with Benny. It seemed best to trade for a blade or two and a traveler's pack. I've heard only praise for your work, and as I have little weapons knowledge, would appreciate purchasing from the source instead of a tradesman in search of greater profit."

Matthias wondered at such a strong Kinetic sitting so prim and proper, as if she were the forgotten queen of his home. He drummed two fingers along his thigh. "But would a Kinetic trader cheat his fellow countrywoman?"

Willow lifted a brow. "We both know he would try."

"And where are you staying in town?" cut in Anya. "There's just the one inn, and it was packed full this morning. Come look. The rain seems to be worsening again."

"We've made do in worse conditions recently. We can camp in the public woods." Willow's smile was tinged with truth, ropes of loss hanging like a noose from the gallows of her gaze.

Anya and Evan darted glances at their head of house, the request for permission in their eyes clear. Matthias nodded with a resigned huff.

Evan stood up. "You must stay the night in the loft."

"Oh, but we couldn't," said Willow.

"You're the one who made the space available by moving our cauldron, so refusal is futile," laughed Aya. "And I promised to make that cap for Benny tonight. This way, you can have some say in the pattern."

Willow leaned over to give Anya a quick hug, and Matthias rubbed his scruffy chin in agitation when she returned it. He stood. "I should check on the forge. I trust my children will see you settled."

"I'll come with you, Father," Evan followed him out with a pack in his arms. Just outside, he handed it over and said softly, "Look at this."

Matthias pulled out a long swath of sand wyrm hide, remarkably lightweight for such tough, stone-like material, and held an edge up to a lantern, eyes wide as he confirmed its authentic shade, texture, and thickness. He dropped both hands in surprise. "She's met Victor."

He hurried back to the forge with his son and shoved an entire arm into the void.

Nearly every forge location was determined foremost by the presence of a void pool, and because of their unique ability to feel external ether and tease it apart from the void, the Exoskia traditionally made for far better voidsmiths than did the voidsmen.

Even so, the external void to Matthias felt different than it might to anyone else. It was an emptiness that rippled, one through which messages sent with shadow ether flowed from one pool to another like leaves along a lazy river. This void pool had been empty of late, nothing from the Twisted Forge in a while, its owner likely lost in some complicated design.

Matthias stepped back and considered. He wrote a message on parchment, then stripped away a sheath of ether from its surface into the pool, essentially sending off a shadow of the note until a voidsmith noticed its existence. "Who is she, Marsden?"

He waited, wondering how Victor could have let loose an exiled Kinetic.

A reply came through a couple hours later signed from the south: "Strong, but harmless."

Willow listened to the rain hitting the rafters, with Benny curled into a ball at her feet. Blankets piled layers thick and warm around them, the space felt comforting in its constriction. She wanted to sink into it. Relax.

She knew letting down her guard could spell death even if Anya had taken a liking to her, yet Willow's body felt looser than it had since leaving the East Skia Trading Village. At that thought, she realized— the Tug had ceased. She went cold with panicky elation.

Is Zeph here?

She sat up to look out the window, into the dark evening mist. She pushed it open without thought and pulled herself with a twist onto the cottage roof. The maneuver required kinetic power, and just as she landed on wet thatching amid swinging trees and thrashing winds, she could have sworn someone hurtled off the edge.

She jumped after them and began to search the perimeter like a madwoman.

Matthias found her like that in the rain, her clothes soaked through and stumbling about like a sleepwalker.

He approached, carrying a swinging lantern and with a waterproof hide over his head. "Alright there, youngling?"

She looked at him with wide, terrified eyes and screamed through the storm, "I have to find him."

"Has Benny run off?"

"No, my Guide—he's here. He's got to be here."

Matthias's eyes widened as well, but he took her arm with a gentle touch. "Come into the forge and warm up. The fire's blazing. Come along now."

Willow allowed herself to be tugged into the smithy and plopped before the promised roaring blaze, which dried the front of her clothes in a mere minute. Matthias coaxed her into turning around, and as he did, she doubled over into his arms from acute, slicing pain.

"He's left, has he?" asked Matthias.

Willow burst into tears. "He led me here. Why would he leave?"

"Guides are notoriously fickle."

She leaned back, desperation in her voice. "What do you know of them?"

"Not much. Although they often meet quite tragic ends, don't they?"

Willow blinked, eyes wet. "What do you mean?"

"Never heard of the most famous Guide pairs in history?"

When she shook her head, Matthias gave her another once-over. "It's a rare Kinetic that shows no contempt for my kind, let alone has never heard the most famous tales. Where were you raised? It can't have been Maddooinne."

She hesitated before saying, "Outside the Sky Realm, near a village not unlike this one."

"A Kinetic from a village and not a sky clan. Rare, but not impossible, I suppose," he replied. "Well, get comfortable by the fire and I'll tell you some key Ingressian tales. Just bear in mind that stories don't dictate your life, you follow?"

She nodded, more at ease to look around the famed Farrow's Forge as its master stepped away. Barrels and banners, tools and weaponry alike leaned against walls, hung from the ceiling, or covered the tables—all filling the warm space to the brim.

Willow drew a thick rug forward with her powers and placed a chair by the fire for Matthias.

He had handed her a cup of pitch-black tea and a blanket just as dark by the time he spoke again. "You're too close to the forge. Step back."

"It feels so much like home, though. A good fire."

Matthias smiled and let it go. Taking his seat in the chair across from her on the rug, he said, "Well, let's see, then. Most things Ingressians talk about concern the wealthy, the ones who have the money to travel more safely or matter most to the economy, so usually we hear about your kind in these parts."

Willow nodded.

"The most famous tale begins the day Kinetic royalty visited the Shadowlands for a celebration."

"What?" she gasped.

"Yes." Matthias's voice grew softer at her surprised fascination. "Thirty years ago, the distrust between fellow Exos was not so great, and some Kinetics lived on the outskirts of town, were permitted within the borders for supervised events and gatherings. But royalty— they were even granted lodging at the Steelie Inn. You wouldn't know this, but it's our oldest and most venerable site, though it has since lost its luster. Exokinetic Queen Liliana arrived there with her daughter, Lavender, to honor the newly born Shadowland prince."

She cocked her head, surprised again. "The Shadowlands have a prince?"

"Yes, child, just as the Metas build hierarchical republics, the Exos have always leaned toward clan-based monarchies. Our king is now old and sickly, but his two sons are grown and said to be quite striking. They say that Lavender, a maiden just on the cusp of adulthood, was so taken with the Skia heir apparent that she followed him about like a spoiled puppy."

Willow tried not to see too much of herself in the woman.

"But," he continued, "when she discovered the existence of his Guide, a defenseless girl of common birth, she had the other woman slain in her sleep. The princess must have thought a Guide would prevent the elder Skia prince from following her home out of loyalty or sheer pain. So she had her problem solved permanently."

"But didn't that hurt him into hating her?" Willow scooted forward, looking up at him. "Seems counterproductive."

"The prince won't talk about it publicly, but of course, the Shadowlands has never welcomed them back. Ever since that hateful murder, ambassadors have been sent between our borders for political matters in place of monarchs. And they say both mother and daughter were cursed for what transpired, dying as they did just a few years later."

Willow gaped at Matthias, her eyes wide in the firelight. "And what about other Guides?"

"Ancient pairs have included the Shadow warrior Elijah and the child Danika of Skia Clan Rameen. He died on the battlefield trying to reclaim—"

Willow interrupted in a rush, "Child? But aren't Guide pairs romantic?"

"Who in the void told you that?"

"No one," she said slowly. "I suppose."

Matthias seemed truly shocked. "Are you in love with your Guide, dear? Is he the husband you mentioned?"

"No, sir, I was just under a misconception."

He placed a heavy hand on her shoulder. "Guides are always of the same designation, but they should never enter into a romance. You be careful."

Willow took a moment to let that sink in, the implications manifold. If Zeph were a Kinetic, she was correct in heading north to the

Sky Realm. But then, why had he kept his powers secret from her, spending all that time helping hers grow and his suffocate? And then there was the other issue, the one just as hurtful.

"Why be careful?" she asked, voice small.

"The tragedy of it all. Lost love tends to be the most heartbreaking of relationships, and Guides are more often parted than not."

"Then what's the point of a Guide pair? Why do they exist?"

"Well," he said, slowly, and selecting his words with care, "it must be true they serve an important function for each other—able to lead the other back home when lost or separated. But like my prince's Guide, many often meet early ends if they don't ignore each other altogether. An annoying or even painful sensation is not enough to convince everyone to leave safe harbor and journey forth into Ingress. I assume that's what you're doing? Unmarried and frantic?"

Willow nodded, a timid smile on her face for having lied.

"That's alright. You have a little one to protect."

"Oh, Benny! I left him." She made to stand.

He gave her a hard look and said in a hard voice, "He's in no danger from my family. You have my word. Now, may I ask you, child, how did you end up in the Southern Portal Mines?"

"I'm sorry?"

"A sand wyrm is found nowhere else."

"I traded for the hide."

He raised a brow.

She sighed in defeat and sat back down, retelling her own tale of the Guide flare she witnessed.

"Amazing," Matthias muttered. "No wonder Alden spared them. You understand now why we have a softness for Guide pairs in my land." He leaned forward and tapped her nose in amusement.

"They're not yet adults," argued Willow, "only Meta children being hunted. Wouldn't Alden have spared them just for that?"

"Perhaps. Perhaps not. Our kingdom protects its own first and foremost, as do they all. Now I think we had best tuck in. You'll be needing weapons forged with bright eyes on the morrow."

Benny was having a damned good time watching Matthias work.

"Please," he begged.

"For the last time, child, you may not use the hammer. You could fatally injure yourself."

Benny pouted, his legs swinging back and forth from his seat on a high table.

Matthias continued to slam iron against anvil. He worked the metal with clear vision, from roundness into a thin, sharp dagger as small and well-suited to the child who watched its conception as possible.

But Willow had wanted an ax, claiming the most familiarity with its use, and he was still developing its design. Axes were rarely requested from smiths of his caliber, being an unusual weapon choice in general. She intended to use it for more than felling trees, and he quite liked the multipurpose way she seemed to think. It wasn't like a Kinetic to be practical instead of lofty.

He returned to the void pool and extracted more wild ether, coaxing it into the iron with unmatched deftness. A blade forged with shadow ether strikes true to the soul, or so the Skia say. He could see the strand shimmer with the colors of the rainbow as it blended into metal, adding an ethereal ductility that increased both its toughness and cutting-edge hardness with minimal flexure.

Never had a blade of Farrow's making fractured.

He grunted as he dumped this one into water to cool and got to work on the handle, the image of the ax evolving in his mind as he moved.

Anya's voice reached him softly. "Father, I've convinced our guest to come to town for some shopping."

"Hello again, sir," said Willow, appearing at Anya's side. "We'll take Benny off your hands now."

Matthias grunted. "Take Evan with you too."

Anya laughed from her place at the door, the heat of a working forge not healthy in her condition, though she could rarely ever stand it. "I'll be the one with a Kinetic by my side. You may need Evan. We're not free of thieves even here, Willow."

Matthias grabbed the bellows and waved a hand in dismissal as Willow scooped up Benny.

The boy called out, "Make it really good, okay? Super pointy and full of diamonds."

"There will be no diamonds," grumbled the smith. "Kinetics and their damned diamonds."

The trip to town proved uneventful, Anya waddling along with a long list of shopping Willow had volunteered to levitate back.

"And you're sure I won't come across any patrollers from the East Skia Trading Village?"

"Oh no," replied Anya, "patrollers are not a centralized sort. They vary from town to town, too far from each other to communicate regularly. How would they recognize you anyhow? You're a long ways away from there, both in distance and portal direction."

"I suppose my exile was lucky in the overall goal of heading north. I would have had to locate six separate portals to reach this far otherwise."

"A silver lining, then!"

"To a very dark thundercloud," said Willow, linking her arms with Anya.

The village proved to be so crowded with Kinetics that no one looked twice at them. Willow overheard conversations, took note of interesting bits of information about Maddooinne, and floated small things here and there until the traders dropped their guards with her in the periphery. And finally, with all of Anya's shopping bundled up into a burlap sack that Willow kinetically carried, they made their way back following the road to Farrow's Forge.

Benny was hopping over puddles ahead with another spear-like stick when thunder cracked.

"Oh dear," said Anya. "That is unexpected."

Willow looked up to see clouds sailing into the clear sky as if from a great distance, roiling darker, at unnatural speed. "What's going on?"

"Perhaps a Winged mage is casting an Exo spell." Anya held Willow's arm tighter, and at her questioning look, said, "When someone takes power by controlling external chaos, sometimes the environment retaliates or, well, tries to add balance with chaos."

"It's just a bit of rain, though, isn't it? Let's speed up."

Anya shivered hard. "The dark is dangerous with so many bandits and animals in these woods. We should turn back for the village. Wait it out."

"Aren't we more than halfway to the forge? Wouldn't it take longer to turn back?"

Anya looked around. "Yes, but just ahead, the forest gets thicker, and…do you hear that?"

Willow turned.

"The meat," Anya whispered. "I shouldn't have bought it so fresh."

Glowing eyes stared back at them through the brush.

A low growl sounded. Then there was utter quiet.

"Anya," whispered Willow, "meld with shadow ether and go home."

"I can't. I'm pregnant."

Anya stepped away in distress and tripped over onto her back with a gasp, unable to stand with her belly so round, arms pulled over her eyes in hiccupping fear. Beside her, Willow knelt, her gaze trained on the shadowed one staring back at them in the tenuous calm.

"Benny," she whispered. But the boy did not answer.

A creature pounced, a fiend wolf the size of a bear. It reached an impossible height in midair as Willow stood up with her arms out, focusing with all her might on its body instead of its snarling green face.

She slowed it down, but it was still coming.

Willow stared into its yawn of a mouth and cried out, shocked into stillness.

Benny had appeared atop the wolf's shoulder as if dropped from a portal onto its body. Clutching a tuft of fur, he sank dripping teeth, sharp and elongated to Willow's incredulous eyes, deep into the wolf's neck.

The creature fell to the forest floor, landing with a loud thud, unmoving at her feet.

Benny scrambled off with a worried look at Anya, still flat on her back. He stared at Willow and put a finger to his lips.

Soon, they would hurry back to the forge to a litany of Anya's thanks that Benny had found a sharp stick for Willow to kinetically shove into their attacker's neck. Soon, her husband would envelop them all in a choking embrace. Soon, Matthias would promise a proper show of gratitude.

But after all that, Willow would make sure to take Benny aside for an overdue interrogation.

"Metaporter, then?" she asked, hands on his shoulders outside the empty smithy.

"Uh huh."

"How do you have fangs?"

He pulled back his top lip with a finger, revealing a canine only slightly longer and sharper than average. "Only Porters have these. But they get bigger when we use them."

"Is this why you never really smile? To keep your secret?"

"Uh huh."

"What's in the fangs?"

"A sedative."

"A deadly one?"

"Depends on the dose."

"And you couldn't just tell me?" Willow knelt before him, a new worry in her gut.

"Nuh uh."

"Why?"

He swung his little arms in the air. "I'm a Meta, for one thing. For another, my people have been in hiding for over a century. We want to be myths, forgotten and happy."

"Then why aren't you with them?"

He hung his head, this strong boy who had survived solitude to save her from that and more, just before bursting into tears.

Through the sobs, he managed to tell her of a loving family: handfuls of cousins, scores of aunts and uncles, and the parents who taught him how to metaport. But he learned too well and too soon and made a mistake in anger, never able to find his way back to a people of nomads, their main base unnamed and unmapped.

"But that's why we have fail-safes. The Skia trading village was mine. They were supposed to come for me there if I ever messed up. I waited for months. In clear view! They never came. They just…left me there."

He could only port to a place he could clearly visualize and thus believe in, the key element of source control for Metas, the many tribesmen falling under the Line of Reason. So Benny's powers had stopped working the more he lost sight of home.

Willow hugged him underneath a black sky that had not yet spilled forth. And even when it did, she knew it could not match the force of an orphan's anguish.

"I really like your fangs," she whispered, gratified by his watery smile.

Willow set the table five days later, the work a delicate kinetic exercise and one she still wondered at doing in front of others, when Matthias entered the cottage with two sacks slung over a brawny shoulder.

"Done already, Father?" asked Evan.

"Yes, presentation before dinner," he said, removing his boots and taking a seat by Willow, Benny scrambling over to lay on his belly at their feet. He handed them a camping sack of materials before digging out weapons from the other bag.

"Me first," sang the boy.

Matthias pulled out a small, fine dagger, so thin it nearly disappeared when viewed from the side.

"The hilt is just slightly large for your current fist, but it is an average size, so it's one that you can use when you're older as well," he said, holding it out with two hands.

Benny squealed even as Matthias forced him to practice sheathing it.

"And for Willow," he said, pausing. "I have a specialized version of mirrored ax, or mirrax." Willow gasped as Matthias Farrow's eyes glinted with pride in presenting a double-headed, double-sided ax the length of her forearm.

"That looks brutal," breathed Anya.

Willow accepted the weapon, taking the long body of the mahogany handle in two hands, admiring the deep curves of its four beards and the dark gleam of its blackened cheeks. She ran a finger over the Farrow clan crest, two intertwining spirals of smoke within a triangle, engraved into both eyes of the mirrax handle.

"So heavy," she murmured.

"I used more shadow ether than usual," whispered Matthias, solemnity infusing his voice. "It will cut and kill with less force. Use it wisely. Carry it with care. Speaking of which." He unfolded a square of material. "Try this on."

Anya helped her don what proved to be a protective vest, buttery soft and yet the texture of brick rocks—the reworked sand wyrm hide sported arm bands for her weapons and a quick-release cross-body harness to hold the mirrax against her back.

"But, sir," breathed Willow. "This is too much."

He shook his head, face scruffy from days shut away working. "Take it. May it protect you and yours as you protected mine." He placed a similar, smaller vest over Benny and stepped back with a satisfied nod.

Not far from Farrow's Forge, they located a veiled portal headed north, albeit unidirectional and bifurcated; they could not jump back in to return, and it would send them by chance to one of two places: close to Maddooinne itself or close to its official entry point on a mountain peak.

Praying for the latter, Willow held Benny tightly against her chest as they fell.

On the other side, Willow was too much in awe to be upset over which exit they used. "It actually exists."

"A floating diamond mine," said Benny, his eyes just as wide.

Their exit portal landed, unfortunately, on a low rise in the Voidsrange section of mountains, almost directly beneath the Sky

Realm where it hovered over the Northern Portal Mines, a dead valley churning with the familiar sound of crowded portals. The bottom half of the kingdom was the nonliving portion, a volcanic mass of diamond mines visible beneath cloud cover. The living half existed unseen above floating curls of white.

Willow looked at it from afar, overcome. "Now I really have to see the top."

Historically, the Kinetics had constructed a prospering kingdom at the peak of Mount Onstel, but half a century ago, they tore the whole territory out of the mountain, along with much of the diamond mines below. Maddooinne thus became the Sky Realm as it rose into the blue abyss above, with a bountiful supply of untold riches at its feet. The kingdom came to a stop above a swath of portal mines for added protection, though the exact way the land hovered so constantly remained a mystery.

The floating, coal-colored rock Willow could see gleamed with gems, and it decreased in diameter toward the bottom, like a sharp stalactite hanging from the heavens. The sight was so sublime it stole her breath away.

Traders in town, when discreetly prodded, had mentioned there was only one way in: a kinetic ferry from the highest point above the cloud cover, right by the titanic crater Maddooinne had left behind.

So the physical journey to higher elevation began, in a heat so overwhelming at first that they stripped off everything but their hides and trousers within an hour of the hike. The rugged landscape swept before them in its overwhelming vastness—there was nothing here, no mapped portals, no water, no greenery. Just rock faces as far as the eye could see.

Benny grumbled.

"We can see our destination, Benny. It's only a matter of time."

But time again refused to be neither friend nor foe. By nightfall, as they camped in the mouth of a warm cave, Benny recalled an old

Ingressian saying that went, "Where did the time go? Down a portal again?"

Willow lay on her stomach, tracing the map in the dim firelight along her arms, tapping areas to enlarge them over and over, memorizing again and again what she could of the Sky Realm. "I've lost so much time, more than I can quantify." A tear plopped onto her arm.

"Are you scared we won't find him?" came Benny's worried voice. "Or that he's dead?"

"No, I'm…just lost. So lost. But I have to get home." She lay her heavy head on crossed arms. "And interrogate him within an inch of his life."

A pause. "What about me?"

"You're sure there isn't any way to find your people?"

"Not if they don't want to be found."

She tousled his hair. "Then you're my people now. You'll like most of us. Especially my mother. And I…Well, I miss her. Does that make me a child?"

"Maybe," Benny replied softly, "because so do I."

They tried to sleep then, as the earth beneath them shook throughout the night, so abruptly at first that they grasped hands. Willow stared up at the pitch-black and reminded herself to breathe. She would have to scale a mountain on the morrow.

In the morning, they discovered skeletons in the far end of the cave. Mangled bits of flesh clung to the bone, not yet fully rotted.

Benny tugged her hand. "Okay, time to go."

They discovered a trail lightly indented with footsteps and followed it, aiming for the highest peak they could reach.

"What now?" asked Benny hours later, rubbing his weak leg and staring up at a sheer rock face.

Willow took a breath. "Think you can port up there?"

Benny shook his head.

"Then we scale it." She reached back for her mirrax, grabbing it with a snick of its holster, and knelt. Benny scrambled onto her back to hide his face in her neck.

"Don't be scared," she whispered, scared.

Great heights like this always dampened her powers—or the fear did, as Zeph once tried to tell her. It all compounded the greater difficulty of moving a living body compared to a thing. But something about carrying Benny reduced the full weight of fear she might have felt, as if he took its place on her back. With him there, falling was not an option.

She and Zeph had climbed many a wall. This would just be another.

The mirrax followed, pet-like, beside them; she maintained it in her peripheral vision while keeping her center of gravity close to the wall, using her power to tether herself to the rock face like a harness, because flying reliably at this elevation was too hard for her.

When reaching a section without a reliable handhold, she would kinetically slam the mirrax into the rock, a blade on either side sinking deep, so she could grab the horizontal handle like a bar.

Up and up they went, tamping down the urge to shiver at the precipitous drop in distance and temperature, until she pulled them over the edge and onto a flat patch of earth once more.

"You can open your eyes, Benny."

As soon as he did, he pointed straight ahead and yelled, "Clouds!"

They walked into the mist holding hands, breaking through to see Maddooinne for the first time.

CHAPTER
12

HEIGHTS
ABOVE
THE REST

Strays, so starved so sick so sad,
May mean much more
When once we've wandered worn.
However home has harkened
Amidst an army, adrift
And asking,
Do dreams deliver, does daylight darken

W aist covered in a thick sea of cloud, Willow breathed,
"And there it is."

"What? Where?"

Looking down at their joined hands to see Benny's hair barely
breaking through the white line of cold mist, she pulled him up
into her arms and delighted in his shriek of wonder.

Because across from them stood a veritable island in the
sky. Half a league away, a castle the color of matte onyx pierced
the firmament at the far-off edge of a land of pastels and sunset

brights. Homes clustered together to rise in multiple tiers so tall, the sight struck Willow with its technical impossibility for space-maximizing brilliance. So much floated unattached and unidentifiable at this distance.

Yet the very first thing she saw had little to do with buildings or people.

The tallest spire of the castle rose through the clouds adorned with a monster.

A long and narrow body curled around metal a mile high, its arms and legs covered in the same scales as its torso, each one obsidian rimmed in bright orange. The creature's ghoulish face gleamed with the sly features of a fox, dark as the castle it held in its saber-length claws. Its skeleton showed clearly against the stretched black skin of an underbelly covered in streaks and splotches of color. It had the same markings above its eyes—such human eyes, yet they were lacking iris and pupil, both blown completely white. The thing's two long whiskers and the bristly white fur running along the spine down to its tail were all that moved in the wind, until—

It turned its head their way, almost as if it could hear Benny's outcry from such a distance.

Below the creature, a round platform stood at the bottom of its spire. Robed Exokinetics lined its circumference, still and trancelike, hands clasped.

"What do we do now?" whispered Benny, his own eyes on the monster.

"We wait."

And sure enough, across the yawning distance came a flat, floating chunk of rock the size of a large bed frame. It halted with a thud against the mountain edge before them.

Willow stepped forward, but Benny pulled at her hand.

"I don't know about this," he said.

"You want to try going back down the way we came?"

He sighed. "Good point. Let's go."

They hopped onto the kinetic ferry, noticing an iron peg attached to the center with rope, like reins to a horse. The ferry commenced a smooth glide through the air, and Willow marveled at the strength of the bearer's powers. No Kinetic in the trading villages had shown such vast ability.

Her free hand lifted into the bright air to touch a wisp of cloud, and she felt the cold vapor and accompanying shiver break through her adrenaline rush. She pulled out their cloaks and wrapped them both, concealing her mirrax in the streaming fabric and ignoring the staccato beat of her pulse.

As they retreated from Mount Onstel, Willow could see how near they had been to a massive crater, likely the kingdom's original location, and how dangerous it would have been to fall into it.

More pressingly, the closer they came to Maddooinne, the larger the reality of her actions loomed, especially with the Tug so plainly loosening.

She could now see ramparts at the realm's perimeter and a high tower growing larger at the edge, where a man watched them with eagle eyes, arms out, royal blue robes flowing behind him.

They stilled in the air just feet away from the destination of many weeks' travel.

The robed man cocked his head and boomed, "Source?"

Willow stood. "Exoself."

"Designation?"

"Kinetic."

"Display."

Willow kinetically lifted her mirrax, letting it swing through the air with a flourish.

"Approved. Now the boy."

Benny made himself as small as possible, clutching at her neck. "My son has not yet developed his powers enough for display, sir."

"You vouch for him, then?"

"Yes."

The guard narrowed his eyes at them. "Reason for entry?"

"Returning home from trade."

A pause as he took in their lack of goods.

Willow lifted her mirrax again. "This was my main objective. A Farrow's Forge blade."

She allowed the weapon to soar into his outstretched hand. The man's eyes gleamed as he inspected it before him, expertly keeping the ferry in his line of sight as well. "Approved."

The ferry moved forward once more, coming to rest near the sentinel's feet.

Willow carried Benny onto the landing and bowed. "Thank you, sir."

He nodded and identified himself. "Master Jamison of the High-Level Guards." A smirk broke through beneath his large blond mustache as he handed back the mirrax. "Got screwed by the bifurcated portal, did you? Tough luck. I take it, then, you lost all your other traded goods in the climb?"

"Yes, Master Jamison. Very unfortunate."

He turned away, resuming his watch. "Still, you have good timing. The tournament ends today. Best sign the entry log and head to the arena."

Willow nodded as if she understood and took off down a ladder leading to blessed, blessed ground.

Benny looked up at her with eyes of awe. "We did it. We really did it."

Willow spun him around once before setting off.

Navigating the kingdom was itself a climb, for the ground was a literal chunk of mountain, one with nearly all patent portals, making it the safest, largest piece of inhabited Ingressian land she had yet come across.

Although the streets were empty.

"Everyone must be at that tournament," said Willow, just as a shiver ran through her. She looked up to see the white eyes of the monster still trained upon them, though it made not a single move.

"Creepy," grumbled Benny.

It huffed and turned its eyes away, as if looking off into the distance.

Willow followed the direction of its blind gaze, only now hearing the dull, distant roar of thunderous applause. "I know where the arena is. It's on my map, but we don't even need it."

They traipsed through narrow roads that fed wide boulevards, packed on either side with shops rising so high up she could barely make out the top of many signs, except from afar. They headed for the other side of the realm, toward the castle and arena, from which the roar intensified for a moment, swelling and ebbing with whatever tournament raged. Even the Tug agreed that everyone must be congregated in that direction.

Willow soon halted, holding out her arm. "Wait, wait, wait. What is this thing I'm walking on? Did someone place pebbles in the road? On purpose? What would *possess* them?"

Benny looked down at Ingressian cobblestones and shook his head. "I don't know. No offense, but Kinetics are weirdos. Powerful weirdos."

They shrugged and dashed off again with a swish of their frosted cloaks.

Crowds closer to the arena pushed people together, the sound reaching deafening levels and the Tug falling silent.

Zephyr was here. He had to be.

Just past the wide-open castle gates, the arena sank below them, looming much larger than it had appeared on her map and featuring wraparound stands full of thousands of spectators.

A body flew past her face.

If she'd had any doubts about the Winged before, she did no longer, as two of them dueled it out before her.

Wings so large they spanned twice a man's body length, both midnight black but for a streak of white along the larger one's right wing, carried two figures enmeshed high in the sky and hurtling toward the earth as the crowd screamed in exhilaration. The man beside Willow had gone flaming red from his howling, and Benny clamped his hands over his ears.

The larger of the Winged strangled his opponent as he pushed them both down toward the arena floor. His captive furled his wings, tilted his body, then snapped his wings open with a burst of power that propelled away his aggressor.

They landed with feline grace on all fours upon the dusty ground near Willow's side of the arena. She could see now the heavy paint covering their entire torsos, the smaller mage slathered in bright blue and his opponent in yellow. Other than that, they sported only leather trousers and bloody gashes as they navigated an arena twisted with labyrinthine columns of stone.

"They're massive, and they're real," squealed Benny into her ear. He flagged down a woman beside them. "Hey lady, what are they fighting over?"

The grandmotherly woman, dressed in gauzy white, turned to Willow instead. "Should he be here?"

Willow shrugged. "Eh, he's seen worse."

The woman inched away from them.

Willow turned back to the tournament to see the larger yellow mage roll over just as a column beside him spontaneously turned to rubble. Benny gasped and poked the old woman. "How? How? HOW?"

"Mind your manners, boy," she said, though she humored him. "Some Winged mages know how to combust ether." She went quiet,

then elaborated, "All adult mages above grade-six mastery have to par-
ticipate in the annual Champion's Tournament to quantify their worth
to the king." She leaned toward a thrilled Benny. "Today, we crown the
champion."

Benny bounced atop Willow's shoulders. "We just got back from a
business trip. How long've they been fighting?"

"Close to two hours now. Had to defeat all the others in the maze
first." She bowed her head. "I'm Mandarine Rose of Clan Wallek, a
kitchen maid back at the castle."

Willow nodded, smiling, though her eyes remained glued to the
warriors circling each other on foot. "How strong are those two, then?"

The woman seemed to enjoy lording her superior knowledge over
them, drawing herself up and crossing her arms. "The yellow mage is
on a higher level, grade eight, but though the blue mage has only just
reached level-six mastery, he's managed to stave off defeat very well.
It's been driving us all batshit mad. New to the arena he is, yet he's
made it to the final battle with the reigning champion, Vivek Azakor."
She spoke the name with reverent fear. "The Winged are all nameless
to the public unless they've been champions."

Mandarine stopped to clap as multiple columns blew apart.

The yellow mage, Vivek, straightened and with a ripple of the muscles in his back, he pushed off against the ground into a breathtaking
vertical takeoff. He exploded into the air before his feathers, together
at first on the downstroke, delaminated and spread into sun-dappled
beauty.

The blue mage stood still, however, his back to Willow's side of the
arena as his opponent flew higher. After a couple hair-raising seconds
of silence, he touched his chest and spun around with a look of shock.

Willow could not speak. Her heart pounded, wet and painful in
her ears, because even at this distance, as long as she could see those
eyes, she knew.

"Zeph," she screamed, the word pulled from so deep within her gut that it sounded like crushed gravel in the din. "Benny, that's him. The blue one. He's no Kinetic."

Benny's mouth dropped open in a gasp, though she did not hear it. Her entire world had narrowed.

Yet the fight raged on.

Zeph's shoulder suddenly gushed blood, running in red rivulets down his bare chest, with the other mage nowhere to be seen.

"Black magic, that is," gasped Mandarine, the crowd going wild in the stands.

Willow readied herself to intervene.

But Zeph just shook his head with the force of a wet dog and instead of flying off, knelt and muttered to himself.

He held his hands above his head and intertwined his fingers, pushing his linked palms outward. The arena had gone silent. Vivek careened out of the clouds toward him in a haze of feathers and sunlight, but Zeph refused to move.

Moments before his opponent reached him, Zeph pulled apart his fingers and blood spurted from Vivek's forehead into his eyes. Zeph took off straight into the air with the ease of a hummingbird, allowing his blinded rival to slam into the ground where he had just been.

Only flying feels like flying.

Zeph had said that to her once. After she had flown his frozen body up the Western Hill and tried to convince him he imagined it.

"Oh, Zeph," she breathed.

He was hovering in the air, wings gusting the sand in the arena, looking at her with a body dripping crimson even as the trumpets blared his victory—

Just as a louder sound cut through.

Willow ignored it until Zephyr turned to look. A castle turret was crashing, falling off the nearest corner of the perimeter walls and onto the spectators. It broke off slowly with a bone-chilling grind that blended with the screams below.

Thousands of hands flew into the air, youngling and old alike, staving off the stone with their powers.

"Damn. All the high-level masters are on Hover Duty," grunted Mandarine, both her arms straining from the focus.

The turret was so large and falling from such a great height that even the combined strength of a Kinetic kingdom seemed only able to paralyze it against the formidable force of gravity.

Willow stopped focusing on the frozen threat mostly obscured by the crowd and looked around. She began to walk away.

"Hey, girl. Girl, where are you going? Come back here, you traitor."

The crowd started grumbling at her as she ignored their jeers.

She and Benny raced over to the nearby castle wall and climbed up a ladder to the ramparts for a better view of the falling tower.

From there, she saw what looked like bright copper strands, thick and ropelike, encompassing the stone. Some were thin, others thicker, but they all settled around the turret's curves and fissures the harder she focused. Running even closer to amplify her powers, she drew the stone away from the people—the strands straining as if to help—and with a great heaving breath, dropped it kinetically back to where it came from. The threads disappeared from her vision, blending into the coppery hue that had shimmered around her so constantly from the moment she awoke in Ingress that she had forgotten it was there.

She could hear her own harsh breathing, the pound of her pulse, and a deep voice.

"Well, that was something."

Willow pushed the words away and wondered at what she had just seen, glad but confused when the turret did not fall over again. Looking closer, she realized the crack of separation had been completely horizontal across the stone.

She collapsed against the onyx parapet behind her, Benny patting her shoulder, and turned to see an older man, deep gray hair at his temples and in his sleek black beard, staring down at her bent form. His face, unusually long, was smiling a great big smile. "Come now, girl, what's your name?" he seemed to ask again.

Willow glared a moment, trying to think of a way to avoid the answer. "That was no accident."

"My robes, Ivan," barked the man, now hopping on both feet as if to relieve an excess of energy.

A tall, rail-thin boy carrying a cane he did not appear to need stepped forward to help the man into diamond-encrusted robes emblazoned with the silken Sky Realm crest. To further highlight their point, Ivan manually seated a large crown atop the speaker's head, dropping it down at the last moment with an emphatic plop and a widening of his hands.

Willow wasn't sure she could manage a bow at the moment.

The king swept out his arms. "Which of my subjects, then, might you be? Neither of you have been to court."

Ivan smirked. "His Highness never forgets a face."

"Too true, Ivan."

Willow pushed herself up and with a clumsy bow, recalled the cover story Farrow helped her create. "Willow and Benjamin Erifson of Sky Clan Munster, my king."

Ivan slammed down his cane. "You will refer to the monarch of Maddooinne as Your Highness on first greeting and sire thereafter."

The king crossed his arms. "Not to mention, no such clan exists."

"Yes, Your Highness. You see, my great-great-great-grandparents left Maddooinne on trading matters but were unable to make it safely back in their lifetime. They settled in a minor trading village to start our tiny new clan. My parents passed away this year, and that's when I resolved to see the land of my forefathers, hoping my own son could be raised here. As I was not."

180

The king tilted his head. "A commendable desire." He tilted Benny's face up toward the light. "Hmm." Willow's heart dropped, but he seemed to accept her explanation and snapped his fingers. "We celebrate our champion tonight. You will join us, and we will come to know each other."

"Sire, I'm hardly worth knowing."

"Oh, I doubt that, Miss Erifson. Or is it Mrs. Erifson?"

"Neither, really. Lately widowed, sire."

The king clicked his tongue. "Tragedies such as these are only too common outside our realm. But you have chosen to return to our safekeeping. Well done of you." He nodded at Ivan, who raised his arms. Two of the Winged landed beside them. "Your escorts. Torrent and Flynn, take our honored guests to the best available room in the court wing."

"But, sire—"

"I have spoken." He turned and left with Ivan.

Willow looked up at the Winged, their unique outlines looming so large before her, and she realized with a start that their kind must have been the cloaked figures on the rooftops at the Kinetic beheading months ago. Eyes dark as coal expressed not a single clue to a stray thought.

She steeled herself. "Hello. Um, how well might either of you know Zephyr?"

They stood stock-still.

Willow sighed. "Lead the way, then."

Torrent and Flynn turned on their heels with military precision, flanking Willow as she picked up a dazed Benny. She stole a glance over the rampart to notice the silent arena staring, then with a yank she was in the air, each mage holding an arm about her waist to fly them off toward the castle.

"I'm glad you didn't say anything to him, Benny, because you're going to have to play mute. That way, they can't find inconsistencies in our story as I make it up." She peeked out behind the drapes of their room to see a massive private balcony, with Torrent and Flynn crouched like breathing gargoyles on either side of the thin ledge.

"What? No. I already talked to that lady in the arena!" whispered Benny.

Willow looked back at him curled up on the softest, lushest bed either of them had ever seen. "What are the chances we see her again though?"

"She said she works in the castle. Are you deaf, or what?"

"I don't like this condescending tone of yours. You do realize I'm the adult here, right?"

"But you're not *from* here."

Willow opened her mouth, then shut it. "Fair enough," she finally said. "At least we seem to have the favor of the king, right?"

He flapped his hands around his face. "Lady, he has a chin dimple. I don't trust men with chin dimples. It's like they've got two faces."

A knock sounded at the door. Willow smoothed out her shirt and stood straighter. Only to be disappointed.

A young lady's maid entered with a bobbed curtsy. "Begging your pardon, ma'am. I've come to prepare you for the ball."

Benny groaned, plopping back onto the sheets. "Ugh. Ew. I'm not going."

One painstaking hour later, his hair was slicked back and his face cleaner than Willow had ever seen it.

"This is just unnatural," said Benny, glaring down at his little ensemble of formfitting black trousers topped with a gauzy white shirt. "And where's my cap?" He stuffed Anya's gift into a pocket with a suspicious glance at their quietly exasperated maid, Marina, whose fine powers were so exquisitely controlled she soon had Willow's hair braided and pinned with elaborate little bows, dripping down her back.

Willow stared into a floor-length mirror as Marina helped her into a dress being tailored before her eyes with a floating gold needle and thread. She had refused to take off her protective vest beneath the dress, so Marina finished sewing on sleeves to the odd ballgown and watched Willow affix her mirrax to the cross-body harness she wore over it all.

"There you are, ma'am. All set," said the maiden, although she did not look pleased with the final touch of weaponry.

"May I wear this?" asked Willow.

"Yes, ma'am, but most people take a small blade or bow to formal functions, so as not to ruin their finery."

"Oh, well, I'm not bothered about that."

As they walked out, Torrent and Flynn flew forward in a burst to guide them down the empty hallways ahead.

Marina chattered nervously on the way. "The court wing is the only inhabited wing. The central wing is used for parties and the like, while the weapons wing includes the armory as well as special exhibits."

The air crackled around the mages like static, and if she tried hard enough, Willow could swear she saw translucent tendrils of copper straining toward their massive forms in thicker bunches, similar to what she had seen around the falling turret today. She lifted a hand to touch them but felt nothing.

One of the Winged tossed her a suspicious look, as if assuming she had been trying to reach for him, before looking straight ahead again with a grunt.

Willow had been too stunned to look these two strange beings in the eye on their flight over, but now she took her fill of their profiles.

The mage on her right, Flynn, bore a twisted, sunken scar from chin through Adam's apple that disappeared beneath his high collar, and long graying hair brushed his shoulders as he walked. To Willow's left stalked Torrent, who appeared much younger but just as stone-faced. Torrent was female, bald, and magnificent, with thick black lashes and eyes the color of the sea.

They marched in silence down ornate hallway after ornate hallway, twisting and turning until they came upon the antechamber to the throne room, guarded by men in the king's livery who drew the doors open in mute obeisance.

Before them appeared a huge staircase ending in sky, which a lady dressed in swaying fabrics currently ascended. Willow watched her reach the top, and suddenly, the woman's train of split fabrics and flowing sleeves danced around her as if along the wind. She was announced, took a step forward, and vanished from view.

"I'm never climbing nothing again," grumbled Benny, just as they too reached the zenith of the inverted staircase.

"Willow and Benjamin Erifson of Sky Clan Munster," roared a voice.

Willow reached down for Benny's hand as they stepped over the threshold into a room full of clouds.

No walls held the room together, only marbled floor and stone pillars supporting a latticed ceiling at the realm's edge. Willow looked away from the sheer drop around them and stared ahead, where an ice-blue carpet led up to a raised throne.

Scores of finely dressed Kinetics lined the area, their clothes leaning toward wispy and sheer, perfect to play in the breeze. But their eyes were veiled too, curious and silent, in an open hall warmed by large ovens of coal tended by liveried servants.

"What's a munster? Sounds like a sneeze," laughed a sharp voice in the crowd.

The king looked upon them, practically vibrating in his gilded seat, with Ivan standing at his side and Winged mages poised in line behind the diamond-studded throne like an open set of knives.

Willow's eyes drank them in, so anxious for a view of the one person she had traveled farther than she could comprehend to find. The last time she walked into such a council of vultures, he himself had remained steady at her side. Now, she could only take in a deep breath as she walked along a velvet carpet with Benny's hand clammy against her own.

A train of deep forest-green silk neatly matching the ribbons in her braided hair streamed around her, and she used a bit of power to help it flow forward with a ripple. As she walked, a domino of gasps fell behind her once the guests noticed the mirrax at her back.

The king's fingers tapped a quick beat against his closed lips when she and Benny knelt before him. Willow suppressed a shudder at a blast of cold in her veins.

"Do I speak first? No one mentioned," said Willow after a lengthy silence, eyes turned to Ivan.

The room held its breath.

Benny trembled.

Ivan raised a brow.

The king hopped to his feet and waved a floppy hand in her direction. "No one else boasts a Winged escort to the ball but you and I, dear, so talk as you please, preferably as we dance. I'm damn tired of sitting around."

He offered a hand. Willow choked back the fear of her cultural ignorance and took it with a soft, "Yes, Your Highness."

Lofty music rose up the moment he pulled her into a hold, and the other guests were coaxed back into dance as well, even as they stole glances over their partners' shoulders each time they veered close to the king and his odd guest.

Leading her to an open space away from the edge, the king finally spoke. "How did you convince Farrow to give you those blades?"

Willow could not focus on his curious eyes, hers dancing around in search of someone else's gaze. "I simply paid Matthias what he asked."

"No Kinetic just pays Farrow."

She looked at him then, at that cocked head and twitchy eye. "Well, I did."

A smile bright as a sunbeam split open on his face. He took her arm and placed it on his shoulder, moving them into a familiar waltz set to unfamiliar music.

King Soren floated her a bit too fast through wisps of cloud and the musings of the crowd, even past a rapt Benny in the corner stuffing his face with finger food. The king danced on the tips of his toes, pushing past the tempo like he had no time for it. The Winged guard encircled them even now, each well over six feet tall and solemn in their sentry work.

"Tell me about yourself," said the king.

"I wouldn't know where to begin."

"Well, the best way to get to know someone would be to ask this: What do you regret most in life?"

Surprised, she looked up at black eyes gone soft with curiosity and answered, "Hesitation."

"But hesitation shows forethought."

She shrugged. "Or lack of trust. What do you regret most, sir?"

He chuckled. "Nothing." At her raised brow, he explained, "Anything can be made right again with enough effort. Just look at our people. Centuries ago, we had nothing. Decades ago, we had war. Now, thanks to my reign, we enjoy peace and untold riches."

"How did you do it, sire?"

He looked up with a grin, and said, "By embracing the sky," just as a dappled shadow passed over them.

Willow gasped as something monstrous circled above the lattice.

The king paused, following her gaze, and raised a glittering hand to command the room's attention.

"Ah, now who would have thought this day would come?" he said, pointing above him. "The young Azakor, who molted for so long we began to wonder whether he would ever return, but knowing that if he did, it would be with great strength and even greater resolve. He has more than proven us correct today, marking the start of a new era, one where the Exokinetics write their own history.

"So I give you the king's champion, Zephyr Azakor, Wielder of the Black Forge Scythe!"

Across the open edge, Zeph flew into the room, wings sleek and wide enough that four people could stand beneath them. Covered in flowing black robes with a hood lined in gold, his clothes matched the way his external night-black feathers were tipped with gold talons at the shoulders. For a long time, he hovered at the center of the vaulted ceiling above them all to widespread applause—very light, very polite, as the Kinetics' clothes rippled from the wind of his wings. Willow pounded her hands together, outdoing them all.

The king chuckled at her in surprise.

"Next order of business," he called out, grasping her fingertips with an outstretched hand. "Willow, what would you like for your welcome gift to the kingdom, one which we offer in gratitude for the great service, which I must say you did not hesitate to render, on your very first day in the Sky Realm?"

Zephyr never looked down, one hand clutching a scythe so long and sharp it gleamed with lethal promise above them all.

Music swelled, and Willow could feel the import of the decision on her skin, as though the wrong answer swayed against her neck with its own razor edge.

At last, she said, "A dance with your champion, sire."

The king of Maddooinne startled. "The Winged can't waltz."

"Is that a fact?"

CHAPTER
13

CHAMPION'S BALL

He says the Winged can't waltz.
Well, I'll waltz with you
And relish withering eyes turn hard
While wagging tongues turn blue.
Furthermore I'll say,
Let all the wine here spill
If frigid forms fall still
With fury as we fly
Our waltz—surrounded, so alone—
Along a saffron sky.

Naive or brave, Ivan?" asked the king.

"Moronic, sire," came the loud reply.

"Hmm. I suppose so," said the king, but he stepped back to allow the request.

Willow's racing heart pounded harder at the thought of an impending explosion, her hand reaching out to her old friend ever so slowly.

Aside from Torrent's raised brow and Zeph's abnormal

stillness, only the Winged guard looked unfazed at the scene. The courtiers showed open wonder at the woman reaching for a mage, the exotic Kinetic who dared dance with domestic danger. Willow expected some felt pity at her artlessness, but most of them displayed the same suspicious scorn with which Spinor Falls had first welcomed Zephyr, that strange boy who now gathered her into a dance hold as a man, but in the same way damp wood takes to flame—reluctantly resigned to its flickering fate.

Willow gasped as he pulled her in.

But no explosion was forthcoming, and the afternoon light soon faded into a lavender dusk that darkened Zeph's face just as much as it stole her breath by highlighting the new harshness etched into the sunken hollows of his cheeks.

Moving into a closed position, she felt dwarfed in his shadow but fell into step as the music started, the first notes so hesitant it seemed even the musicians could not believe what they were seeing.

Zeph refused to look down at her, guiding them a beat too fast.

"Look at you," breathed Willow into his ear. "How are you?"

The king's champion dipped the young woman low rather than answer her, glancing a moment to the side of her head, where the sharp blades of the mirrax peeked over her shoulder.

He remained silent even in their bent hold, taller than she remembered by at least a foot, his face as aged as hers but his bandaged body leagues broader. She glared up into one unchanged feature: those eyes, which she worried, not for the first time, had fossilized the skeletons of an unreachable past deep within their amber.

Those eyes that narrowed just a tad when she dug her heel into his toes.

"I've come a long way to be ignored," she bit off as he pulled her up, a light hiss escaping his lips. "But considering you abandoned me for fifteen years, why am I not surprised?"

"What?" he finally snapped.

"Don't you talk to me like that. I'm the one who gets to be angry."

"You don't know the whole of it."

"Then tell me."

"Here?"

Willow could see the king staring at them in curiosity, like everyone else. She composed her stormy expression, and her eyes strayed to the strange beauty of Zephyr's wings. "Only flying feels like flying, or so said a youngling I once knew?" she prodded.

The tiniest hint of a tease touched his lips even as he looked away again. "Very good, nestling." Her breath caught, the origins of the pet name finally searing through her as he continued. "Seems you've flown the nest too. A fledgling now." But the words were whispers, falling featherlight.

"Where *is* home?" She brushed a stealthy finger along the wingtip near the palm she rested on his shoulder. "And why do they call you Azakor?"

"It's my family name. My real family name."

"Which you've known all this time."

He sighed into her hair. "Which I've known all this time."

She leaned her head against his, trying not to shiver at the contact. "You kept a whole world from me. Yours and mine."

For a moment, he held her waist so tightly it hurt, yanking her forward to ask, "Is your final promise to me on that cliff clear now?"

"Sentience," she whispered back with just as much urgency, the strange new feel of him against her a heady rush.

His eyes flooded with that familiar look of approval they often tossed between them during a joint heist. "Never use your powers on people. Or yourself if you can help it. It could get you killed."

"Only if I'm caught."

He stopped moving for a shocked moment. "So you already have? But I left you the book."

"How useful," she snarled. "A puzzle book instead of yourself."

"Well, where is it now?"

"I lost it on my way to you, so sorry. But don't sidestep." She pushed her body closer to his, flowing forward with him even as he tried for distance. "I want to go home. *Where* is Spinor Falls?"

His lips thinned, voice dropping even further as he pressed his lips against her blushing ear. "Out of your reach. For now, just hush."

She let out a shaky breath, glancing at her small hand in his rough grip. They had held hands many times before. But it looked and felt so different now. Her fingers seemed longer and more slender against a calloused hand with prominent veins and corded muscle.

Zeph led them all the way to the edge again, where the world dropped into cascades of yellow light warming a blanket of domed clouds. No one dared step close, a fear in their eyes that Willow had missed at first when Zeph landed into a kneel before his king.

Once the waltz drew to a close and another song lit the air, Ivan cajoled the crowd back into dancing.

Zephyr deposited Willow before the king with a half bow, taking his place behind the throne and widening his hands, lightning-like strands of bright copper flashing between his moving palms and fingers as he plucked at the air. Willow realized that the copper color looked exactly the same as the molten ether of a patent portal, just as Zeph lowered his head and began to chant in a strange, rough tongue, so guttural that she openly stared.

"Just a protective spell, dear," said Soren, chuckling at Willow's expression. "A king can never be too careful, and my Winged brethren provide—what's the phrase we used earlier, Ivan?"

"Brute muscle."

"No, no."

"Living armor."

"Devoted defense. They provide us defense." He waved a hand

with a frown. "Don't mind, Ivan. He's a few sandwiches short of a picnic and can barely move a pin."

Willow rather thought a well-aimed pin something worth worrying about, but that did not seem like the right thing to say to a king.

He paused before turning another one of his large smiles upon her. "Speaking of which, you should try those decadent finger sandwiches before they disappear. We will talk more over dinner. Enjoy yourself for now, weary traveler."

Willow bowed and, head spinning, moved toward Benny, who handed her a massive cream puff with both hands as if he had struck mounds of gold and felt eager to share the loot. She took a bite and moaned herself, the shock of the day giving in to a body starved from climbing Mount Onstel.

Benny gestured to Zephyr. "So that's him, huh?"

"Yeah."

Benny nodded, asking no more questions in public, the Meta in him so often grasping adult reasoning quicker than she did.

Willow was smiling softly at his single chipmunk cheek of food when a nasal voice called out, "Evening, Ms. Erifson."

She turned toward a young couple approaching: a lady with a floating fan flapping at her face and a man with a sneer on his.

"Well, that's one way to win the competition. Get in close with the instructors," said the woman, knobby shoulders leaning forward as if she were in Willow's confidence.

"Excuse me? Didn't the competition end today?"

The woman looked at her escort and sniggered, eyes raised and the fan beating faster to match her mad laughter, sending her hair flying about her head. "What. A. Wily. One." Both laughter and fan stopped abruptly.

The man leered. "You just stood up with a monster. The Winged Reaper himself. What's that make you?" The couple shook their heads and sauntered off.

Benny cupped chocolatey hands around his mouth and called out, "Bye now."

Others introduced themselves with a hair more civility. One old man just patted her on the head. Until at dinner, Ivan seated them by the king along a table so lengthy and littered with delights that Willow wondered again whether she had ever truly understood wealth.

"Care to explain the dance?" asked the king just before he took the first bite, his eagle-eyed courtiers following suit.

"It was a waltz, sire."

Ivan glared.

"What in the void compelled you?"

She glanced at Zephyr, standing behind the king's right shoulder and staring straight ahead.

"Your champion has a handsome face."

The king guffawed so loud the rest of the table looked lost. "The nerve of you. I suspected at the arena, but now I know. You *are* as mad as I am. Now, where do you plan on staying?"

Willow pushed some food around her plate. "We're looking to pay for a room at some inn and find simple jobs."

"What inn? Dear girl, we don't have visitors here. Only verified Kinetics are allowed in my realm, usually only returning after trading journeys. No, no. I will find you lodging with a courtier if you like, but I have a better proposition. As you must know, I've no living heir. I'm not interested in siring another, and so we are in the process of naming one."

He looked at his hands, milky white and threaded through with large veins that bulged when he fisted them on the gold tablecloth. "Blood binds nothing but blindness. We will choose the strong, some-one with the ability to keep us soaring ever higher, and as you've already shown great power and fearlessness in your youth, those being my only requirements, what do you say about entering?"

Stunned, Willow took a while to speak, but finally asked, "How is the competition won?"

He lifted a finger. "The completion of one task. Not too long ago, the master mapmaker stashed the greatest map ever created here in our realm. The first to find the map wins, or naturally, the last one standing does."

"What do you mean by that?"

"The last one to evade elimination secures the throne by default."

"Elimination?" asked Willow.

"To keep the field of contestants thin, you face a series of duels to prove your superiority in power, as any worthy heir or champion must. If there is more than one competitor remaining at a time, I reserve the right to add another between duels, as I am doing now."

"But how do you know such a map could even be found here?"

The king waved a hand. "The mapmaker invaded our land and was imprisoned for it. We know that ultimate trespasser must have used the master map to penetrate our sanctuary, but it was missing on their person during capture."

"So where is the mapmaker now?"

"You have many questions."

"You have a big proposition."

The king rested his head on steepled fingers and locked his eyes on hers. "Died by suicide. Our dungeon is not designed for the weak."

As Willow could not get him to reveal the mapmaker's gender, she had to consider he knew the truth. Maybe the master map truly was here. "And what if I'm not really interested in power?"

He lowered his voice. "Too late for that. You were born with it. And you're clearly attracted to it." He tilted his head to the right, where his champion stood guard. "Time to step up, youngster."

"Sire—"

"Did I mention all the benefits of competing? Set aside the bounty of food you see here and the castle lodging. My potential heirs are assured full access to all restricted sections of the royal library, kinetic dueling lessons, and lectures from our foremost instructors on everything from portalcraft to Ingressian history to chicken wrangling—if you so desire."

The king leaned back, clearly scenting victory in her widening eyes as they filled with the realization that she could learn it all and throw a duel when she discovered the way home.

She looked at Benny grinning across the wide table from her, holding up a turkey leg the size of his head.

The king smiled. "Think what a life you could give him as the future monarch of Maddooinne."

Willow glanced up at Zephyr for direction, even though she knew he could express none.

The king held out a cupped hand dripping in diamonds, his fingers spread wide. "Royal offers never sit on the table, dear. I place them in the air between us"—he snapped his fingers into a white-knuckled fist—"and you must seize them before they vanish."

Willow set aside hesitation. "Alright, then. I'll give it a shot."

They shook on it, his gleaming gems cutting into her calloused hand.

CHAPTER
14

LET US
BEGIN

Don't you see these sizzling zealots
Simply keep us just to sell us?

I told you not to trust that man. He's genocidal."

"You said he has a chin dimple. That's hardly the mark of a mass murderer."

Benny was aghast, railing at her in their room the next morning for agreeing to something he claimed she didn't comprehend. "But he is. What made him kill all those Metas? What if he sees who I am? You ever think of that?"

Willow sat down beside him on his bed. "If there's anything I've learned here, it's not to trust rumors that travel farther than people can. The king can't be all bad, not if Zeph protects him."

"But—"

"And you can't even use your powers. How will he figure out your designation? Think. We can learn anything we want and then leave. There's an entire world I missed out on as a child, so much of my past that doesn't add up. And the answers are all here."

Benny just shook his head, little eyebrows scrunched in concern. "That's a bunch of assumptions there too, lady."

Willow tried to tamp down her agitation, explaining away a rash decision that still felt right even if it settled with an edge of unease in her belly. "And what about my home? If we find the master map, it could lead me back to Spinor Falls, where my mother would love to have a son like you. Metas and Exos don't even exist there."

"But what if the king gets his hands on it like he wants? Good maps are power. Real power. And this is a map of everything!" Benny stood up on the bed and waved his arms. "He could take over *everything*."

"I won't let him have it."

"You could try. And what if *your* map is the master map? It's possible."

"Hardly. It has a whole swath of land missing to the southwest. And Spinor Falls is nowhere to be found on it. More than anything, I need the master map to get home."

"Well, can't your Guide just take us?"

"I don't know. He acts like there are eyes and ears everywhere."

"There are," came a voice like snapping thunder. Torrent glared at them from the terrace, its glass somehow *missing* and a rim of light shining along her open wings from the waking sun.

"You can speak?" Willow tried joking.

The mage stalked closer. "Watch what you say, dolt."

Benny started to full-body shake as he asked, "How long have you been there?"

Her lip curled. "Dueling lessons begin in a quarter hour." Torrent picked up Willow's vest from across a chaise and tossed it at her. "Gear up and come along. Leave the kid."

"You mean my son?"

"No."

Fighting through his limp, Benny streaked up to the mage. "Are you gonna tell? About me?"

198

Torrent gave him the side-eye. Rising to her feet in alarm, Willow thought the young woman would either strike or stay silent, but she only said, "I have better things to do," before sprinting off the terrace edge.

The long tassel of a curtain tieback wrapped around the mage's waist and yanked her back into the room, using her momentum against her.

Willow straightened her spine. "I'm afraid that's just not good enough."

Torrent's right arm shot out at a crooked angle, and with a flick of her bent wrist, copper smoke smothered Willow's face. "You're an untrained, ungrateful little girl—out here playing with fire."

They charged at each other, Willow soon trapped underneath the massive weight of the mage as Benny poured a pitcher of water over them both in panic.

"What in the Putrid Portal is going on here?"

Taking a gasping breath and shaking her sopping head, Willow looked up to see Zeph holding Torrent's throat against the wall. "I expected better from you," he said softly to his kin.

"The boy's a Meta," Torrent grunted back, standing still against his hands as they roiled with ethereal smoke. "I overheard."

His arms dropped and he blinked, turning as Willow pushed Benny behind her onto the rug, her outspread arm and shoulder covering his small, shivering body.

Zephyr stepped forward, dropping to one knee, wings of blackest night settling behind him. "Come here, child." His voice sounded different from the one Willow remembered, unflinchingly dominant and without a slip of softness.

She tightened her grip without thinking.

But when Zeph looked over at her, she felt a shiver totally unrelated to fear.

"It's alright, Benny," she said. "This is my Guide." The boy crawled beneath her arm to glance up at the mage. "Zeph, this is Benny."

Zeph placed his middle and ring fingers against the boy's chin, staring into wide little eyes for a frightful intake of breath as both their sclera went black. When he spoke, his voice sounded deeper, more distant, "Neither Ferver nor Shifter. Your kind are very old, youngling."

Benny swallowed, the whites of his eyes returning. "Not as old as yours."

"Have they left this plane without you?"

"I don't know."

Torrent cut in, "We can't cover up another fucking voidsman in the Sky Realm, Zeph." She leaned against the revived glass of the terrace doors with her arms crossed.

Zeph pushed onto his feet with a flap of his wings. "Say that to me again."

Torrent glanced down in deference, but persisted. "You know I'll keep my mouth shut, but can they?"

"They'll do it or die. It's that simple."

"And why should I trust her with this, Zeph? With Benny?" asked Willow harshly.

"Because *I* do."

Willow and Benny exchanged a hopeless look before she asked, "And what about trusting the king? Is he truly after all the Metas, Zeph, or are people acting in his name?"

He looked down at her, brow raised. "This is the last time we speak of anything bordering on treason. You're late to training. And we don't know each other."

Willow rose, ready to burst, saying, "Wait. How do I get home?"

But she was too late. He was gone.

The arena looked different. Thorny vines and yellowed weeds strangled the space, carving maze-like pockets into yesterday's open, grassy
field where the Winged champion had emerged a victorious revelation
to his travel-weary friend, one still in search of herself and him.

As Willow's feet touched the arena floor today, the ground rumbled and a boulder the size of an Exowinged mage streaked toward her.

She looked around, seeking the Kinetic in control, but no one
moved a muscle. A trio of curious young faces, one little girl with a
pixie cut and two blond adults, merely stared back at her by the open
weapons shed across the wide field.

The boulder sped up, and she pushed it aside at the last moment,
slamming it into dust against the arena sidewall.

"Was that some sort of test?" she called out.

Daggers flew in answer as the trio jumped apart and turned on
each other.

"Choose your weapon," shouted a mage in the stands.

Willow unfastened her mirrax, testing the weight of it in her grip,
but just as soon bent her head back to avoid a flying blade. "Time to
move, I guess," she muttered, zig-zagging her way to cover behind a
mound of vines.

The child, who looked about Benny's age, peeked over her target
destination just as Willow neared and let loose three arrows. Willow
deflected one with her powers, one with her mirrax, and took the last
one in the chest.

The girl stared as Willow pulled it from her protective vest with a
grunt and lunged in a different direction.

A small Winged battalion arrived to watch from above with the
disposition of a circling murder of crows, until finally, one of them
landed beside her huddled form where she was shivering against a wall
of thorns despite herself, terrified something would come at her from
behind, her legs and arms already oozing blood.

Bare-chested before her in leather combat trousers, the mage opened wings spanning twice his body length, offering a brief reprieve from the barrage of blades in the breeze.

She glanced up with a gasp. Vivek, last year's champion, looked her over. "Close your eyes."

"Here?" she asked. "It's like they're trying to kill me."

"They are. What part of 'last one standing' did you not understand?"

"He meant standing *alive*?" Panic skipped across the waves of her pulse with the beat of a pebble about to sink. "Shit. Oh, fucking shit." She fell to all fours and moaned, "I thought you just get eliminated from the competition, *not from life*."

"Hmm. Well, you only get eliminated if you die."

Willow's doe eyes grew even rounder as she looked up at him.

"Enough of that. Close those eyes. Go on." He added when she hesitated, "I'm the instructor today."

She lifted her chin but did as he asked.

"Kneel properly and feel the floor with your palms as it shakes. Good. Now anchor yourself."

"What?"

"Concentrate on something stable within."

Her eyes snapped open. "Nothing is fucking stable within!"

A burst of wind slapped Willow onto her back. She lifted her eyes to Vivek's glowering hazel gaze set in a sun-weathered face, large jaw jutting forward. "Then strangle the void inside you," he growled.

Willow glared as she regulated her breathing, tried to recall the way she and Zeph would sometimes meditate in their hallow to fight off the cold, and tied that memory into the present.

"That's it. This can't be new. Use that focus to connect with the chaos around you. Can you see the concentrated ether in my hands?"

"No," she whispered, staring at his cupped palms with the hopeful blindness of a newborn pup.

"Then look harder. Do you see any copper strands?"

"No. What are they supposed to be? Ether?"

"Stop it, Vivek!" came a male voice. "No fair. Let us at her."

Vivek cocked his head. "You even met her yet?" he called behind him. "That's it. Everyone gather round. Ceasefire!"

Vivek stepped aside as her three foes finally stepped forth into the open. He pushed a middle-aged woman and a young man about Willow's age forward. "Sienna Lafette of Sky Clan Warren and her cousin Philip Emslie of the same clan," he said before pointing to the little archer girl, and announcing, "Reynor Marten of Sky Clan Vermilion."

"And how old are you?" asked Willow, kneeling to her level.

Reynor kicked her in the chest with one foot. "Old enough to get you first."

"Eleven. She's eleven," laughed Sienna, who looked so much like her cousin they could have been twins, despite the age difference. They stood stocky and freckled, with long blond hair tied back, his into a bun and hers braided around her head, their wide hands bearing broadswords.

Willow got up, swaying from pain. "I thought the point of all this was to find the master map."

Amused, dark looks passed over each face. Even Vivek's lips turned up at the corners.

"Yeah, like that's ever gonna happen," muttered Philip, Sienna's expression a mirror of his.

Willow quickly learned the map had eluded the entire kingdom for nearly three decades. And more importantly, her fellow contestants had thus decided against the bloodless route to victory.

She was now just another body in their way.

"I will also remind you all," Vivek said, too casually for Willow's liking, "that the interior of the castle is neutral ground. Commit your murders elsewhere, or lose by default. If someone dies over their porridge bowl in the dining hall, you all lose eligibility."

Combat training continued with basic instruction on sword fighting, affording Willow the chance to hold a broadsword for the first time, something she could not do without her powers because of its great weight.

Her body was shaking by the end of practice, and her nerves were torn apart from a constant state of vigilance. She watched the others, gauging their vast differences in style and proficiency; the twins attacked with rough, raw power never quite held in check, whereas the girl relied on agility and stealth. She wondered why the king had chosen a child, worried it meant nothing good about him or for herself.

"What kind of armor you got under there? Care to show us?" asked Philip as he kinetically lifted her shirt near the end of the day.

Willow declared, "I'd rather smoke your grandad's dried turds."

"What in the void kind of expression is that?" laughed Sienna.

Slapping the garment down, Willow fled the arena as fast as she could upon dismissal, a reading list from Vivek clutched in her hand.

But as they hurried back into the castle, everyone's eyes on each other despite the Winged guard, no one was willing to change pace, walking in an awkward, tense line until they passed through the main archway and into safety.

Hours later, Willow watched Benny float to the library ceiling, a manuscript held above his head that an academic was trying to shelve at the very top. But he was having too much fun to let the woman do her work, what with flitting about, grabbing at the books that bobbed past the stacks. Since only the largest of tomes seemed to have enough heft to raise his little body, he lunged for those.

Willow smiled at his chance to act the child for once, even as worry beat a separate, erratic pulse in her throat.

She had located the two volumes on her list and a thin one on metaportation to stash away. She read for hours, trying to make sense of it all, until Benny started spinning like a top, the night librarian clearly so much more ruthless than his daytime counterpart that Willow brought Benny down herself before leading him by his collar all the way to bed.

"I hope they finally scared the trust out of you," he whispered to her later that night.

"What a terrible thing to say. I thought you were asleep."

"That's Ingress for you." He offered no recriminations, just a brutal understanding of a world she still struggled to internalize.

Willow grimaced and thought of the coming day, when she would start learning at ERA, the Exokinetic Royal Academy. Getting to class would be the most dangerous part because it required cutting past the castle to a gray stone building down a winding, open-air road.

"And about trust," said Benny, dropping his voice so low she had to strain to hear it. "I was thinking you shouldn't tell Zephyr about the skin map. No, don't shake your head. Listen, lady. We should feel this place out first."

"Zephyr already holds my greatest secrets, Benny, so I don't see why that's necessary."

"Okay, but you don't know what kind of loyalty, or even power, this king has over his secret guard. I mean come on, they're *his* guard!"

"Benny—"

"Have I been wrong about this land yet?"

Willow bit her lip. "Alright, just for now, we'll keep the map to ourselves."

She woke around midnight, dripping sweat and heart pounding with anxiety over a different sort of climb in the morning. She stumbled over to the balcony to step outside, gulping in the star-drenched cold in gratitude when a couple of the Winged flew past, dancing below in the night air. She turned with a scream trapped in her throat when someone landed behind her.

"Name's Flynn. I've been assigned to you. Permanently this time." He bowed low.

Willow stepped close and whispered, "To protect me or to spy on me?"

He straightened, gray hair falling back from a face gaunt as the night, and like most of the Winged, stood at least a foot taller than Willow. He smiled.

"Spy it is, then."

"Each competitor has an assigned Winged guard."

"You're no one's guardsmen. You're assassins."

He cocked his head. "Then step back."

"No."

"Careful. He's not here to protect you."

"From you?"

"From anything."

Her classmates at ERA were children—unlike the instructors wobbling about as old as their subjects, including the castle's Introduction to Ingressian History director, Ms. Wintern, a lithe old maiden who sent chalk flying around the room during her spittle-ridden rants.

Ms. Wintern stared her down from the start. "What came first, contestant, the Original Void or the Great Portal?"

"How could we ever know?"

She smirked at Willow, who sat straight-backed yet folded up in her too-little chair, and stuck her face much too close to her pupil. "An academic always knows."

When they moved on to the topic of seeing ether, Willow was further confused.

"Exos see external ether, and Metas claim to feel an internal void. That is our core difference, what separates us into chaosmen and voidsmen, and what allows us to manipulate the visible world. A powerful Kinetic finds the thickest line of ether within their target and pulls it in the direction they want to see movement. If you're really strong, you can pull on many strands at once. So, the first important skill for you little beginners is to determine what ether looks like. For example, what shade are the lines you see, contestant?"

Willow looked around at expectant faces before swallowing. "Lines?"

A piece of threatening chalk flew over to tilt her chin up.

"Yes, of copper ether. Come, come. It's not some secret you need to keep to yourself. It bears no true significance."

The chalk tapped her cheek at the same tempo as Ms. Wintern's foot against the floor, all while Willow recalled the "lightning" she had seen flashing in Zeph's hands and the identical lines that had surrounded the falling turret. Had that all truly been ether at work?

Willow replied, "A very bright sort of yellowish copper. I think?"

"You think?"

After being treated like a belittled moron the entire day, one with no clear understanding of how anything worked, the humiliation bubbled for hours under her skin. Flynn followed along, keeping tabs on her whereabouts, the rare impatient rustle of his wings reminding her of the larger inky pair that should be above her instead of his. Her mood grew ever fouler as the day wore on, her vigilance and suspicion heightening off castle grounds. How could Zeph allow someone else to watch over her? Especially a cruel, threatening presence like Flynn?

But when she returned to their rooms, safe so far from murderous competitors, Benny wisely avoided her moodiness with a nap. She sat before the fire in silence, considering for the millionth maddening time why so much had been kept from her all her life.

"Flynn says you didn't enjoy your lessons."

Zeph stood by the balcony doors, arms crossed, an amused look on his face.

His arms opened to embrace her as she ran to him, but she barreled Zeph over with her whole body onto the stone balcony beyond and punched him in the nose just to wipe off that infuriating look. Clawing at his face, she shrieked in small bursts, making noises like a trapped cat spitting fire.

"How could you keep all this from me? How could you?"

Zeph's arms came up to cover his face in an X. "Stop."

"Answer me. Damn you."

His hands fisted the air as his arms uncrossed, and suddenly, she was dazed and staring at walls of smoke.

Reality returned. Leaning against one of the balcony doors within her room, he was holding her in his lap, blood dripping onto her from his nose.

He admitted, "I might have deserved that."

She huffed but reached up to wipe his face with her sleeve. "Why are you even here?"

"The voidaggen was looking away, so I was free to come by," he said, pulling her closer, voice soft against her hair.

"The what?" came her shaky voice, tired yet furious.

"The creature on the spire by the Hover Council."

She punched his chest, this time without force. "Explain something for once then. What is that thing?"

"Not a thing at all. It treats that place like a nest. Hasn't left its perch in decades."

"How's that even possible?"

"It's not. Voidaggens were never meant to live like gargoyles, and so it seems to be enchanted, which is all the more concerning as it was not bespelled by one of my kind. They're...marauders of the void, happiest slipping in and out of portals, rarely staying still, at times following in the wake of a trusted tribe of Metaporters. This one is definitely not behaving as it should."

"So what's it to you if it spies for the king? Don't you all?"

"I don't know who it spies for, fledgling." He sighed. "Thankfully, it's pitch-dark tonight, with heavy enough cloud cover. A quick drop down a few stories before I take flight, and no one should see my exit."

She rubbed her face against his chest a moment, holding on to the one piece of her past she could. "Fuck, Zeph, I have a million questions."

He shook his head in such a way that she knew he would not provide the answers before he even said so. "I promised my kind many things." He stroked her head, arms still wrapped around her. "But there are loopholes. And Torrent isn't here."

Willow was quiet before she nodded. "I can't really believe *you're* here right now."

"I'd say you're the one who's impossibly here." He held her tighter a moment, voice changing, wondering. "You've always known I keep a lot from you."

It was a question wrapped in fact that she answered anyway. "I believed you'd always include me when you could. But has it really been fifteen years since we left, Zeph?"

"No."

"No?" she practically screeched.

"Months. It's only been a few months. Close to a year."

"How is that possible? Just look at me. I've aged. Evie and Jerald said—"

"No more questions. I swear to you. It's barely been a year since we left Spinor Falls."

"Are there a hundred months in a year here or something?"

He chuckled, his chest vibrating against her with the rumble of it. "No, just the usual twelve."

She bit her tongue and pulled back, thinking. Then she said, voice urgent, "Okay, Zeph, one more thing, please. Just promise to answer one thing?"

His eyes searched hers, careful.

"If I'm a Kinetic, then is my mom…is she really my mom?"

He let loose a breath. "Yes. Yes, she is."

She closed her eyes. He pressed his forehead against hers as she wondered aloud, "You sound so sure."

"Well, I *was* at your birth."

She pulled back. "We met before?"

"How else did you think the Tug started?"

Lips round from relieved surprise, she clutched at his shoulder. "You know my mother will be worried sick about the both of us. You know it, Zeph."

He looked unsure for a moment. "If you learn enough and work hard enough here, you will find a way back. No." He pressed a finger against her parted lips. "My little Guide, there are implicit ways of getting what we are not explicitly allowed. You follow? Keep searching for that master map. Study it to find your answers."

"Yes, sir, Master of Loophole."

He laughed.

"Any leads you can offer on finding it?"

His lips pursed. "My kind knows it was left with the mapmaker's most precious valuable. But what could be more precious than that map? It would be the greatest find in all of Ingressian history. Speaking of which, that's partly why I'm here."

"What do you mean?"

"I don't want you learning about our origins from these Kinetics. They don't even understand how light came to exist."

"From Mother Phoenix, Light Bearer of the Void."

"Hmm," he snorted. "Sort of. No, you see, from within the Original

Void came the first Guide flare—the great combustion of ether that littered the land with portals." And with that revelation, he stood and walked farther into the room, wings opening behind him, sweeping the floor in an almost playful manner one moment before he sat on his haunches against a wall. His feathers spread out as he stretched his neck.

"In the beginning, there was only nothing next to everything, the stillness of the Original Void separated from the Great Portal, and in it swirled tangled strands of the most concentrated, chaotic ether ever to exist. When the two collided, the multiverse was born from what resulted—an explosive Guide flare. She was the void, you see, and he was her ether."

"Mother Phoenix and Father Orelio?"

"Yes, the concept that Guide pairs must be of the same designation arises simply from pure statistical chance, considering the aversion to travel—the Guide pairs most likely to meet each other in this land are those who happen to be of the same designation. But look at us, fledgling. And look at them."

She sat down beside him against the wall, careful, unsure of leaning back against his feathers until he curled them around her, staring out at the dark while she marveled at the smooth softness of this new aspect of her old friend.

"Yeah," she said. "Just look at you."

He stopped breathing when she stroked the sharp talon of a wingtip.

"So, Zeph, what does ether look like for you?"

He cocked his head, exhaling. "Well, your kind see only lines, so they're always tugging at them to move things. Exoskia see waves of flat shapes they can pull around or over themselves. The Exowinged, however...we see multidimensional folds."

"Then what power do your spell words have?"

He touched the starburst scar near her chin, an affectionate smile on his face. "Want to know a secret?"

"If sir wouldn't mind sharing."

He laughed. "Nothing. No power. They just aid in focus. Root us in tradition."

"And confuse the rest of us?"

"Actually, yes. Because viewpoint is key, isn't it? Like when you see folds instead of lines, you can effect more complex change. When a mage casts something especially intricate, say an enchantment, we often link them to previous ones of similar complexity, all interconnected, all dependent on the others to remain folded in their new form. It's more casually called the Rule of Rings."

"What are these folds like?"

He grinned, looking around as if with genetic glasses that speared the world into separate parts. "The way ether is folded within the voids of space is with dependably mathematical precision, and that determines everything about it. Impossible to explain without years of study practically from birth. But it's so beautiful"—he lifted a hand out in front of him and twisted it—"that I'm curious—what do you see here?"

"I don't see anything." She said it like a secret. "I don't think I see ether at all. Everything here has a strange copper shimmer, and I might see separate copper strands being used like tethers to move things around at times. But usually, I just manage to connect with what I'm kinetically moving, and it does."

He smiled, something satisfied in his expression. "You had to get used to using your powers differently in Spinor Falls. Just keep doing what you're doing."

"But no one else could do *any* of this back home. Why?"

He looked at her, almost confused a moment, and shook his head. "How about I continue our history of time?" And as if he could distract her, he rambled on, "Mother Phoenix and Father Orelio oversaw their new multiverse, slipping between dimensions as their children grew into distinct lines after being geographically isolated. That's how each designation evolved suited for travel in new ways."

"Except the Fervers," cut in Willow.

"Perhaps."

"And the Kinetics have no idea?"

"It's all theory, really, as the beginning of time must be, but we have more reliable sources than they do"—he glanced over at her open, riveted expression—"what with being direct descendants of the Purveyor of the Night."

She cackled, delighted, grabbing his face between her palms. "Orelio? Is that why you played him each year? All this time, you were laughing at us all."

The smile at the corner of his mouth shriveled. "No, fledgling, *they* were laughing. I was only hungry."

The shock of it ran through her harder than any admission thus far. "Wait. The Norwoods didn't feed you?"

From his expression, she suspected that was not the worst they did.

Her hands froze in the air beside his cheeks.

Benny chose that moment to walk over, awoken from his nap on the bed, to stand in front of Zeph's crouching form. "Why would a mage ever know hunger?"

"I could cast no spells within Spinor Falls," said Zeph, looking up at the little face and stumbling limbs before him.

Willow grabbed Zeph's shoulders and shook them. "Why?"

"Does that hurt?" Zeph asked Benny instead of responding.

The boy cocked his head.

"Your limp?" clarified Zeph.

"Yes, it aches," said Willow when Benny refused to answer.

"Come here."

The boy shook his head, but Zeph was already tugging at the ether in the air like he often did, his fingers swirling and wrists crossing over each other until shadowlike strands of copper grew around his hands, so thick they began to travel up his forearms. "I'd need at least an hour to heal such a chronic injury, but I can decrease the inflammation for now. May I?"

Benny looked at Willow. She nodded.

"But that's dark magic. You'd do that for me?" asked the boy.

Willow looked over at Zeph. "What's that mean? Dark magic?"

Zeph placed both his hands on Benny's left knee, massaging the shadows into the joint. "Just that it upsets the balance in the world, to use an internal source on an external target. Exos use external ether to affect the external world, and Metas use their internal void to affect themselves. Magic is only called magic because it is a disruption of the natural world, so in that sense, it's always dark."

Benny stretched out his leg in suspicion. He shook it. Then he hopped a little and smiled. "Thank you."

Willow, however pleased, was not interested in being further distracted. "Aren't there consequences to this, then?"

Zeph stood, smiling at her question, as he said, "Our council spends many holidays throughout the year restoring balance and giving thanks. A mage does nothing without thought to the repercussions."

"Like coming to Spinor Falls? Where in Orelio's name were your wings?"

"That's enough for now, I think." He stood, heading to the balcony, but she followed close behind.

"At least—"

"Willow, you promised no more questions, but you've been leading an interrogation."

"Just—what does your kind know about me? About us? I deserve to know!"

He pressed a finger to her lips. "They know of our upbringing, our Guide bond, and obviously the strength of your powers, but I will never bring up the sentience issue to them. A promise is a promise, right?"

She mumbled, "Yes, but do they hate me? They seem to."

"They're split on how to treat you, perhaps. Loyalty above all else, you know."

"To the king?"

"To each other." And with that, he must have had enough, because he vaulted off the balcony without another word, dropping into the alien abyss of a sable sky. She nearly fell after him in her rush to look, seeing only the ghost of his wings snapping open far below.

CHAPTER
15

MAZE OF
WARNINGS

If ether forms tethers,
Could they ever sever?
Or are we doomed to dance this damn dance forever?

The first challenge came before dawn.

A few weeks after her last private conversation with Zeph, the contestants had been ferried down to the land beneath the Sky Realm in the darkness of early morning, shivering from the cold and trying not to look below as a crashing sound grew louder and louder.

The swarm of patent portals whirling beneath Maddooinne flowed across the dry mustard-yellow earth with a moderate tremble, but it was the silence of the veiled ones that left contestants nauseous at the thought of wading past the Northern Portal Mines.

The Winged had cast an enchantment around the area to manifest as a circle of smoke that would signal the first and final contestants to leave the perimeter, like a tripwire of chaos.

Extending just past the overhanging Sky Realm, this separate section of the minefield was only about a couple miles in diameter and would have been terrifying if not for Willow's map. She took a breath to remind herself how much smaller these pockets were than the southern ones she had already conquered.

Five. I can remember five.

There were only five veiled portals of concern here, all of them following a common pattern to naturally occurring portals, which Victor had pointed out: tight clusters of patent portals laid out like concentric rings of a tree around one veiled entrance.

She looked up to gauge how soon the sun would rise. The sky was already lightening. And as always, silent wings circled above them at a great distance.

A sword slashing back and forth at her side distracted her sky gazing as Philip looked her over, the skilled movements of his blade so incessant they grew blurry.

He grinned, saying, "There's a portal around here somewhere marked just for you. I hope you're ready to meet those dead bastards in Void Valley."

"Is there really?" She decided that must be the one veiled portal on her map without destination markings. "I thank you for such vital information."

He smirked the smirk of a brat born of endless money.

Willow thought of the one-way portal just ahead of them leading to the Southern Portal Mines and imagined kicking him into it.

But she only swung her head in the direction of Vivek, who was crouched on his heels upon a nearby ledge of mountain rock above jutting out from one of the many towering faces of Mount Onstel.

"When I say the word," called out Vivek, "you each head for the center of the mines, right where you can see that large tent. Your task is simply to return with what was taken from you."

As Willow possessed nothing here that she was neither wearing nor carrying, she raised a hand like they did in the children's classes she still attended.

The contestants laughed.

Vivek smiled. "Yes, Willow of Sky Clan Munster?"

"What did you take from me?"

"Your son."

Her hand fell. This time, no one laughed. But neither did anyone ask what they were all thinking.

"The formal rules are as follows. If you fall into a portal, no one is to go searching for you. If you return alone, you forfeit by default. If you are the last one to make it back, you will under no circumstances be allowed to return for your loved one. And finally, to the winner goes the glory." Vivek stood, one talon-tipped wing outstretched. "Turn and take your places."

Mages flew them to opposing ends of the mine, in each cardinal direction about a mile from the center, while Vivek flew above the tent in the middle.

His baritone voice boomed loud and clear, "On the count of three. One. Two—"

Willow's hand shot up again. "Seems only fair the others know who they're missing too," she shouted.

Vivek tossed her such a well-controlled look of exasperation she knew he must have children. As he rattled off some more names, Willow gazed up at the clouds. *So close.*

"Alright, if there are no more questions," he said, looking over at Willow. She smiled up at the pinkish color the dawning sky had just turned and pulled a fistful of pebbles out of her pocket, just before he bellowed, "One. Two. Three!"

Willow sprinted off as the others stared blankly after her. She weaved through the molten copper of the patent portals with the nimbleness of a farm mouse. "Seven, eight, nine, this one."

She sent a spray of pebbles into the portal she had in mind and watched them erupt from an exit much closer to her goal, showering down to earth. Satisfied, she turned backward and plopped into her confirmed gateway. She landed deliberately without rolling over, then tossed a pebble over into the center of a cluster, watched the veiled one turn pink like the sky for a flash, and avoided it in her jump across.

Ahead of her, little Reynor ran to the tent from exactly opposite Willow's direction, slower than the rest, glaring daggers and raising a longbow at her from over a mile away. Willow turned again, fell backward, and felt a sharp prick between her shoulder blades. Landing on the other side of the portal, just a few paces closer to her goal, she felt the arrow pushing deeper into her vest. She lifted her torso immediately and dug it out. Tipped with an odd silver color, it had managed to pierce her sand wyrm hide.

"How is she so good at that?" Willow muttered, stuffing the arrow in a pocket while at the same time pushing herself up. She threw another pebble where she now expected would be the veiled portal leading to Void Valley.

The pebble remained firmly on yellow land. She tossed another near it and…nothing. Tossed a shower of them. Confused, and now perhaps lost, she stood still, chest heaving as she considered her position: south of Mount Onstel, just a mile or so off to the side of the northeast wall of the Sky Realm, where the nearest patent portals were all accounted for, in their expected locations.

Her map bore a mistake. Nothing had ever frightened her more.

"Oy, Willow, how are you doing that?" asked Sienna across from her, waving both arms madly.

"Like I'm gonna tell—"

Philip slammed into her from behind, pushing her into the patent portal just ahead.

She emerged, tumbling too fast for a controlled fall, coughing up dirt and jaw stinging from an impact to her face she could not even soften with a roll. "Fuck. They tricked me."

Nearly outside the mines now, she landed where Vivek sat against the mountainside, expressionless face pressed against a single fist on his drawn-up knees. "Having fun out there?" he asked.

The rock shook as she tried to control her anger.

"Whoa," he said, taking flight in an impressive flash. "Rein it in."

She huffed and ran back into the competition, the earth around her quaking harder from her internal turmoil. Philip was now closest to the tents, with Reynor the farthest behind and visibly unsure of where to step. The vibrations surged forward and dipped Sienna into a portal that sent her farther back. Light-footed enough to avoid a similar end, Willow flew past the trailing girls and took her chances with multiple patent portals she tested with her rocks until she ended up in clear sight of the tent.

Just ahead of her, Philip reached out a hand, lifted the tent's blue cloth entrance, and ducked his head into it.

Willow sent her mirrax soaring to push against the back of his neck. A trickle of blood seeped down onto his collar. "Step back."

He lifted both hands and retreated, the blade edge circling around to his throat as he turned to face her. "You witch," he whispered. "You cheated."

"Head up if you want to keep it," she growled, forcing his neck to the sky to keep his eyes well out of sight of the ax.

Her gaze on his, she pushed one hand behind her into the tent and called out, "Benny. Come on out. It's me. Benny?" Her voice rose.

"He's not coming."

"Why?"

"Take a look," demanded Philip.

"I'm rather fond of my own neck. Thanks."

"They're all injured," he growled. "Recall your weapon and let me tend to my mother."

She pushed the blade closer to his left pulse point. "Benny! Come out right this instant!"

"You idiot, just let me *in* there."

Willow stripped him of his weapon, grasping the broadsword with a rope of ether and sending it flying into a veiled portal that she would much rather have sent him into.

"Hey!" he shouted, eyes clouding over.

She recalled her mirrax into its holster and burst into the tent.

It was a mess of limbs, bodies tossed about the small space without care. Gasping, she ran to Benny's side and flipped him over. "I'm here. Oh, I'm here now. Let's go. Benny?"

She looked up to see Philip haul an old woman over his shoulder. "Don't waste your breath. They're clearly all enchanted."

"What?"

"They'll sleep until those dirty fucking mages decide otherwise."

"They're not dirty—"

"Oh yeah, and you're so tough you've become obsessed with those monsters?"

"Watch your mouth," she said, lifting her mirrax.

He backed up, one hand raised. "Power attracts power. I get it. But those butchers aren't worth a passing piss in a portal. That's Reynor's dog over there, all she has left. Her entire family is dead because of them. Even the Skia smith who tried to hide her away paid the price when that Zephyr champion took him out to bring her here. Just for this. More death." He sneered as he tenderly cupped the back of the old woman's white head and escaped the tent, tossing his final words behind him without looking back: "Not everyone had the grace of a royal invitation."

Willow looked down at Benny, her heart hammering away with a realization that showered her in ice water.

Almost blindly, she ran out the tent after Philip to look for the one-way patent portal headed right where she needed to go—the very one he had pushed her into earlier.

Finding it, she appeared directly in front of Vivek and stepped through writhing copper smoke, shooting up into a circular wall that met in the middle to form a transparent dome encasing the mines behind her.

"First one back by quite a margin. How's that?" asked Vivek.

Willow glared, holding Benny tight to her chest. "Is this what you did to me? Was I enchanted all those months, lying asleep in some backwater village until you decided I deserved my own life?"

Vivek seemed taken aback, struck silent for a searing moment, eyes not leaving hers. "That was not our choice."

"Then whose was it?"

"There are forces in this world—"

"More politicking and lies. Lovely."

With a deep sigh but no visible guilt, he reached both arms out. "Well done to you once again. May I?"

She did not give up Benny, only scowling at Vivek and his questioning expression until she noticed the mountainside decorated with his brethren, standing or stooping on outcroppings with inhuman stillness. Zeph was nowhere to be seen. Flynn's suspicious gaze tracked her as usual, but the force of all their combined attention proved oddly frightening, pushing in on her like a cave of glowing eyes that had snapped open all at once.

Fuck it. Neither the king nor the Kinetic guard was here.

So she pulled a Zeph—

She burst out, "You're all gathered like flies around a corpse, but where were any of you when Zeph needed you?" She pointed up at them. "When he was secretly hungry and publicly shunned, where the hell were all of you? And you know what else? I know a thing or two about absent fathers, and whoever you are, you should be ashamed of not being around to teach him what it means to be a man."

On a defiant exhale, she turned her back to them and stared out at the mines, struggling not to shake. Philip was now caught near the center of a cluster of patent portals, and she almost wanted to call out a warning when Vivek abruptly barked, "Zeph!"

He was there in the space of a breath, dropping out of nowhere somehow to land at her side with a nod to Vivek. "General," he said before he questioned Willow more softly. "So how'd you do that, fledgling?"

"I already asked," said Vivek.

"Well, it's not like she would tell *you*."

Vivek seemed to accept that. They both looked over at her, Vivek a bit more hesitant than before.

Turning her back to them all once again, she said with heavy petulance, "I learned a lot on the way here. It would have been easier if *someone* had been willing to teach me instead of throwing me to the fiend wolves of his world."

"Hey, I left you Father's book on the Primordial Clan, but *you* lost it."

"*She* had my book?" Vivek sounded alarmed.

At that, Willow spun around.

"Did I forget to mention it?" muttered Zeph.

"It's been missing for years. You said nothing."

Zeph crouched onto his haunches, cracking his knuckles. "Is anything really missing if someone somewhere knows where it is?"

Deadpan, Vivek let him know, "I'm going to kill you. One day soon, you will be well acquainted with death. Because I will personally make the introduction."

"Someday soon, *I* will slip you a diarrhetic so strong you shit yourself in the sky."

Willow could not stop staring at them smiling at each other, heart in her throat, as she realized they had the same exact smirk.

But she nearly fell over when Philip suddenly pushed past her with a shout. He had run through the smoke dome and clear of the portal mines to lay the old woman at their feet. "Bring her back. Do it. Do it right the hell now."

With Benny still comatose in her arms, Willow piped up, "Yeah, bring them back."

"Not," said Vivek, soft and sure, with Zeph standing serenely at his side, "until the last contestant is determined. The sleeping enchantment is interlinked with the border spell, such that they will all awaken together."

Philip spat at their feet and sat down to pull the woman into his lap, brushing back her hair with his knuckles.

Recalling the Rule of Rings, Willow looked over at Zeph, her brows drawn.

He just nodded his head at her in confirmation, turning to watch Reynor and Sienna. But the outcome remained all too obvious. Sienna neared the border of the mines with a young man she was dragging by the torso, whereas Reynor had yet to even reach her dog.

Once Sienna pulled past the last portal, the littlest contestant collapsed. She wailed, forehead against the dirt, as they all looked on.

Vivek ordered his son to retrieve her.

Zephyr rose into the air.

"Stop!" yelled Willow.

"Yes?" Zeph raised his brows at her, a different question peeking through at the edge of his mouth, great wings flapping to keep him in place.

"I'm going back for the dog," she stated.

Philip startled, staring over at Willow in confusion.

The mages all stood together at attention.

Flynn flew down, his massive body pressing in too close to hers, danger crackling at her hip.

Vivek motioned with his wings, and Zeph landed on her other side.

"That's against the rules," said Vivek, cocking his head.

Willow stepped toward him, the two mages beside her following suit. "No, it's not. You said we wouldn't be allowed to return for our own loved ones. Reynor's dog is not one of mine."

A beat of silence.

Vivek turned to Zeph and snapped, "This is all your fault, isn't it?"

"And how might that be?"

"As the king's champion, you worded the rules. If anyone knows how to get around something—"

Thrusting Benny into Zeph's arms, Willow turned her back and rushed once more into the portal-filled fray.

After each challenge, the king hosted a royal celebration in the winner's honor. But tonight, there had been a hesitance within the castle, some question whether the king would allow the party at all, which left Willow and Benny in a state of unease. When Marina came in toward the evening to prepare their attire, the pair glanced at each other in relief.

An hour later, Willow stepped into the royal gardens with Benny, his hand clammy in her own, hundreds of candles in little cages flickering around the costumed guests. A large mesh mask covered the top half of her own face, and Benny's silk face scarf was tied behind his head with an elaborately long bow.

They walked down the brightly lit runner leading to the king and knelt.

"I hear you have a soft spot for animals, today's champion," Soren said, the words light, but the king's voice not as chipper as it usually sounded. His mask was composed only of face paint, slashes and swirls of color around his eyes. His feet tapped with his usual impatience, though he placed a hand against his cheek in affected boredom. That smile beamed bright as ever, but Willow imagined it tinged with a crazed light, his costume more like war paint. "Or did you mean to disrespect the games?"

The ensuing silence pushed in on them all.

Benny's lips started to wobble. Willow held his hand tighter, but he could not help the words and tears spilling out as he cried, "A large dog saved my life once and Mom never forgot it. She had to save that one for me."

Willow grew still, glancing back at the king. As he watched Benny break into heaving sobs, the man's legs started to bounce up and down on either side of the throne. "How thrilling, quite thrilling. Rest assured we have very few dogs here, child, as they do tend to fall off the sides of our territory." He stood, his smile stretched too wide for any face. "Congratulations, young champion. You've won a battle in a great big war. Now go. Celebrate." He waggled his fingers in the air.

And never having said a word, Willow bowed in farewell as the people applauded. She pulled a crying Benny into her arms and rushed off.

"Nice," she whispered once they were a distance away.

"Genocidal maniac. I'm telling you," he hiccupped into her neck.

She stroked his back and walked through the throng to sit at the sidelines, settling him in her lap. Philip arrived not long after, walking toward the king with a cocksure ease, dressed in long gray velvet fabric that trailed behind him like his identifiably ice-blond hair, tied back tonight with a leather thong. When he dropped to both knees and stretched his arms out onto the ground, the king's voice boomed with delight.

A different voice, soft as a snake with a suggestion, spoke from behind her, "Get out of this realm while you still can. *No, don't turn around.*"

In the veiled gloom of the hedgerows, Torrent stood half within the curling shrubs.

"Are you talking to *us*?" asked Willow.

"No, I'm talking to these bushes, idiot. Stop looking my way."

"You seem like someone I can trust for life advice."

"Don't be snarky."

"You started it."

"Children!" snapped Benny. "Can we talk more about keeping me alive?"

Torrent just said, "If you have any loyalty to this child or his life, you will leave as soon as you are able."

Willow held Benny tighter. "Why?"

Silence.

"I don't like cryptic warnings. They sound more like threats."

"Do as you like."

"Give me a reason. Hey, what—" She turned around to see Torrent had disappeared, just as a deeper voice said, "Evening."

Philip was holding out a hand. "Care to dance?"

Benny slapped it away. "No."

Philip smiled, small and cheery. "I wasn't asking you, but I suppose your permission matters too." He knelt before them. "May I have this dance with your mother?"

Benny's eyes narrowed. "No, actually—"

Willow placed her hand over his mouth; he mumbled against it as she said, "I don't want to leave Benny alone."

"Well, that hurts. You left him once to dance with a Winged beast."

But he said it with an exaggerated hand to his chest, and perhaps that was why she offered, "How about a stroll instead?"

Philip nodded and they walked on in strange silence, leading to where the guests spilled out into hedgerow mazes in the garden, coming to a small space where the crowds thinned. After a long silence, he asked, "Why go back for the dog?"

Willow recalled the copper dome of smoke dropping away at the exact moment Benny returned to consciousness in the mines: a rippling breath passing through his entire body before a single convulsion and the sudden opening of his eyes, staring at her in shock; her relief, even though she knew he was alive; the gratitude swelling in her breast; the devastation ready to consume her if he had not opened them; the way Reynor's dog was running in circles around the red-eyed girl.

"I know what it's like being left to the mines. Someone once helped me find my own way back."

The music seemed to fall away as he stared at her. "Which mines?"

"Does it matter?"

"Perhaps. Perhaps not." He looked up at the bright stars as he began, "Look, since we're all stuck in this shitty situation—"

"Help me find the map." The words spilled from her lips before she'd even considered them.

"What?"

"Why should we all kill each other like a pack of brutes? Let's join forces and find the map. If we can recover it, no one has to die in these challenges."

Philip dropped his voice as he said, "But it's not real. It's just a myth we've been force-fed for years. The king simply wants to believe the thing exists."

"It does exist. It has to," piped up Benny.

"And how would you know that?"

"If the mapmaker is real—"

"He's not."

Willow pointed at the sky. "Outside these walls, they say the Winged aren't real. They're wrong about that too."

"That logic does not follow. Not every conceivable thing must exist because one unbelievable thing does."

"You sound like a Meta," noted Benny, a bit too pleased for Willow's taste.

She ignored him. "Yes, okay, but do you really want to reach a point where you have to fight your own cousin to the death? When there's even a slight chance you can avoid it?"

Philip yanked at his hair in frustration before dropping both hands to his hips with a huff. Turning to the side, he asked, "If we do find the map, Willow, do you know what that would mean?" He looked around before stepping back to her, his face inches away, such that she could feel his breath when he said, "The monarch of Maddooinne, the man who set fire to thousands of Flamethrowers from leagues away, could finally set fire to everywhere else."

"So it's true?" Willow's eyes widened. "And he could do that from here?"

"Yes."

"And why would you care?"

"Do you have such a low opinion of your own kind?" In that moment, with her confused face fetchingly turned up to his, he swooped down to press a quick kiss to her parted lips. He sounded a touch surprised as he murmured, "Now I really do hope I don't have to kill you."

"How…romantic."

Willow would recognize that condescending drawl anywhere, but this time it was laced with violence. Wings pointedly rustling as they stretched behind Zeph's back, he rolled his shoulders and stepped slowly out into the torchlight.

"No one asked your opinion," said Philip, hand falling to the blade at his side.

Zeph lifted his chin. "Fuck off."

Philip took a step forward, but dark copper threads began to swirl at their feet as Zeph's fingers danced by his sides. A large hand crafted in smoke curled around Philip's legs and up toward his chest.

"Dark magic?" he breathed. The steely-eyed contestant held still until the hand took hold of his throat, at which point he choked out, "I give."

"Of course you do. Willow of Sky Clan Munster, the king requests your presence at the Hover Council."

"'Orders' is more like it," gasped Philip.

But with that, Zeph turned on his heel and stalked off, Willow and Benny scrambling to follow. Zeph kept tight against the darkness of the hedgerows, his entire being merged with shadow like one of the Skia. He growled, "This is a formal event, and he is your literal blood rival. Of all the idiotic—Benny, why didn't you stop him?"

The boy waved his arms. "Well, somebody was talking sense *for once*. Right before it got disgusting."

"That so, voidsman? Well, you both better bear in mind that he could be dead tomorrow."

"So might we all," sang Willow.

Zeph slowed his breakneck speed across the grounds. "Are you enjoying this?"

Some devil took hold of her as she said from behind him, "Had my first kiss tonight, so a little bit, yes."

At that, he paused and spun to face her, his eyes flashing. "Would we really call that pathetic display your first kiss?"

Willow tilted her face up to his and stepped closer in the gloom. "It only counts if you don't apologize afterward."

"I didn't—"

Before he could finish, a clawed hand took hold of his arm, and a wizened old voice sang, "Hello again, my little baby Azakor."

Zeph pulled away as if burned from the contact. "You. What are you doing here?"

Willow could see no wings. But that hand looked familiar. She wore a covering over her entire face, bent over, back hunched like—

"Come now, boy, where's my hug?"

"Don't be obtuse."

"Is this your Guide?"

"Dear Father of Darkness—" he swore. "Shut up."

Heart thudding, Willow interrupted, "Do you know me?"

"Of you, dearie, just of you." She let loose a very familiar cackle. "Glad to see you made it. I knew any Guide of my nephew's must be of strong constitution."

"Aunt Tempest, are you trying to get us *all* killed?"

"So paranoid you've become. Tsk. Your father is rubbing off on you."

"Speaking of your brother." Zeph raised an arm straight into the air and tugged hard—a bright copper spark went off into the sky. Vivek dropped out of the air before them in response, his eyes narrowing before his feet even touched the earth.

"Dad," said Zeph, voice low.

"I see. Leave her to me."

"I don't need minding, you silly boys. I'm only here to deliver a message."

"Well, fuck us all," breathed Zeph.

Vivek roughly pushed Zeph away. "Go on, son, I've got her. And the boy. Don't keep the king waiting."

Willow stood straighter. Zeph's father he may be, but trusted he was not. "Benny comes with me."

The boy shook his head. "No, it's okay. I'll stay."

"Why?"

"He watched over me before, when they came to get me for the mines. It's alright. Look. I...I really don't want to face that king again."

Zeph had already stormed off.

"Keep him away from Torrent," Willow warned Vivek before rushing to catch up with her friend, all while trying not to stare at the hag patting Vivek's face with visibly unwelcome fondness.

On entering the castle, she could see no one else around and confessed, "Zeph, I think I've met her before…in a Skia marketplace all those months ago. Benny even tried to steal from her. But she's a Kinetic, so how can you be related?"

Willow didn't think he would answer, but he said, "Split parentage."

She grabbed his arm, though he pulled away with an admonishing look. "Wait, are you telling me that the Exowinged and the Exokinetics can have children? Together?"

His stern expression gave way to something heated, sending shivers rushing through her skin as he brushed the corner of her jaw with a bent knuckle. "Yes, fledgling, I am. Exos have proven they can reproduce across designation lines. It's rare but possible, since they are of the same source. My aunt is a Kinetic by designation." His thumb and index finger tightened on her face. "And the king took her wings for it."

An errant vision melted away like cotton candy on her tongue, an aftertaste of sweetness the only evidence it was ever there. Instead, Willow's face went red in anger. "Why would you serve such a monster?"

He clapped a hand over her mouth, just as footsteps turned a corner at the end of the hallway. "Come on."

They walked for so long, entering stairwells that grew progressively steeper, before exiting into the cold night air. "Feels like we've been here before," whispered Willow.

"Stay calm," he said, somehow without moving his lips. "I'll be watching."

A chill ran down her spine. She looked behind her to see Zeph step away into the darkness beside a massive metal spire, around which the tail of an unmoving creature curled. Straining her neck up as her mouth grew wide, she could see the voidaggen's white eyes trained on her.

"Hello, young Willow."

Her head whipped to the side.

With a flat smile, the king looked over from the edge of the platform on which they stood. He stood ramrod straight and unnervingly still, especially for him.

She walked over when he held out a hand.

Soren pulled her into his side and patted her arm. "Welcome to the Hover Council, dear." He pointed down at a different circular platform below them, rimmed only by a railing of sky and a battalion of robed Kinetics.

These men and women stood in the very center of the realm and stared out at the land, fully visible to them at this altitude.

"Take a good look at some of our strongest people," said Soren. "They keep us soaring in safety."

"How are they doing this?"

"They can see the entire perimeter of Maddooinne from here, so each councilor pulls up as many strands of ether connected to our land's edges as possible, until we have essentially built something like—"

"A parachute of power."

He raised a brow, impressed but unsurprised. "Yes. Done that yourself a time or two, have you?"

Willow wisely deflected. "But what if their attention breaks?"

"They've proven they can do this with snow belly snakes crawling up their naked torsos. And of course, they take shifts. But I agree with you. We should test them some more." The king pulled a hefty metal comb from out of his robes.

"No! No, I trust you, of course, sire."

"Alright." With a shrug, he tossed the comb behind him with deceptive force, hitting one of the councilmen in the leg. The man lifted it in silent pain and balanced on the other without moving any other part of his body. "But do you truly trust me, Willow?"

"Yes, of course, sire."

The comb sailed back into the king's hands, and he began twirling it between his fingers. "Your performance this morning was utterly incredible, dear. Consider me even more impressed than before. But the sort of portal knowledge you displayed. Well—"

She tried not to flinch. "Sire?"

He pulled her forward by the hips, facing him, body pressing tight against hers, mouth hot against her ear. "Have you found the map already, Willow? Are you holding out on me?"

"No, I would never—"

"This land is mine. Its every treasure is mine. Is that clear?" he asked, hand stroking up and down her bare back, searing her skin with its ice, as the other used the comb to pull her hair away from her neck and playfully outline the starburst scar so close to the soft skin of her throat.

"Yes, sire." She tried not to shake at the cold metal against her pulse. "I only know how to avoid the veiled portals. That's all."

"How's that?"

"I just wait until the sky turns a deep color, then toss a spray of pebbles or sand wherever I mean to step. Veiled portals turn the color of the sky for a moment as the ether in them is disturbed. It's common knowledge...where I'm from."

He considered her a moment. Pulling away, he crossed his arms and hopped once before bending over in laughter.

Willow worked to keep her face controlled.

"Ah, you're really like a daughter to me, Willow. Dear girl. You remind me of her actually. My little Lavender."

"I'm sorry," she whispered, shivering as the silent wind of a sad history tore through. The council somehow grew more still around them, so still it seemed even their robes refused to stir.

"Yes, I suppose you should be. She was dead before she could live, you know. Her brother came out squalling moments after his twin, already destroyed at the death of his Guide, but she just lay there, unmoving in her mother's arms, with that foamy cord for a necklace."

He yanked Willow forward by the shoulders. She could see Zeph staring narrow-eyed at them from behind the king's shaking head as the ruler's voice rose, his eyes gleaming, to say, "But don't you see? I'm so strong that I brought her back. Time holds no power over me. She lived again." His hands dropped to tap away at his thighs. Tap. Tap. Relentless. "That is, until she didn't."

Willow remembered to exhale.

"Time," he whispered, chuckling. "It will turn, as it always does."

"I don't understand, sire."

"Become my heir and you will, dear girl." He kissed her forehead and tugged her ear. Then, patting her cheek as if disinterested, he called out, "Take her back now, Azakor."

Zeph stalked forward, stopping short as screams rose up from the gardens below them. He flew over to the edge in a burst to look down for the cause.

"Damn it," he bit off.

"Get your petal-soft, rosy-colored royal ass back down to your own party," shouted that old voice. A bare pinprick in the distant gardens, and with a ring of fire encircling her, Tempest waved wildly up at the three of them, who stared as the partygoers fled from the crone like the plague. "He's coming. I want you to know that he's coming! You won't have much left for long, darling."

Soren turned to Zephyr to demand, "What's that crazed mongrel doing here?"

"I wouldn't know, sire."

"Well, what are you staring at me for? Arrest her!"

Face blank, he soared away from the platform and down toward the hag. She held her arms up and wrapped them around her nephew's neck so he could fly her to where she clearly wished to be.

Clapping her hands upon arrival on the platform, Tempest asked, "Why are you Kinetics always so fearful of a little fire?"

The king charged forward as Zeph angled his aunt behind himself.

Soren promised through gritted teeth, "Kinetic law prohibits your death, but I can still make you wish for one."

Her gleeful face finally flashed a sour expression, chin pressed on the hand she rested on Zeph's shoulder. "And how much worse could you do now, you royal prick?"

"You have other limbs you could live without, I'm sure."

Tempest pushed Zeph away and jumped off the top ledge, landing behind a council member and locking her bony but muscular arm around his windpipe. The man stared on as she looked at the king and whispered loudly in his ear, "Oh, I think you'll listen, my little love."

"You were banished," Soren screamed. "Get out of my realm."

"Oh, no, no, no." She held up her free hand. "My people never banished me. We don't share your puritan views. But never mind that." She squeezed tighter in warning, until the man turned blue and the platform shook. "I'm here to do you a favor, so go on and say thank you."

"Never."

She pulled out a thin blade and held it to her hostage's throat. "Say it."

"Thank you," he spat down at her.

"Kneel." She drew blood, a thick stream of it that finally broke the councilman's attention. The platform began to wobble, the entire realm growing destabilized. "Isn't this the head of your precious Hover Council in my embrace?"

Soren fell into a crouch for support, one hand against the ground. "If you kill him, the realm will tip over. You'll kill scores of people."

"*Your* people. Mine can fly."

"You bitch."

"Kneel!" she screeched, turning the blade onto its point. "Or watch your subjects plunge to the literal ground."

Soren screamed as he complied, "I can destroy the entire Flock right now, and you know it."

"Oh, but listen. Listen," she said softly, dragging out the words and drawing that blade point in circles against the man's stretched, wet throat. "He's coming. So you can't."

When no one else spoke, Zephyr broke the silence. "Who?"

"That which walks through the void. That which brought us to our knees. That most putrid of beings."

"Aunt!"

"The Voidroamer. He comes."

Zeph took a thunderstruck step backward as the king's frozen face turned even paler.

Willow forced herself to say nothing.

"Why does he come?" demanded Zeph.

"Oh, our darling Soren can tell you that too, I'm sure. He comes to collect."

"Liar," growled the king. "I was promised longer."

"Did you get it in writing, lovey? A blood pact, at least? No? Oh, pity. What a pity."

"And why would you warn me?"

"I warn my children. *You* I hope to make suffer in expectant agony. The agony of knowing your days with power—hell, your days *alive*— are almost up. And as much as I want you dead, I don't wish to see my clan pay the consequences of your greed." She cocked her head totally to the side while eyeing the king, the tease in her voice falling away.

"You were so little when you were crowned. Look at how it's ruined you. Better think of a way to hold on to those siphons, baby Soren."

The king's stubborn facade cracked as he crawled forward to look down at her. "How?"

"I wouldn't know." She pressed a kiss to the back of the councilman's head. "What a good little puppet," she crooned into his hair. "Now, bye bye." She fell off the side, her laughter echoing in the midnight air until it abruptly cut off. They all rushed over but could see no broken body upon the ground.

CHAPTER
16

ONCE MORE
INTO THE
VOID

Within myself there is a Void
all that's left once Chaos freed
so slowly means
not all of me
bleeds black or white.
But when the Void stares hungrily
at some sliver of myself
I see
when wading
past the gray so deep
I catch the waters darken
too late, or maybe
no, wait—

I can hear you thinking from here, Zeph. Just come in."

"Can't. It's turned this way."

She herself stood facing away from him while slumped over her balcony railing, with Zeph hidden a few feet above on a ledge, blending into the dark. His shadowy form crouched on all fours and his open wings pressed tight against the castle wall.

Yawning, Willow forced herself to stay awake despite the late hour, as she hadn't seen him since the ball two nights ago.

"It's blind," she insisted softly.

"Doubtful. Don't turn around."

"You sound like Torrent."

"We all sound like Torrent." And then, like he couldn't help asking, "What exactly did she say?"

"Warned me to get out of here. For Benny."

"You should get out of here for *you* too. I just can't figure out how to make it happen without implicating my people." He sighed. "But I'm trying. Fuck. If the next challenge doesn't kill you, the Voidroamer will."

She lifted her head as far back as it would go, baring her neck to the sky. "I'm scared to ask why he frightens you. Is he a Metaporter?"

"He doesn't frighten me."

Willow's head fell forward as she laughed.

"He's a threat. I take all threats seriously."

"And just what sort of a threat is he?"

Zeph's voice grew ever softer, falling around her like snow, as he answered, "No one really knows *what* he is. My people have fled from him for what seems like millennia. But fifty years ago, he forced us into this…slavery. Used our own spells to create siphons that trap pieces of our internal void, all as a way to boost the power of the siphon bearer. Gave them to a seventeen-year-old grieving father gone mad."

"Why would he do all that for Soren?"

"A deal. Soren spends the actual time needed with us for siphoning, and perhaps when he has collected enough or some specified amount of time has passed—we don't know the details—we suspect the Voidroamer will take the siphons back for his own use."

"Why can't you all just leave?"

"He has pieces of us, of our metaphysical souls. If he destroys the siphons, he destroys *us*. No one can risk angering our puppet master, even if he himself dangles from much longer strings."

"But *you* came to Spinor Falls. You spent years away."

He sighed. "A loophole. We're allowed the time to molt, as our infant feathers fall and the new ones grow in. I don't have that excuse anymore, feigned as much of it was. And there's no leaving for me when there's another challenge for you on the morrow."

"So soon?"

"The king's in a rush now. The Winged get no say in this one. That means he'll make sure there are deaths this time."

"Like with that turret?"

"You know about that?"

"It was a clean break—and he was standing right there!"

"Yes, he enjoys reasons to act the savior. It foments his power and just shows off his face, really. But if you knew that so early on—why did you agree to enter this competition? Willow, why'd you make that awful choice?"

"To be near you."

She heard his sharp intake of breath, the loudest her spy had been all night. She continued, "And to learn, and figure out where I come from, maybe. Also, subconsciously I think I knew he was never going to give me a real choice."

"I've always loved that about you."

It was so hard not to turn around that time, not to see his face when he continued, "Your instincts are spot on. And you don't overthink like I do. That's how I knew you'd get here. I knew you'd make it, even when it killed me not to carry you over from Farrow's Forge on my own back."

"Then why bring me to Ingress only to steal months of my life away? How could you do that to me?" She struggled to lower her voice.

"I didn't. I swear it wasn't me, Willow. Please believe that, fledgling."

"You won't tell me who or why, though, isn't that right?" She wanted to murder his guilty silence to pieces. Tears sprang to her eyes, a light mist of twisted fear, as she asked, "How much longer can I last like this? Sometimes it feels like I can't even use my powers properly, Zeph. I don't see the ether I use, not like the educators say I should. Sometimes the lines are there, but I think maybe I'm just imagining them."

"Like I said before, you're running off instinct. Like a baby who's just opened her eyes but has the strongest and most innate form of control I may have ever witnessed." His wings rustled. "I'm curious. What shade of copper is ether to you?"

"Yellowish. And very bright. When I manage to see it."

His voice was full of wonder. "The folds I see are also a very bright shade. There must be some undefined connection between our abilities. Come to think of it, the Tug is thought to be—at least, in certain circles—a long strand of nascent and internal ether that would naturally begin to hurt when pulled taught over long distances. But why does it never stop burning once severed? And while its formation makes more sense for twins, how could it come to exist between an unrelated Exowinged and a Kinetic? Perhaps I should write a paper on the apparent commonalities between Guide pairs. Even if our evidence is anecdotal, that may be all we ever have."

She chuckled at hearing him sound more like himself than she had since arriving in Maddooinne. "There's no taking the academic out of you, Zeph. I've always loved that about *you*."

They were quiet for some time before she bent over to rest her head on her forearms with a sigh, stare into the sea of dark unknown below, and say, "I was glad to realize you have your father here. Is he good to you?"

"My dad's been bearing the price of generations worth of

mistreatment and mistakes, fledgling. He's not the most sentimental of beings—"

"Neither are you."

"Does that bother you?"

"No, I like you as you are."

He paused, the silence pregnant with something neither of them could bear for long, before saying softly, "I would recognize the sound of Father's wings anywhere—they still mean safety, still mean home. Sometimes in Spinor Falls, the wind would tease me with a whisper of them. But I'd look around only to be disappointed."

"And your mother?"

"She died while I was away. Fell sick."

"I'm so sorry."

They fell quiet for a while, just basking in the calm after a difficult day, as they used to back on the island, when a knock sounded on her bedroom door.

Benny woke and moaned, "Who's there? Go away."

Willow flipped around, glancing up at Zeph, whose gaze was ablaze and trained on hers, as if he knew without even looking who the caller might be.

The knocking grew insistent just as Willow swung open the door.

Her mouth dropped.

Philip leaned against the frame. Sienna was there too, arms crossed and nose in the air.

"I'm taking you up on your offer," said the young man with his perpetual smirk.

Willow looked pointedly at Sienna, then back at him.

Sienna said, "We can't trust that you won't off him in some secluded corner of the castle and make it look like an accident."

"I see," said Willow before calling out behind her, "Benny, come along."

"Now wait a second—" said Phillip.

"So I'm supposed to be the one who's outnumbered?"

"How about we all go, then?" Reynor stepped out from behind a large sconce, her small dog in her arms. Willow was glad to see his panting little face now wide awake, framed by long brown ears and a sweet white spot on his forehead. Scratching away behind those floppy ears, Reynor looked a bit like him in her brown-haired pigtails.

Sienna whirled on her. "Go where?"

Reynor scoffed. "Please. I know what you're up to."

Willow tried not to sound as suspicious as Sienna when she asked, "How?"

"These two are really bad at sneaking around," said the little girl. "They've been fighting about searching for the map with you all night. In a lot of castle corners. And I'm much better at hiding than they are."

"We can't all be the size of a mine mouse," scoffed Sienna.

"Or sound like a banshee," shot back Reynor.

Sienna lunged.

Philip grabbed her by the shoulders as he said, "She's just a kid."

"She could kill us all if she wanted." Sienna flapped her arms with dramatic flair.

"Yeah, don't underestimate kids," said Benny, finally appearing at Willow's side and sleepily rubbing an eye with his fist.

Reynor looked him over and scoffed. "You can't even use your powers enough for display. Everyone knows that."

"Hey!"

"You're the definition of an infant."

"Am not."

"Are too."

"Am—"

Willow pulled him into her arms. "We all go. Civilly, and with the understanding that if the map is found, we take equal credit."

"The king won't like that," said Reynor, voice dropping. "He really does want an heir."

Phillip looked over at Sienna, who tossed her hair back as he spoke. "Sienna wants the position. She'll take it."

To Willow's surprise, one by one they all nodded their agreement and filed into her room.

Sienna perched on the edge of a bed and asked, "Where do we start, then? Anyone got information?"

Willow offered, "I know the master mapmaker left the map with the most precious thing they possessed. But I don't know what it was." She did her best not to look out at the terrace, where her source might still be listening to the contestants bickering back and forth.

"What kind of valuable would someone leave with a map?"

"Should we start in the treasury?"

"Why the hell would the mapmaker leave anything in the Exokinetic treasury?"

"Because he was a Kinetic."

"I'd bet that's not true," said Willow.

Phillip flopped back onto her bed, sprawled out like it was his. "Oh? Kinetics are the strongest beings in Ingress. We are the *only* successful merchants. Who else could safely travel this place so well?"

Willow shook her head at his typical Kinetic ego. She was unwilling to bet that one of her kind would save or even know a Ferver like Victor, but she kept that to herself. "I think the Winged or the Porters are best suited for travel here, no?"

Reynor cocked her head. "But the Winged are tied to this place. They can't be traveling the world. And the Porters are long dead, if they were ever even real."

Benny leaned against Willow's thigh and glared at the ground. She stroked a hand through his hair and asked, "Where was the last place the mapmaker was seen? Let's retrace any and all steps we've heard about."

Phillip bit his lip.

"Speak up, then," said Willow, catching the hesitation in his expression.

"I don't want to go there."

"Oh, the great Philip Emslie is scared? Scaredy, scaredy Kinetic," smiled Reynor. "I just turned eleven. You more scared than me?"

"Ha! You're eleven!" said Benny.

"I'm older than you, infant."

"By one year!"

Sienna nudged Phillip. "Come on, then. Where was the mapmaker last seen?"

"The Sky Dungeon."

Willow wasn't sure why, but Sienna's face tightened. Then Reynor tried to back out of going without saying as much, which led to a loud mocking argument with the cousins.

Benny tugged her shirt. She bent down to his level so he could whisper in her ear.

"I got an idea from what you said in the mines. You think the Winged mapped this place together? Like with every mission or whatever, they just added to their map? Maybe the master mapmaker isn't a single person."

She was taken aback once again at his mind. "That's a brilliant thought, Benny. But it would mean Zeph is lying to me."

"He's lied to you before."

"Only by omission. And if he had the map, he could save me from all this...I don't think he'd do that."

"He would if his people order it. We can't just break the duty to our kin here, lady. Family is all we've got. Most of us anyhow."

She wrapped him up in her arms, rocking for a moment.

The trio were staring.

"What?" she asked, eyes daring them, Reynor especially, to insult Benny.

"We should get going. It's only a few minutes to sunrise, and we're all in. Are you?" asked Phillip.

At Willow's nod, the five of them set off, passing by clusters of Kinetic guards at their posts who could not hide their surprise at the sight of them together. Multitudes of eyes traced their steps, some guards even trailing behind.

The cousins knew the way to the dungeons, and Willow learned they were distantly related to Soren.

"I stayed here many childhood summers," said Sienna, making her dress float around herself as she walked, just like the imperious ladies at court looking to make an impression.

Willow couldn't help it. She kinetically tugged at the hem a little.

Sienna spun around, glaring at Willow and Reynor, before marching on.

Reynor laughed. "Are we really gonna help her be queen?"

"Better the devil we know," Willow answered loudly at Phillip's deep chuckle.

Reynor smiled, her dog pressed tight against her chest, and looked up for a moment to say, "This is my puppy, Sprite. He says thanks."

Willow rubbed the little canine's head and nodded.

"I was standing by your room tonight on purpose, you know, to thank you. With a warning."

Willow sighed. "Such a common thing here."

Reynor skipped a little as she walked, the child in her shining through. "You danced with the king's champion like he's not evil. But I promise you, he is."

Willow halted.

"My family was hunted down for leaving this place after the king demanded I join his competition."

"Your family fled? Why?"

"The rightful heir fled too. The crown prince could return any day and take back his birthright. Why would anyone want a throne like that?"

"I see."

"Point is…the Winged killed them all. My family. And then the recent champion came for me himself."

"On whose orders, though?"

"What does that matter?"

"I think it matters when you don't have a real choice. Or when you use what little power you do have to save a small creature in a portal mine."

"You did that."

"No, he's the one who—"

"We're here!" announced Sienna.

They had crossed the entire distance of the castle and come to a small stone door. "People are only ever sent here to die in agony," Philip said, glancing around. No one had followed them on the last leg of their journey.

"Why are there no guards?" asked Willow.

"Apparently, they're not necessary," said Sienna. "And no one knows why."

The door was shut, and no amount of jostling or slamming or kinetic pressure on the lock worked.

Reynor stepped forward, looking very serious even as Sprite licked her face.

She stared at the door, unblinking for so long it grew frightening, when for a moment Willow imagined she could see the wood wobble in place just before the entire door turned to dust.

"How?" she whispered.

Reynor shrugged. "They tell me I see tinier strands of ether than

A WORLD OR TWO OVER

you can. Because I see the dots in the lines. So I just pull them apart. All at once."

"But can you do that to clothing?" asked Phillip.

"Why does your mind always go there?" commented Willow as Sienna laughed.

A hiss. Their heads snapped to the side. They were now all looking into a dank dungeon.

"Are there any portals in there to worry about?" asked Willow.

Philip shook his head. "No, it's not built on ground. We only hear rumors of the worst criminals ever to live, and of monsters even worse than the criminals."

"Maybe we shouldn't have destroyed the door, then," huffed Benny with a pointed glance at Reynor.

"Shut it. They're all locked up…probably." Reynor marched inside, holding Sprite so close the poor dog squirmed.

Philip and Sienna shot each other an unsure look as they followed.

The corridor was long and led down an endless flight of stone stairs, but the dank darkness gave way to light, of all things. Specifically, the sun.

At the bottom, a pile of writhing soot in the corner of a cell seemed the most worrisome thing about the place. Willow could see other cells, some with shackles and some without, but they were all adjacent to each other on the opposite side of the chamber and completely drenched in dawn. Because instead of a wall to confine the prisoners, just past the bars was an open drop into the sky.

"Wow," said Benny, looking impressed, but not for the reason Willow expected. "None of the bars have doors."

"What?" she asked, realizing he was right. "How does that work?"

Benny chewed his lip a moment before exclaiming, "I bet the Winged fly the prisoners right into these cells from outside!"

A loud hiss echoed once more. They all jumped. Then realized it was coming from that pile of soot against the bars, swarming, unfolding into the form of a captive.

"Got any real food?" he rasped, milky blue eyes shining.

"No, sir," said Willow.

Out through the bars, he extended his arm, wrapped in layers of old, fraying cloth that fluttered. He beckoned her over, but Willow didn't move.

"What?" she whispered.

"Come here."

"Not on your life."

"You look familiar. Have we met?" he said, head cocked.

Willow knelt to his level without coming closer. "No, sir. But I am here looking for something of great value."

He barked a single laugh that soon rolled over into a few. "Not even my life's got value, and that's all you'll find here. For now." He turned onto his back, staying close to the bars. Holding on to one with his right hand, he looked over at the open wall. "Gonna jump today."

"But that's suicide!" said Reynor.

He snapped his head back over toward her. "You the brains of this operation, then?"

"No, I just meant—"

"You just meant?"

"How long have you been in here?" cut in Willow.

"Twenty-eight years and thirty-six days." He smiled. "How long you been alive?"

"Not quite sure anymore."

He smirked at her, sitting up, wavering as though drunk. "I'm going to jump."

"And for how many years have you been saying that?"

"You think I won't? I've seen a lot of jumpers. Years and years of them. Men. Strong men. A lady's maid. A child. Even a pregnant woman. They've all taken refuge in the sky. Sweet, sweet abyss." That hiss grew more pronounced. "Figure it's about my turn, don't you?"

Philip pushed his way forward, impatience taking over. "Where's the master map? You seen it around here during all these years?"

The prisoner cackled and curled back up into his pile of soot. "Go away. I'm busy planning tomorrow."

"A lot of planning needed to step into the sky, then?" asked Philip.

The man refused to acknowledge them after that.

So they searched the empty area but ultimately did as he said, returning to their separate rooms feeling very disappointed and a little disturbed. But Willow and Benny remained awake two hours past dawn, unable to sleep, chatting about recent events—from the tempestuous ball to their fragile alliance with the others. They nodded off while discussing parts of the castle they should search next for the map, the monotony of list making lulling them to sleep.

Willow shot up later when something banged, realizing after a few seconds that it was a knock.

"Yes?" she yawned, opening the door to a liveried courier with a silver tray. "What time is it?"

"An hour past noon," said the man. "I have urgent news, miss."

She plucked a note from the outstretched tray that bore very formal instructions to present herself to the main hall immediately. The messenger had already rushed off by the time she finished reading, presumably to deliver more notes.

Turning to where her roommate's little head peaked out from the covers on his bed, Willow said, "Benny, I think it's another challenge. You sleep. I'll go."

Willow caught Philip's profile as she stepped into the hall and felt a deep concern at how uncharacteristically serious he looked. A small crowd had gathered, ranging from staff to residents, all pushing to see the dais, and Willow had to shove herself forward to get near the front beside her fellow competitor.

"What is it?" she asked, neck straining to see.

"Someone's dead." Philip nodded to where a closed coffin rested, covered in banners of red-orange. "And I think our plans just went to shit."

"Those colors belong to Clan Vermilion," said Sienna's panting voice from behind them as she fought her way through. Willow bared her teeth in anger as the words sunk in.

"Do you mean—" Willow started, but was cut off by the announcement of the king's arrival.

He stood at the front decked in black robes, Zeph and Vivek on either side of him, chanting.

The king opened his arms and said, "We are gathered here today—"

"For some sort of black wedding, apparently," muttered Philip.

"—to mourn the loss of Reynor Marten of Sky Clan Vermilion."

Willow felt the blood drain from her face.

The king continued, his face somber but serene. "This heartbreaking loss comes as a great surprise to us all. But our once potential heir will be long remembered for her unique and precocious powers. Born able to do what no others have displayed so young, she was an asset to our thriving kingdom—that is, until her desire to take the throne must have made her too rash in judgment. She was found slain in the dungeons this morning, having ventured into that most dangerous of areas in the night, no doubt in search of the master map."

"Lies," whispered Sienna through gritted teeth. "He did this."

Though Soren kept speaking, Willow heard nothing else.

"This is my fault," she whispered, struggling against the urge to vomit.

"Yes," said Sienna, pushing her aside and disappearing into the crowd, but not before saying, "Our truce just died too. I'm not turning out like her."

Philip sighed. "He killed her because of the dog. A life taken for the one spared."

Tears tracked down Willow's pale, frozen face. "I really did make this happen. I should have left Sprite in the mines."

Philip shook his head. "She didn't want to live without that dog. He was all she had left."

"But I shouldn't have made that choice for her."

"No, this is how it would have always gone. He wanted someone dead in that challenge. You skirted his rules. Then we formed a public alliance by traipsing around last night. He didn't like that either. He's breaking us up."

Willow leaned against his steady side for a moment. "You're surprisingly intuitive for a pervert."

"You're expectedly judgmental for a woman."

"You little—"

Ivan stomped his cane for silence and glared their way.

"In other news," said the king, looking over at them too, his voice now peppy and upbeat. "We have three final challengers and one potentially final challenge this afternoon."

Willow clung, barely breathing, to hot stone with her fingertips, her body dangling leagues above ground.

The kinetic ferry challenge had started out simple enough. Instructed to sail to the other side from the ramparts of Maddooinne to the closest edge of Mount Onstel, the winner was promised immunity from participation in the next challenge.

Until the goal of getting there first switched to getting there at all, for it was clear the king was intent on narrowing down his heir, just like Zeph had predicted.

At the start, they had lined up next to each other along the ramparts at the perimeter of the realm, where the ferries used to transport travelers back and forth docked. Except all of those before them lacked any reins or footholds.

Willow was distracted a moment when she noticed Benny struggling up a ladder to reach them and settling down to watch, which allowed the cousins to take the average-sized, drier chunks of rock for their own, leaving her with either the most massive or mossiest boulder to jump upon.

Philip shot her an amused smile from his perfectly sized boulder.

And for the first time, Soren watched. Decked in robes of red and gold, bright as the sun that weighed them all down with a near-blinding shower of its rays, the king, holding a scepter, stood above the competition on a huge, protected ferry with a dozen of his off-duty Hover Councilmen and a full legion of his Winged guard.

At the start, the contestants sailed forward at about the same pace, Willow barely keeping up while trying to maintain her footing despite the size of her ferry. Until suddenly, the air turned into a zone of floating stone and rock that jolted without warning.

The Hover Council was in play.

Keeping both the ferry and what was ahead of them in sight at the same time proved a tricky task for them all.

Instinctively shifting to all fours, Willow refused to look down. The world below was a dizzying array of blended colors that made her feel ill. She could tolerate heights but no longer enjoyed them, not since the fall off that bleekmere tree or Zeph's terror-filled gaze when she woke sprawled across icy ground.

She worked now to pull at the edges of her rocky conveyance like the Hover Council held up the land, though she kept hers floating without actually visualizing any lines of ether.

Sienna tore past, getting close enough to whip her braids into Willow's face. Willow ducked in time, but pitched forward and slipped off her ferry.

For a frantic second, she simply knew she would die. And there was a peace in that, a sort of stillness in the air that finally allowed her to notice a thick rope of ether she tossed over at her falling ferry, yanking it toward her plummeting body until she crashed into its side.

Willow quickly formed a parachute of power she could actually see to stabilize its position in the air, forcing the mossy boulder to a halt. Holding her breath, she gripped the edge with a grunt, lifting her body kinetically just enough to retrieve her holstered mirrax with the other hand and slam one end into the rock. With that physical anchor, she pulled herself back over.

Adjusting her weapon, she sank a blade on either side into stone and positioned herself perpendicular to its handle. Sitting down on her haunches, she could now hold on more safely using both hands and keep her body away from the two exposed blades.

With a stable grip achieved, she finally had the confidence to build up speed.

Sienna stared, mouth agape, as Willow soon soared by.

Willow looked over her shoulder at the other girl, raised a brow, and sent dust flying into her face.

"Hah!" Willow said, then streaked away as Sienna tried to regain the balance of her eyesight and the spinning ferry.

Her lead was short-lived.

The other girl zipped ahead of them all within minutes, completely uncaring of deadly heights and wholly intent on her goal.

"Hey, Willow," called Phillip from beside her, eyes gleaming. "Race you!"

"What the hell else do you think this is, Emslie? A sunny stroll?"

she asked, steering her boulder away, but he slammed into her, tailgating her ferry.

"Sharp blades you've got there." He sounded quite pleased as he asked, "You know what? You like deals, right, Willow? Sienna's going to beat us at this rate. Let's join powers to get well ahead of her, but as soon as we do, it's every contestant for himself."

"*Her*self!"

"Sure."

She looked back at him in suspicion. "And why not join forces with your cousin?"

"Simple. I have to win to live. And she won't trust anyone after this morning."

Willow reached behind for his hand and yanked her body onto his better ferry, slamming her ax down into stone again, and watching her former boulder plummet. Philip slipped a hand around her waist for stability and grinned before kneeling beside her, the two of them holding the mirrax handle to catapult their stony steed forward.

They neared Sienna, everything going well, just as the sky turned a murky green.

Everyone and everything paused, including their breathing.

No clouds rolled in. No winds tore through. The world simply changed color in the blink of an eye. Then deepened so much, she was afraid she'd lost her sight.

The king started shouting something she could not decipher, his ferry and the Kinetics atop it a hazy blur of colors in the dark.

Willow held back the urge to scream for Zephyr when her entire body broke into a cold sweat.

Philip cursed beside her. "This must be part of the challenge. Keep your eyes on the ferry, Willow. Stop looking around."

She felt as if she still had a hold of the boulder, though, and she was so scared, she grabbed his arm. "Philip," she gasped out.

"What? Hey, why'd you go silent? Willow?"

Through chattering teeth, she managed to say, "The Voidroamer. He's coming."

He barked a laugh. "And I'm High Queen of the Faeries."

"It's what that woman was screaming about during the ball, or don't you remember?"

"Oh, yes, *she* seemed very sane."

"Where's Benny?" She spotted him behind the ramparts. "Philip, we're going back."

He pulled the ferry forward. "What? Absolutely not. We can't just turn around in the middle of a contest."

"Can't you see it's already over? Look inside yourself. Can't you feel the sickness in the air?"

"Nonsense. We had a *deal*. Why—"

He was cut off.

A bright light opened in the middle of their field of sky, directly beside the king. It expanded into a crimson orb through which a large leg stepped out.

Willow pulled the ferry back toward the ramparts, with Phillip finally too shocked to put up a fight. A body entered the sky, five times the size of a man, as large as the king's ferry and its occupants. But it was no man, more like a bipedal creature with the deformed head of a jackal. Wings forged of flashing fire sprouted from where its neck met its back, lighting up the sky and hanging like two massive scythes on either side of its body.

That amorphous body constantly shifted in place, giving the general shape of a person wearing smoke for robes that merged into the surrounding thunderclouds. Worst of all to Willow, its mouth had no lips—it was a wide-open void she could not force her eyes to look into, as if a destroyed universe and all its horrors resided within.

Their ferry soared so fast that it slammed down onto the ramparts, its edges crumbling into pieces of stone. Willow and Philip tumbled over just as the creature fully arrived.

"Willow!" whimpered Benny.

Willow knelt for her boy and scooped him up, his little arms tightening around her neck. High above, the voidaggen's eyes blinked, crimson pupils suddenly flashing into existence.

Philip lay frozen at the edge of the wall, staring out at the great conflagration in the sky.

"It can't be," he whispered.

Willow nudged his shoulder with her own. "I've been saying that for months now."

"Let's get out of here already," urged Benny.

Willow and Philip nodded, turning for the stairs, as everything went blindingly bright and a deep voice intoned, "Mine."

The word held a strange power that seemed to call to something primal inside everyone present. They all froze as the Voidroamer grabbed Soren's ferry and shook it. A curdled laugh cut through the air.

It distracted Willow from the haze overtaking her mind. "Where's Zeph?"

Phillip turned to her sharply. "On a nickname basis, are you?"

She shot him a glare and tried to make her legs move, but they gave up. She fell to her knees, that sick feeling spreading through her faster now. Benny could feel it too. He was turning green in her arms as they both struggled not to vomit.

"Sienna!" Philip's sudden scream sounded yanked from his soul. He tried to lift their ferry from the landing with his powers, but he was shaking so hard it barely moved.

Willow dragged herself over to the edge on her knees, an arm holding Benny and the other hanging over to grip the short, broken pieces of the wall.

She could see Sienna was no longer on her ferry. She floated stationary in the sky, arms splayed out, held in place by the Voidroamer, or some part of it. An extra limb like a tentacle sprouted from its chest, forming a black tunnel that shot into her torso. The Voidroamer pulled it out of her mangled body with an abrupt slurping suck, and she dropped dead to the cold earth far below.

Benny started sobbing even as he held still.

"We have to go." Willow tugged on Philip's pant leg, but he couldn't move, shell-shocked, looking down into the darkness that now held his cousin.

Willow called on her meditation training to focus, reining in her fears just enough to get to her feet.

The Voidroamer whipped its head in their direction and licked at the air. "Sweet," it said in a whisper louder than a scream. "Thick, clear void."

It sailed toward them, wings of cold fire swallowing up the distance and dropping the temperature in its wake.

Willow ran, rushing along the narrow pathways bordering the realm, with Benny tight against her chest and Philip close behind. She'd reached a battlement with a stairway exit when one of the Kinetic guardsmen grabbed her.

"What are you doing? Let me go!" she screeched.

"Orders," he grunted, face pale.

The Voidroamer came to a stop before them, one clawed wing having dragged Soren's ferry with it. The king dismounted with his men—including Zephyr, the only one standing ramrod straight instead of quivering.

Soren himself pulled Willow over to the creature, one hand on her neck and the other on her elbow.

"The strongest Kinetic in all our land," he said with a shake of her head in his shuddering grip, "I give to you as payment for leaving my kingdom in peace."

The creature cocked its head, mouth widening, teeth somehow growing sharper. Then it laughed. "*Your* kingdom? Hmmm. So much chaos you've stored. But the void. The true void is rare." He swayed forward.

Willow's world turned ever colder, his meaning sinking in.

"Benny, it wants you. Port," she said under her breath. "Please."

That black limb started to extend. "Mine. Yes," the creature hissed.

Benny breathed so harshly, his body convulsed from fear.

"Wait!" Philip stepped forward, bursting between Willow and the murderous creature.

The Voidroamer shoved him aside, right over the ramparts.

Transfixed, Willow stared at the roiling mass lengthening toward them, unable even to watch Philip plunge to his death. This thing before her seemed to drink up all the rational thought and feeling she once had.

It grew closer.

She swayed forward, numb yet yearning to touch it. *What would it feel like to feel again?*

A hand pushed her hard from behind. She toppled over into the sky too, just barely able to hold on to Benny, gravity taking them both down without mercy.

Zeph had said to her in training once, "You can't fall faster than I can fly."

He proved himself right. She felt large arms wrap around her, along with the parachute-like force of his wings, slowing them down gradually as they reached the lowest tip of Maddooinne's floating diamond mines.

Willow pushed her lips against Zeph's ear to pant, "Get us far away. Please."

"No," he said.

"No?" she shrieked.

"We go where it can't follow," he shouted over a clap of thunder.

Willow shivered, worried, when the sky started flashing strange colors in an epileptic warning of oncoming slaughter. "Just get Benny out of here."

He maneuvered Willow more firmly against his front, his arms beneath her legs, as Benny crawled onto Zeph's back and sunk his little fangs between Zeph's shoulders for a better grip.

"You're not going to let go, are you, voidsman?" asked Zeph without a flinch.

Benny didn't lift his head.

"Good." Zeph shouted over a sudden wind. "Now find the void pool within you when you need to port. Tie a memory, something calm and emotionless, as an anchor into that pool. Fall into it. Feel nothing."

Benny whimpered.

Zeph neared the Northern Portal Mines, coming to a hover, trying to navigate them in the dark without stepping down to the earth.

The *thing* whooshed past and came to a stop before them.

"Foolish, foolish," it repeated, a curling tongue darting out in their direction.

Its form grew blurry, encompassed by its own smoke. The smoke cleared all of a sudden, and the thing was now a stunning woman, hair dressed in gold-brown fire and its body robed in ombre hues of sunset, skirt a carpet of sky that curled and furled in waves indistinguishable from the night air. Tendrils of it dipped into the portals around her. Yet its face was still empty and blank, but for a gash of a mouth.

"I *am* the void." It smiled somehow—a lovely, becoming smile. "You hold what is mine by right." She held out long, long arms, both so welcoming. "Come."

A voice like sugar, like the long-awaited call of family, swept over Willow.

She held out her hand and would have stepped forward if Zeph weren't holding her in a death grip in the air.

"That won't work on me, ancestor," he called as he rushed away, gaining height, high up in the sky within moments. But the thing slithered after them, visibly amused at its prey thinking it could escape.

Its smug sluggishness might have given them an advantage…if Willow had not noticed it already had Benny. Emotion crashed back into her body.

"No," she shrieked.

Benny's chest shook with the vibrations of the tunneling arm that had just reached into his tiny back. He lifted his head from Zeph's neck to look Willow in the eye.

"Go," Willow commanded Benny. "Port! Think of something."

Zeph was still flying them away as fast as he could.

Benny's eyes glossed over in a way she had never seen before now. Was this the emptiness of an approaching death?

His neck swung back as if pulled by a hook, his little body flinched, and he vanished.

"Yes!" screamed Willow.

Zeph took that moment to hurtle down to earth.

CHAPTER
17

TOGETHER
AWAY

A tree won't bend for just a breeze
Though a sapling may,
With naive ease, transform
Should a zephyr
Fly by his willow
To herald a storm

Zephyr had always likened the coppery gold of Willow's eyes to the molten appearance of a patent portal…though he was never quite free to say so.

And now, after the squeezing force of the portal exit pressed her body against him and her stricken gaze lanced through his own, he was still not quite free to say so. Not while death tapped its feet nearby.

"Fledgling, don't forget to breathe." He snapped open his wings at the height of their exit launch, parachuting them a moment before flying down through the twisting limbs and leaves of a dark forest fraught with manducaré.

He had soared them right through a penta-directional portal

to the Shadowlands, one of the riskiest territories for the Flock to enter, but also the closest multi-destination portal he had recognized.

"Try to keep your eyes open," he said before dropping them both into another portal by a massive rosebush. Willow suppressed a shriek as she only just missed a thorn in her eye.

Zeph led them through one hidden gateway after another, from damp forest to snowy mountaintop and finally to scorching hillside, where he landed.

Hands on his hips, he finally let loose a deep breath. "Good. It won't find us here."

"But how sure can we be?" asked Willow, still trembling with the aftershocks of a fear so innate that Zeph knew her body had disconnected from her mind in the Sky Realm.

"Ninety-five percent sure. It was the best I could do in a matter of minutes."

"Zeph, this is not the time for making fun of me with numbers."

He shot her a look, the same one he used to give her in class when she was not paying attention. "That first portal had five possible destinations, the next one two, and the final one two again. Do the math."

"Oh, so you actually do know the probability. Good. Great. Good. That makes me feel better." Voice as shaky as the rest of her, she dropped to her knees, visibly willing the adrenaline to subside. It only got worse. "All of them. They're all *gone*. And Benny must be so scared. How will he ever find me now?" Her head snapped up. "And what about you?"

"What about me?"

"The king could kill you at any moment. You *left*."

"Life is not without its risks. Rest." He placed a hand on her shoulder, stopping her as she made to get up. "And what excuse would I have if I went back?" He bowed low, holding his other hand to his chest, and announced, "Sorry about that, sire, but she simply matters more to me than you."

"You could be dead at any moment." She rose anyway and threw her arms around him, clutching hard. "Just like Benny."

"Willow, stop that. He's not going to kill me now. He has a much more important matter on his mind, and he'll need every siphon he's got to deal with it. The Voidroamer is the ultimate distraction, I promise you. And if that thing can't get to us, it will be dealing with Soren. There may be no kingdom left to worry about by now." His voice dropped off at the end.

She pulled back to say, "Your family is a very formidable bunch."

"I know."

"Look at how you all seemed so in control, while I've never felt as useless as I did back there when that *thing* took over my whole sense of self."

"A void trick. You always had control. It just felt like you didn't."

"There's a lot to unpack there."

"Yes."

"But let's start with—where are we?"

He smiled. "We should be quite close to the Emberlands, actually."

"As in Void Valley?"

"No. The Emberlands is a massive realm, the one to which Void Valley belongs. Its other lands are mostly barren now. The Metashifters had multiple villages nearby. The voidsmen of old used to reside here, and then a tribe of Metaporters spent an uncharacteristically long era tied to the region. We should be closest to their ancient lands."

"Why are the voidsmen always the ones dying or disappearing?"

"Metas are people of the mind, in a sense. Much less combative, less likely to raise armies for a cause. Exos can be…unreasonably aggressive against those they do not understand."

"Much like my people back home," she observed.

He laughed. "When it came to me, certainly. Perhaps they could just tell I had blood on my hands."

"Did you? Back then?"

He sighed. "No. But I was raised to consider my family's actions my own. What one has done, we all have done. We take responsibility for the choices of the unit. I know it's hard for you to fathom. Your mother never thought that way. She wanted you to be your own person."

"You're right. I was lucky."

"I'm not elevating one approach above another."

"You spent your childhood thinking you have blood on your hands just because your parents did. How is that healthy?"

He looked down at her with eyes that shone more with admiration than judgment. "You spent *your* childhood believing you had to single-handedly save your mother's estate from ruin. How is that healthy?"

She smiled. "To each their own flaws, I guess."

"Yes." He pulled her tight against him with a desperation at odds with the moment.

"Zeph?"

"Just a second."

He looked like an avenging angel staring out at the green expanse of rolling hills in the dying light, with his scythe held in a white-knuckled grip, his black wings spread wide behind him, and his sweat-soaked shirt tossed over a bare shoulder. She stepped forward after a long while, interrupting his thoughts with a timid hand on his slick back. Hard muscle bunched beneath her touch.

"We need a plan," she whispered. "That includes finding Benny."

He tilted his head a fraction, a lock of dark hair falling into his eyes. "First things first. Food and shelter."

Willow looked down at her outstretched arm, feeling guilty she had not said anything yet about her skin map, but Zeph always had everything in hand. He even seemed to know the area well enough, leading her off toward a forested region in the distance with sure steps.

"Will you tell me how to get home now that we can talk freely, Zeph?"

He shook his head. "I'm sorry, fledgling. I really am."

She felt considerably less guilty as she stalked off in the opposite direction.

He followed, clasping her shoulder to spin her around, and said with a firm sort of reluctance, "But you will get there. I'll make sure of it."

"What's that supposed to mean? Zeph, how long can you keep me in the dark? Why did you even lead me to Ingress in the first place?"

"Didn't you want to know the truth about what you are?"

She slapped his chest, the sun glaring at him from behind along with her. "Couldn't you have just told me? You had years to do it!"

He pulled her closer, wrapping an arm around her waist. "Would you have believed me if I did?"

"Yes, of course."

"Would you have believed me about the voidsmen too?"

"Yes. Maybe. But either way, if you'd been honest, at least I would have had a choice in leaving everything behind."

He shook her. "You did have a choice. You chose to jump."

Her hands rose to grip his shoulders. "Is a decision made without all the facts a choice?"

Zeph's head dropped, and he took a deep breath in. After a long moment, she cupped his chin and lifted it, unable to bear the regret-riddled silence.

"It was selfish of me," he said, eyes flashing, "and so is this." He tossed his scythe to the side and pulled her body into his own, arms wrapped tight around her back, lips slanting over hers in a fierce kiss that felt like a lick of flame against her soul. Willow's hand rose to his jaw with a groan, her thumb pressing hard into his cheek and body melting against the force of a moment that arched her spine. She felt his wings curl around her back to steady her against him when he lifted both his hands to her face.

Zeph's lips trailed from hers down her throat, light stubble scratching against the soft skin of her neck as he whispered, "We shouldn't."

"Why?" she murmured, distracted. "'Cause we're Guides?"

"That too." His head lifted, ocean-deep eyes searing into hers, then turned to the side at the sharp caw of some large beast flapping above them. "It's just a bearded stork. But we should go. It'll be black as pitch very soon in this region, and there's a stream up ahead. It's a fail-safe location that my cousin swears never runs out of fish."

"Huh."

He tugged at her hand, but she remained frozen in place. "Willow?"

"Zeph…I think I know where to find Benny."

"Where?"

"His own fail-safe. And you're not going to like it. Incidentally, have I told you about how I was once exiled?"

Later, seated on a log beside a fire, roasting their speared fish, she told him of the clocktower Benny used as a family meeting location in case of separation, and they decided to kill two birds with one stone.

"My great-uncle Xavier has a long-term post in the East Skia Trading Village," Zeph explained, turning the spears. "He kept an eye on you for me. Made sure that old couple was keeping up their end of the bargain. Alerted me when you'd left for the Shadowlands. But now I know why it was so hard to track you to Farrow's. You took a pretty hairy detour. Xavier might also have word about the status of Maddooinne and whether we should return."

She tugged his ear. "If you were at Farrow's like I thought, why didn't you talk to me then? On that rooftop?"

"Farrow was watching, for one. And I could barely steal a small enough slice of time to check on you when I knew that night's storm would slow me down getting back to the king. But your stint in the Southern Portal Mines just before that had me worried—the Tug had become excruciating with you so far away. I had no clue you were in those fucking mines. When you reached Farrow's, I spied you speaking with his family and confirmed you were headed to Maddooinne."

"Is that how good a spy you are, then?" she asked, bumping her shoulder against his.

He laughed. "I've never seen you flutter your lashes before."

"ZEPH! Shut up. Zeph!"

He pulled her in with a wing and helped shut *her* up instead.

It took a few veiled portals, but Willow happily learned firsthand that if you could fly over your obstacles, you could take the most efficient string of portals to any destination. And as it turned out, Zeph knew quite a few.

Deep within the Voidsrange Mountains at one point, he pushed her forward against the edge of a steep drop.

"Our final portal is right down there," said Zeph.

"No." She turned to face him, clutching at his neck.

"You can do it, fledgling. I've seen you soar."

"But Zeph, it's too high."

"The Exowinged routinely push our young off great heights to teach them how to fly."

She held him tighter. "Don't you dare. May the Putrid Portal consume you if you try."

"Well said, just like a little native. Alright, I won't force you. But you will have to learn one day. And soon." He kissed her forehead, visibly disappointed, then flew them right through their destination despite her loud shrieking.

They erupted high into the sky from that same exit portal within Thornhaze Forest they first used on escaping the Voidroamer. Willow realized she had also ended up here with Jerald all those months ago, by accident, when she first visited the Shadowlands. She sighed into Zeph's neck at the thought, relieved to be here in the arms of the person she had sought, instead of stuck with the Skia.

Zeph's glorious wings unfurled, spreading out around her to control their descent, until their feet gently touched the frostbitten earth.

Tucked beneath Zeph's large cloak, she pressed against his warm torso when hit by the region's typical cold and smiled in relief as he spelled a gray fog to camouflage their movements in the night.

Through the manducaré-thick forest they trekked, before flying across the Border River and finally reaching the familiar pebbled road toward their destination, heat replacing the chill the closer they came to the East Skia Trading Village.

Willow wished above all that Benny had not lost hope she would come, that he'd hold on to the thought of her harder than to his parents' promises.

It began to drizzle, the sky foreshadowing a worsening downpour with a thick, natural fog.

They snuck into the village, deserted by this late hour, the townspeople long since tucked into their beds, supposably avoiding any assassins in the night that fit the description of her travel companion.

Upon reaching the town square and noting the rebuilt roads and locked-up stalls, Willow headed straight for Benny's fail-safe location.

"Over here." She sprinted away from Zeph's cover spell to kneel at the clocktower. Her face fell at the distinct lack of Benny's presence. "He should be here."

"Well, would you look at this?"

Willow groaned at a deep voice that always sank through her stomach like a rock. She turned to see the official figure of a man she had hoped to forget, and breathed, "You again."

James Alden lifted a blond brow. "Please. It's more of a shock to see you, a flagrant idiot returning to the scene of her crime so soon after being convicted. How in Orelio's name did you manage it?"

Behind him, like a black suit of cards unfolding from out of the ground, six men stepped forth in a V-shape to lock her in against the clocktower.

"She's a bit impulsive, as you must have noticed."

Zeph stood tall behind the Skia, the dim light of a lantern he had stripped off a store nearby held high for protection and sparking off his hair, raindrops dripping down his hardened face, and the ticking of the clocktower impregnating his every pause.

Willow noticed he kept his wings furled back and shoulders shrugged in a less threatening pose than usual. It did not help.

"Azakor." Alden spoke the name like something reviled yet revered, before turning on his heel. He lifted his palm to calm his visibly shell-shocked men, who had all raised their weapons against the distinctive spy. "What do you want?"

"To take the girl and go."

"Is she your next mark, then?"

"Clearly."

Willow tried pushing past Alden, but he grabbed her, his fingers long enough to wrap around her upper arm while his other hand snatched her mirrax from its holster. He inspected the crest with interest as he commented, "She doesn't seem all that afraid of the Winged Reaper."

"We've established she's got strange instincts."

Willow tried her hardest not to glare.

"You're lying to me, assassin. Are you even any good at what you do?"

Zeph chuckled, dark and deep. "How's your Guide doing again?"

"Shut your murderous mouth."

"Thanks, but my mouth isn't quite that talented."

Willow snorted a soft laugh.

Alden gave her a curious look, something in his face changing, mouth widening, and his next words coming slowly, "No, don't tell me. Is she *the* girl, or *your* girl?"

Willow decided she did have terrible instincts after all.

Zeph glanced up at the heavens in apparent frustration and without even appearing to look back over at them, sent a dagger deep through Alden's ankle.

Alden folded to the damp ground with a scream, his guards circling to cover him as Zeph shot up into the clouds.

One Skia melded away and reappeared hanging from the spire of the clocktower by his thighs. Limned by the moon, he raised a crossbow into the sky.

Another guard accosted Willow with a blade against her pulse before she could bolt.

"Bill, is that you?" Willow asked through gritted teeth.

"Knew you were trouble the second I laid eyes on you." A jolt of lightning flashed his craggy face bright. The same old gruff tone and mustached smile made her shiver.

"Let me go or I swear he'll kill you," she said, wriggling only until she felt a sharp sting against her throat.

Bill chuckled. "Stories say he might skin me alive or turn me inside out, my innards flopping about for all to see. But you know what I think? I think the Skia fight dirtier, and lookie here, don't we have ourselves a pretty hostage?"

She tried to move the knife, but she couldn't see it. When she peered over their joined shoulders, what she did see sent her into a panic, her body thrashing despite her bleeding neck. "Stop. I am not going back there! Stop it."

He was backing them up against the clocktower and panting, breath fetid as fresh refuse huffing into her face, their cheeks pressed together. Calloused fingers moved to wrap around her throat. "You found this portal, girlie. Only fair you get to use—"

A strong wind knocked them all off their feet, the gale force of Zeph's descent slamming right into two of the smaller men and knocking them unconscious. When Zeph turned, face feral and clear in a blaze of lightning, he held the Black Forge Scythe parallel to the ground with both hands.

Willow could barely recognize him.

Zephyr Azakor stood in the middle of seven men, one fallen from the spire above into a broken heap, one bleeding from an ankle with exposed bone, and the rest grounded and groaning.

Yet his face still read murder.

He snapped his wings closed, raised the scythe, and swept a full circle, culling the air as four new men burst into existence out of the shadows around him, torsos separating from their bodies just as they materialized.

Bill struggled to rise from the ground, one arm shaking to push himself toward a patch of shadow. He grabbed the edge of it and pulled.

Lightning flashed. And he lost hold of his escape in the glow.

Willow woke from her frightened stupor long enough to jump onto Bill's back, pushing his head down and wrapping her powers around his neck to aid her trembling hands.

"Zeph! I've got the last one!" she called out.

"Hang on," he shouted back.

In her peripheral vision, she could see Zeph holding Alden up in the air by his neck in a bright area beneath a swinging lamppost. The usual chilling apathy in her old friend's eyes had long since given way to cold fury.

Alden's rugged features twisted as he spat, "You have no sense of justice, you fucking fiend."

"And what of your justice? The exile of innocents?" Zeph brushed the man's exposed neck with a wingtip, the caress full of promise.

Alden managed to say, "If you kill me, this leads to war. Soren will have your head for it."

"Ah. The princeling thinks he understands politics."

Willow blinked up in surprise at the title, allowing Bill to flip her around and switch their positions, her face now planted against stone running wet with rivers of rain and gore.

"I warn you. Skia are without mercy," rasped Alden.

Zeph tightened the choke hold. "As are we."

"Let His Highness go or she dies!" screamed Bill, both hands now squeezing Willow's windpipe.

Willow wheezed.

Her vision faltered—

—and returned to find Zeph standing above her between flashes of light and shadow, thunder clapping and Bill's fish-dead eyes staring up into hers from his position face down on her stomach. With the sharp toe of the Black Forge Scythe sunk deep between his shoulder blades, Bill's body jerked against hers as Zeph yanked the weapon smoothly down his back and out his fresh corpse.

The Winged Reaper stood still a moment, his weapon washing clean in the deluge. The clock struck midnight, dinging twelve loud clangs, while Zeph secured his blade to his back and avoided eye contact.

The storm cleared.

He held out a hand in the sudden silence.

Willow's fingers twitched as she reached up, her very being numb in more ways than one. "You caused the storm?" she breathed.

He nodded, pushed Bill off her, and gathered her into his arms. "Show me the portal to the Shadowlands," he demanded.

Willow's round eyes grew even rounder.

"We're not going. He is." Zeph jerked his chin to the side, where Alden's unconscious body lay shrouded in flickering light.

"Did you—?"

"He's alive. We'll toss him home for medical care and get the damned void out of here."

"You spared him."

"My people don't need the political headache."

"How...virtuous."

His head dipped down toward hers, corded arm tensing beneath her back. "When someone tells you who he is, it's best to believe him."

"I do," she said, wondering at the taste of those words in her mouth. "I do. And I thank you, Zeph. Whoever you think you are, I thank you for saving me."

He pushed her hair away from her face, fingers threading through the sopping strands, before his head leaned down, pausing as a voice rang out—

"So you didn't listen. Again."

He dropped his face against her bleeding neck with a groan. Willow looked up.

The Flock stood on every roof and gutter within view, their wings outspread and weapons at the ready.

"Oh, hello," Willow said rather weakly.

After a beat, one of them sailed down, an aged man she had not met with a twirling gray beard to match his tired gray eyes. He took a long look at them, the lines bracketing his mouth tightening as Willow's arms rose to loop around Zeph's neck for support.

"It's too cold out here for these old bones," the mage said, walking off to the nearby town tavern.

His bones did not seem very old when he kicked in the door.

Zeph put Willow down with a look of warning, then he followed, one arm still around her waist. Cold inside and out, she kinetically recalled her mirrax from out of the hand of a decapitated guard as they walked past.

"Take your time," drawled the Winged mage from where he was stoking a fire to life within the tavern.

"Evening, Elder Linus," said Zeph in greeting, pausing in the doorway to remove his arm from around Willow to rest it before her on the doorframe.

"Get in here already."

"You're the one who said never to get into an enclosed space if I can help it."

"With an enemy, boy. Not your own grandfather." The fire was a little thing now, but alive. Linus dragged two of the stools stowed on the bar top over to a table by the hearth.

Willow figured they were quite outnumbered anyway, so she ducked under Zephyr's arm to say through chattering teeth, "That fire is just pitiful."

Linus watched her, brow raised, his expression blank.

She grabbed the bellows peeking out from behind a potted plant and got to work, coaxing the flames into a blaze and leaning into it with a sigh of pleasure, trying to banish the image of a pair of eyes boring into hers as the life leached out of them.

"Rare for someone to turn their back to me," Linus commented mildly.

Remaining tight-lipped, she could hear Zeph walking in and the sound of a seat being pulled back before he said, "We were about to get in touch."

Linus replied, "Save it. Xavier let us know you're here."

"I figured. He could have at least made contact with me first. The traitor."

"Funny *you* should call him that."

Now that really made Zeph angry. "Grandfather—"

"Soren has my son."

"He has all of us. I know that."

"No, boy, he has my son—your father—threatened with execution if you do not return."

Willow's head snapped back to them.

Zeph made to get up. "Then I will. Of course I will."

"The both of you."

Zephyr froze. "You'd have me trade one life for another," he said after a moment.

"We have no reason to believe he'll kill her. But we know for sure what he'll do to Vivek. And it will not be as swift as turning to wild ether from the crush of a siphon."

At that, Willow chimed in, "He'll feed me to the Voidroamer."

"That creature is gone," said the elder.

"Forever, or for now?" asked Zeph.

Linus sighed.

"Thought so," said Zeph, sitting back down.

"It wanted the boy, not her."

Willow offered, "I'll come if you tell me where Benny is."

Linus banged his fist against the table. "Done."

Zephyr grabbed that very fist and looked his grandfather in the eye. "Enough lies. The only tracking device that exists on this plane is the Tug. And not even you can manufacture that."

Linus pushed his grandson's hand off in anger, but persisted. "The Voidroamer made another deal. Soren will start siphoning the girl—"

"Fuck that!"

"Don't interrupt your elders," snapped Linus.

Zeph's lips thinned, but he bowed his head. Willow tied back her dried hair and kinetically slammed down a wingback chair at the circular table. She gingerly took her seat and looked between the two large men discussing her life. How many times had they done this without her present, she wondered, sighing.

The elder ignored her. "To siphon the girl, he must keep her alive. It's a fair trade for Vivek's life."

"I am not yours to trade. You can't even look me in the face as you say it," said Willow.

Linus finally turned his great shaggy head her way. "I wish I *could* say I know what to make of you, youngling. But I hear such differing accounts. Let's see. Vivek considers you unpolished but upright. Flynn wants you gone, in any way imaginable, some being quite inventive. Torrent would probably die for you—"

"What's that?" blurted Willow.

"I'm her favorite cousin," explained Zeph. "She wouldn't let my Guide die."

"Favorite? You choked her against a wall."

He smirked. "How better to show my affection?"

Linus's head swung over to Zephyr. "Quite a lot of affection you've left out there for us to clean up." The elder stroked his beard, curling coarse ends around a finger, and shook his head. "You know, I thought she would break by now—after how she arrived, reached the Sky Realm on her own, even how she fared in the hands of our fair king. We all wagered she'd be a deranged mess by this point."

Zeph put a hand on the back of Willow's chair. "She's always been exceptional at accepting harsh realities. Maybe because she grew up with such power. Maybe because that's simply who she is. But she bends more often than she breaks."

Willow blinked once before staring like an owl, flattered but frowning. "Doesn't mean you should test my limits."

"If that's the case," Linus said softly, "you may break last, but you'd probably break hardest. Even so, it's not my desire to pressure you now, only my duty as a father."

"I'm willing to come if you can find Benny and ensure his safety."

"The little Porter boy? Done."

Willow leaned forward, eyes gleaming, ready to shake his hand, when Zeph cut in, "You have no means of finding him."

Linus smacked his fists down again, but Zeph looked straight at his grandfather, mirroring his position with both palms pressed flat on the table, and said, "Let's be totally honest here, sir. The Voidroamer might even be able take down the universe with all that power siphoned away. Who knows how much it's already hoarded?"

"I don't care about the universe right now. All I care about is my son."

"And so I will come with you. Alone."

"You alone are of no use to me."

"We are the *Flock*." Zeph said it like it meant everything, and tonight Willow was finally seeing firsthand how true that was for him. "If we can't lead an extraction operation for one of our own, then what is the point of us?"

Linus leaned back in his chair, rubbing his eyes and chuckling. "Oh, my boy. My dear boy. You really are always looking for the loophole."

"Just like Mother always said," murmured Willow.

Linus eyed her. "And what was she like to our Zephyr? Your mother?"

Surprised at the question, she took a second to consider. She had pushed away the memories of her formative life. Perseverance had demanded it of her, but damn it, she could feel her eyes watering now that she was being asked with honest curiosity to remember.

Finally, she offered, "She loved him like a son."

Unimpressed, Linus waved his hand as if swatting a fly. "Hmm."

She leaned forward. "When I couldn't see he was hungry, she fed him. When I couldn't see he was cold, she clothed him. When I couldn't see anything past my own troubles, she kept his secrets from me to protect his pride."

Linus glanced at Zeph, who nodded and looked away.

"Aurora," said Linus slowly, "was always good to a fault."

Willow took the opportunity to say, "Zeph mentioned he was at my birth."

Zeph groaned. Linus glared at him.

Willow continued. "And if you knew Mother, then clearly she's been here, all the way to Ingress. Now how is that possible?"

Linus stood up with the ultimate deflection. "My son's life, his very head, hangs by a thread. So will you come willingly, or will you not?"

CHAPTER
18

FIRST BLOOD

Look! Galaxies fall quiet before
The tears on her face, as they wait
To hear them fall into a branching portal
And perhaps reach a world or two over
Where they have no meaning
But joy.

Willow did appear on the ramparts of Maddooinne once again, but this time, no one saw her coming. She did not struggle to scale Mount Onstel and certainly did not bother to use a sanctioned ferry.

As her head broke through cloud cover to face Master Jamison of the High-Level Guards, his mouth dropped open, quickly snapping shut when a pair of wings behind her back flapped open hard enough to send him sprawling from the gust.

Large hands gripped Willow's waist as the king's champion helped her onto the stability of the walkway from behind.

"You could have waited for me to carry you," he complained.

With her powers, Willow had steered up a chunk of rock that had fallen below the diamond mines during the chaos of the ferry competition. She let it fall once more as she stepped back onto Maddooinne.

"It was good for my nerves," she whispered before saying aloud, "and I didn't see the need for climbing up a whole mountain again, Master Jamison. Been there. Done that. As you well know."

"Very smooth," muttered Zeph.

Sweaty from panic, Jamison lifted the ram's horn hanging around his neck and blew.

A Kinetic guard of no fewer than twenty men rushed forward to strip them of their weapons and lead them through crowded streets, all the while emphatically refusing Zeph's offer to fly Willow to the castle.

Many of the residents lingered in the entrance hall for a glimpse of the pair being escorted past. But that was all anyone could do.

Willow and Zeph were ushered into a sterile, empty throne room without the usual stained glass windows—just lattices filtering in light, nothing hanging on the walls, and no runner along the ground. It was merely a long room with a throne at the end, where the king stood flanked by a small army of Kinetic guardsmen and no Winged.

Zeph strode up to the dais and sank to his knees, fist pressed to his chest. "Your Highness."

The king looked on, his face the strangest mask of apathy Willow had ever seen, especially stripped of those too-wide smiles.

"Took you quite a while to return from that heroic drop, Azakor," he said after a lengthy silence.

"I took portals I did not know in order to escape the Voidroamer, sire, so we ended up lost—

"And yet you return so easily once your father is threatened?" He clicked his tongue and cocked his head.

"My family found us—"

The king lifted a hand. "You want to know what I think? Of course you do." He stepped forward, his guards stepping with him, faces uneasy despite their number.

Soren looked between the pair of them, noting Willow's heavy breathing, and placed a hand on her waist, pulling her forward. He sniffed her hair. Laid the side of his heavy head against hers. Started to stroke a hand up her thigh. Willow gritted her teeth. Soren glanced back at Zeph to say, "I think your hand just tensed."

He let go and started laughing, bent over in hysterics.

Wiping his dry eyes, he returned to the throne and sat with his legs tossed over the cushioned armrest. "I *also* think I remember a day nearly thirty years ago. You were all but two, just a toddling little useless beast who was supposed to lead my guard—" the king's voice rose "—and instead, you tore this hall to pieces with the flare of your betrayal!"

Willow looked over at Zeph, who for once looked to be on the verge of stabbing his king, even while on his knees.

"Guide flares are not a choice," said Zeph through gritted teeth. "Sire."

The king's voice calmed to a snake hiss. "Yet at your core, you are tied to someone else. To people not of my kingdom. Your loyalty is divided. You know what that means. What that meant then. And what that means now."

"My Guide is dead. Just as *you* ordered."

"Oh, are we still playing this game?" The king snapped his fingers. Ivan slammed his cane against the wall behind them. The door there opened, and Vivek was pushed through with his mouth gagged and hands tied back to the root of his wings with twine, held in place like an animal prepared for roasting. The guard manhandling Vivek smirked as he pushed the mage down.

Someone started tying Zeph's hands together as well, but Willow could not stop staring at the new guardsman.

Just as he could not stop staring at her.

Because he was no guardsman.

He was the executioner from the East Skia Trading Village.

"Recognize each other, then? Well," spat Soren, "imagine my shock when Gareth arrived from his post across our borders with a tale of power, deception…and you." The king swung his legs down and stalked over to Willow, who screamed when he pulled a tuft of her long hair to yank back her head. "A unique scar beneath her jaw and an ExoSource traitor. One who thwarted the direct royal order of an execution. Not only that, but worse—my own Winged saw it all. Vivek was there! Yet not a peep out of my long-standing champion when a fugitive shows up to infiltrate my court."

Zeph's eyes flitted between Vivek and the king.

"So I ask you, young Azakor, for whom else would my own spies keep their silence, hmm? For whom else—but your Guide?"

Zeph rose, his voice disrespectful for the first time ever in the king's presence as he snapped, "It's not possible for me to serve her people. There is no danger to you."

"Hmm. This much is true. She is just about the last of her kind. But look at her." He circled Willow, stopping to grab her chin with a pinch. "So grown up. So strangely powerful in her youth. What do you have to say for yourself?"

Willow's eyes were rimmed red as they moved over to Zeph. "The last of my kind?"

The king's mouth went wide, his gaze like two bright beetles in an overstretched face. "Don't you know, child?" He leaned in to press his moist lips to her ear and asked, "Don't you know he killed your mother too?"

The broken look on Zeph's face sent Willow straight to the ground, saved only from fully crumpling by her chin in Soren's grip. He stroked his thumb over her lower lip.

"The Azakors slew them all, in fact. They were the only ones powerful enough to do it. But I suppose he had to go and save his Guide, didn't he? I thought you could be my heir, my chosen child!" He stepped on her hand, increasing the pressure slowly. "But you were lucky you were ever even *born*."

Zeph had never led her away from Spinor Falls to show her the truth. He simply got her out before the massacre. Or maybe just as it started, when he set fire to Areida's home as some sort of signal to his brethren. Then stashed her away in some backwater village, enchanted against her will, all so he wouldn't have to live with the physical agony of her death? The horrible way it all made sense pushed bile up her throat.

"Couldn't you have at least spared Mother?" she sobbed up at her Guide.

Zeph's face twitched into an expression she did not recognize, some strange mix of fury and regret. "No, she's gone. They're all gone."

Willow shook, shot through with shock, as she accused, "You swore you'd get me back to her."

"And what good is the promise of a beast?" commented Soren, inspecting his fingernails. "He lies even to his own king. They all did. And such treason calls for swift and exact punishment. Now, Gareth, I believe you were swindled out of an execution at Willow's hands?"

A part of Willow understood what was to happen, and another part of her was simply not present. Her mother was gone? Could the kindest councilor, the most attentive of single parents, have raised her own murderer as much as she had raised her own daughter? The sound of bubbling blood rushed through Willow's ears to swallow up the entire space.

A deep breath. A prayer for calm. A call for reason as it fled.

"Stop!" someone screamed.

And somehow, in that vacuum of calm she often found herself

sinking into during her life's most chaotic moments, she thought of Benny…of how he dealt with orphanhood so young…how he always said never to trust anything at face value here. Zeph would have found a way to save her mother—he must have, just as he had covered up her rescue—and if so, he could never admit to that now. So maybe that meant—

The current agony on Zeph's face finally registered. He was begging. Zeph, of all people, begging? A sound of sheer horror cut through—

"No," screamed Willow, her kinetic instincts slamming the swinging sword out from Gareth's hands with such force it thrust upward into the executioner's throat. He gurgled, stumbling back, arms flailing toward the weapon and slicing his palms.

Vivek flipped around onto his feet and kicked Gareth in the chest in one smooth motion.

Some of the guards surged forward as a handful of intelligent cowards like Ivan fled through the back door.

But everyone froze when, from out of Gareth's corpse, Willow recalled the only weapon present to hang, dripping blood, between two sides of a room divided. The army, the king, and Vivek on one side faced Willow and Zephyr on the other.

Pure, wary silence.

The Exokinetics gulped.

"Willow," called Zeph. "Release me."

"Zeph," whimpered Willow, his name a plea.

"It's alright. Come here."

"But, Zeph, I…just…I *killed* someone." Entire body shaking, she fought the onslaught of tears that threatened her vision and her hold on the sword.

"No, you didn't. Stop shaking your head. Listen to me. Darling, you *protected* someone."

A sob tore its way through her throat. "And you? Did you protect my mom?"

"Nestling, you know who truly raised me. Don't you?"

She nodded frantically, every part of her panicking.

"Then trust me," commanded Zeph, turning to give her access to the binds. "Please."

She stood, reaching for him blindly, hands sliding down his long arms to untie him as she kept staring at the broadsword with single-minded focus, holding tight against the considerable force of a couple dozen Kinetics using their high-level powers against her own.

She tried to summon the sword, but it would barely move. So much opposing ether was concentrated around the weapon that she could see the coppery strands of it, and she could even feel it slamming against her own mind like a mental attack.

Freed, Zeph burst to his feet.

"Where do you keep the siphons?" he demanded, taking a step toward the cluster of men covering the king.

Vivek was eyeing the sword like everyone else. His deep voice rang out, "Willow, I know how strong these guards are. Do you have control?"

She yanked at the deciding factor in the room, the strain turning into a physical ache, just to get it to move an inch her way. The king's men collectively pulled at the sword with their powers too, but she doubled down, sweat streaming down her face. "For now," she managed to say.

Vivek crossed the room, hunched slightly given how he was tied, as Soren screamed from behind his wall of men, "Step aside."

But the guards were not listening, all trying to cover their monarch in panic.

As soon as Vivek moved far enough away from the enemy, Zeph rose his arms in that familiar X before uncrossing them with a vicious roar, sending a cover of copper smoke onto the floor and surging to the other side. The guardsmen dropped to their knees, one by one, convulsing, until only the king remained standing.

"Where are the siphons?" boomed Zeph as he untied his father's binds.

Vivek started coughing at his son's side.

Zeph pushed. "Speak or you die."

The coughing worsened.

"General?"

The mage fell to the ground.

"Dad!" Zeph knelt to cup his father's face.

"You think I don't always have them?" sneered Soren.

In a flash, Willow lost hold, and the broadsword went sailing right into the king's raised hand.

His eyes had gone white with the invocation of some unspeakable power, his voice morphing into a facsimile of the Voidroamer's banshee pitch as he said, "The siphons are not physical, you fools. You have two options—"

"Zeph," croaked Vivek, "this only goes one way."

Willow stumbled over to them, uncaring of the king's next move at the realization she had never seen Zeph cry before.

Vivek's face turned puce, skin sinking into itself, decomposing before their eyes. "Son…I let you…alone…too young…sorry…"

Zeph pulled his father into his lap, the entirety of his arms now covered in the healing ether he was pushing into his father. "Hold on. Just…please. You're clan leader. Head of the family. Everyone. You're…I need you, Dad. Please." Zeph was turning paler and paler.

Everything in Willow had gone so cold.

"Stop, don't give…that…Stop!" Vivek pushed himself up against all odds to grab Zeph's shoulder, but his eyes rolled back. He dropped down again and forced out, "You need the ether to end it."

Zeph's tears fell onto his father's face as he rocked him, never giving up.

Willow glared back at the king, hair swimming around his face despite the eerie lack of a breeze. She focused her anger on that throat, wrapped a world of ether around his windpipe, and *squeezed*.

The king bent over in shock. Vivek stopped choking as the king started.

Zeph looked up in hope. "Willow?"

"He won't take another parent. He can't!" she cried, compressing harder.

Before the king could lose consciousness, his nostrils flared wide, and the sword shot through Vivek's throat faster than Willow could rearrange her kinetic focus.

Zeph roared.

She lost her hold at the shrieking sound of her failure and his grief.

CHAPTER
19

THE PAIN
OF BEING
ON EDGE

Mother would often insist,
"Don't cry over spilled milk!"
But that was well before I said,
"And what if what I've spilled runs red?"

No meaning lies hidden in tragedy other than what we choose to give us peace. But what we choose—that makes all the difference.

Soren Everly of Maddooinne, the first of his name and the youngest-ever ruler of the Kinetic Kingdom, came to power when his parents died together on the battlefield. A warrior couple, they led their people to greater victories at greater distances than any monarchs in recorded Ingressian history, and yet Melissa and Leonard Everly's expectations of their only child rose greater still with each success.

Despite inheriting their looks along with their kinetic strength, Soren never possessed their shared thirst for a good fight, perhaps because he was more like a Meta than any Exo would ever care to admit, always preferring wits to brawn in gaining the upper hand. The way his twelve-year-old self saw it, Ingress would never prosper in the hands of a child ruler unless he outsmarted the world, and so he plotted a meeting with the most powerful being rumored to roam the void.

But he always fell a step behind, a moment too late, or a tip too short in grasping the great creature that haunted his graveyard of goals.

Five years later, the sea itself screamed across the many mountains of the Voidsrange at the stillbirth of a future ruler, a girl who Faeries foretold would herald untold riches for the Kinetic Kingdom. And it was in that state of grief, while his sobbing young wife clutched their breathing son next to their dying daughter, in that moment of true desperation, that the Voidroamer found Soren, instead of the other way around. Such that when the sea screamed next, it was fifty years ago exactly, and scores of the Exowinged were dragged from their preferred plane to witness the resurrection of a babe on the precipice of death, one that would ensure the enslavement of an entire designation.

"And then she still died early," Soren whispered now, remembering fully and willingly for the first time in about two decades. "She fell mad for a Skia instead of her own kind, and they assassinated her with my wife rather than let our girl live alongside their damned prince. That's when I stepped up once more. I pulled us into the sky, where nothing bad could ever touch us again. Not even time."

"Liar."

He looked over, across bars of spell-enforced metal, at the accursed girl who reminded him so much of Lavender. He had never wanted anyone dead so much.

"She killed the Skia prince's Guide," Willow reminded him, even as she lay on her side, clutching her knees in a puddle of despair.

"You bitch," he snarled.

"Then you ripped your home from Mount Onstel with stolen

powers, all to escape the consequences of who and what you had raised, choosing only to see what you could do."

"Quiet."

"The queen's life was taken early by the balance of time to repay the years you stole for Lavender."

"Silence, you insolent chit!"

Willow sighed. "Zeph told me all about the great, young Soren. The desperate boy who wanted too much. Stole too much. Hated too—"

Soren stood, shaking out his robes, "You have quite the mouth for a prison rat." He pressed his face against the bars and smiled. "Any day now, I could have you hanged, beheaded, or simply pushed over the edge of your cell. You might just fall asleep and find yourself rolling to your death. It's how most delirious dogs leave this place."

The king's words rang in her ears like a siren. Willow glanced over at the edge, where a moonless sky would soon give way to dawn. The kingly coward standing safe in shadows had chosen total darkness for his visit. But he was right. Two days she had gone without sleep so far. Two days she had dreaded the night, and now even the light.

Oh, how she wished she had learned to overcome her fear of great heights and fly freely, the way Zeph had urged.

Calming down at her silence, Soren's silhouette sat back on his heels and swiped a hand over his mouth. "All of your choices have led you here. So why travel where you're not wanted? What was your true purpose?"

Her gaze remained fixed on the edge. "I want to know who I am."

"You are *not* one of us. You never were."

Willow stood and grabbed the bars. "What am I, then?"

He laughed, his head cocked, eyes locked intently onto hers. "I thought dear Zephyr Azakor told you everything?"

"Don't you *dare* speak his name. You fucking murderer."

"He belongs to me. I can call out his name right now and order him to push you over. He would do it, or die."

"Slaver."

"Ownership of a beast is not slavery. It is a hunter's *right*."

Willow kicked the bars with a scream, hanging her head. "Ugh. I want to go home. I can't stand you backward maniacs."

"Now we're talking." He stepped toward her, inches now from her face. "Where is home? Where are the rest of you?"

She raised her head slowly. Spinor Falls. He didn't know of it. And he was here to find out. She smiled.

"You said you killed us all." A theory was forming, something slotting together at the far reaches of Willow's mind, something that seemed so impossible that it might yet be true.

"Some of you escaped. You must be the reason we keep finding stragglers. You half-breeds must have slipped through the parameters of the spell."

There it was.

He'd only ever wiped out a land of Metafervers, not Exos.

And years ago, after Zephyr had seen her lift him up the Northern Hill, even he had spoken words that now finally made sense: "You moved a person with your mind."

"My mind," remembered Willow, taking a deep breath and releasing a great fear. "So you aren't my father."

He spat, face twisting with horror. "I would never debase myself so low as to sleep with a Meta."

Willow looked down at her hands. She chose in that moment to believe—not in the king, or her salvation, or the words of others. She chose to believe in herself and the long-ignored bubbling in her blood.

Flames erupted from her fingers, flying far enough to set the king's robes on fire.

"Just had to make sure before I did that." She laughed, strange tears of relief streaming down her face, all as he screamed like a startled child. The flames were traveling fast across his gauzy, sheer garments, burning his neck. White-faced guardsmen with buckets ran down the stairs into the Sky Dungeon, one of them Winged, to usher their sovereign away.

But that mage paused to glance back over his shoulder, brow raised.

"Surprised?" asked Willow.

He tossed his head and resumed walking.

"Yeah, well, next time don't keep me in the dark!"

The mage halted, looking up at the stairs where the king had vanished before stepping back in her direction. He whispered, "The general reports Aurora Erifson is alive and well," and sprinted away after his master.

"And what about Benny?" she called after him, but when she received no response, Willow dropped to her knees. Her face fell against the bars with a sob.

"Hells," came a rasp.

She looked over at her only prison mate, the pile of grumpy dirt lying on the ground three sets of bars down, and asked, "What is it now, Stellan?"

"You are so dead, Ferver."

She pointed a flaming finger in his direction.

He held his hands up and laid his head back on the stone floor.

"This explains my map," she murmured, crouching to hold on to a bar with one hand and stare in awe at her other one, flipping it over again and again. "It's flame-locked for a reason."

Willow spent the next few hours staring at her arms, stroking her lit skin up and down in a tired haze, trying to keep herself from falling asleep or fixating on what the Kinetics had planned for her.

First, she imagined holding Zeph as he mourned, the thought an ache. Wondered instead how Benny was enduring their separation, but that thought was just another ache. Grieved for Philip, Reynor, and even Sienna. Finally tried to memorize her skin map so well the images might burn a distraction into her brain. She muttered, "Voidsrange is north of Maddooinne, which is northwest of Farrow's Forge, which is northeast of the Shadowlands, which is south of the trading villages at the Border River, which are all still quite north of the Emberlands."

Eyes narrowing, her voice rose, "But why is all of Void Valley uncharted? Hey, Stellan!"

He lifted his head.

"Is it true what they say, that the best maps don't burn?"

"Yes, idiot. That's why they say it."

"And why don't they burn?"

"They just don't."

"You ever seen one like that yourself?"

His grimy, long-nailed fingers danced in the air. "No, but I've been stuck here a while."

Willow let go of the bars and set one hand on top of the other. On a deep inhale to gather her courage, she tried to burn her left forearm. The flames felt cold instead of hot.

Maybe this really was the master map, or a good copy of it. Victor was a Ferver. It stood to reason that his young mapmaker friend had been a Ferver too.

She tamped down her excitement. "But it has two big flaws. That portal in the mines was missing, and this huge region of Void Valley in the Emberlands is blank. Fuck. Think, Willow. Think your way out of this. Come on."

She pressed her forearms against her face until something that Jerald had said came filtering through, about how a designation would never leave portal markers in their own territories out of caution. Would the mapmaker record Void Valley if she were a Ferver?

She wouldn't want or need to map her home.

"She was definitely a Ferver." She brought her hands down and slammed her head back. "But how is any of this going to get me out of here?"

To her left, the sky was lightening into those beautiful pastel colors under which she had danced with Zeph on her first night in this realm. It was hard not to wish he would just come sailing through the open air and spirit her away. But she knew the king would have threatened more of his family to take precautions against her release. She hoped he was safe. She hoped he wouldn't do anything stupid in his grief.

People acted stupid when they were sad.

Like how the mapmaker had killed herself in here, or so the king had told her. But the king *was* a liar.

"Stellan," she called out.

"I'm sleeping."

"No, you're not."

"Okay, I'm not."

"There are scorch marks in the corner of my cell."

He lifted his head to give her a look of pure annoyance. As if he had anything better to do. "Were you expecting silk sheets?"

"Was a Ferver ever in here? In this very cell?"

He flapped a hand in her direction.

She snapped, "Besides me."

"Not sure. Been here awhile."

"So you keep saying. But I bet you'd remember a flame-spraying Meta."

He twirled a finger in the air. "There was someone. A crazy woman. Or at least she went crazy."

Willow perked up. "Go on, then. How'd she get out?"

"Killed herself."

Her heart sank. "How?" she whispered.

Stellan sat up to face her cell, jostling mental cobwebs with a toss of the head. "What did you ask me again?"

Willow slapped a hand against the ground. "The Ferver who killed herself in this cell. Who was she, and how'd she do it?"

"I don't recall."

She stood up and walked over to the edge in frustration, staring out at the greatness of untold history beyond. Far below, the Northern Portal Mines looked like one great soup of concentrated ether. Her teeth chattered from the cold and the fear snaking through her soul at the sight.

"Maybe if I fell, I would just land into a portal and survive."

"Nope." Stellan was smiling for once.

"What's that?"

"Stupid move. Go through a portal with too much speed, and bad things happen."

She slammed a hand against the metal bars between them. "Yeah, I know. Shut up."

"You exit the way you enter, so you'd burst out the other end just a short distance from the ground with all that velocity you had gathered as you fell in—"

"I know!"

"—and gravity would take care of killing you. Gravity," he said, slapping his palms together, "always gets the last word."

"Why, thank you."

He saluted. Seemed he was always most talkative when it came to the topic of death, no matter his or hers. Willow looked back out, staving off tears, needing a deep breath of air. She held tight to the prison bar at her side and sat at the edge to watch dawn break in peace.

"Yes! Just like that," shrieked Stellan.

Willow jolted, for once actually grateful for the bar in her fist.

Stellan breathed, "She sat right there for hours before she jumped off the edge."

"You're sure? She really did kill herself?"

"Not a sight so easy to forget."

"Yet you just did!"

He shrugged.

She shook her head. "I don't believe you. A woman doesn't survive nearly every region of this land only to give up behind open bars."

"Respect your elders, you filthy Ferver."

"When I get out of here, and I will get out of here, I'm leaving you behind. Just like she did."

"Sure, don't take me with you into the great void of death. I'm crushed."

She ignored him, continuing to scan the view before her instead.

She had been staring at these clouds for days. Long enough to realize the wind never trespassed so close to the Kinetic forces holding the kingdom aloft.

So the clouds here never changed.

Yet something was different about them. Something was off.

And that's when she saw it—a strong glint above a uniquely small white patch nearby. Her gaze zeroed in on its familiar coppery ripple.

"No," she breathed. "I didn't think that was possible."

A portal in the sky.

CHAPTER
20

CHAOS FREED

Falling feels like losing
Despite ground's promise
Of a stable place to start,
If ever at rock bottom
A hardened heart lands open
Even as it falls apart.

I t was too high to jump down. Much too high.

She stood with a gasp. "The location of the portal that was supposed to be in the mines was correct. The map was right. But the elevation was off. Because a map's just two dimensional."

Her heart thundered at what this meant.

"I can't. No."

She started pacing, holding on to the bars and marching along, away from the edge, back toward it, away, back, away, and back, again and again. She paused to groan, "What if the only way out of this mess is the same way I got in?"

"Wow, now you really look like her, with all that mumbly pacing."

"Shut up!"

"Testy."

"I'm gonna do it. My powers can slow down the fall."

"Great—another jumper. No, don't. Your life is worth something," he deadpanned.

"You were planning to jump the very day I met you."

"Bullshit. What makes you say that?"

Rolling her eyes, Willow walked back to the very edge, facing the open wall, her left hand clutching cold iron, fisting and unfisting it in terror. She lifted her other hand and tried to toss forth flame.

"Ugh," she grunted.

Again, and again, and again, until a shower of fire arced before her to illuminate the full breadth of the portal ahead.

"I know I can do this. I know it. I know."

She tossed her right arm straight out once more, locked her eyes onto the portal, wrapped as much wild ether around herself as she could, and jumped face-first into open sky.

It felt as if lightning crackled through the air when it woke her up, zipping across her skin and pushing her eyelids apart.

The Flock crowded around her prone form, within a thick pit of feathers. The sheer power of dozens of them, the potent concentration of ether they attracted just by default that danced off their skin, now suffocated her in this small, dark space.

Willow pulled herself up from a massive, downy nest into a shaky fighting stance that amused them all, until her fists erupted in fire. She turned in a circle, using Ferver light to see wary faces taking stock of her, some of them unable to rein in their shock and pushing others aside to see.

"Air portals suck the energy right out of you, huh?" asked a sweet voice.

A youngling stepped forward, barely a teenager, and Willow realized she was seeing a child mage for the first time. Her blond hair hung impractically long, kissing the floor when she cocked her head, framing a round but tired little face. Her spread wings were a fluffy whitish gray instead of smooth black, and she stared in awe at Willow before saying, "Soren won't find you here."

"Where is here?" asked Willow, flames rising to crawl up her forearms in panic.

"The Mage Caves just beneath the mines. We already sent someone to tell the general you're here. It's okay." She held out a tiny hand. "My name is Skyler Azakor. You can come with me."

"How—"

"He's my cousin." She took Willow's hand from her side, uncaring about the flames. Willow tamped them out immediately. "Come this way. But watch your head, okay?"

The ring of mages parted, silent but following close behind their youngling. Skyler led them out of the dank room Willow could barely make out into a well-lit serpentine tunnel, where sconces illuminated black walls embedded with raw diamonds.

Willow asked, "Are we really beneath Maddooinne?"

"Yes, we made caves that connect to some of the abandoned mines—best way to stay out of sight nearby. Smart, no?"

Willow's hand swept against the wall beside her for support, and not a little out of sheer wonder. "How could a portal lead here, into what used to be solid rock?"

"It's not a natural portal. We crafted it in one of the voidaggen's blind spots when the prison was not yet in use. Most of the energy let off was within the rock, so no one else could see it happen. And crafted portals still have a little shimmer when veiled, which makes them easy to hide, but not impossible to find. It was Uncle Vivek's idea." Willow's chest tightened and Skyler's voice trailed off just as they reached the end of the current pathway. It opened into a vast cavernous space.

Willow spun in surprise, taking in a ceiling vaulted so high it had no clear end. Gem-studded rocks jutted out of the walls in chunks so large that mages reclined upon them with their wings spread. Hammocks and other nests strung across corners, where women held or nursed their young. She had never seen these people so relaxed or their faces more at ease, at least until they took in her presence and sat up.

Willow stepped back as Torrent landed before her with a sudden swish of bright-colored robes, nothing like her practical black fighting leathers. "Look at you." She circled Willow. "Bet you wish you'd listened to my warning before you had to free-fall your way to freedom."

Willow laughed, hummingbird heart still pounding, just as Torrent's face cracked into a smiling sort of smirk. "I had my wits to keep me steady."

"And she does have great wits," called a deep voice from above, its location so high and so dark she couldn't see who said the words.

But she didn't need to see.

With a relieved smile, she lifted her arms up in welcome.

And he came, flying down into them, landing on bent knee to help even their heights as he embraced her.

"General!" shouted Skyler.

Willow looked up, trying to find the general as Zeph groaned.

"Yes?" he asked, turning to stand. Confused, Willow dropped her arms.

"Coven Code forbids the general kneeling before anyone but the king," Skyler whispered, her urgent voice echoing through the cavern anyway.

Willow blinked. Zeph just nodded at the girl and said, "It also commands leniency for Guide pairs, so we can agree to disagree."

"General?" asked Willow.

"Title passed to me." He shrugged one shoulder, which Willow only now noticed was dressed in his father's old garb—fitted black fighting leathers ruched along the arms, with a high-neck collar, obsidian shoulder plates made of metal feathers arranged in overlapping rows like scales, glinting leather boots, and of course, an empty weapons harness that crossed his spine.

"What about Linus?"

"He passed down the position to my father years ago."

Willow stepped back to allow him to rise somberly before her. "You stand differently. Responsibility looks good on you. Heavy, but good." She brushed a hand down the front of his chest, and before she could help it, tears blurred her vision. "I'm so sorry. Your dad—"

He turned away, refusing consolation to look out at his people for a long moment. "I owe you some answers."

She lifted an arm, sending fire soaring up to her elbow with a chuckle. "I'd say you do."

"Told you!" Skyler whispered to an even younger child mage, his little eyes wide as saucers.

Zeph seemed fascinated but unsurprised, outstretched fingers asking to close the distance and test the licks of flame. "I hoped for this. You have no idea what an important theory you've proven, literally in the flesh."

But Willow doused them and grabbed his shoulders. "How is this possible for me? Were we all capable of this back home? Did we just not know we were Fervers?"

"Yes and no." He took ahold of one of her forearms and flipped it around, inspecting it.

Willow lost her saintly patience and pushed him away. "Where is Spinor Falls, Zeph? Where is everyone?"

"They're in Void Valley."

"But we were just there! Why didn't you take me to them?"

"Because Spinor Falls isn't there."

"What? But you just said—Then where the fuck is it?"

"Right here." He stepped forward and tapped her right in the forehead.

"No." She froze, voice stuck somewhere between a laugh and a scream.

Zeph continued. "Twenty-seven years ago, the year of your own birth in fact, my great-grandfather led us in casting a grand enchantment."

Angry voices started to interrupt, but he hushed them with an arm roiling with copper.

"I have the authority to speak now," he barked at them. "The Sequester Spell enslaved any Ferver Folk residing in Void Valley into a collective plane. First Elder Balen called it a shared prison of the mind. Because while the bodies may lie in Void Valley, their souls live in a mental plane of amnesia, where memories of the past and their powers are long gone."

Willow pulled her arm away and fell back. It took her a minute, glancing around at all the rapt faces taking in her reaction. She finally said, "Soren wanted us dead. So you made it look like we were."

"Exactly."

"Meta powers center around belief, around our minds, so—"

"So if you can't remember who you are or what you can do, then you can't do it."

"And since that's not true for Exos—"

"Yes, fledgling. Go on."

"That's why I could still use my kinetic powers growing up."

He nodded. "You must be a blend: not Meta or Exo, but somehow both. Mixed children carried to term are so rare, and they only manifest one source. But you? We've never seen anything like *you*."

"Benny once joked about Metakinetics." With a shaky breath and palm on her forehead, Willow realized, "None of us ever really thought about the past, or how we came to be on the island. I could barely bring myself to ask about my father. It made us all so uncomfortable to think of what we couldn't remember."

"And quite rude to foreigners."

She glanced at his face, surprised at the joke, but that was Zeph, darkly humorous, even in the dark.

"We were always happiest within our hallow." She looked around the cave, where the mages muttered urgently to each other. "Guess it reminded you of home. But…where were your wings in Spinor Falls?"

"They're a visible manifestation of my Exo source, and anything to do with sources or the time before the enchantment were wiped from the memories of everyone trapped within. It's a theory, but I think I couldn't manifest something that no Meta remembered. Because everything physical in that plane is a shared memory."

"Like the empty books in my mom's library?"

He chuckled. "Yes, people probably read those titles but never finished them."

"So how old are we really, Zeph?"

"I came for you at my age fourteen, when you were actually twelve but believed you were eight. Time slows down in one's mind, and it moves fifty percent faster here than in Spinor Falls. The ten years we thought we spent in there together were actually fifteen."

"The same fifteen years Jerald and Evie kept my body?"

"Exactly. I left you with them before I entered the enchantment. So you're now twenty-seven to my twenty-nine."

"Twenty-seven. I thought I turned eighteen last year…So I lost over nine years of my life?" she asked, pacing, staring out at the hundred or so faces that followed her every move. She came to a stop with a shout. "How do we fix this?"

She had directed her question at the crowd, but frantic cries from a connected room interrupted them: "General! Where's the general?"

Zeph tossed his head back, groaning. "And this is my life now," he muttered before responding, "Over here, Castor! In the main den."

Willow fell back against Zeph as a mage flew so fast through the chamber, she was almost blown over by his wings. Thinner than most, the mage landed, gasping, on both knees with a hand crossed in deference at his chest. She recognized him as the one who had offered news of her mother in the Sky Dungeon. This time, he announced, "General, the king just ordered his armies to assemble." He looked up. "They head to the Emberlands."

Zeph pulled him up. "Why? What's left to fight there?"

"They take no armor or heavy weaponry to slow them down. Soren must suspect something of what we've done. He ordered his men to dismember the bodies of all Ferver Folk—in case they're not truly dead."

"Mother!" breathed Willow, grabbing Zeph's arm.

"Castor, does the king go with them?" asked Zephyr, pulling her into his side.

The mage shook his head. "He stays here, sir."

Zeph looked at Willow's alarmed face, his hand wrapping around her jaw, a finger stroking the scar beneath her chin. "It will take the Kinetics at least four days to reach their destination, but only a matter of hours for us. We simply adjust the plan."

"The plan?" asked Willow.

"Yes."

His arms swam with bright copper ether, swirling to illuminate his face, as he flew up into the center of the den and faced his people, pointing as they ran to do his bidding. "Torrent, it's time to notify the sleeper cell. I'll take Willow to the Veil to give her instructions before I meet you in the war cellar. Castor, wake any molting younglings old enough to fly and send them with a contingent of healers to Void Valley. Skyler, you fetch my blade."

The youngling was ready for him as soon as he landed, passing over the Black Forge Scythe with deep respect, bowing and stepping away. He nodded, securing it to his back before reaching out for Willow.

"I'm sending you home now, as promised," he said to her.

Taking Zeph's hand, she followed as he rushed off too fast to speak, heading through more tunnels, all too small to fly within until they reached a wide opening in the floor.

"Whoa," she said, coming to an abrupt stop as Zeph yanked her back.

"Up you get," he said, motioning to himself.

Climbing onto his back, adjusting to the feel of those massive wings unfurling around her on the takeoff, she asked, "So you're ending the enchantment? We'll be able to defend ourselves?"

Zeph fell forward and down into the darkness below.

As they sailed through what seemed the Original Void itself, he said, "The only mage who could end such a spell is the one who cast it, but Great-Grandfather is dead. So, if we can't end it, we break it. And breaking free of a prison of the mind can only happen from within. That's why we'll return you home through the Veil, something he quite cleverly folded into the enchantment."

"The wha—"

He made a sharp right, and Willow screamed as he laughed. "I get my dependence on loopholes from him, by the way. You remember the Rule of Rings? The Veil isn't a real portal, more like a connected spell that can splinter your mind away. Now that you know what you can do, your job is to convince the Fervers to get out too."

"How? Am I supposed to push them all off that cliff? One after the other like some serial drowner?"

He scoffed as if she weren't joking. "If only it were that easy. That fail-safe portal is Exo-locked by the very nature of the Sequester Spell. Pure Ferver Folk cannot leave that way. You must get them to believe they can throw fire, gather them at the highest hill points possible, and finally, you melt down the metaphysical walls surrounding the island with the combined force of all that Ferver flame."

"No way."

"Then they all die."

"But you won't let them die, Zeph." She squeezed her arms around his neck.

"No, *you* won't." They had flown through many linked chambers, connected by tunnels above or below, until they landed in a very small space, a dead end with a strange black wall full of cracks bursting with coppery light. "I am still beholden to the king. And awake or not, the Fervers cannot truly live as they are now. They will always be half-dead in Spinor Falls." He swung her to the ground, spinning her to face him. "There's more to say, but not enough time to say it. Look, we...*I* need you to do your best to get this done. Breaking this enchantment has been the focus of my people for years, but we have long since realized that you're the only one who stands a real chance."

She reached a hand up into the hair at his neck. "Why didn't you explain all this to me in Spinor Falls while we were growing up? We could have broken the spell together."

"Because your fire," he said, taking her hand and pressing it to his cheek, "was only something you had a chance of manifesting for the first time here. A realization you had to come to on your own, with the proof of your origins. It's a Meta power, one you must see to believe. And until you can show the rest of your people their own fire is possible, they will never be capable of it either."

Lower lip trembling, she said, "I think I understand."

"Promise me." He pressed his forehead to hers. "You'll get it done."

"Mother's life depends on it."

"Yes, and so I'll hold you to it." He stepped up to the shining wall behind them, pressed his middle finger to a specific point as his ring finger and thumb came together in a sweep, and whispered a short chant while he gestured her over to face it. "This is it. The Veil. Now remember, time moves differently here compared to Spinor Falls. Don't get sucked into thinking you have long. Just over a couple of days, at most."

"You said it would take four days for the Kinetics to reach us!"

"Time moves fifty percent faster here in the Land of Portalcraft. Remember?"

"That's right." Her anger resurfaced. "I won't forget those nine years I lost stuck with Evie and Jerald."

With a nod, he said softly, "I entrusted your body to them just before I first entered the Veil, so that you wouldn't awaken one day in a land full of, well, what would look like corpses. But this time, my own people will be here to watch over you." He kissed her temple before speaking against it. "Your body is of no use without this. So if all else fails, get to the fail-safe and save yourself."

He pulled his hand back, a gossamer-like material tenting forward out of the stone as if it were attached to his pressed fingers. "Now, are you ready to enter the Veil?"

At her nod, he pressed her face against the pulsating mass. She gasped as a mouthful of some intangible substance flowed down her throat, recognizing somehow the peppery taste of madness, before Ingress simply began to melt away.

Zeph caught her body when it crumpled. His face hardened, and the last thing she heard him say was, "Better fly home fast, fledgling."

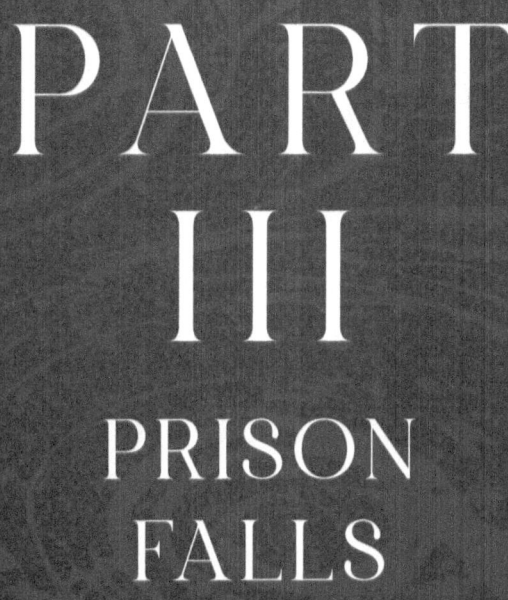

PART
III

PRISON
FALLS

CHAPTER
21

A VENTURE
FOR REVIVAL

Here be the rules.

$v = 1.5w$ $x = z + v$ *Willow:* $z = 0$

                          $y = z + w$ *Zephyr:* $z = 14$

                                          $[z] = years$

v = *years passed in Ingress*
w = *years passed in Spinor Falls*
x = *current Ingressian age*
y = *current Spinor Falls age*
z = *Spinor Falls entrance age*

Depend on consistency even in variance.

A person who disappears may never notice the answers they seek blazing behind them, but someone who returns may have better questions to ask. And so it was on the day Willow Erifson snuck past old Robert Larsen's kabob stall, she finally knew exactly where to head first. Not to the council. Not to the town square. And definitely not to the enforcers.

She had awoken in the sea, drifting on her back not too far from shore, feeling dazed, until she bumped against a wall in the water, of all things. To her left, Spinor Falls rose cold and blustery as ever, but to her right, an invisible barrier pressed hard into her side. She pushed herself up, slammed her freezing hands against it, and called forth her fire. Edges of a material that felt like the Veil singed before they dissolved around her fingers, revealing blades of green, green grass beyond where there should have only been more water.

"We're going to burn you down," she whispered to the borders of a prison she could finally feel.

So ignoring the gut-wrenching, fishhook pull in her chest, she moved with new stealth, the kind taught to her by a kingdom far off but headed her way.

It took all her new kinetic control to avoid the whirlpools around her. Heartbeat in her ears, the panic softened at the sight of her home cresting before her in the setting sun. The Western Hill rose even higher than in her memories, the house that settled at its peak not visible from the wide base at this angle. She set aside the weight of her mission to topple it all, her legs kicking up the pace at her eagerness for home.

The snow had thawed, and it looked like midsummer—as if she had been gone six or seven months instead of nearly a year.

She reached the hill without encountering a single person, but once she came to the main path, she could not help sprinting past the stables and into her house, sidestepping into the vestibule, hiding by a pillar, ducking into her mother's private study, and finally coming to an abrupt stop.

The room was dark, with only a few candles weeping on the desk and a fire dying in the hearth. The scratch of a quill seemed louder than her bated breath. Until it stopped.

The woman who looked back at her from across a colossal desk was tiny. So tiny and frail.

"Mother?"

Aurora sat stock-still, her fire-red curls pulled into a severe bun.

"It's me," whispered Willow.

Silence, until—

"You're ruining the carpet."

Sopping wet, Willow looked down at the handwoven material that she had crawled across once upon a childhood and heard herself laugh. "You know what? It's not even real. The carpet isn't real."

"*You're* not real."

"Depends on how you look at it. But I *am* really here with you." She stepped forward. "Are you ill, Mother?"

Aurora stepped out from behind the desk, face motionless, to touch Willow's wet skin. Her fingers trailed down her daughter's cold cheek until they reached her jawline and began to twitch at the rough, familiar feeling of her daughter's scar.

"Mother? Are you alright?"

With her other hand, Aurora abruptly shoved her. "How can you ask that? What happened to you? What happened?"

Clutching at Willow's shirt, she shook and shook until she broke, a dam falling in slow motion until it spilled over into her daughter. The two of them were at a loss, Willow spiraling in her apologies, and Aurora pushing and hugging her all at once. At some point, they fell to the ground against the desk.

"Well?" pressed Aurora.

Willow stood silently, leading her soaking mother to the roaring fire. "I have so much to explain, but now that I'm here, I don't really know how." She peeled off Mother's damp outer robe and pulled all that long flaming hair out of its bun. "I think I'll start with this."

Aurora yelped as Willow's hand turned to fire while still within her hair, holding her kinetically in place, gentle but firm for a moment as the hair dried without burning. Willow moved her bright hand to Aurora's cheek.

"You can do this too. You've only forgotten," she whispered into the stunned silence.

Trembling, Aurora took her daughter's hand in her own and raised it to her eyes, but before she could speak, the room was alight with a different fire—the sudden blaze of hot voices and an inferno of threats.

Enforcers from every region, armed with arrows and knives, burst through the study door in the one second it took for Aurora to push Willow behind her.

Detective Reid stepped into the room, straight-backed and smug, and pointed a long finger at Mother. "You swore you had no idea where she was, *Councilor*."

"Have you been spying on my home?" asked Aurora, incensed.

"Patrols are nothing more than standard protocol."

Aurora scoffed, her face twisted in disgust. "Then you'll know Willow has only just returned. She is my daughter, and I will be the one to question her. Now get off my property."

"And normally, we would comply, of course, but I'm afraid you're both under arrest."

Willow stepped forward. "And I'm afraid you're a saggy bag of—"

"Willow!"

"Apologies, Mother, but we don't have time for this."

Aurora looked at Reid. "And why am *I* under arrest?"

"On charges of harboring a fugitive."

"Fugitive? Since when?" screeched Willow.

"Since you burned down a councilor's property and disappeared. Areida Sampson is pressing charges, as is her right. Now, if you'll follow me, the council will convene immediately given the high status of both families involved."

"I *am* council," warned Mother.

"Not for this."

Mother actually *hissed*.

Willow pulled her close, speaking in her ear, "Actually, this could be the fastest way of gathering everyone to hear me out."

"Hear you out? Willow, you and Zephyr have decimated us in the court of public opinion. Where the hell have you been?"

"Yes, where *is* Zephyr Norwood?" asked an enforcer.

Willow held out her clasped hands. "I answer first to the council."

"Where is the fugitive, Zephyr Norwood? Tell us and we may grant you leniency."

Willow looked around at the courtroom from her place in the Bowl beside Mother, their hands tied before them with mounds of thick, abrasive rope, and wondered aloud, "It should be the height of summer here. And yet, it's still too cold to step outside without a cloak. Why do you think that is?"

Councilor Ignatius Ren peered down at her through iron-framed spectacles with a look of livid wonder. "We are all well aware we live in an arctic climate."

"Yes, but I'm realizing now that the cold dampens our powers. Our minds have been frozen like our bodies. Let me start at the beginning—"

"You will answer the court's questions, and only the court's questions."

Willow had been the very opposite of a demure miss these past few hours, shouting her voice away as they were led to the Academy building, calling everyone and their uncle to come witness her court proceedings. And they had—so many people were here, Yonsoon had been unable to close the doors. He fumed at them all from the back of the room, likely forced into watching a trial for the first time himself.

Councilor Sampson pulled down the hood of his official robes to reveal his craggy face. "Aurora Erifson, we turn to you for some semblance of reason. Your role as councilor was to safeguard our community against any and all threats, yet your own daughter nearly kills mine in some vengeful attempt at late-night arson. Do you admit now that you have been hiding her from us?"

Mother bared her teeth. "First of all, you have no evidence she did such a thing. Motive and proof are not one and the same. You are allowing your personal desire for vengeance—"

The audience and even some council members roared and booed.

"—but I know my rights. And like anyone else, I have the right to defend my case."

Ren raised a hand to calm the crowd. "Peace. Everyone be at peace. Aurora, I agree that you have the right to finish your response before we question you further. Go on."

Mother lifted her chin even higher. "Seven months ago, my daughter disappeared. Even I have not had the chance to ask what has happened or where she has been. We must turn to her for answers. Willow?"

Willow looked down at her hands and took a deep breath. She lifted them up over her head in full view of the crowd and incinerated the restraints.

"Bright be the judgment," she called out, "like a blaze."

The room erupted into chaos. All the councilors stood, taking a step back even as their torsos curled forward with intrigued disbelief.

Willow allowed the flames to travel down her raised arms all the way to her shoulders, slapping her hands down at her sides to form a clear arc of fire for all to see. "I have a long story to tell," she shouted across the din. "Quiet."

Everyone vibrated in shock, and she knew her flames tugged at their memories. Even a display of her kinetic powers would not have caused such a horrified reaction.

"You are all capable of flame like this. *We* are the Metafervers of Ingress, the Land of Portalcraft. We are not isolated from the world by waters around an island. We've only been enchanted to believe it, our minds wiped clean of the past and our powers, to keep us in a prison of our own control."

"A prison?" asked Mother, voice heavy with suspicion.

"Our minds were spelled together into this plane, but our bodies are lying motionless at home in Void Valley. Consider this. Can anyone present even recall how we arrived on this island? Councilors?"

Some people were shaking their heads, others suddenly clamoring to leave.

Her voice rose painfully as she stared up at the council. "There are people we never ask about, never wonder about, and never even speak about. The ones who came before, or ones we lost. My father, for one." She took a deep breath. "Councilor Ren, you speak of Matthew as your heir, but sometimes your wife calls him her baby, even her littlest boy. But he only has younger sisters here. What child did she lose? Lady Ren?" She turned around to see the woman staring at her in hurt confusion, eyebrows drawn together so tight they strained. "Do you recall?"

"I will have you hanged," boomed Ignatius, slamming his hand against his seat.

Great anger swelled in the room, the product of dry, confused minds fighting the infiltration of doubt the way umbrellas violently snap open against the rain.

Willow scanned the crowd, finding the sprightly but wizened Bastian Eldur. She spun, turning to face him. "Mr. Eldur! I went back, Mr. Eldur. I went back with Zephyr and I met your grandson, Gideon.

He is so proud of your work, sir. Do you remember him? Curly black hair and eyes bluer than your own? Can you remember Gideon?"

Bastian, unlike the others, cocked his head without outrage.

Many other people, however, started to cry, great heaving sobs that triggered her own tears. "It's hard to look at all of you, knowing our lives depend on what I do here, and yet you must hate me for it. It's hard." She swallowed. "I'm sorry. I'm sorry that sometimes pain must come before freedom. But if we can't accept it, we will never be free."

It was suddenly silent enough to hear a pin drop, so Willow yanked at the pin of her last grenade. "When was a child ever born here?"

Devastation became furious denial.

"Witch!" called out her old friend Moira, still pregnant in the back.

"What?" whispered Willow.

The chant grew louder.

"*She* burned down Areida's house. Look at what she can do! She's admitted to the crime!"

"Who could be safe with such a monster roaming the streets?"

"Seize the witch!"

"Lock her up!"

Willow turned to Mother, whose resigned, terrified face told her all she needed to know. Willow asked, "Unreasonable Metas? This is bad. Shit. Shit. Shit. Mother, let's go."

"Willow, *be careful.*"

But she was already slamming people kinetically aside and dragging Aurora off with her. At the door, Yonsoon stood tall, glaring down at her. But when her arms flared, he stepped aside, terror bright on his face.

"Is it true?" asked Aurora. They sat in one of the treetop homes of the lowland forests of the valleymen, where Willow used to help Zeph teach. The families here remained disconnected from the rest of the island, and they readily opened their homes to the councilor who always opened hers for refuge in the winter.

"Of course." Willow was on her knees, clutching Aurora's hands in her own. "Can you do it, Mother? Try."

Aurora looked down and shook her head.

"Then you don't believe me. Belief is the core of it. You just have to believe."

"My girl, for years I've wondered at what you can do. For years, something inside me has screamed an answer that I just can't hear."

"Who is my father?"

Aurora looked up into her eyes, face slack, tears welling. "I don't remember. It feels as though…what they call me sometimes…maybe it's true if I can't remember."

Willow took her by the shoulders. "Never. And I can prove it to you."

"How?"

"Can you remember my birth?"

Aurora went still, the tears spilling over with a scrunching of her brows.

"Don't you see? Obviously, you were there. But I was born just before all this. Right before the enchantment that brought us here. And when we try to remember the before, it hurts like hell that our reality doesn't line up with the facts. But only until you accept it. So accept it, Mother. Please."

"I don't know if I can," she whispered, her fingers clenching and unclenching, leaving crescent-shaped marks on her palm. "Why this urgency, Willow? Why couldn't you just have taken it slow with us?"

"Because they're coming—our enemies, the ones who trapped us here, they're coming for our bodies, and if our minds don't reconnect, we'll be defenseless against those murderers once again. Only this time will be the last time. We have to wake up to fight. We have to wake up to live."

Mother's hands gripped hers so tightly that Willow resisted the urge to cry out. After a long moment, she fell forward into her daughter's arms. Willow let loose a loud breath, holding her mother close but battling panic. If Aurora could not believe her, then who could?

Her thoughts fell once again on Bastian Eldur and that singular look on his face.

Night had fallen hours ago, but Bastian still sat by his forge in the southern valley, mind racing in the pitch-dark and his wife long gone to bed. He was a large man, as muscled as when his hair was jet black instead of gray, his right little finger misshapen for reasons he never managed to recall, and with sharp, severe features that rarely softened in joy.

Flashes of a little boy came and went. A toddler who ran between his feet and nearly straight into the forge. Head of coarse hair singed to the roots. And a laugh he imagined or mistook for the near-constant clanging against his anvil.

"Gideon," he said, tasting the combination of sounds and feeling the shape of them in his mouth like pieces of a painful, old prayer set aside for too long.

"He found his Guide."

Bastian bolted from his chair, reaching for a lantern until a flaming figure lit up by the door.

"Willow Erifson?"

"Yes." She hummed. "Fire son."

"What?"

"The origin of my name. I once read in a life-altering book that Metafervers naturally favor anagrams for important names. I'm beginning to see it now."

"You're a wanted woman."

"Too bad I'm on fire. With everything on the line. And therefore untouchable."

The old man chuckled, rubbing his beard and retaking his seat.

The first councilor barely noticed. The second nearly screamed his house down. Willow learned to gag the third one sooner, and by her fourth kidnapping, she was quite adept at using Bastian's master ring of estate keys to float her targets out of their homes in a way that ensured everyone else remained none the wiser.

She took her last gagged captive, mother's dearest friend on the council, Eliza Sholeh of the Northeastern Tribe, to the edge of the Northern cliffs, upon which Mother stood watch over the others.

Aurora rose at the sight of them. "Oh, Liza." She touched her friend's shoulder before giving Willow a concerned look and rushing off to ready their docked boat.

Willow placed Eliza beside her fellow councilors, but she refrained from tying up the calm woman, unlike the others they had hooked to a bleekmere tree. With the sounds of waves crashing in the distance, she considered her next words carefully.

Councilors Sampson, Ren, Norwood, McKay, and Sholeh lived closest to the north, and Willow did not have time to gather any more of them before first light.

She sat across from them now, legs tucked under her thighs. "First of all, thank you for being here. I'd call you to the Bowl, but instead, I'm sending you as our emissaries to the wall. Second, I hope this might be enough to finally get you to listen. Third, our people depend on your open minds, so please, put aside any past prejudice while you judge our current situation for yourselves."

The wind was howling, sunrise teasing the horizon, and she knew they didn't have long before they would be spotted by waking homeowners.

"Right. Here we go." She floated them all down to the shoreline.

Choppy waters lapped at their oarless boat, hanging lanterns swinging. Willow's powers pushed them forward from her posterior position by the stern, the best place to see everyone and everything, as Aurora sat opposite her. Once far enough from shore that shouting would do no good, Willow kinetically removed all the gags with a flick of her wrist.

"How fucking dare you?" Ren, typically the calmest of them all, shouted.

Norwood just scoffed.

Eliza said serenely, "The whirlpools will kill us all."

Sampson, old and tired, glared straight at Aurora. "If we make it back alive, we'll make sure you lose everything."

"Oh, suck a tiny turtle dick, Niles," snapped Mother.

"Excuse me?"

"No. I've taken care of your old sack of bones through rain and snow and hail. Even when your own children refused to help you take your seat on the council, I offered my arm. But when my daughter stood before you begging for help, you wouldn't so much as hear her out. So if you're sitting here trussed up in the dark, then it is entirely your own fault."

Aurora tossed her flaming locks and looked out at the water, all while Sampson sputtered and Eliza chuckled, leaning back against the boat edge.

But Aurora was not finished. "And my daughter's powers, as you may have noticed when she plucked you from your beds, are considerable. None of us will be dying just yet."

Willow smiled at her mother's patrician profile, at the way that beloved button nose was tossed up and flared.

"Mother?"

"Yes?"

"I love you."

Aurora turned to her with a sniff. "Then tell me where you're going next time."

The boat jerked back with a thud, the councilors looking around in shock at the hard stop.

"Is there a creature in the water?" grumbled Idris McKay, clearly trying not to sound worried.

"No, but we're here," announced Willow. She turned the boat until the hull came to rest against the invisible wall. She closed her eyes and reached out a hand to burn away a piece of the barrier. This time, she could see movement on the other side, something like a pair of wings flapping. "Can you see that? Reach out and touch. Come on."

At first, no one moved, then the boat was tipping over as they all lunged to run their hands against where Willow's pressed in the air. With a gasp, Willow pushed the lifting side of the hull back down with her powers, taking in the shock and anger from around her as a dozen hands roamed across the metaphysical wall that closed in their minds.

"Your own light is all that can save you," whispered Willow, her hands flaring brighter, creating a larger space to see beyond. "This is the wall we must break down before our enemies arrive."

"Damn it all. Is that me?" breathed McKay.

A body lay before them in the fire-rimmed opening, and as Willow widened it, they could see a face—Idris fallen on his side, a Winged youngling kneeling over him, pressing healing ether into his skin.

"What is that *thing* doing to him?" demanded Sampson, failing to push his wrinkled hand through toward the fallen Idris.

Willow slapped his fingers away with her burning ones. "That *mage* is healing his disused limbs, so he can move once he wakes." Her fingers curled against the wall. "Zeph is one of their kind."

Norwood stared hardest of all, a sort of dawning fear crawling into his eyes. "What exactly is he capable of doing?"

Mother took Willow's hand before she could respond, and her face was filled with awe as she asked, "So he's alright?"

Willow squeezed and nodded, but as she pulled away, the hand clutched in her own remained ablaze. "Mother?" she breathed.

Aurora lifted the hand before her own face, flipping it over, again and again, when with a sudden smile, she lifted it up. And the fire didn't just remain, it flew so high above them it poured down sparks that singed their clothes.

"Aurora," complained Eliza, laughing as she scooped water from the sides of the boat onto herself. "I liked these robes." She sighed, wearing a determined look, the wet hand gliding through the water lifting suddenly as her own powers emerged and she shot fire into the wall before her.

The men sat down in shock, faces alight with dancing shadows and disbelief, both melting away as all three women shone brighter and opened the barrier farther. Until even Sampson was staring at his hands, trying to make flame.

"Careful you don't burn the boat," Willow whispered to them, floating up a bit in her relief.

The sky was on fire.

Willow had loved a good blaze for as long as she could remember.

The smell of it, the smoke in her lungs, and even the heady danger of its spread. She and Mother were always in charge of keeping it from doing so, but now, all she could do was hope it would catch on. So naturally, they started with the sky.

Spinor Falls had woken as it usually did to the morning light, except it was not yet morning.

The stars were out and there were seven people hovering above the town square in a burning circle, their interlocked arms now torches.

She could see valleymen in the distance come running out of their homes in excitement, her old students screeching in awe. Even Amos and Areida looked up from the square without fury.

Willow was sweating with the effort of holding so much sentience in the air a few feet, her blood bubbling in that newly familiar way, when people filtered out of their homes, eyes wide, red-rimmed, and even weeping.

Detective Reid seemed to be shouting, "I told you all! I told you so."

Mother was the brightest, with even her hair on fire. She called out to the gathering crowds, "We come to you as your council. I come to you as the head of the Western Tribe, and I offer the entire store of Erifson firewood to our cause."

The gasps grew louder. People started looking over at each other.

Willow tossed flame at Areida.

Instinctively, she tossed it back.

And finally, finally, the individual sparks Willow had wrought billowed into flame. A whole village began firing up.

Mother shouted orders. "Everyone, get to the perimeters of the island, up to the main estate in each direction. If you're from the north, head north, and so on. Immediately begin tossing fire at the perimeter. Willow will deliver wood and help you send it flaming to the walls. We don't have much time...I don't see Councilor Vesta. Norwood, you're closest to her. Pass on the instructions she needs to coordinate the Southern Tribe."

Willow placed Norwood on the ground, and he went running.

"Mother, I have to get to the police watchtower for the best view."

"Go on, then. I can manage this."

She hugged her parent hard, descending all of them gently. "I see that."

As she too ran off, her people parted, staring after her in a match-box mob of flame.

Once upon that open landing high above Spinor Falls, where she had once come of age, Willow watched everyone rushing to do Aurora's bidding like fire ants in the distance. The Northeastern Tribe was sprightliest due to Eliza Sholeh's efficiency, already gathered and working together.

Willow focused on the store of firewood behind her home and sent a portion over to the perimeter, where her people set it aflame, and she slammed it forward until it reached the wall. Again and again.

Until the world around her was falling to ashes.

She looked down a moment to see the town smithy sprinting to the tower with his wife in his arms.

"Willow, please help. What's happening?" he called out.

Moira Halifax's left hand was…missing. Her face remained motionless as her entire arm disappeared.

She was turning into nothingness.

"Hold on!" She rose Moira into the air, but before she reached the landing, her friend was gone.

The smithy fell to his knees, staring up in disbelief.

"They're here," whispered Willow. "They're killing us."

As holes broke through the walls, shrieks rose up at the scenes behind them. The Winged younglings were hiding from intruders in the Emberlands, and the Fervers in Spinor Falls were dying as their souls were ripped from their bodies.

The prisoners moved with more wood, more fire, more effort.

They tore gashes harder. And when all seemed lost amid the screaming, strange light began to break through.

Willow zeroed in on the last of the firewood, a pile so massive it could have built ten homes, dipped it into a rampant blaze she spotted nearby in the north, and sent it sailing into one of the largest cracks in the east.

Those lines in the wall spread, out and out and out.

Until it all splintered like fireworks through her soul, and she knew it finally for a fact.

The Metafervers were back.

CHAPTER
22

CONFLICTING
SOURCES

A mind will fight
Itself
Before it breaks—
Walls
It may have meant
Or meant not
To fake
Against the truth
Of what it means
To wake

She lifted her lids in a new world, looked around for Zeph, and instead saw mountains flying by beneath her.

"Stop screaming or I'll drop you."

Twisting, she could see Torrent holding her up by the strings of a makeshift harness.

"He left me with *you*?" screeched Willow.

Torrent landed, sending Willow rolling across the ground to the lip of a cliff, grabbing her by the shoulders just in time and searching Willow's eyes for something. "I'm babysitting you when I should be beside my general. So answer me, and do it quickly. *Did you use the fail-safe?*"

Gasping, Willow raised herself onto her hands. "No."

"But you're awake." Torrent leaned back, taking her in. "You're fucking awake. Shit. So you did it. Did you do it? Oh, damn, you actually did it." Torrent hugged her hard, something like pure joy on that austere face, though she pulled away in a flash. "I have to get you home."

"No," said Willow, backing away at the outstretched arm to tug off the harness and hop around until she was free. No one would be chaining her up again. "I'll follow on my own," she said, rising into the sky with her powers.

Torrent went gray with shock at that display of rule bending, and it took her a full minute to whisper, "Stay close. One portal left to arrival."

She shot away, with Willow hot on her heels as they zipped past treetops. The woman's wings were practically lightning as she made turns and drops as if at a whim. Willow held her breath at a sharp left that turned into a steep descent toward a shimmering patent portal at the base of a mountain, which they soared through at a dive.

On the other side, they erupted into the hottest sky Willow had yet experienced, and it made her soul sing to turn her face up into the sun, at least until she looked down.

The eight main hills rose high as ever, but there were dead bodies strewn in the town center, each pierced through with arrows. All Fervers, many of them friends. Moira lay in her own congealed blood, arm severed from her pregnant body.

Willow felt the rise of bile in her throat and tears in her eyes.

Fervers throughout the land struggled to stand, bodies atrophied and powers untapped for over a quarter century. Weeds strangled structures as well as fields. Time had torn its way through here without mercy. But worse than that, the Kinetics had already cut through the square and were making their way up the nearest hill, the Eastern, for a stronghold at the summit.

"There's a whole army of them. Where are the Winged?" asked Willow, sobbing. "Why aren't they protecting my people?"

Torrent glared. "The Flock are not here. Our younglings are healers, not warriors, and they can only tend to your atrophied muscles."

"But aren't the Flock coming?"

"Depends on the general's orders."

"Then, what do we do right now? You're one of them. You know how to fight."

Torrent shook her head. "I fight on the general's orders only."

Willow looked at her in disgust and said, "You were ordered to protect *me*, though, weren't you?"

"Now hold on—"

Willow spiraled down into the battle on the leeward side of the Eastern Hill and began to rain fire. The Kinetics looked up in shock, loosing their arrows, all as she dodged with sloppy skill.

"How is any of this possible?" one of them was screaming at another as Willow set him aflame, and he went rolling down back to the square.

An arrow shot through her shoulder, piercing only the skin but hurting like hell.

Willow raised a hand to touch it when Torrent slammed into her from behind, taking her captive into the clouds. Willow thrashed and kicked, finally sending fire rippling up her arms, burning away the arrow and Torrent.

The mage shouted, "Even you can't fight a whole army on your own."

"I'm not on my own," Willow barked back.

"Great Father of Darkness, you're the least rational Meta I've ever fucking met."

"Look at me," she said, widening her flaming arms. "Even *I* don't know what I am."

They heaved up there above it all for a moment, until Torrent suddenly laughed a weary laugh. "Alright, but we need an actual plan. The Kinetics can't know I'm on your side in case any of them survive to tell."

Willow opened her mouth, but the sound of a very distinct crisis horn cut through the air, the one belonging to the Eastern Hill. She and Torrent dipped down just past the cloud cover to see Yonsoon, in all his large and silent glory, gunning up that very hill. Both his cannon-like arms were spewing barrels of flame from a mile away, razing clusters of Kinetics.

"Damn," said Torrent, whistling. "Heard about this giant once."

The enemy split up, some still heading up the hill while others roasted below.

"What else do you know?" asked Willow. "Who are the most powerful of my people?"

Torrent looked out at the dire landscape, her long lashes sweeping against her cheeks as she blinked in the bright sun. "Well, the easterners in general are Throwers. Isn't that why they're the hunters of your region?"

"The McKays? Well, fuck." Willow turned her body toward the Eastern Estate. "Alright, I'll get to them. You find my mother."

Torrent laughed, then said, "You're not serious?"

"What's the joke?"

Before she could answer, another crisis horn blew. This time from the Western Hill.

Willow felt her blood run cold. "That's Mother. Fine. Alright. No more babysitting for you. Just direct the easterners and help them find their feet."

"Willow, wait!"

"What?"

"Stay alive. And here." From the satchel over her shoulder, Torrent passed her the Farrow's Forge mirrax.

"Thank you. But no promises." Willow glanced at her bleeding shoulder before soaring off.

Her home looked different from a high altitude, she thought, gazing down at the windows she'd once shattered and the pathways she'd overrun with childhood abandon. Willow tried to tamp down her panic when Mother was nowhere to be found inside the house, unlike the staff, who had not yet been reached by the healers and were unable to stand. They had fallen immobile throughout the space ever since the Sequester Spell had overtaken the land.

One of them called out to her from where he lay on the walkway near the back door just as Willow rushed out. It was Colin, their stable boy, who no longer looked like a boy.

She knelt at his side and repeated a version of what she had said to the others. "It's alright, Colin, your muscles will be better with time. Let me just get you inside, where it's safer."

"No...miss...soft hay," he croaked, eyes rolling.

She patted his cheek and floated him over to one of the stalls. She was upset to note all their horses dead or fled. "I have to go now. I need to find Mother."

"Stacks."

"What?" she said, placing her ear at his lips.

"She ran out...back door...five minutes." He closed his eyes, tired just from speaking a broken sentence.

Willow's eyes widened. "Thank you."

She recalled the bone-deep ache of first waking and let him be.

Mother was right where he said, by the stacks and carrying stores of wood relentlessly over into carts despite heaving with exertion. "Willow! I was thinking we could use the same tactics as in Spinor—"

Willow just sprinted into her arms. "I know there's no time, but—"

"All the more reason." Mother stroked her hair. "And there's so much to say, darling."

"How are you walking so well?" asked Willow.

Mother answered, "I woke to a Winged girl named Skyler working healing ether into my muscles. She said all the councilors were treated first as a matter of priority, but I sent her away to hide as soon as we heard the Kinetics. She reported some of the east, west, and southwest should be up, but not much else. The lowlands of those areas would be our best bet for finding able people—"

Voices called out to them. "Aurora, we heard the horn!"

Norwood and Sholeh were racing over, the youngest councilors arriving in response to her call, as protocol dictated.

"We need a gathering point for anyone willing and able to fight," Mother said, quickly reassuming command. "And a plan. Our powers may be hard to manage after so long, but firewood can intensify them if Willow enhances their long-range capability, just like she did before."

Willow had already walked over to the crest of the hill, from where she could see most of what she now knew was Void Valley.

"The enemy have congregated on the Eastern Hill, Mother." Directly across the territory, it was the farthest hill she could see and currently engulfed in flame, a clear battle raging. "I can't tell who I might hit from this distance. I sent one of the Winged to help the easterners better band together. We should make our way over there. We need the Throwers. And they need us."

With quick nods of agreement, they headed down the hill, as hard as it was to do past screaming people lying frozen and scared. Mother carried with her a few weapons, as Willow focused on controlling the pile of firewood she rolled kinetically before them.

"Quiet," said Eliza, catching a sound in the brush. "Someone's coming."

They abandoned the firewood and crouched behind a small thicket of trees to watch a couple of Kinetic soldiers stomp up the path around a bend.

"What's all this, then?" asked one of them.

"Pretty decent firewood," said the other, picking up a smaller piece. Willow forced his own hand to slam it into his face, knocking the man out as his partner laughed.

"You fuckin' idiot," the first one said, before the logs around his feet began to roll. Two of them slapped his backside. He turned in confusion, tripping as the wood pushed him off the hill, down and away.

Norwood laughed hard, stepping out to watch the man roll, until a louder sound than Yonsoon's horn blew, a distinctive alarm from the southwest.

"My home," he shrieked.

Willow lifted the wood into a consolidated pile so Mother could set it alight at the base of their hill. They burst down through the main path leading southwest and used their pyre to tear through large swaths of Kinetics on their way up to the estate.

With the firewood soon depleted, they crested the hill, where a large group of the strongest of the Kinetics clustered.

Norwood's estate, fully encapsulated by forest, hovered high in the air, ripped away from the first floor, as people screamed from within.

"Surrender, or else," came a growl from one of the enemy, heaving as he focused on hovering the building.

"Or else what?" asked Aurora, stepping forward, holding up her flaming arms, though they were too far down the hill to reach the Kinetics.

"We tip it over," said a bare-chested man, sweating rivers from kinetic exertion.

"Emory," screeched Lady Norwood, her head emerging from one of the windows to call her husband. "Do something."

Willow locked in on her, pulling her body out kinetically in a move that shocked the enemy so much they dropped the house, its foundation crashing and breaking to pieces.

They all finally turned to face the Fervers, visibly shaken, trying to deny what they had just witnessed or discover who had done it, when Willow realized a few Kinetics standing up by the tree line behind the house were disappearing.

It became clear how when just then, Torrent silently dropped down to lock her thighs around a man's head and twist. She flew off with the body, her legs holding him beneath his lifeless arms.

Willow stepped closer to distract the Kinetics from looking behind them. "There are only about thirty of you, and this is our territory. We know the land, and you don't. Now leave. You've taken enough."

"Oh, and you'll just let us ride home, will you? Offer up a couple dozen dead horses for the trip?" piped up one of the men.

"Traitor!" screamed another as he raised a hand—and toppled the house onto its side.

Willow's entire arms burst into flame without conscious thought.

But her anger morphed into shock when she realized who hid in their enemy's little cluster.

"Ivan?" she asked, taking a step forward.

The king's right hand smirked at her, and before she knew it, he had kinetically wrapped a whip around her torso and yanked it.

"Nothing bigger than a pin, my ass," shouted Willow, face down on the ground.

"Five Fervers against thirty Kinetics," he snarled. "The odds are not quite in your favor, are they?"

The tips of the whip snaked up to her flaming neck and squeezed, the material proving to be fireproof.

Mother tried to move toward them when an arrow shot her in the thigh.

"Mother!" screamed Willow.

Ivan laughed, stepping over her body. "He was so fond of you, just because you could move a few pillars. But the rest of us could see a worm for a worm. Decaying everything in her path."

Willow gasped as the coarse leather caked in metallic, old blood began robbing her of breath. Eyesight beginning to fail, she twisted her head enough to see what looked like Devlin Norwood at one of the house windows—wearily pulling himself over the sill, falling over behind the Kinetics, and raising a fiery hand that shook—

Air returned. Ivan flailed about, in flames. Willow shot into the air, Torrent holding her around the middle.

"Rain fire, Ferver," shouted the mage.

Willow sent spirals of it down toward their enemy. She engulfed half of them in seconds, but the rest charged at the few Fervers and easily pinned them all down before looking up at Willow in triumph.

Ivan, burned but somehow still bombastic, called out, "I think I'll start with cutting off your mother's leg here if you don't surrender."

He picked up one of their fallen axes and Willow tried to think clearly enough to focus her powers on him from such a distance. Her ears were still ringing.

"Let me go," cried Willow at Torrent. "I have to get to her."

"No, you're my priority right now. And I don't care if you burn me—"

But Willow didn't have to turn on her Winged ally because suddenly the Tug in her chest cut off in deeply visceral relief, just as every Kinetic standing on that hill was shot through with an arrow—including Ivan, right through the eye.

To her left, the Flock lowered their bows, Zephyr at their helm in the sky. Twenty of them hovered in attack formation, assessing the small but weathered battleground below in steady silence. Their faces loomed more ominous than usual, covered as they were in black V-shaped warpaint resembling birds in flight.

Zeph wore the lightweight battle armor he favored, the Black Forge Scythe glinting from the harness at his back and dark hair curling over a forehead dripping with sweat. Willow imagined she could see something triumphant in his aerial stance, those rolled-back shoulders and that lifted chin. Her heart thumped in her chest.

Flynn nodded over at Torrent. "It's done," he said.

Torrent actually whooped.

"She's slipping, cousin," growled Zeph. Willow felt her head dip, the blood loss making her a bit woozy and the adrenaline rush disappearing along with the Tug.

A bloodcurdling scream rose up.

Ivan, gored eyeball oozing blood, was pulling Lady Norwood's unconscious body against him down the hill like a shield. Walking backward, he crashed trees down with his powers to block the Fervers from following.

The Flock's archers raised their bows again, smirking at how easy the shot would be, when Zeph raised a hand bent at the elbow and crisply ordered, "Wait."

Emory Norwood, trying to pull himself over fallen trees in pursuit of his wife, looked up at that. He shouted, "No. You must help her. She's not well. You know she never has been…son."

"You are not my father," bellowed Zeph, sharper than Willow had ever heard him speak in Spinor Falls.

Norwood, the most stone-faced of all the councilors, dropped to his knees and cried up to him, "Please."

Zeph's hand remained raised. Willow tried to lift her head from Torrent's shoulder so she could push away the dawning blackout enough to speak.

But her vision suddenly went so white it was blinding.

The world disappeared, then reassembled, the brilliant rays ebbing—from Aurora's skin, of all things—only after the light had given

Mother enough cover to dive over the final fallen tree blocking her from Ivan. He turned on her, dropping his hostage and lifting his arms.

Zeph lowered his hand. Ivan was dead within seconds, riddled with so many arrows in the face that it could never again be used to identify him.

Wide awake now, Willow pushed Torrent off in a tired motion, trying to get over to Aurora but falling through the air in a weary whoosh—

Zephyr plucked her into his arms.

He sailed down to seat her on the ground directly before her mother.

Voice deep and official, he bowed his head at Aurora to say, "Hello again, Master Mapmaker. And welcome home."

CHAPTER
23

TURN THE TABLES, RUIN THE FLOORS

betrayal bleeds black ooze atop my open spine
to drip
> *drip*

between butterfly bones laid bare
where all sense and sensation flow bloody
in their lair of human
existence
persistence
and care.
so
> *fine!*

bury the poison
fling that fire
and sing your song
of backstabbing pain
and the sable—but fabled—
corrosion
you blame.

W hat?" breathed Willow, looking up and between the two of them.

Zeph lifted his head. "It's an honor."

The Flock landed silently behind him, one by one, into a formal line.

And Aurora, despite how brave and quick-thinking she had proven herself today, began to tremble at the sight. She clasped her shaking elbows to steady herself, eyes darting between the many stoic yet somehow eager faces before her, only to land on one.

"Zephyr Azakor. How you've grown." She reached a hand toward his face but dropped it. "It's too much. I can't...just can't untangle the flood of old memories from the new ones. And it hurts. It all just *hurts*."

"The mental storm will die down," assured Zeph. "Center yourself in the void. Do you remember how?"

Aurora looked up a moment, eyes bright. "The last I remember, I had returned home to take Father's seat on the council. Because he died." She shook her head as if to jostle the cobwebs in her mind. "My father. He only just died. Except it's been *years*."

She went silent in shock.

"Mother, I'm sorry," Willow cut in quietly, not sure what to do, knowing her own surprise paled in comparison to Aurora's state of mind. "But is it true? You're the master mapmaker?"

Aurora's voice shook as she said, "I think they used to call me that."

"Does that mean you can help me find someone I've lost?"

Aurora did not seem to hear the question. With a spastic jerk, her gaze landed back on Zephyr. "First Elder Balen? May I see him?"

Zeph's face tightened. "No, Great-Grandfather is dead too. He took his own life...after he took yours."

"No. That can't be true," said Aurora, falling to her knees and visibly crumpling in on herself. "I need him. Only he knows...he helped me with the birth and spells and...I can't think straight. What kind of beast would torture us like this?"

"Soren!" Willow rose from Aurora's side in a stumbling haze to grab at Zeph's shoulder. "Won't he notice how long you've all been away?"

Zeph only seemed to stand taller. "No, it's over. It's all over, Willow. He can't get to us. I'm king now."

"But I thought you were general?" Willow rushed forward to help her pale mother sit on a mangled tree stump before she glanced back up at his familiar face, now cast in the coiling shadows of the leaves draped over them all. "Do the Flock have kings too?"

"No, Willow. The Sequester and Siphon Spells were linked."

At that, she unbent slowly at the waist, a crushing sensation in her chest at the pieces of another hazy puzzle slotting into place. She was angry before she fully understood why.

Zeph continued. "Great-Grandfather cast them both. When one fell, so did the other."

"So you mean you're king of the Sky Realm?" asked Willow.

"Yes. He can't hurt us ever again."

She dug her toes into the ground. "So you used me?"

"No, not—What? Not in those terms."

"Did you kill him? Were your hands the ones to do it?" She scoffed at his silence, voice rising. "Did my actions help you murder a man? For his throne?"

"He was not a man. He was a monster—"

"Then, why take his place?"

"Why not?" He looked at her and seemed so unruffled, unbothered, and unfeeling. So *regal*.

As for Willow—she felt so much it burned. And so she screamed. Harder than she ever had before. Until it shook the soil of the entire Eastern Hill.

A couple of the Winged looked concerned. Torrent even snatched a bow from an archer and notched an arrow.

Willow glared at them all, her eyes scanning back and forth in growing panic. Trying to breathe, she said, "All this time, you acted like you came for me. To enlighten me and free my people. But everything you put me through…it was for you, not us. Our bondage was just tied to yours. Our plight stood in the way of *your* rise to power. If you thought I'd be alright with this plan, you'd have told me before carrying it out. Right?" Again, that searing silence from her opaque friend. Her voice calmed and dropped low. "I always made excuses for your lies and half-truths. But not this time."

The Fervers and the Flock stared, some of them taking a step forward. Only Mother remained bent over and moaning, her head buried in her arms, not from the physical ache of her gashed leg but the even greater pain of remembrance.

"All my lies were designed to protect you. To keep the secret of *your* people safe from a monster." Zeph reached out a hand. "Willow—"

"No!"

Zeph swept the hand out instead. "Just look the fuck around! We've helped free you all."

"But have you freed us into another prison? How would we know? How? And this was never about helping us. You were all just keeping our bodies safe to buy our minds enough time to break the enchantment. Weren't you? *That's* why you and your Flock showed up so late. My people were dying here as you took your throne. But you were always a great actor, huh?" A blackness bloomed like a swift rot in her soul, and she resented him all the more for it, for this new ability to hate. "*You're* the monster. You've always been the monster."

His tense face relaxed and went totally blank. "I didn't expect this from you."

"Yes, you did. Or you'd have told me the truth."

"And have you always been so honest with me?" he questioned softly.

"Of course! I—"

"Then you haven't had the master map all along?"

Aurora glanced up, her gaze locking on Willow's left arm.

Willow spluttered, "That is not the same thing! I wasn't sure of what I had. *You* had a whole plan set in motion for years. How could you do it?"

"Do what?"

"This! How could you do this to me?"

He charged forward, taking her by the shoulders. "He asked me the same thing before I pulled my blade out of his gut."

"And what did you say? What answer did you give your prize victim?"

He pressed his face so close to hers they breathed each other's air. "Are those the sort of reassuring words you want from me right now?"

Through gritted teeth, she answered, "What I want is for you to be *honest* with me for once in all our damn time together."

He spoke slowly and with relish, "I was groomed to train, kill, spy, and bleed. But more than anything, you *asshole*, I was groomed to lead."

Willow shivered up into amber eyes finally alight with the answers she had wanted for so long. "And just like that...Maddooinne's yours."

He laughed. "And you're such a saint? Angelic Willow, who let my only parent die, even though I saved hers."

"How can you even—"

"—yet you can't see—"

"Oh, I see," she roared, stepping back in tears. "For once, I truly see. I see it always meant more to me than it did to you. How...how embarrassing. If I could take *your* world, burn down *your* dreams, stop cold *your* heart—you'd see a mirror of my memory. Then I'd shatter it like I'd shatter you. In utter. Fucking. Effigy." Shrieking the last word, she sent her mirrax flying at his chest. He grabbed hold of the handle, resisting the force of the most chaotic ether she'd ever used with sheer force of will.

Hardened eyes bore into hers for a long moment. Until they slid closed. Until he slammed her blades into the ground and those great inky wings took flight.

His flock followed, the archers facing her.

"Aren't you afraid of this kind of power?" Willow couldn't help but yell up at him. "Didn't we all just see what happens to someone who falls from heights like this?"

"I'm not afraid of falling," replied a king from the center of his people, "because I've always lived on the floor, and it was from there I rose to lead a rebellion."

She could only see his profile in the harsh sunlight—the upturned nose and stiff set of his jaw as he hunted some unseen portal.

And if she thought she saw him glance back in pain a moment, it must have been a trick of the light.

Willow Erifson turned to look at her own people, most of them fortunate to be tired and many of them unfortunate to be dead, with the firm resolution that they were all that should matter to her now.

ABOUT THE AUTHOR

Golmah usually lives in a far-off realm halfway between fantasy and reality, where bad things happen but always resolve to her satisfaction. It's a world of her own making, and she likes it just fine.

The rest of the time she spends firmly grounded in American soil, cajoling her way with admissions essays into studying history at UCLA and dentistry at Harvard.

In college, she wrote over forty articles for the *Daily Bruin*, attained authorship and scientific citations as a brain tumor intern for a neurosurgery lab, and swapped as many in-class exams as possible for florid history papers. While at Harvard, she blogged for the dental school website and squirreled away time to write this very book.

Because the yarn she most loves to spin for fabric are total fabrications—stories full of people and places that manage to entrance away our pain, poetry that communicates a lot with very little, and epic romances that stand up to the nastiest villains.

Join Golmah's newsletter for updates on her sequel, bonus reading content, the Verbal Alchemist podcast, and more exclusive extras.

Sign up at **golmahz.com**.

♪ / @golmahz
🅕 / golmahz
🅞 / golmahz